AFRAID
TO
HOPE

ANCIENT PASSAGES BOOK 2

SUTTON BISHOP

 NliveN, LLC

NliveN, LLC
880 Lennox Drive
Zionsville, IN 46077

Afraid to Hope, Ancient Passages, Book 2
Copyright © 2020 Sutton Bishop
ISBN: 978–0-9898816–6-1
ISBN: 978–0-9898816–7-8 (e-book)

Printed in the USA

For more information, contact: thesuttonbishop@gmail.com

Cover by Ally Hastings, Starcrossed Covers
Edited by Victory Editing

 NliveN, LLC

dedication

For You:

Tenacious, fierce, and intrepid.

a note to readers

In conforming to American English rules, some of the Arabic and English words have been capitalized within *Afraid to Hope*.

المغرب كا الشجره جذورها في افريقيا واوراقها تنفس في هواء اوربا.الكتاب يبدا بهذه المقوله.
وهي مقولة الملك الحسن الثاني

※

Morocco is a tree whose roots lie in Africa
but whose leaves breathe in European air.

※

King Hassan II
(1929-1999)

prologue

H E MOANS IN PAIN AND heaves out the words: "Help me… Help me…"

The dancing circle of light punctuates the dank blackness, surrounding the man lying contorted in the shallow, murky water. Somehow he's alive. It's impossible to tell if he's bleeding, but he is broken. His arms and legs are bent at impossibly unnatural angles, mangled like twisted metal after a car accident.

The man sobs loudly, like a young child, and pants like a dog in the heat of summer. He wails, then gasps, "Pushed… someone… hard…"

Eyes tightly closed, I try to dismiss the image of him and quell the bile that rises closer to my throat with each rolling shudder passing through my body. It's not working, so I open them and focus on the obsidian wall directly in front of me. Its uneven, wet surface is awash with reflections of torchlights, headlamps, and flashlights. Everywhere else is a blacker-than-black space. The slimy, uneven footing beneath the deepening water slows my pace as I falter toward the wall, intent on distancing myself from my team, the medics, and the Maya who gather around the man, discussing how best to get him onto the basket and out of the ruin.

Perspiration races from my hairline and armpits, drenching my face and arms, racing down to my fingertips. My wet clothing adheres to my skin. *Breathe deeply,* I chant in my head. Breathe. Nausea is a swallow away. Fear mushrooms within me, as do panic and light-headedness. My hand slips on the slick wall. It undulates under my touch, moving my fingers in a wavy motion. The outline of a monstrous face appears, and I barely save

myself from face-planting in the cloudy water as I jump back. I have to get ahold of myself.

"Dr. Jordaan, you okay? We need you." A voice reverberates in the rock chamber.

I nod and hold my hand up, signaling that I am and that I'll be with them soon. It's hard to get my breath my heart is pounding so hard. I glance back at the wall. The face stares at me and fades away. I inhale again, deeply through my nose, then wipe at my face with the back of my clammy hand, rubbing off the sweat, adding the excess moisture to my pants. My heart slows to the point I can no longer hear it in my head. I tell myself this is no worse than many other things I've seen.

But it is.

Death mingles with the pungent, earthy wetness and an overpowering scent of sulfur. Not reeking and nasty like sewer gas but different, as if matches have been lit—lots and lots of them, as if to cover the stench of rot permeating the space. None of us have burning torches, so where is the stench coming from?

My nausea is diminishing. Carefully I bend and dip my finger into the water, which covers the tops of my boots. With everything else assaulting my senses, I didn't notice the water is terribly warm, bordering on hot. The water smells full of minerals. My booted feet are growing uncomfortable. Thermal spring? What the hell is this place?

Something sinister is here, and it waits. Goose bumps break out all over me, and the hairs on my neck rise. My gut screams, *"Move! Get out of here!"* My body ratchets into alarm mode. I want to flee, run up the uneven and broken steps to the temple above and outside to the steamy, sun-drenched day. Jesus. I'm stronger than this.

I slosh back to the shallower water, careful to minimize splashing as I near where everyone gathers around Eric Schaus. The American.

The paramedics and my men are busy immobilizing his injured body with help from the Maya. Schaus's face is partly submerged, turned away from where I stand. His loud moans and whimpers are frightening, and then he yelps, the sound echoing out of the black void. His rambling words make no sense.

The Maya freeze their movements. Disbelief and fear fill their expressions.

"Do you understand what he is saying?" I ask of the Maya closest to me.

His voice quakes as he responds, "It is Q'eqchi,' our language. But it is not. It is more ancient. It is as though the voice comes through him. It is not his."

My stomach knots, and I gulp down the nausea again. Resorting to academic logic, I'm able to back away from the sensory details and accompanying feelings assaulting me, and I rush to compartmentalize. Something I excel at. Aloud, I say more to myself than anyone else, "Interesting. His creds don't mention he speaks any Mayan dialect."

"Dr. Jordaan, we can use you here." A medic points to the American's head after he secures a cervical collar. "Can you talk to him while we immobilize his limbs? Try to keep his mind off our manipulations."

So what should I say to him? Hey, there. Did you know I've been tracking you for years? Did you ever think you'd be caught? Instead, I move to Eric Schaus's head. It's wet and caked with black silt. I direct a question to the medic next to me. "His neck? Is it broken?"

"It doesn't appear to be, but we're taking every precaution." The medic shakes his head. "I don't know how in the hell he ended up here, so far from the steps. It's as if he was thrown. We are not taking any chances. He's in rough shape. We'll know more after we get him to Belize."

Eric Schaus's screams pierce the black chamber and echo into the unseen voids leading out of it. As the medics and my men skillfully restrain his arms and legs, Schaus screeches like he's being pulled apart.

Another medic inserts an IV line into Schaus's trembling arm and administers something from a syringe. "I'm giving you something to manage the pain," he says, emptying the syringe into the clear, snaking tube.

To disassociate, I sort through my research on Xibalba, the Mayan underworld. The paintings on the upper tiers did not escape my notice. The depiction of flesh separating from bodies. The massive river of blood filled with scorpions. The gaping centipede jaws. The glyphs, the smells, the water. The foreboding undercurrent of death. It all adds up. Gulping, I struggle to inhale. This place has to be a portal to Xibalba.

Schaus whimpers. The sedative has kicked in.

"We're going to move you, sir," one of my team states calmly.

The medic closest to me bellows and crosses himself as Schaus's face rotates upward while he is positioned on the basket. The Maya scramble back, crying out in terror, causing the medics to adjust swiftly to keep from dropping Schaus.

I lose the fight and surrender to the overwhelming urge to look, immediately wishing I hadn't. His eyes are open. I am paralyzed by the palest blue eyes, almost spectral in his burnished-tan face. He pins me with them and smiles manically. His words bubble through the spittle. I can barely make them out.

"Fear the ghost."

A charred image extends from above Eric Schaus's singed left brow to his jaw, within the angry and pulpy skin. The mark of *Xquic,* the Blood Maiden, the Hero Twins' mother. The Serpent.

diverted

دق الحديد وهو حامي.

Strike the iron while it's hot.

chapter 1

Morocco…

"MISS? MISS?" THE FLIGHT ATTENDANT reached across the empty aisle seat to softly touch the shoulder of Natasha, who slumbered next to the shaded window.

Natasha jolted awake, blinking furiously as the scene faded and the present came into focus. She stretched her kinked neck this way and that, smiling, hoping to soften the fearful scowl she'd first given the woman upon waking abruptly.

"We are preparing to land, miss. I'm sorry I startled you. Please make sure your seat back is in its full upright position and your seat belt is securely fastened. Thank you."

"Thank you," Natasha responded, shaking her head in an effort to cast out the remaining dregs of her recurring nightmare—the all-too-real dream of her last moments in Guatemala that would haunt her for some time, perhaps forever.

She slid the window shade up and peered out. The plane reduced speed and dropped below the fluffy cumulus, banking sharp left, revealing the white city nestled between the terra-cotta desert and bluish-gray Atlantic. Emotion closed her throat and wet her eyes as memories assaulted her. It had been far too long since she had been back to Casablanca.

The plane righted itself and dropped lower, buffeted by crosswind. In

short order, the wheels bounced and the plane lifted slightly before they touched again, scorching the tarmac, reverse thrusters on. Now fully awake as the plane taxied toward the Jetway, Natasha reflected on the last days that had put her on this flight to Casa, the nickname she and others affectionately called their beloved city.

After transporting Dr. Eric Schaus, the American, to a hospital in Belize to address the injuries he sustained in the fall—or push, as he claimed—Natasha had looked forward to going home. She had not been to South Africa in nearly two years. Assignments had taken her all over the globe, and after finally nabbing the elusive looter and having him charged with international trafficking of national treasures, Natasha intended on taking a very long and well-earned holiday.

✄ ❂ ❀ ✄

South Africa, Two days earlier…

Natasha had only been back in Cape Town for a few days, fully believing she had time to settle back into her town house and address its sparseness and obvious lack of occupation when her cell rang.

The caller identified herself as Mrs. Bradley from INTERPOL, Executive Director Emmet Cantrell's assistant. "We need you in Morocco, Dr. Jordaan," she said in a clipped British accent. "A package is arriving by courier within the hour. Your flight leaves tomorrow morning."

Natasha's door buzzed as she disconnected the call.

Sunlight slanted onto the hardwood floor, warming her bare feet as she padded to her front door in the early hour. Survival habits kicked in. Natasha looked through the peephole, contemplating the tall, suited man on the other side. Surely it was the courier. After checking the sidearm at her hip, she opened the door carefully.

"Dr. Jordaan?"

Natasha nodded but didn't speak.

"No flowers yet?" he asked, glancing at the large empty ceramic pots baking in the hot sun next to the walkway.

She replied with the designated code. "So, can you suggest a good nursery?"

"Sea Point has a nice selection." He handed the large white cardboard envelope to her. "Enjoy your day."

"Thanks. Have a nice day." She backed into her town home and closed the door, locking it and waiting for his retreating steps. A fresh blanket of fatigue wrapped around her. Natasha felt far older than her thirty-six years.

During the Red Notice debriefings on the agency jet while flying from Guatemala to Cape Town, Natasha had not been able to reconcile the paranormal aspects of what she had witnessed. Neither had Assistant Deputy Drummond. The last hours spent in Guatemala haunted her twenty-four seven, awake or asleep. It didn't matter. Any sound sleep broke into nightmarish fragments. She was exhausted.

Natasha's throat burned as she stared at the framed photos in her kitchen, on the shelf to the left of the coffee maker—one of her grandparents and her, taken weeks before Pépé died, and the other was of her parents, brothers, and herself—the last family photo taken before she lost all of them. She kept smaller copies in her wallet. God, how she missed them.

The envelope felt more substantial with each step toward her long-untended garden. Plopping into a chair shaded by the pergola, Natasha drank deeply from her cup, fortifying herself with steaming coffee before extracting the contents. The Disney Princess mug—a silly exchange gift from a departmental party when she taught at university—mocked her. She didn't feel like a princess. She felt like one of the old, wizened crones Disney favored in its fairy tales. INTERPOL was giving her little time to recover from the ordeal in Guatemala or to catch up on much-needed sleep.

Heaving a long sigh and rubbing the bridge of her nose, Natasha placed her SIG and cup on the wicker table next to her and opened the cardboard packet, shaking the contents out onto her lap. Two envelopes, several out-of-focus photos of a building that looked old and tired, and a small key attached to a rusting Fatima.

The Fatima was heavy, larger than her hand. The key reminded her of the one her grandmother had given her when she was twenty-one. She shifted it in the sunlight. It was engraved. L-91. What did it open?

A large solid brass Fatima had graced the beguiling blue door of her grandparents' riad in Casablanca for as long as she could remember—a symbol of protection—and she had been enamored with it. Natasha had wonderful memories of time spent there.

She rotated her left hand, revealing the small Fatima on her wrist just inked after her grandmother died last year. Tears pricked her eyes as she considered what the tattoo

signified. It was in remembrance of Mémé, who had loved her deeply and provided wise guidance and emotional support to her after her parents and two younger brothers were killed in Madrid's Atocha Station bombings in 2004.

Natasha was supposed to have been with them, but she had accepted an invitation from her best friend the night before to see a limited still-life painting exhibit at the Prado. The plan was for her to meet her parents and brothers later, after they returned from their day trip to Alcalá. Natasha slept while the coordinated terror attack killed nearly two hundred and injured thousands during the morning's rush hour. Upon waking and hearing what had happened, she was unable to reach her family. She and her friend never made it to the Prado. Instead, Natasha stayed with her friend, barely functioning, alternating between fits of sobbing, rage, and vomiting until her grandparents arrived from Morocco. She insisted on accompanying them to the morgue but was forced to remain with authorities in the sterile hallway. No amount of screwing her eyes shut could make the morgue disappear, and her hands covering her ears did nothing to block the keening of Mémé and Pépé as they identified their daughter, son-in-law, and two young grandsons.

She placed the Fatima and attached key next to her mug and wiped her eyes, swallowing her sadness and bitterness, and opened the first envelope. The short memo—embossed with INTERPOL's logo—stated she had a new, open-ended assignment and details would be provided when she arrived at the Moroccan office. It was signed by Executive Director Emmet Cantrell, Rabat, Morocco.

The second envelope held a visa and one-way, business-class ticket to Casablanca, early afternoon the following day, and a generous check for incidentals. Only INTERPOL would be able to finagle the Moroccan visa required for South Africans on such short notice. She swept the photos that held no meaning, the executive director's memo, Fatima and key, and plane ticket back into the packet.

Dammit. A full day of flying. Just what I need. Grimacing, Natasha chugged the rest of her coffee, then stood and stretched. She had a lot to do before she left for the airport and took a notepad from the counter to write her list: finish laundry, shop, go to the bank to cash the check and exchange money, request her grandparents' *riad* be freshened up for her arrival, and check her PO box. Her travel tote and red suitcase were still lying open in the living room from her trip to Guatemala. She had pulled clothing from the suitcase when she needed something to wear—a tee, her favorite cargo pants, underwear—but her mostly depleted travel toiletries remained untouched.

Guatemala. Those last days had worn her to the bone. Scared the shit

out of her. Shaken her spiritual foundation—something she was not aware she had or relied upon until then. Sleep continued to be broken, and she often woke from the recurring nightmare, gasping for air when her throat had closed, muffling her screams.

It was early September. Cape Town was transitioning out of the damp winter into spring, a shock for her after months spent in the hot humidity of Guatemala. The director had not indicated where Natasha would be working while on assignment in Morocco or in what capacity. The country was more temperate, and modesty was expected. She would need options—layers of clothing and a few shawls. If she traveled south, the temperature could be hot, but not muggy like Guatemala.

The check, notepad, phone, and keys went into her purse. While she was thinking of it, she searched her kitchen drawer for the key to her grandparents' *riad*—the grand, traditional Moroccan home that was now hers—and secured it within an inside pocket of her travel tote.

Screw finishing the laundry. Time was at a premium. Smiling to herself, Natasha closed the door, deciding that shopping at her favorite local boutique was in order. It might just take the sting out of this trip, and she would get herself a few extra niceties too for the inconvenience.

chapter 2

Morocco...

THE HAIR ON THE BACK of Natasha's neck stood up. She continued her pace through Casablanca's bustling airport, her eyes sweeping the people and activity in her periphery and to the front of her, the feeling of being watched growing more pronounced. Whoever was surveilling her was behind her. She had felt the presence of someone after she handed over her landing card and had her passport stamped in Customs.

Natasha stopped abruptly and was bumped from behind. She held her ground, turning with an apologetic smile. "I'm so sorry."

Her eyes scanned behind the tiny elderly woman swathed in a hijab and wearing a djellaba, catching the retreat of a large man, a baseball cap obscuring his face and hair. His stealthy movement as he faded into the crowd indicated he was military, paramilitary, or former military.

Already on heightened alert, her system went on full red. *Why am I being watched?* She closed her eyes briefly, checking in with her senses. They had quieted. Natasha was no longer being observed, but her mind continued to be unsettled as she continued with her baggage.

"Dr. Jordaan?"

Turning around, Natasha released the bag she was in the process of claiming from the carousel. Irritable from over twenty hours of traveling, Natasha groaned inwardly. She'd have to wait for it to come around again. "Yes?"

13

A dark-headed man bowed slightly. "How was your flight?"

Access into airports was restricted to passengers with travel documents. Despite the fact that he had to have special clearance to be here, Natasha took in her surroundings, particularly the exits, then assessed him. She was tall and had him by at least two inches. Like her, he was slender, wiry, and probably deadly if the need arose. He wore an earpiece. Dark sunglasses were tucked into his jacket pocket. Her driver, as mentioned in the letter. Natasha cocked her head, looking down into light brown eyes, challenging him, not responding.

He cleared his throat and shifted, his suit jacket moving enough that it revealed a holstered piece. The man displayed his ID covertly. "Specialist Geoffrey Malcolm. Welcome to Morocco, Doctor. The director wishes to see you immediately. I have a car waiting outside."

Natasha raised her eyebrows. "I'm waiting to retrieve my bag."

"Right. I interrupted you." He inclined his head, a dusting of pink flaring under his fair skin. "Your luggage is coming around again."

She had dressed casually for her long trip from Cape Town to Casablanca—a long, flowing brown skirt; low, closed-toed sandals; a pale yellow tee; and a muted, patterned linen wrap. No makeup other than her favorite lipstick, and most of her shoulder-length, tousled hair was hidden under a colorful Mayan scarf. Despite having gotten some sleep, her eyes burned, and jet lag nagged at her. She only wanted to sleep. For days. And forget.

She remained mum, hoping to appear composed even though she felt otherwise. Natasha turned away from Malcolm and grabbed the handle of her oversized red luggage, hefting it from the conveyor belt and standing it on its wheels, snapping up the pull bar. She pushed it toward him. "Thank you."

Confusion showed on his face before she stepped in front of him and headed toward the exits. Natasha pulled her smaller red carry-on and called back over her shoulder, "Come, Malcolm. Let's get moving. I'm bone tired." She strode in front of him, headed for the final baggage security point.

Natasha smiled wryly and shook her head. Men.

chapter 3

N ATASHA STRETCHED HER ARMS OVER her head and inhaled deeply. Apparently Specialist Malcolm had not been briefed or he would have known she had spent a good portion of her younger years growing up in Casablanca. He droned on and on during the drive from the airport, reciting this and that about Moroccan culture. Natasha might have nodded off more than once, lulled by the rocking car and Malcolm's dry as a witch's tit delivery, jolting awake when he slammed on the brakes in Rabat's heavy traffic. She was only too glad when he departed after bringing her through security and into INTERPOL's offices.

She checked her watch, noting thirty minutes had passed. The large desk just off of the director's door reminded her of a sentry and remained vacated. Natasha was the only occupant in the enormous space, aside from an occasional person passing through the common area or into another room. No one approached her as she waited, although they glanced her way. Natasha rose from one of the carved benches, her impatience growing. She could have been sleeping in her grandparents' home. Her home.

She positioned her carry-on on top of the larger bag and pulled them to the huge desk in the open room, where she drummed her fingers on the neatly organized desktop. *Come on. I'm tired as hell.*

As if summoned, the heavy doors opened. A distinguished and slender older woman appeared and paused, her bright blue eyes alighting on and assessing Natasha. She clasped her hands together in front of her hips. A

soft burr coated her words. "Hello, Dr. Jordaan. I am Matilda Bradley, Executive Director Cantrell's administrative assistant. He will see you now," she said firmly. "Leave your luggage with me."

"Thank you."

"Come with me, please."

Natasha followed Mrs. Bradley into the inner sanctum.

"Director, Dr. Jordaan has arrived," Mrs. Bradley said and left Natasha, the doors closing with a soft click behind her.

Rays of late-afternoon sun poured in through the window opposite Natasha, temporarily blinding her. She blinked rapidly as the director moved from behind his massive desk and extended his hand in greeting.

"Dr. Jordaan. Thank you for coming. I understand the flight was long and we gave you insufficient time to recover from your successful deployment in Guatemala."

"Sir," Natasha answered, extending her hand. "I look forward to working with you." She appraised him. Trim, her height or just a bit under. Late fifties to early sixties, short white hair, cornflower-blue eyes that missed nothing, and wrinkles that looked as if they sagged from all the world's worries. His English accent indicated he was a member of the United Kingdom's upper classes.

"How was your flight, Doctor?"

"Long."

"You didn't sleep?"

"Off and on. Sleep has been difficult, sir. I expect Assistant Deputy Drummond informed you about what occurred in Guatemala?"

"Right. The damnedest thing."

"It was," she said, her face breaking into a large smile, standing taller, feeling pride down to her toes. "But we got him, sir. So you—"

Something shifted behind her. Natasha whipped around.

A mountain of a man rose from the sofa in the shadowed corner and stepped into the rays of light. He dwarfed her five foot ten by a good six inches. He moved forward with easy grace, invading her personal space.

Natasha's eyes had a mind of their own, and she was helpless as they traveled his lean, powerful body at a record rate. He was the most beautiful, unabashedly male, exquisite man she'd ever laid eyes on. Rugged. Ripped. Devilishly handsome.

Confidence and raw sexual energy buffeted her, but Natasha refused to step back, to surrender her space. Wavy, dark brown hair tapered to a short fade, resembling a week's growth of beard. Heavy, dark brows framed expressive hazel eyes—bedroom eyes—that had a keen interest in her. *Jesus.* Natasha couldn't look away. She snapped her mouth shut to keep herself from drooling. *What in hell was I doing while I was blatantly staring?*

His eyes twinkled and his crow's-feet deepened. His mouth drew up in a crooked, sexy smirk with a hint of dimples, and he spoke so softly that she doubted Director Cantrell could hear him. Every word he uttered in his deep timbre vibrated within her, setting off delicious, hot sparks. "You can look, Dr. Jordaan." His smirk broke into a devastating white smile. "I'm even more impressive naked."

American. A tinge of a Southern accent. Natasha didn't dare break eye contact, but she backed up abruptly, stunned by his brashness. She glared at the man and her posture stiffened, disdain pouring from her eyes. "Excuse me? Since you're here, I assume you're more than just eye candy." Turning to the director, she cleared her throat. "Sir?"

"Bane. Knock it off," grumbled the director.

Deep laughter erupted behind her. "Sorry, Emmet. Eye candy. That's a good one." He chuckled. "I've never been equated with eye candy, but whatever floats your boat, Doctor, is fine with me."

Who the hell was he, calling the director by his first name?

"Dr. Jordaan, please sit." Director Cantrell pointed to the chairs in front of his desk. "Bane, you too." He took off his glasses and rubbed the bridge of his nose before sighing heavily and amending his demand. "Please."

Bane seemed to accidentally graze his leg against Natasha's as he folded his large frame into a chair that was too small for him. He regarded Natasha with eyes that hinted at a melting pot of ancestry and danced with mischief and humor even though the man was not smiling.

"Well. I guess I should start over." He held out his large hand, his eyes looking deeply into hers. "Bane Rua."

Never one to let anyone get something over her, Natasha extended her hand even though her body was already humming from being grazed by his leg. He clasped her hand, softly stroking the palm with one of his fingers. All reason evaporated as electricity shot through her system again. Appalled by what he was doing and her reaction, she squeezed his hand

harder, fighting like mad to get ahold of herself, calling on her training to slow her heart rate.

"Dr. Jordaan," she said, her voice cracking with irritation.

A cocky grin and a glimpse of his straight white teeth flashed again. He nodded perceptibly. "You're strong. I like that. Since we're going to be working together, don't you think we can be on a first-name basis?"

Working together? Oh no. She could not work with him. She would not. Natasha shook her head in disbelief and pulled her hand from his.

Bane leaned in, his smile open and confident. "You don't want to work with me? Oh, Doctor, you might want to rethink that." His voice was teasing, sexy.

Natasha grappled with the embarrassment flooding her, disconcerted that he had been able to read her. His scent—clean male, sandalwood, and spice wafted over her. It was heady, seductive, and she had lost control of her emotions, which she normally had a firm grip on. With little effort, he had stripped Natasha of her long-useful defenses, and in front of Director Cantrell.

"Enough, Bane." The director cleared his throat. "Dr. Jordaan, you do not have a choice in the matter. I called this meeting to acquaint you with each other. We require particular expertise, experience, and skills for this assignment. Bane is former special ops and, like you, fluent in French and Arabic. One of the best specialists we work with. Granted, his methods"—he ran his hand through his hair and replaced his glasses, his tired blue eyes scrutinizing Bane—"and humor can be a bit taxing."

The director came around between them and leaned back on the edge of his desk, crossing his arms in front of his chest and one ankle over the other. "Well, let us jump to it. Water?"

Natasha was suddenly parched. "Please."

"I'm good." A ghost of a smile lit Bane's features.

The director poured water from a glass pitcher etched with a gold-and-teal design. He handed a matching glass to Natasha. "Doctor, I'll keep this meeting brief in light of your long travel day. The three of us will reconvene tomorrow morning and go over the assignment in more detail. Plan on a full day. Bane, Dr. Jordaan is a classical archaeologist specializing in archaeometry, which means she excels at the archaeological details such as dating and authentication that are essential for accurate identification. We require the doctor's skills in addition to

her field training and your specialties." His eyes moved back and forth between them. "Inasmuch as the focus is in Morocco, repatriating looted items, the scope of the assignment impacts the world. INTERPOL and AFRIPOL, specifically you as our representatives, are tasked with recovering recently discovered treasures. Of note, there's a codex that went missing from Ouarzazate, suspected of being similar in age to the Codex Sinaiticus, which was written in the fourth century. The other treasure is human remains, *Homo sapiens,* believed to date back some three hundred thousand years, excavated from a newer pit in Jebel Irhoud. Again, the authenticity and ages of these discoveries are unconfirmed. If verified, they will be considered priceless, possibly revealing astonishing scientific and historical significance."

Natasha's heart sank. That could only mean one thing. "A private buyer."

The director turned his eyes to her. "Yes, and the clock is ticking. There is fear that the Ouarzazate Codex may already be in private hands because that bidding has stalled. The bidding on the *Homo sapiens* is slowing, indicating a purchase is imminent."

Natasha finished her water. "How much time do we have, sir?"

"I'm unable to answer that." The director paused and regarded Natasha. "There's more. Intel gleaned from multiple sources confirms that the American orchestrated the thefts and that bidding commenced prior to the looting. Of course, crushing or seriously damaging the American would be outstanding."

She sat up rigidly. "Excuse me? That's im-impossible, sir," Natasha stuttered. "I took the American into custody in Guatemala. Eric Schaus let it be known that he was the American. He cannot have recovered from his… his… accident in Petén. He was in critical shape. I witnessed his injuries."

"You are correct," he said. "Eric Schaus was in critical condition but has improved greatly. Our people used skills at their disposal to convince Schaus that it was in his best interest to talk. The man became quite cooperative. One key piece of information he has given us is that the American is a *network,* not an individual as we long believed. The American has been operating since World War II and has a presence on most continents."

Natasha would have toppled over in disbelief had she not been sitting. How the hell had this been missed?

"Doctor, you were sent photos and a large Fatima with an attached key. The Fatima and key were found, it seems, in an abandoned outbuilding of an old cheese farm outside Imouzzer du Kandar, a small town situated between Fes and Ifrane. The pictures were taken by a team that was following up on a credible lead, but they were called away on another urgent matter, which never materialized." Emmet frowned and tapped his pen on his notepad, temporarily pulled to that moment, and said under his breath, "Strange that was." His laser focus returned. "I apologize for the quality. The photos might prove useful when you are further into your assignment."

Director Cantrell reached behind him and turned back with two identical-looking, thick binders, which he handed Natasha and Bane. "It should go without saying, but bloody hell, I'm going to say it anyway given the escalation in activity related to the American and its interests. The information within these binders is confidential. Should it be seen by anyone outside of us, your safety and the mission would be compromised. On that note, Dr. Jordaan is tired. Matilda will call for the car to take you to your *riad*, Doctor. While you are waiting, please use my office and begin studying the materials. I have another meeting. As I said, we will meet again in the morning. Oh eight hundred sharp, Bane."

"Got it," he answered, still slouching in his chair.

"I need to get supplies—food, basics," Natasha protested, still wrestling with the revelation about the American.

"Provide a list and I will give it to Matilda on my way out. All of the items will be in the car when it is here to collect you," he said, handing her a notepad from his desk.

Natasha wrote quickly and handed it back to Director Cantrell. "Thank you."

"Simon Wade is your driver and can assist you with anything else you might require. Try to get some restive sleep. You too, Bane." He stood, indicating that the meeting was over. "I'll see you in the morning."

※ ▨ ✳ ✕

"You grew up here?"

"We're supposed to begin studying the information while we wait, Mr. Rua."

"Bane," he said, smiling devilishly. "I'm going to study tonight. I want to know more about you."

"Maybe another time," she said evenly, giving him what she hoped was a look of indifference. "I'm going to read." Natasha glanced away quickly, afraid she would be unable to stop herself from staring at him.

"Always a rule follower?"

Her eyes snapped back up, right into amused hazel orbs. They had become greener in mere seconds. "I follow orders. Are you always a nonconformist?"

"I follow orders too. Emmet didn't give us an order."

"Suit yourself," Natasha said dismissively. Her eyes dove to the open binder in her lap. She focused on shutting out his presence.

Bane slid his binder into the waxed canvas messenger bag on the floor by the leg of his chair and crossed his ankle over his knee. He clicked his pen rhythmically, like a metronome, while regarding Natasha thoughtfully.

No longer able to concentrate, she stared at him.

"Am I bothering you?" he asked, smirking, continuing to click his pen.

"Can you please stop?" Natasha reached over and stilled his thumb, partially covering his hand. Belatedly she realized what she had done. The connection between them flared and electricity sparked and raced like wildfire through her body. Rattled, she withdrew her hand as if burned.

Bane's eyes sparkled with mirth. "Stop what? I'm sitting here quietly, minding my own business."

"You are annoying me with your pen clicking."

"Oh. Sorry."

Natasha made it to the end of the second paragraph before more clicking pulled her from her reading. She glared at him.

"Guess it's a habit." He smiled mischievously. "I've never had a woman partner before."

"I'm not surprised if you're always like this."

"Ouch. That hurt, Doc."

The doors opened behind them, and the director's assistant popped her head in the room. "Bane. Dr. Jordaan. Simon is waiting. Dr. Jordaan, your luggage and shopping items are in the boot."

"We're sharing a car?"

"Yes. Bane will be dropped off first."

21

Bane drawled, "Aw, Tilly. If it's not too much of a problem, let's drop the doctor off first. She's wiped from traveling."

A girly smile broke over Matilda's staunch features. She held up a finger to Bane and tapped on her earpiece, quietly issuing a change of plans to Simon.

Natasha's temper was close to boiling over, but the words died on her lips. Bane winked at her, then gave her that devastating smile.

chapter 4

THEY RODE IN SILENCE, NATASHA snagging the seat up front with Simon to avoid sitting with Bane, who'd draped himself over most of the back seat. Her mind reeled from the knowledge that the American was a network. Actually, it was a brilliant deception. Why look for a network when the singular name clearly indicated the looting was the work of an individual? It made more sense when she reflected on the immense scope of the Guatemalan operation. It was impossible that Eric Schaus had orchestrated all that by himself. He had to have had substantial financial backing—from either exceptionally wealthy private citizens and organizations or from the coffers of countries. The team left in place in Guatemala would be figuring all that out.

So, did the network more closely resemble the mythical hydra? Had she helped to cut off one head of the network only to have it grow more? And if so, who or what was behind the American? What was Natasha getting herself into? *Actually, check that.* Her entanglement had begun when she accepted the previous assignment in Guatemala, and now she was mired in more deeply. Excitement and fear about what she might further discover played tug-of-war within her. Incessant drumming on the back of her seat pulled her from her musing. *Jesus, what now?*

Not bothering to turn, she snapped, "What do you want, Mr. Rua?"

"Wow, Doc. Where were you? I've been trying to get your attention for a few minutes. Maybe I should have clicked a pen." He sat forward, his rough voice much closer now, his breath caressing her neck, sending delicious chills over its surface, reawakening the sparking electricity she'd

23

experienced in the director's office. "Are you up for dinner and studying together?"

Dammit. He was like some obnoxious little boy who wanted candy. She was not going to be his flavor of the month. Natasha dropped her voice and enunciated each word. "Listen carefully, Mr. Rua. I'm not into your games. I do not wish to be more than professional colleagues. So other than that, keep your distance."

He moved closer, testing her resolve. "It's Bane, Natasha. And you're as interested as I am. I see it in the erratic pulse in your neck and the dilation of those fucking amazing eyes."

"It's anger, you ass."

Bane chortled and sat back quickly, throwing his hands up in the air in surrender. "Whatever you want to call it, sweetheart."

The car slowed to a stop.

"Sorry to interrupt," Simon said, poker-faced, preparing to exit. "We've arrived, Dr. Jordaan. I'll help you with your things."

She sprang from the car, key in hand, slamming the door. Bane opened his, but she pushed back on it with her hip. "Stay in the car! I do not require your assistance." To Simon she said, "I won't need to be picked up in the morning. I'll taxi in. Good night, Mr. Rua."

"It's early, but sweet dreams," Bane offered, having rolled down his window, his expression oozing sexual confidence.

What an incorrigible ass. Speechless, Natasha ignored him and all but marched her way to the *riad,* pulling her red carry-on behind her. Simon followed; his arms laden with supplies. She paused in the soft glow of the lamp and inhaled deeply as she counted to ten, seeking calm, gazing at the Fatima door knocker against the freshly painted blue door—her favorite blue—the flash of annoyance at Bane dissolving to nothing. Her fingers moved over the knocker reverently before inserting the heavy key in the lock. Opening the door, she reached to her right to flip the switch, euphoria and sadness mingling as she stepped inside, beckoned by the warm lighting. So many memories.

"Please. You can leave it all here in the *setwan.*" Natasha pointed to a spot just inside the door. "Thank you so much, Simon." She stroked the Fatima wistfully again before closing the door and sliding off her sandals in the small and welcoming entry and sitting area. She continued through the short, angled corridor with her bags, depositing them at the base of the stairs. Natasha turned and soaked in the elegant, beautiful space—her

riad. Her home. The resplendent and traditional Moroccan elegance felt like paradise. Soon lantern light would illuminate the traditional red-pigmented Moroccan *tadelakt* plaster walls, archways, and through openings in the intricately carved wood.

The late-afternoon sun played hide-and-seek in the clouds above the rooftop terrace, casting moving shadows over the atrium. The fragrance of jasmine mingled with scents of the lemon and orange trees and the trickling, sparkling water of the *sahrīdj* welcomed her and soothed her frayed nerves. How often she had sat in this courtyard, dipping her hand in the tranquil fountain? After her parents and brother died, Natasha slept next to the fountain for weeks, its vital life-force providing peace and, eventually, balance. She blinked rapidly at unshed tears.

Tiles displaying different artistic interpretations of the Hand of Fatima had been inset in the four cardinal points of the base of the *sahrīdj.* Natasha rotated her left wrist. One of her tears dropped onto her only tattoo. The Fatima connected Natasha to an integral aspect of her Moroccan history—her grandmother. What was it Mémé had told her every time she asked about the Fatima? Natasha closed her wet eyes and allowed herself to drift back to her last visit with her grandmother.

⁂

She had stroked Natasha's soft, sun-streaked brown curls. "The Fatima wards off negativity and evil, Tasha. Fatima's hand channels good, healing energy. Always keep her with you, my darling heart."

Then Natasha prayed in unison with Mémé, as she always had. "Let no sadness come to my heart. Let no trouble come to my arms. Let no conflict come to my eyes. Let my soul be filled with the blessing of joy and peace."

⁂

Her grandmother died suddenly while Natasha was on assignment. As was her wish as a French expat, Mémé was buried in the Catholic cemetery managed by the French Embassy within twenty-four hours of her death, honoring the Muslim custom of the country she dearly loved. Unable to return to Morocco in time for Mémé's burial, Natasha had wandered the streets of Phnom Penh, bereft. A blinking neon Fatima drew her into a tiny tattoo shop, where she had let go and mourned her grandmother, tears sluicing off her chin as the artist inked the tender skin of her wrist. It was the last time she could remember crying.

Natasha wiped at her eyes and nose and then walked the perimeter of the courtyard, peeking into each of the large rooms through the open ornately carved double doors—extra bedrooms, office, and baths, happily noting how cared for her grandparents' home was. It felt lived in, warm, and inviting.

"No. My home," she said softly, correcting herself.

Clara and Oliver—her grandparents' longtime help—lived in the small home on the back of the property. Their part-time responsibilities had morphed throughout Natasha's life, depending on what the property or her grandparents needed. After the tragic deaths of her parents and brothers, the couple were more present as Mémé and Pépé grieved and focused on Natasha, particularly Clara. Natasha had grieved for her family with Clara, believing that sharing her pain with her grandparents was too much for them to bear on top of their own grief.

Natasha suspected Clara and Oliver had made extra preparations ahead of her arrival, beyond what she had requested, after she called them from Cape Town. It had been wonderful to hear their voices after months of no contact, and she was eager to see them again.

Natasha paused in the kitchen. Like the rest of the *riad,* it was just as she remembered. It wasn't large, but it was functional. Her eyes traveled over the Moorish-inspired carved cupboards and open shelves. Cubbies made of the same red-pigmented plaster that formed the walls and ceiling were laden with tableware and serving dishes. Vibrant blue, yellow, and white tiles of differing patterns created a backsplash behind the sink, and larger deep blue and white tiles covered the floor, playing into the warm color scheme. Small collections of brass lanterns hung from the ceiling in three of the corners, and there was one to the side of the french doors that led out to the tranquil gardens and large lawn. How many times had she and Mémé prepared food and pastries in the kitchen with ingredients from the gardens?

Natasha walked back to the front of the *riad* and climbed the steps to the second floor with her luggage. The first door on her right was her grandparents' master, and it took up the majority of this side of the house. She flipped on the light. Per her instructions, all the bedding and towels had been replaced. Clara and Oliver had outdone themselves in the master. How well they knew her.

Joyful reds, blues, oranges, and pinks, and layers of patterns and textures should have clashed, but they worked beautifully against the architectural detail, delighting Natasha, making her feel very much at

home; she could not wait to crawl into the lush bed and sleep deeply after addressing her assigned homework.

Among the pillows was a note card addressed to her. It was brief, from Clara, welcoming Natasha home and inviting her to come see Oliver and her after she got settled. Natasha smiled, warmed by their thoughtfulness.

She did a cursory check of the rooms on the other side of the open corridor until she reached the room her parents used when they'd visited Mémé and Pépé. After the bombing, Natasha had not entered that bedroom or the one her brothers shared next to it. She stepped back and considered. It was time that she found the courage to face her long-buried grief. But not today.

Reacquainted with her surroundings, Natasha made her way downstairs and moved to the fountain, spray from the trickling water wetting her skin. She had stood there so many times, dipping her fingers in and out of the water until her grandmother called her out to the gardens. She could almost hear Mémé now. "Tasha! I would love your company, darling heart!" Natasha wiped a tear from her cheek and hugged herself.

They used to have tea parties with her troop of stuffed animals when Natasha was little and, as she grew older, lunch made with garden treats amid adult conversation. Sometimes she and Mémé would slather on the sunscreen and lounge on the rooftop terrace, shrieking and giggling like young girls when they jumped in the unheated plunge pool in the late spring and early fall, avoiding the scorching summer sun.

She could do this. She would use the house as her base while she was working in Morocco and rely on Hama's Prayer to help heal her shattered soul.

The amplified *adhan,* the call to prayer, flowed over the rooftop from minarets in every direction. Although not Muslim, Natasha's body vibrated in response to the magical and melismatic tones. Completely overcome, her heart melted at the familiar and beloved sound of home.

chapter 5

WEARINESS OVERWHELMED BANE AS HE unlocked the door to the company apartment. Three months of reconnaissance had taken its toll. After turning on the lights and walking inside, he shed his boots and tossed his messenger bag to the couch in the living room, noting again how sterile and devoid of natural light the space was. Furniture blending into the cream-colored walls and floor, absent of any Moroccan architectural features or art, something that had not bothered him until now.

Maybe at the age of thirty-six, Bane was getting tired of the grind, of twelve years of collecting intelligence undercover. It felt like a lifetime. Losing Atticus, his partner and trusty German shepherd, six months earlier while working in Syria had affected him. This wasn't the first time he had mulled over wanting a change—like a new focus, a place to call home, and a meaningful relationship.

Bane had missed lunch, but military training had taught him to ignore his hunger pangs. In the small, functional kitchen, he took a plate and fork from the dish rack and cracked open a cold beer, pulling deeply while patiently waiting for last night's leftovers of stewed chicken and lentils to reheat. Once in the living room, he settled himself on the couch, his thoughts turning to the enigma of Dr. Natasha Jordaan as he ate by the meager light from the kitchen. She was a stunning package but with an invisible DO NOT APPROACH sign flashing. Perfectly arched brows and fringes of dark lashes framed gunmetal-gray, cat-shaped eyes. They flashed silver when her emotions ran high. That intrigued him. Very much

so, and he hadn't missed how her pupils dilated and the nostrils of her dainty nose flared slightly, reacting to his nearness. It wasn't fear. It was heat. A lot of it. She was molten under that icy splendor. He'd bet his life on it.

He had observed the gorgeous doctor from the corner of the room when she had first entered, his eyes raking up and down her luminous golden-brown skin. Tall. Volumes of sun-streaked, tousled dark hair, long enough for him to run his fingers through and hold on to when he lost himself in her. Full, kiss-me lips and an elegant neck begging to be nuzzled and bitten.

The flowing silk skirt and loose, sleeveless tee had done little to conceal her long, willowy form. If anything, her clothes had whetted his appetite, as had her sexy, hard-to-pin-down accent. The sunlight streaming through Emmet's office window provided an enticing silhouette of her lean body, and later, when she had unconsciously licked her bottom lip and bit down on it, his body revved in response. He'd had to shift to make more room for himself.

Bane had resorted to teasing, testing Natasha and her guard, challenging her focus eye-to-eye, concerned that she would realize the state of his arousal. That she stood between Emmet and him was fortunate. Although Bane was sure Emmet knew he was interested in the lovely doctor, he didn't wish to display his body's telltale interest in her. He washed down his final bite with the last of the bottle, then reclined and closed his eyes. Visions of her naked limbs entwined with his replayed over and over in his mind. He grew rock hard.

"Fuck," he muttered, opening his eyes, standing and stretching his arms up toward the ceiling. Thinking about Dr. Natasha Jordaan was getting him nowhere but unfocused; he had a lot to read through before tomorrow's meeting. Bane prided himself on being ready. He chucked the bottle, fork, and trash and headed to the bathroom.

Bane stripped and then studied himself in the mirror while he waited for the water to get hot. His thick dark hair was in need of a trim and his beard needed to be shorn back to the heavy stubble he preferred. He was tall, six foot four, broad shoulders and narrow through the hips, the build of a linebacker—the position he had played in high school. A series of tattoos covered his left side, from his shoulder and chest, cascading down his obliques, and stopping at his flank. What stories did her body hold? The image of Dr. Jordaan had his erection hovering at his navel, nestled in the flat planes of his abs, aching for attention. He

smiled to himself. She could probably accommodate his length and girth with no problem.

He hardened more at the thought, then fisted himself and stepped under the spray, his other hand bracing against the shower wall while he stroked roughly, his release quick and explosive as he thought about sinking into the beautiful Natasha, riding her deep, and the pleasure they could have. After his heart slowed, he toweled off and slipped on a pair of joggers and a tee, then headed into the kitchen for another beer. Time to review their assignment.

Bane adjusted the lamp next to the couch and pulled Emmet's binder from his messenger bag. He read the short, dull bio and studied the poor-quality black-and-white photo, which did nothing to describe or highlight the evocative and mercurial woman he had met earlier in Emmet's office. Her credentials were impressive, but he was sure there was far more under Natasha Jordaan's hood, possibly more than even she realized. As Bane suspected, the majority of what he had discovered the past three months had found its way into the material, along with his and others' analyses of the American.

Their assignment was delicate, and that Eric Schaus had been identified and apprehended in Guatemala made infiltration and success far more difficult. Suspicions ran high. It had taken him months of work through layers of intermediaries throughout Northern Africa just to acquire names and contacts.

The American used violence to keep others compliant. Many assumed to be connected to the network stayed mum, had been found dead, or had simply disappeared. Surgical precision was imperative.

He and Natasha were in place and ready to proceed to the next step of the operation, which he hoped was efficient and quick. Bane was overdue for time off and a visit home to see his family in the States.

He read for a while, finishing his beer while mulling over the information about his thirty-six-year-old partner and the mission they were undertaking. Bane opened another bottle and continued reading, going slowly over the finer details of the assignment, occasionally closing his eyes and thinking through the material, committing specifics to memory. He returned to reading. The next page brought him to a stop. Bane burst into laughter, scrubbed at his beard, and ran his hand over his damp hair. The cool, carefully controlled Dr. Jordaan was not going to like this. Not one bit.

chapter 6

NATASHA SHOOK HERSELF AWAKE. SHE felt grounded in a way she had not experienced in far too long. She had relaxed in the chaise, captivated by the sky's retreating watercolor of pink, orange, and yellow, the *adhan* finishing as twilight disappeared. The night was pleasantly warm. At peace, Natasha closed her heavy eyes, intent on doing so for only a few minutes.

She glanced at her watch. Thirty minutes had passed. The heavens above were now dark and awash with stars, but their brilliance was diminished in Casablanca's lights. Natasha sat more upright and stretched her arms up, yawning deeply. She reflected on the decisions and issues facing her.

Cape Town served nothing by being her home base. She was alone except for university colleagues. Her father's family had not exactly welcomed her upon her move there, and since she traveled so much, the chances of her being accepted by them were likely nil. That hurt. It more than hurt.

Natasha wanted more. She yearned for connection and belonging. She loved Morocco. She had retained her citizenship, along with her South African status. Possibly she could negotiate with INTERPOL to help her move back and inquire about becoming a visiting professor or adjunct. While the assignments were exciting and stretched her in a way teaching did not, Natasha missed working with and mentoring students at university level.

There was also the issue of Bane Rua. He was a force to reckon with, and she was more than drawn to him. That was a problem. Natasha sat up fully and crossed her legs, her hands securing her thick hair into a ponytail with a hair band from her wrist.

She glanced at her watch again; fifteen more minutes had passed. Despite her nap and the early hour, Natasha longed to surrender to sleep, but she had one more thing she wanted to do before going to bed. She left the rooftop terrace and entered the *riad,* then exited the french doors of the kitchen and crossed the expansive garden to the smaller house on the home's property.

※ ※ ❋ ※

"Natasha! Come in! Come in!" Clara bear-hugged Natasha after opening the door.

Natasha folded over the petite woman and returned her hug enthusiastically. Past Clara, she noted the center of the kitchen table was full of serving dishes and plates containing couscous, olives, a stew, and bread. Her stomach rumbled audibly.

"Is that who I think it is?" Oliver asked, raw-boned and towering over his wife. He gently pushed her aside to hug Natasha ardently, then pulled her deeper into their cozy home. "How we've missed you, young lady. We're having a late dinner. Have you eaten?"

Natasha hugged Oliver just as tightly. Her words rushed out. "I've missed you so much too. No, I haven't, but I don't want to intrude. I wanted to pop in and let you know I'd arrived and then head to bed. I'm sorry it's so late. I had a meeting and then I was going to come over, but I heard the *adhan,* and, well, I fell asleep on the terrace. I can come back tomorrow."

"Nonsense. You will sleep better with a full belly." Clara chuckled, guiding Natasha to the table and sitting after Natasha got situated on her pillow. "Sit. Oliver, get our girl a plate."

Oliver sat and served Natasha a heaping plate of vegetable fish stew from the center of the table, then served Clara and himself. Each helped themselves to the bread and other food in the communal dishes.

"Oh my god! The stew smells heavenly." Natasha scooped some of her stew onto her bread and took a large bite, holding it in her mouth and savoring the fish, chickpeas, and tomatoes cooked in warm spices.

She talked with her mouth full, then swallowed, adding, "Delicious! It's been ages since I had this."

Natasha drank hot tea and continued to eat with gusto, answering questions between bites, observing how the couple looked—rested, healthy, and happy. Both of them retained their full heads of hair, now more salt than pepper. Their blue eyes twinkled with vitality and warmth.

"She looks wonderful," Clara said to Oliver.

"She does, but tired," Oliver observed, answering his wife.

Natasha found their habit of talking about her in the third person comforting. "It's a long flight from Cape Town."

Clara turned to Natasha. "Yes, but there's something else."

Natasha smiled at each of them. These two people she had known all her life, roughly the same age her parents would be if they were still living, were aging well. Clara was still beautiful and Oliver handsome. Hired by her grandparents when the property became too much for them to take care of, the couple oversaw the maintenance. Natasha loved them and considered Clara and Oliver her aunt and uncle. She spoke with both Clara and Oliver when her schedule permitted it, and on many occasions had joined them for a few days when they were on holiday, but not over the past year.

"I'm good," she responded, fudging the truth. "My last job took a lot out of me, more than I expected. I was still adjusting to being back in Cape Town when I received this job, a hurry-up-and-get-here directive, which is why I gave you such short notice. Thank you again, by the way. I love the linens and pillows. And I love you."

"We love you too, child. I told Oliver they looked like something you would enjoy."

"I never thought a career in archaeology would keep a person so busy," Oliver said.

"Neither did I, but I certainly love it." Natasha put her fork down and grasped Clara's hand, then reached for Oliver's. "You have no idea how happy I am to see you." Her eyes became watery. "Sorry for the emotion. I am tired," she said wistfully.

"You've no need to apologize to us." Oliver smiled at her, his eyes twinkling.

In a stronger voice, Natasha said, "After this job is over, I'm going to explore relocating to Casablanca. Most of my history is here. I have a

home, friends, and"—she looked from Clara to Oliver, smiling—"family. I still have networks I can plug into."

"That's the best news!" Clara's entire face lit up. "Our girl is coming home."

Oliver covered Natasha's hand with his and squeezed gently, swallowing convulsively and blinking furiously.

"Let's finish up here and get you to bed," Clara said.

Natasha started clearing the dishes. "Let me help."

Clara held up her hand. "I'll not hear of it. Oliver will help me clean up."

They stood, and Oliver pulled Natasha into his arms for another heartfelt hug before planting himself at the sink. Clara led Natasha to the door and embraced her, and again Natasha was reminded of how much she had missed her home.

challenges

اليد الواحده ما تصفق.

❈ ❈

One hand does not clap.

❈

chapter 7

H AVING FINISHED THEIR TEA AND small talk, Natasha and Director Cantrell sat in silence, waiting on Bane.

"Right. Well, let's get started," the director said, somewhat irritated at Bane's tardiness. "Do you understand the scope of the assignment?"

"I do, sir, but I have—"

The doors opened and Bane strode in, carrying a paper sack and his messenger bag. "Sorry I'm late. Stopped at the bakery. Busy as hell." A slow smile lit his features when he glanced at Natasha, his words taking on additional nuance. "I needed something sweet this morning. How about you, Doctor?"

Natasha swallowed, but not from wanting pastries. She bobbed her head, not trusting herself to speak, her heart racing, her body buzzing. She pretended to drink tea from her empty cup, which didn't go unnoticed by him. Bane Rua was gorgeous—a walking billboard of tall, dark, and handsome. One hundred percent sexy, confident male, all encased in lean, corded muscle.

His smile grew cocky. Over his shoulder, he called to the outer office area, "Hey Tilly, can we get some more tea? I'd like a cup too please." He settled himself in the chair next to Natasha, offering her first dibs to the contents of the now-open sack. "Parched, huh?" His eyes twinkled in his olive-toned face. "Me too."

"Bane," warned the director, his voice rising.

All mirth disappeared from his expression. Bane placed the sack on the director's desk. "Emmet. Your favorite's in here. Wasn't sure what you liked, Doctor, so"—he ripped the bag open so that it lay flat, then sat back—"I got a few of mine, in addition to Emmet and Matilda's." Winking at Natasha, he said suggestively, "You can sample what I like."

Natasha rolled her eyes. The man did not let up, and his words from yesterday had created a vivid dream where she had all kinds of sex with him. It was still fresh in her mind, and being in his presence was uncomfortable. Her sheets had looked like a tornado had torn through them, and she'd woken up wrung-out. If she were a blusher, Natasha's face would resemble a ripe red tomato.

Emmet cleared his throat and glowered at Bane. "Where's your binder?"

"In there." Bane pointed to the messenger bag at his feet. "I brought my notebook." He reached into the large pocket of his field vest, then leaned forward and helped himself to one of Emmet's pens.

Matilda arrived with the tea, breaking the tension. "Here you are." She placed an empty cup in front of Bane and filled it, poured fresh cups for the director and Natasha, and left the ornate teapot on the desk.

"Bane, you spoil me," she said after taking her pastry. Delicately biting into it, she moaned before closing the doors behind her. "This will be my undoing."

The director had opened his computer and was focused on the screen. Bane leaned over and whispered in Natasha's ear. "What's your undoing, Doc?"

"Someone else will be joining us at eleven hundred, so let's get down to it," Emmet said, his voice steely, glaring at Bane over his computer. "Questions?" He snapped the laptop shut and pushed it to the side, his eyes bouncing between them.

"I have one, sir. The information indicates we may be traveling quite a bit. Can you provide more details?"

Smirking, Bane put his notebook on Emmet's desk and slumped back into his chair with two pastries and his cup. That was clearly not the question he'd expected Natasha to ask.

The director sat forward earnestly. "Such as, Doctor?"

"Mr. Rua, you and I function as INTERPOL's first response team, command central, coordinating with local agencies who are involved in this case. Correct?" Striving to get the upper hand, Natasha gave Bane a

hard stare that he returned with squinted eyes and an amused smile, as if he was swallowing laughter. She ignored him and continued, addressing the director. "The initial correspondence I received indicated the duration of this assignment would be open-ended. However, the details were not specific." She scowled at Bane before opening her binder and flipping quickly through the pages. She stopped, her finger on a highlighted spot, peering at the director. "We may possibly be moving all over Morocco, sir?"

"That is correct," Emmet replied.

"So actually, that leads me to another question. Of course I brought clothes, but I will require additional items. How long do I have to purchase them? I apologize. I realize that's another question. So apparently I have a few."

"Doctor, you are correct. Rafiq Nasir, our Moroccan liaison, will be joining us shortly. He can fill you in further. As to your questions, you have time to shop before departing and can be expensed. Please provide Simon or Matilda with your receipts. I advise purchasing a good rucksack if you didn't pack one. At this time it seems you may be in the Atlas Mountains, and most likely in other regions of Morocco, as necessary for a successful outcome. I expect you may be moving around quite a bit. The movement of the American is amoeboid. We can be on top of the network, say, in Marrakesh, and then it vanishes and pops up in Tangier. I understand you spent much of your youth and teenage years in Casablanca, Doctor, but you should be prepared for time outside of metropolitan areas." He glanced at her and back at Bane. "I realize you both are aware of this, but it is Standard Operating Procedure that I go over it. The more rural your travels are, the more modesty is required. This includes your dress and manners. Social cues and interactions. Be very mindful of proxemics, particularly touch."

"Okay. Fine. Thank you." She sat back and sipped her tea.

"Wow!" Bane guffawed, his mouth full of pastry. He took a large sip from his tea and swallowed. "That's it? Thought you'd fight that harder. Glad to know our cover won't be an issue."

Natasha's face twisted.

"Dr. Jordaan understands this cover is best for the success of a mission."

Unease prickled within Natasha. She shook her head. "I have no idea what the two of you are referring to."

"You read the binder, Doctor?"

"I did. I—" Her unease grew into foreboding.

Bane's rugged baritone broke in. "I for one am relieved you don't have an issue being my wife." He pulled his notebook from Emmet's desk and flipped it open. "I made a note of that. Page forty-three, second paragraph. First sentence. 'Traveling as husband and wife—Mr. Bane and Dr. Natasha Rua.'"

Natasha's hand jolted, spilling her tea before she set the cup back on the desk. Her wet fingers worked into the zipped compartment inside her bag and withdrew the navy passport Matilda had given her when she'd arrived this morning. American. She opened it. Dr. Natasha Rua. A few stamps, reflecting recent travel from Egypt to Morocco. *No, no, no!* She scrambled to reopen her binder. The sinking feeling became more like quicksand when Natasha realized two pages were stuck together, probably by the sticky honey phyllo that had flaked off the baklava she had eaten last night while reading. *No!*

"Damned baklava," Natasha muttered loudly enough for Bane and the director to hear as she wedged her finger between the two pages at the bottom, gently prying them apart.

Her eyes skimmed the page she had passed over. Page forty-three. There it was, second paragraph, first sentence, just as Bane had said. *Traveling as husband and wife—Mr. Bane and Dr. Natasha Rua.* The sentences after it justified the undercover ruse. And the need for the same sleeping arrangements for the duration of the assignment. *Surely not.* The blood drained from her face.

She stiffened and looked at Director Cantrell, her eyes huge, her voice strained. "Do you feel this is necessary, sir?"

"I do. Given Moroccan social customs, particularly in the outlying towns and villages, it will be easier if you are married. Under this guise, you can work as a team, communicate with one another easily, and be most effective. The primary reason your covers were selected was to provide you both with more flexibility, especially when you are outside the cosmopolitan areas. In rural areas and villages, social status is relative to the woman's marital status. So being married elevates your status and also affords you the respect you will need and are entitled to, Doctor."

"I concur," Bane joined in, amusement lighting his eyes.

Natasha shot Bane a seething look and steeled herself before asking, "Separate beds, sir?"

Emmet squirmed in his seat. "I cannot surmise what your sleeping arrangements will consist of. You will share a room. Always. I expect you to appear married. Happily married." His focus turned to Bane and he raised his eyebrows. "Respectfully married. The two of you acting as husband and wife does not negate the cultural expectation of no outward displays of affection in public."

Bane nodded. "Got it."

Thank god. "Thank you for addressing that, sir."

Director Cantrell's sharp blues regarded both of them. "I expect you to deal with your marriage as you see fit and to be convincing. You are newly married, after all." He opened the drawer in front of him and ripped open a tiny manila envelope. Rings clattered on the desk. "Go ahead and put them on now."

Natasha stared at the smaller ring and swallowed audibly, then slipped the cool silver over her finger. It fit perfectly. Her brows shot up.

Emmet responded to her surprised expression. "We are thorough in gathering what might be necessary, including minutiae like ring sizes. As you know, the smallest details can make or break a mission." He pushed the larger ring toward Bane.

Bane leaned forward and played with the band before slipping it over his left ring finger, covering Natasha's hand with his, squeezing firmly. Her attempt to withdraw her hand was thwarted, and she was unable to read his expression as he said seriously, "I thee wed."

Natasha bathed Bane with her pissed-off expression. "Do not touch me," she warned, her voice cold.

Bane released her hand and lounged back in his chair, his fingers steepled under his nose, eyes dancing with humor. "You may decide otherwise, Doctor. I've noticed you enjoy sugary things. Trust me, I'm among the sweetest."

"Bane," the director barked.

"Sorry, Emmet. I find it difficult to curb myself. The doc has a burr up her ass, and we have to work around that." Bane rose, hooking his thumbs into his front pockets, his fingers loosely pointing toward his zipper.

Natasha's eyes followed the movement, and Bane smirked knowingly. Her body responded again, even as her anger came to a slow boil. "You are the burr in my ass, Mr. Rua," she said heatedly. "And apparently you enjoy being so." Her eyes pleaded with Emmet. "Sir, I don't think I can do this."

Emmet rose and placed his hands on his desk, leaning toward Natasha. "You can and you will. This cover affords you and Bane the easiest and safest mobility. You've been married for a month. Work out the specifics of your wedding date and wedding between yourselves later today."

Natasha pursed her lips and nodded.

"We're having a working honeymoon, Emmet?" Bane slapped his hand on his thigh and grinned. "How nice."

Emmet raised his brows at Bane before going on. "For decades there have been archaeologists who spy on looters. There have also been and continue to be archaeologists who are part and parcel to the looting and trafficking of priceless ancient artifacts. This is your role, Doctor. Your training in classical archaeology and archaeometry expertise is critical to this assignment. Bane, in addition to your role as husband, you will travel as a professional freelance photographer."

On cue, Matilda knocked and entered, handing Bane a large worn camera bag before heading back for the door.

"Thanks for the gift, Tilly." Bane opened the bag to inspect what it held. He whistled as he pulled out the camera and different lenses. He sounded like a little boy unwrapping gifts on Christmas morning. "Nice! You guys went all out."

"The fact that photography is a serious hobby enhances your cover. We have created a private conglomerate shell of interested buyers who employ you. ART Enterprise Global. An acronym for Artifacts, Retrieval, and Trade. You may be asked by those you come in contact with. The shell leads back to the setup in our offices should anyone inquire or check it out. We fully expect that this will be the case."

Natasha pushed her emotions aside to concentrate on the mission's details. "We're posing as ready to purchase for our buyers?"

"Affirmative. We play their game. Convincingly. Everything is in place. The assessment I provided underscores that the time to act is now." Emmet handed Natasha another manila envelope while Bane was absorbed in checking out the camera equipment. "Here is a brief regarding the conglomerate, its financials, notable people, et cetera. I'm sorry it wasn't in your binders, but it is still being fine-tuned. The phone numbers are programmed into your satellite-capable mobiles that you'll have soon. You have additional time to absorb and memorize the particulars tonight and during your travel tomorrow if necessary. The

success of the mission and, possibly, your lives depend on it. Return all of it to the office before leaving Casablanca."

Emmet glanced at his watch. "You have an appointment at the archaeological museum in Rabat at oh nine thirty tomorrow. Afterward, Simon will take you to acquire a car. Insurance and paperwork matching your covers will be in the glove compartment. The plan is for you to leave the following day. He will pick both of you up in the morning at your *riad* at oh eight hundred."

Natasha bolted up. "What?"

Emmet lifted his hand to caution Natasha, his voice serious and expression somber. "Mr. Rua is spending the night. This will provide you additional opportunity to study further tonight. Together. Your *riad* provides the beginning of a solid cover. The American is an exceptionally skilled and nefarious network with people everywhere. We are confident that neither of you have been compromised, but we cannot be sure who might be watching, listening, and reporting, which is why your *riad* is being swept while we meet. You leave together, Dr. Jordaan"—he cleared his throat and corrected himself—"Dr. Rua, as husband and wife from here forward."

※ ▨ ✿ ※

A rap on the door kept Natasha from going ballistic.

Emmet rose. "Prompt as usual," he said, looking pointedly at Bane.

Another knock and Matilda popped her head in. "Director? Mr. Nasir is here."

"Please show him in, and more tea, Matilda. Thank you."

Matilda ushered in a handsome man wearing a light djellaba over his dress pants and button-down shirt. He appeared to be roughly the same age as Natasha and Bane and was a few inches shorter than Bane, his eyes as dark as his recently cut hair and groomed beard.

"Rafiq, *salam alaikum.* Thank you for joining us." Emmet patted Rafiq on the shoulder while shaking his hand, then nodded to Natasha and Bane.

"*Wa-alaikum salam,* Emmet. It is good to see you, my friend."

Bane stepped forward and extended his hand as Matilda left with the teapot. "*Salam alaikum.* I'm Bane Rua. This is my wife, Dr. Natasha Rua."

Her new identity was introduced, just like that. No chances were being taken.

"I am Rafiq Nasir. *Wa-alaikum salam,*" he responded, shaking Bane's hand. "I look forward to working with you." He bowed his head slightly to Natasha. *"Salam alaikum."*

"Wa-alaikum salam, Rafiq," Natasha said, smiling softly. The Moroccan greeting of wishing peace to one another was lovely, and it took the edge off what had just transpired. "Please call me Natasha."

"Let's move to the smaller conference room," Emmet said, taking a step. He led them across the reception area.

Matilda trailed behind, ready with fresh empty cups and a larger teapot as they seated themselves around the rectangular wood table, Bane next to Natasha. "Shall I order lunch?"

"In order to be thorough, we'll likely go into the lunch hour. Are you all okay with a working lunch? We'll make it a light one since we recently finished our breakfast."

They all nodded and murmured yes.

"Thank you, Mrs. Bradley," Emmet said.

Bane added, "Matilda, a reminder that my wife does not eat red meat."

Natasha looked at her sandaled feet, surprised that Bane knew that. She pasted a grateful smile on her face as she looked at him. "Thank you."

Bane's expression softened, but he didn't make any movement to touch her.

"Is chicken fine with you, Dr. Rua?"

"Yes, thank you."

"Does anyone else have a request?" Matilda looked at each person individually to make sure she missed nothing. Her inquiry was met with shaking heads and no, thank yous.

Matilda exited and returned with four large folders, which she placed in front of Emmet.

"You are American, Bane, yes?" Rafiq glanced across the table.

"I am."

"But your accent, Natasha. It's not American. More..." He drank deeply from his cup, then placed it on the table. "I can't place it."

"It's French and South African. My father was Bantu and my mother French."

"I see. How long have you been married?"

Bane deftly enclosed Natasha's hand in his under the table, rubbing his thumb over her knuckles, then tapping once. Still rattled, she was grateful for the reminder and responded, "A month. And you?"

"I have been married for less than a year as well. My wife is pregnant, and the baby is coming soon."

"Newlyweds, like us. Congratulations on the baby." Bane smiled warmly at Natasha, his eyes darkening, almost appearing brown.

Natasha's insides flipped and she found herself powerless to look away.

"Are you staying in Rabat before we begin our mission?" Rafiq asked, watching them with interest.

Natasha wanted to squirm under the scrutiny. Instead, she chose to pay attention to Bane.

"No. Casablanca," Bane responded smoothly. "We realize it requires some extra driving at the outset, but Natasha was raised here, and she inherited her family's *riad*."

"Very nice. My wife and I reside in Casa as well." Rafiq's next question, to the director, allowed Natasha to relax. "How is your family, Emmet?"

"Stella, my daughter, had another child last month. A girl this time. I haven't seen her in person yet," he said wistfully. "My wife thinks the baby looks like Stella, who is thrilled to have a girl after two boys. We plan to head back to England at the end of the year."

"For a holiday or permanently?"

"Permanently. I'm retiring. I took this post for two years, as a favor to my boss. We will miss our flat in Bouznika, wonderful friends and colleagues, and the genial Moroccan culture."

"It has been a pleasure to work with you, Emmet."

"I feel the same. I hope to finish on a high note with this assignment." The director passed the folders around. "Let's give it a go, shall we?"

chapter 8

NATASHA GLANCED AT HER FOLDER. "Rafiq, fill me in on your background so that we understand better how we can assist you and benefit each other. My last assignment had some challenges I'm still dealing with."

His eyebrows knit together. "You and Bane were not together in Guatemala?"

"No." She shook her head.

"I assumed you were in Guatemala together. I heard that assignment was quite revealing," he said, holding her gaze steadily.

Wariness made her cautious. Director Cantrell had not briefed Bane or her on what Rafiq knew. She glanced at Emmet.

"Rafiq knows you apprehended Eric Schaus at the illegal site in Petén," Emmet assured her.

"I'd like to hear more about it," Rafiq said enthusiastically, leaning forward and resting his forearms on the table. "The details may provide deeper insight into the American's operation here. Schaus's apprehension was quite a coup and a vexing blow to the network. They vanished immediately, and their activity has only resurfaced quietly in the past week."

"You and me both. My wife still hasn't talked too much about it." Bane reached over, leaving a trail of sparking heat where his fingers grazed the thin fabric of the shawl covering her shoulder and arm. "Pretty traumatic…"

God, she could barely think when Bane touched her. How did he know her experience was traumatic? Natasha considered how Bane knew anything about her experience in Guatemala. The director must have told him. She'd ask him later, but right now she wanted her earlier inquiry answered. "Circling back to my question, what do you do specifically, Rafiq?"

Rafiq watched them closely as he spoke. "I am part of DSGN, Morocco's national police. I am a forensic anthropologist, focusing on the preservation of Morocco's cultural heritage, which is why I also report to and partner with the Ministry of Culture and Communication, the MCC, and AFRIPOL." Rafiq sat back suddenly, his hands clasped on the table, approval evident in his dark eyes. "The cover should work, Emmet. Natasha traveled to Guatemala on a different passport, under her maiden name, and her exposure was limited to Schaus's apprehension."

"I'm happy you concur, Rafiq. I feel it's our best option."

Natasha's hand flew to her chest. "You knew?"

"Yes. Emmet and I worked on your covers together. With a little more practice, you and Bane will do great."

Emmet looked at Rafiq, Natasha, and Bane, then at his watch. "I have an afternoon appointment in Fes, and the Ruas have some last-minute things to take care of. Let's dive in. Markets exist for every commodity. Similar to many countries and cultures around the world, Morocco's cultural heritage is under threat." Emmet pushed the nosepiece of his glasses up to rub at the bridge of his nose. "What was recently uncovered in Guatemala proved to be brilliant, terribly insightful." He inclined his head at Natasha. "Thank you, Dr. Rua."

He continued. "We are dealing with profit-driven looters, specifically the American, which was confirmed through questioning Schaus. The American is highly organized in its complexity and capacity, from excavation to sale, if you will. An enormous international nexus of professionals spanning areas in archaeology, curation, military, paramilitary, government, and more. They glean their initial and supporting information from satellite-based navigation systems such as LIDAR and drones as well as academic and popular publications and national and regional registries, which is how they target archaeological sites."

Bane shed his field vest and rolled up the sleeves of his shirt, exposing his powerful, tanned forearms. Natasha's eyes were drawn to where his

movements caused his shirt to stretch tautly against his shoulders, biceps, pecs, and abs. Everything about him was lean, hard edges and coiled strength. What would those arms feel like wrapped around her? What would it feel like to have her breasts pressed against his solid form? Natasha sighed deeply and then blinked in shock. *What in the hell am I doing? I'm in a goddamned meeting. I am not some prepubescent girl pining over her first crush.*

Emmet glanced at his open folder. "Rafiq and I provide this information so that you understand the scope and depth of the American. The network has tentacles everywhere. The American's activity seemed to come to a standstill after Schaus was apprehended in Guatemala in August, yet only two weeks ago the Moroccan Navy seized a fishing vessel before it was able to pass the breakwater in Casablanca. The navy was on heightened alert after impounding close to four hundred kilograms of cocaine in sealed containers aboard a South American ship over a year ago in June." He spread a dozen black-and-white photographs in front of the group. "The fishing vessel was smuggling two crates of prehistoric rock engravings that had been chiseled from the Draa River region in Southern Morocco. The engravings were Tazina-style art, dating to 5000 BP. Photos taken by the excavation team helped to identify and repatriate them quickly. There was another crate packed with stone tools and human bone fragments."

Natasha braced herself on the table with her elbows and massaged her temples, trying to absorb what the photos in front of her represented. Her words were clipped and rushed. "Were the tools and fragments from the Jebel Irhoud site?"

"Possibly. Which is what the General Directorate of National Security fears. Forensic archaeologists estimate the dates to fall in the range of other bones and tools excavated from Jebel Irhoud. That is still being determined."

She knew the answer but was compelled to ask anyway. "Is Jebel Irhoud closed?"

"No," Rafiq said. "Despite the vandalism and the fact that several of the guards went missing, the site remains under excavation. The artifacts recovered from the site are greatly significant to Moroccan culture and history. New guards have been hired; they are assisted by rotating shifts of Moroccan police."

"The Moroccan Navy has done a great job. Were they able to determine how those bones and fragments were secreted away?" Bane asked.

"Information points to locals working with excavation personnel who have ties with the American. Of course no one is talking," Rafiq said. "Additionally, 128 ancient Roman coins were hidden within large industrial plastic bags that were full of copper and lead used for smelting. The vessel was headed for Spain."

"Oh my god." Natasha sounded bereft.

Bane glanced from Natasha to Emmet, frowning.

Emmet nodded toward the photos. "At this time, we have not been able to ascertain the intended final destination, or destinations, for the coins, or if they were to be split up for multiple markets. The local numismatic exchanges and collectors were bypassed. The supply chain looks to be extensive. We have a team working on it. I—"

Natasha fell against the back of her chair and sighed loudly.

"I know, Doctor," Emmet said. "As a serious longtime collector yourself, you must find this unfortunate. That said, the coins are not the focus of your mission."

Natasha raised her head and looked the director square in the eye as she dipped her chin in agreement. "Yes, sir."

The door opened and Matilda bustled in with a rolling cart. "Sorry to interrupt. Lunch arrived more quickly than I anticipated." She placed a large communal dish and smaller dishes, all with lids, in the center of the table and gave each of them a cloth napkin, plate, and utensils. "Utensils for those who wish to use them. I'll help with the handwashing. Natasha?"

Natasha extended her hands, enjoying the rosewater Matilda trickled over her skin. She gently shook her hands into the basin, dried them on the napkin, and laid the napkin in her lap. "Thank you."

Matilda then moved to each of the men and did the same. "Bon appétit," she said to all of them before exiting.

"I'm starving." Bane began lifting the lids. "Thought we were having a light lunch?" Succulent aromas and color filled the room—lamb tagine, chicken with apricots, chickpea stew, bread, sauces, nuts, couscous, baba ghanoush, olives, and baklava. He turned, flashing Natasha an enormous smile, indicating the baklava. "Your favorite's in here," he said, his eyes twinkling.

Dammit. Bane had called her out in front of everyone. Natasha could not glare, nor could she do what she wanted to, which was to say something snide, put him in his place. Fine, she would play Bane's game.

Her voice was pure sweetness, her smile full. "I think the baklava got me into enough trouble last night." She widened her eyes at him. "Don't you?"

Natasha's effort backfired. If anything, Bane's smile expanded, the sexy glint in his eyes challenging her. "Wife, we should keep that between us. That kind of banter only makes others uncomfortable."

Emmet appeared amused and spoke up, shaking his head. "I agree with Bane. Let's eat."

chapter 9

E MMET PUSHED HIS PLATE AWAY. "If you don't mind, I'll continue talking while you dine." He checked his watch. "Rafiq must depart shortly." He opened his folder and sorted through the papers. "The current plan is for the Ruas to depart the day after tomorrow, in the afternoon, and travel to Ouarzazate via Fes. Rafiq, please program their numbers into your mobile and memorize them and their lodging information as well. You will continue reconnaissance here and in Rabat if necessary."

Natasha listened attentively while also trying to get food into her mouth with her nondominant right hand, wishing like hell she was eating with her left hand, with utensils, like the director.

"Do you want a fork?" Bane asked. "I realize you're out of practice."

Mouth full, Natasha shook her head. She chased her food down with a few sips of tea, then said, "Thanks, but no. I need to do this. It's like riding a bike. I'll get it."

"Okay," he said doubtfully.

Rafiq and Emmet glanced at Natasha but made no mention of the growing mess in front of her.

"Any changes in the time line are to be approved through me. I predict nightly briefings." Emmet tapped his forefinger on the table, his blue eyes sweeping over Natasha, Bane, and Rafiq. "The assignment is simple and yet it is not. We seek to recover and repatriate

skeletal remains, *Homo sapiens* thought to be over three hundred thousand years old, and the ancient codex I mentioned earlier. The chatter says the remains are still in-country. We're uncertain about the codex. Bear in mind that there is a rumor of another codex, whereabouts unknown, taken out of Egypt, briefly surfacing in Morocco before vanishing during World War II. It's rumored to be of Greek origin and written by Alexander the Great. We are not focused on that one."

"How would a codex purported to be written by one of Greece's great rulers have ended up in Egypt?" Bane asked.

Really? Natasha chewed on the inside of her bottom lip to keep herself from saying something snide, then answered, "You know how complex history is in this part of the world."

He squinted at her, mischief dancing in his gorgeous hazel eyes. "I learned a lot of things in school. History took a back seat to honing my skills." Bane winked at Natasha and offered her a disarming grin. "Educate me."

"Alexander the Great is regarded as one of the most successful military commanders in history with a legendary record of undefeated wars. He conquered Egypt, united the city-states, and led the Corinthian League, and he was also a student of Aristotle's." She paused and glanced at Emmet, who was beginning to look impatient. "So it is believable that it could have been written by him."

Bane rubbed the back of his neck. "Impressive."

"Very, and a codex authored by him would obviously be priceless." Natasha smiled.

Emmet closed his folder. "Let's stay on task here. Unless it falls into our laps during the assignment, the Alexander Codex is of no importance."

"I need to depart," Rafiq said, rising. He looked each of them in the eye. *"Salam alaikum."*

"Wa-alaikum salam," they returned in unison, getting to their feet.

Emmet walked him to the door. "Drive carefully. Be safe, Rafiq."

※ ※ ※ ※

When Emmet returned to the silent conference room, Natasha was rifling through the contents of her tote after having moved to the

opposite end of the conference table from Bane, who leaned back in his seat with closed eyes. Emmet cleared his throat. Bane opened his eyes and Natasha stopped what she was doing.

"Well done, you two. Now I want you to take some time to get to know one another better before becoming roommates this evening, find some common ground. You are among our best contractors. It is imperative that you work amicably. Get your things and come with me."

Natasha and Bane trailed him to a small and empty, windowless office. He flipped on the overhead light. "I'll be back later. Until then, work on your relationship. Work on the wedding details. I'm going to ask you about one another, details that weren't in your bios."

Natasha plopped into the large armchair behind the desk, leaving a smaller uncomfortable-looking, armless chair for Bane. She smiled as the chair swiveled.

"Uh, Nat," he said, changing how he addressed Natasha as she glared at him. "Natasha, don't you think we should switch chairs? I'm the bigger person here."

"No."

"I see. You're trying to put me in my place. Fine." He smiled dangerously. "I'll play, sweetheart."

"Don't call me that."

"Let's start. Favorite color. Red," he said confidently.

Natasha rolled her eyes. "Lucky guess."

"Nope. Luggage. Toenails. Lipstick on those fucking beautiful lips of yours."

"It's vermillion," she fired back, masking that she was warmed by his compliment.

"Whatever. It's in the spectrum of red."

Natasha regarded him thoughtfully. "Blue."

"Nope." He laughed. "I expected you'd try the safe choice."

"Safe choice?"

"Blue. It's the color most people prefer. But we're not most people, are we? You get two more guesses."

"You're making up the rules as we go. Black," she stated, getting sucked into their game.

Bane threw his head back, laughed, and then sat on the corner of the desk, almost next to her. "Black isn't a color; it's the absence of light."

Interesting answer. "It is when I mixed all the paint or crayons together. So only one more guess?"

"Yep."

"Tell me."

"You don't like to be wrong. Or lose."

Natasha pushed back into her chair and grew still. "You're so wrong. You don't know me."

"No, I don't, but I'm trying to. And I am so right. Your body language just gave you away," he announced, watching her. "To save you from lying to me, I'll give you the answer. This time. Green."

"I would not have lied."

"Lie two. As my partner, you've got to do a convincing job. You also have to be able to adlib seamlessly."

"Do you lie well?"

"If I have to."

Hmm. "Why green?"

"It makes me think of life. Rebirth. Spring."

"Your eyes are green sometimes." *Oh damn.*

Bane didn't react as she thought he would, remaining straight-faced, but his eyes changed. To a dark green. "Why red?"

"I've always been drawn to it."

"It's the color of power and determination."

"Yes."

"It also represents love and passion. Are you a passionate woman, Doctor?"

"Your question is inappropriate."

"Mm. I don't know. I am your husband. I should know."

"You are playing my husband in name only."

"My role could evolve into something more. First kiss?"

"Seriously?"

"Okay, I'll go first. Her name was Grace and we were twelve. Summer, at the creek, behind her family's barn."

"Just a peck?"

Bane laughed at that. "Yeah. I was as sure as fuck she could feel my heart jackhammering though my lips. She pushed me in the mud afterward and ran away. Humiliating."

Natasha giggled, fascinated by his admission, never imagining this strapping, gorgeous man could ever have been nervous, even as a boy. She opted for a safer question. "Would you rather go on a hike or see a movie?"

"Hike. You?"

"Hike."

Bane circled back. "First kiss?"

Natasha broke eye contact and swiveled the armchair from side to side. "It was far later than yours."

"Sixteen?"

"Just leave it," she said, prickly, embarrassed that she had been twenty and it was a meaningless, sloppy, mess with a guy she didn't know at a wild party.

Bane frowned at Natasha's reaction. "City or country?"

"I enjoy both. You?"

"Country."

"Have you always been so brash?"

"If speaking my mind is what you're referring to, yes."

"I find it offensive, Mr. Rua."

"Bane."

"I find your brashness unappealing, Bane."

"You just lied to me again. You're definitely interested in me, and I find you as attractive as hell."

"You need to dial it back."

Bane's asymmetrical grin accompanied eyes that danced with merriment. "Liar, liar."

"So, our"—Natasha twisted in her chair—"marriage. What's our story?"

Bane studied her as he spoke. "Our attraction to each other was immediate. Like, boom!" He clapped his hands together, making Natasha jump. "In the hotel lobby. We met when we were checking in at the same time. We were never apart."

Natasha snickered. "What an imagination. You can spin a story like no one I've ever known."

"Work with me," he encouraged. "It was wild and passionate. I proposed and we decided to marry before the second week was out."

"No one who knows me is going to buy this."

"Oh, they will. I am very convincing," he said, grinning wolfishly.

Natasha's insides flipped and fluttered.

"We got married on the beach. At sunset. Barefoot."

Isn't he the romantic? Surprised, Natasha nodded. If she ever married, saying her vows at sunset on a remote beach was her dream wedding. "Where were we exactly?"

"Fiji, and as far as our honeymoon, we're still on it," he drawled, giving her a sexy, crooked smile. His demeanor turned serious. "You can't be uptight or prickly around me. You've got to sell it. Sell us. We both have to. Can you do that?"

Natasha drew a deep breath and sat up straighter. "I can. Next." She squinted at him. "Interests and hobbies?"

"Many, and I'm open to exploring more. I participated in sports growing up. Worked the farm with my family. I enjoy hanging with my family and friends. Photography."

"So, photography plays well into your cover."

"Yep."

"Tell me more." She sat forward and placed her elbow on the table, supporting her chin on the heel of her hand. "I'm supposed to know you."

"I enjoy the outdoors. Hunting, fishing, and tinkering."

"I've never fished, but I'd like to try it. What's tinkering?"

"Tinkering is figuring out how things work or getting them to work again, hands-on, experiential. My grandfather got me interested when he'd work on antique farm equipment. Keeps my mind and hands busy."

Natasha studied Bane's large hands. His broad fingers were long with wide nails, which he kept short. They looked strong enough to kill a man. Could they also be tender? She glanced up and sucked in her breath; intensity swirled in his hazel depths.

Bane's rugged voice brushed across her nerves. "What about you?" he asked softly.

"I love to cook, garden, and stay active."

"I like to eat. You enjoy games."

Natasha nodded. "Very much. And I'm good at them."

"So am I. We're going to make an excellent team."

※ ※ ✳ ※

A few hours had passed before Emmet asked Matilda to have Simon bring the car around. He faced Natasha and Bane. "While we're waiting on Simon, a few things."

Natasha and Bane listened intently.

"Anna Guilford, the Rabat Museum's head curator, is expecting you tomorrow morning. The *riad* is clean. Simon has your key, Doctor. He has also been briefed about your cover since he is part of the team. Get your travel shopping done. It might go more quickly with Simon's help. Itemize any expenses and give them to him."

Simon knocked and stuck his head in. "Ready?"

"Well, let's go, wife. You have things to do, and I need time to pack and move in."

"Quit calling me that," she said under her breath.

"Nat."

"And that," she snapped at him. "It's Natasha."

Bane threw up his hands as if to ward her off. "Simon, can you drop me off before you take her shopping, then swing back and get me a few hours later?"

"Sure, Bane."

"Good luck, and—" Emmet lowered his brows and scrutinized both of them. "Please continue working out your differences. Did you cement a story of your romance and wedding?"

"We did," Natasha said.

Emmet looked from Natasha to Bane. "I don't feel that you made much headway in the 'let's be cordial' department. You are professionals and colleagues. Try to adopt a mode of civility. You were very impressive in front of Rafiq, so I know you are capable. We'll be in communication."

"Yes, sir," Natasha said, shaking his hand before exiting the room stiffly.

Bane extended his hand, preparing to walk out behind Simon and Natasha. "Emmet."

The director motioned him back in and closed the door slightly, dropping his voice. "Be safe. Take care of her, Bane. She has the highest recommendations, very respected. Give her some room to adjust to"— he squeezed Bane's forearm with his other hand—"the manner in which you conduct yourself. You must have each other's backs if what we've heard about the American is true."

chapter 10

"YOU'RE LATE," NATASHA GRUMBLED, ARMS crossed over her breasts and glaring as she let a damp-looking Bane in. The furrow between her eyes deepened as she caught sight of numerous duffels and luggage behind him and the others that Simon held. Remembering her manners, she greeted Simon.

"Good evening to you too, wife." Bane winked at her and flashed his hand. "I'm becoming accustomed to it." His eyes rested on her breasts pushing up from her crossed arms. "Hmm. I think you've missed me. I thought I'd clean up before I got"—putting extra emphasis on the next word—"*home*. I spent some extra time in the *hammam*."

"How lovely for you."

"I'm feeling particularly invigorated after a good cleanse, scrub, and massage." He leaned down, his scent of soft sandalwood, spice, and male befuddling her brain. "Have a kiss for me?"

She dropped her arms, anger propelling her away from him. Natasha stomped around the wall dividing the *setwan* from the atrium and pointed into the darkened hallway on the other side of the arched columns. "Your room is past the last *bâyt*. On the right," she said when his eyebrows rose in question. "All the way in the back."

"Our room?"

"Your room," she said icily. "I sleep elsewhere."

Bane slipped off his shoes. "Then you'd better show me around so I don't get lost. You know, end up somewhere else unintentionally."

Simon remained silent, watching the back-and-forth, amusement evident on his face.

"Please leave his stuff here in the *setwan*, Simon. We'll see you tomorrow."

"As you wish. Tomorrow then. Good night."

"Night, and thanks." Bane locked the door behind Simon, then turned. He held up his hand to her. "Easy. I'm totally safe, that is unless you want to tangle."

"What the hell? Everything with you is innuendo," she said, furious.

"It wasn't innuendo, sweetheart. You're struggling with your overactive imagination. Cool exterior, but you run a little hot under the hood, don't you? Have trouble containing it. Is that it?" He chuckled softly. "That's understandable. I know you like what you see."

Natasha's temper launched, raw and angry. "You arrogant ass." She seethed. "All that crap in the director's office."

"Ah, yes." He held both his hands up in mock surrender, nodding and grinning wickedly. "Guilty. I didn't expect to be introduced to such a beautiful, sexy, strong woman. Remember, I mentioned how attractive I find you. I reacted as a man, not a professional. I'm late with my apology." He rubbed at his beard, then thrust his hand forward to shake, his eyes gauging her, his voice sincere. "Forgive me?"

Natasha remained stubbornly still, arms rigidly at her sides, fists clenched. The memory of how he'd affected her the last time—hell, every time they touched—was all too immediate.

"We're supposed to be working together. Truce?"

Truce. How the hell was she to get to truce? She couldn't even think when he was around. All her common sense and control fled, as it was doing now. It pissed her off. Mightily.

"Natasha."

She snapped out of it and took a deep breath.

"Can you meet me halfway?"

Natasha considered as she focused on her geranium-red painted toenails, then tentatively extended her hand to shake his. Her pulse zinged as they touched. If anything, it was worse than the first time. Startled, Natasha looked up into eyes that were a kaleidoscope of color—an ever-changing mix of gold, brown, and green, fringed by thick black lashes. Some would call them hazel; she'd argue his eyes defied description.

Entranced, she felt her temper cool and she grew silent and then still, overly aware of something stirring deep within. She sucked in her breath and held it.

"Fuck. This is going to be more difficult than I imagined," he said quietly and stepped into her space, pinning her with his sexy, thickly lashed eyes, gently lifting her chin. He paused, gazing into her. Her full lips were parted. Waiting. He lowered his mouth to meet hers.

The knocker thumped heavily against the front door, stopping them when they were a mere whisper from each other. They both blinked at the intrusion, the interrupted kiss hanging heavily between them.

"I'll get that," she said huskily, moving past him and opening the door. "Well, hello again. Come in, Simon."

He held Bane's worn leather messenger bag. "You forgot this." Simon's gaze moved between them, clearly picking up the tension that was different from a moment ago. He squinted his eyes as if thinking. "See you both in the morning. Good night again."

※ ※ ※ ※

"I'll show you around, Mr. Rua."

"Bane. Hell, we almost kissed. Nat—"

"Look. Bane," she said carefully, drawing out his name. "Nothing happened." She waved her hands in front of him. "Let it go."

He opened his mouth as if to say something, then shut it as her "I dare you to disagree with me" stare challenged him.

She spun and headed out the *setwan* and across the atrium into the hall of arches, toward the back with a go-to-hell long stride. Bane kept pace behind her, admiring the enticing sway of her hips.

At the open, carved double doors, Natasha flipped on the light. "Make yourself at home for however long our assignment lasts. Perhaps we'll return next week. Who knows? The armoire has plenty of space, so you can put your things in there. The bathroom is next to you. Try to keep everything neat and clean. I am not your maid, and we need to keep up the pretense that you and I are married. Extra blankets are in the armoire."

The bedroom was large, a melody of color, with rugs layering the floor and two leather chairs flanking the king-sized bed, which was covered with a cream-colored bedspread and tasseled, decorative pillows. Beams

of *zouaq*—colorful hand-painted wood—decorated the ceiling. "You're not sleeping here?"

"Why are you making me repeat myself? This is your bedroom," she said, enunciating pointedly.

"Meaning yours is elsewhere? I'm not bedding down with my wife? Sleeping with you makes more sense." He grinned.

"No, you ass," she spat out harshly. "I went through this with you just moments ago. Think with the head on your shoulders. You're not sleeping with me."

"Whoa." He chuckled. "That's an overreaction when your eyes are telling me you desire otherwise."

"Never."

"Earlier—"

"You misunderstood—"

He raised his eyebrows, his eyes landing on her pebbled nipples. "I don't believe I did."

Natasha crossed her arms over her chest again and huffed then, clearly noticing where Bane's eyes had gone, then dropped her arms to her sides. "Focus on the mission. Please. We agreed to a truce."

He mumbled under his breath.

"What?"

His stared at her intensely, full of heat. "Do you really want to know?"

"I'm a big girl."

He groaned. "We reluctantly agreed. I dare you to contradict that."

Natasha swallowed slowly, sidestepping the question. "So, any questions?"

"A few." Bane dropped his teasing. Time to focus on the tactical situation like the former-special-operator he was. "Where's the kitchen? Alarm system? Where do you keep your piece? Where are all the exterior doors located? Roof access? Show me around 'our' home. I need to be familiar with my surroundings."

"My gun is currently in my nightstand. No alarm. We're in a safe neighborhood."

"Right. But knowing where I am and how to defend that space is part of my DNA. Humor me."

"Humor you?"

"Yeah, it's an American idiom for go along with my request even if you don't see the purpose."

"Just keep the bathroom pristine, Mr. Rua. And the bedroom door closed."

"It's Bane," he ground out. Fuck, she was mercurial. "Get used to it. You're going to blow our cover if you call your husband 'Mr. Rua.' Are you expecting visitors?"

"No, not that it's any of your business. The bathroom is used by guests, everyone. Guests are always a possibility. As you just pointed out, we need to be mindful of our cover."

"I see." Bane's voice turned husky. He thoroughly enjoyed throwing her off center again. "Can I use yours? I like the idea of us sharing intimate places."

She didn't respond immediately. Instead, she inhaled and squinted at him, clearly exasperated, then motioned sideways with her head. "I'll show you the *riad*."

"Yes, ma'am." Bane happily followed her spectacular backside and long legs. "And Nat, it is my business. We're a team. You're my partner, and until we are instructed otherwise, my wife."

Natasha paused and her body tightened, but she remained silent, then continued moving.

Bane appreciated the stately upper-class *riad*, complete with an expansive atrium open to the sky and containing a large, burbling fountain and attractive trees. The walls were adorned with *tadelakt*, the waterproof Moroccan plaster, and geometric mosaics. The passage above ran the perimeter alongside the doored rooms and was open to the atrium, and its railing was a screen of intricately carved dark wood that played off the lattice screens throughout both levels. Natasha had the largest bedroom upstairs, up front, close to the tightly winding steps. It was the farthest from his assigned room.

The rooftop terrace was beautiful and spacious, the high wall affording privacy. A pergola extended over half of it, a raised wood deck and comfortable furniture underneath. He made note of the exterior doors (three; two downstairs, one upstairs). Keeping with Moroccan tradition, the *riad* was interior focused, without windows, allowing for privacy and protection from weather. A small pool and another pergola shading the outside dining area were features of the well-tended gardens and lawn between the kitchen and the caretaker's house. The high wall, matching

the exterior of the *riad* and the caretaker's house, bordered the gardens and lawn and created a fully enclosed space.

"Are you all good now? Comfortable?"

"Shouldn't I sleep with you? For the sake of appearance?"

Natasha looked like she wanted to scream. "Drop it," she hissed, then looked away.

"You enjoy our banter. Our foreplay." He stepped forward and Natasha backed against the wall behind her. Bane casually placed his hands on the wall, bracketing her within his arms but not touching her. She could easily step away if she wanted but she chose not to; he had no doubt she could handle him. He lowered his head. His lips skimmed her jawline, and he felt the goose bumps rise on her skin as his breath skated over her ear. His voice was low and quiet. "Nat—"

She ground out, "It's Natasha."

"We will sleep together." He pushed off the wall and stood straight, looking deeply into her eyes. "I want it. You want it. I'm a patient man. When you can no longer take care of yourself, come to me. I'll sate you and then fire you up, over and over, sweetheart. You and I?" His finger traced the pulsing column of her delicate neck, then paused, his mossy brown gaze lingering on hers. "We're going to be epic."

Natasha drew in a shaky breath and answered, her whisper fractured and totally unconvincing. "Never."

His eyes sparkled and a crooked, sexy smile accompanied his words. "Never say never."

She looked as though she was two steps away from firing off a retort, but then she quickly made her way inside and down the stairs. He followed at a more leisurely pace, appreciating the view of her backside again, amused that she fought the sexual heat between them.

Bane stepped inside his doorway and watched her vanish as she took the stairs up to her room. "Sleep tight, beauty," he said, to himself. "Dream of me. Dream of us."

chapter 11

T HE LIGHT GLOWED SOFTLY THROUGH Clara and Oliver's window. Instead of turning in, Natasha left the *riad* and crossed the dewy garden to the couple's welcoming space. Even when Mémé and Pépé had been living, she often sought the additional wise counsel of Clara or Oliver. Natasha tapped on the ornate wood door, then stuck her hands into the pockets of her skirt, playing with the silver band on her finger while she waited for it to open.

Clara pulled her shawl around her thin shoulders, scanning Natasha with a long look before a smile wreathed in wrinkles broke over her face. "Good evening, dear! I'll make us some tea."

Second thoughts made her reconsider. "I can come back, Clara. It's late."

"Nonsense. You're here, aren't you? And I'm up. Come in. We'll go sit on the patio with our tea and chat. Oliver just retired. He has a long day tomorrow."

Once they got comfortable on one of the outdoor sofas, a lump formed in Natasha's throat. "How do you always know?"

A soft smile filled Clara's face and eyes. "Child, I've known you since you were born. I mentioned it the other night when I thought there was more on your mind than travel and work, like that fine-looking man we saw earlier this evening, the man staying with you?"

"So you noticed him."

"Oliver did. In the garden taking photos. Then, of course, I had to

69

take a peek. I may be older, but I'm not dead. My, he's exceptionally handsome. What's his name, this man of yours?"

Natasha's heart raced at the thought of Bane being hers, of being with him. What would that be like? "Bane."

"What do women your age call men who look like Bane?"

"Gorgeous? Hunky? Easy on the eyes?"

Clara burst out laughing. "Those words sum him up rather well. Tell me about him. I assume there's more to him than his good looks."

"Well, he's American, works as a professional freelance photographer, which explains him being outside with a camera, and"—Natasha inhaled and plastered a huge smile on her face—"he's my husband."

"Your husband? Natasha! You got married?" Clara squeezed Natasha's hands, examining the band Natasha wore. "In all the excitement of seeing you yesterday and tonight, I didn't even notice. When? I should go get Oliver," she said, starting to stand.

So many questions. "Oh, don't do that. I'll talk to Oliver later."

"Child!" Clara moved forward and wrapped her arms around Natasha and squeezed tightly. "Congratulations!"

"Thank you."

Clara's eyes sparkled as she regarded Natasha. "Tell me more."

"It was a whirlwind. We just knew. Both of us were on vacation in Fiji. We met and—" Natasha threw her hands in the air. "Boom! I can't even explain it."

"When?"

"Last month." Natasha said confidently, thankful she never discussed her work with Clara and Oliver.

"Very newly married! Are you happy?"

Natasha paused a moment before answering. "I am," she said, beaming. "I'm still getting to know him."

"Well of course you are, dear. You'll be getting to know Bane for the rest of your married life. People change. I still learn new things about Oliver."

"Our marriage got me thinking about Mama and Papa, which is part of the reason I came over." Natasha unfolded to standing and wrung her hands, then took a few steps before returning to sit. Uncomfortable, she changed the subject. "What do you know of my parents? Mama and Papa

both shared that they met, fell head over heels in love, and married within two weeks. Mémé and Pépé came around quickly and fell in love with Papa too. Papa's parents, well, they never accepted Mama. Or us…"

Clara sighed and ran her fingers over Natasha's exposed tattoo. "That's all true. Oliver and I loved Peter too. Marie and Peter were very much in love, very devoted to one another. They were of different temperaments, from very different backgrounds. However, your parents compromised and theirs was a beautiful union, all the much richer after you and your brothers were born."

"I know Mama's background, but not Papa's. I asked so many times, but Papa never wished to speak about it, and because he forbade it, Mama wouldn't speak of it either."

"That's because it was painful." Clara sipped her tea.

Natasha cocked her head, searching Clara's blue eyes with her gray ones. "Do you know?"

"Yes, dear."

"Tell me. Please, Clara," she whispered. "I have a right to know."

"You do." She set her cup down on the side table and took both of Natasha's hands in hers. "Peter, your father, was a child of apartheid, a system of racial segregation of whites and non-whites. He and his family were classified as black and stripped of their South African citizenship, and much more. They were banished to one of the Bantu homelands outside the White areas. They lost so much. You must have surmised this, Natasha," Clara said, her eyes pregnant with sadness.

"I did. But without my parents speaking of it, well, it's as if it didn't happen to Papa or to his family. It never seemed real." Natasha crossed her arms, hugging herself. "Does that make sense?"

"It does," Clara said. "During apartheid, laws were enacted making it illegal to be intimate with or marry a person of another color. With the approval of his parents, Peter left South Africa with missionaries and received an education. Like his parents, Peter's citizenship was reinstated in 1994 when Mandela came to power. Apartheid came to an end. Peter returned to South Africa to work, falling in love with Marie when she and Henri and Josette—your grandparents—were vacationing in the Cape. Marie and Peter married in a small ceremony on the beach, long before doing so was popular. Henri and Josette flew us down to witness the ceremony of their only child and support the newlyweds. It was a lovely ceremony. So intimate. So much love. Everyone cried."

"Bane and I were married on the beach at sunset."

"Oh, how I wish I—both of us—could have been there."

Her smile and her voice were soft. "Me too."

Clara patted Natasha's hand. "Well, in matters of the heart, you just listen."

"I looked at those pictures so often, wondering why it was only Mémé and Pépé and you and Oliver present." Natasha sighed.

"Peter's parents would not accept Marie, even after the marriage, and that created further strain. Your parents were living in Johannesburg while Peter worked and finished his degree in architecture, so enamored was he with what Henri did. Marie was a guest lecturer at the university. Peter was so excited about your birth and pleaded with his parents to come see you, but they refused. Josette and Henri arrived to help a week before you were born. They stayed longer and helped your parents move to France with you as soon as they secured work. Peter renounced his South African citizenship after receiving French citizenship five years later. You know the rest."

"Papa renounced his South African citizenship? I didn't know that."

"Yes. Peter had hoped your birth would foster reconciliation, but his parents showed no inclination to welcome you into the Jordaan family. He renounced his citizenship soon afterward. Josette and Henri discovered that after your parents and brothers were killed, when they reached out to Peter's family. Peter's parents told your grandparents their son had been dead to them upon marrying their daughter. They would never accept their interracial marriage."

Natasha shook her head in disbelief as the pieces fell into place. "I didn't know. I now understand why Papa's family was polite but aloof. I thought it was me. But it wasn't. They're just close-minded people. We've come a long way in our world today."

"You have. Many have, able to forgive and move forward. But many cannot, remaining entrenched in their experiences, in their pasts. It's really not for us to judge. Try not to blame Peter's parents, dear, but understand their perspective. Marie represented apartheid, the racist system that nearly destroyed them."

"But to put something like that ahead of your child? I don't get that. When does the healing begin?"

"I may be speaking out of turn, but I believe Josette thought she had your best interests in mind when she decided not to share Peter's story,

believing you would not pursue your South African family since you had never met any of them. Henri disagreed. It was one of the few times I can remember your grandparents being cold with one another. Then Henri died. And Josette."

Natasha's eyebrows rose with her question. "So I shouldn't judge Mémé either?"

"What purpose does it serve? Your grandmother loved you with every fiber of her soul." Clara smiled sadly and squeezed Natasha's hand, then yawned. "I need to get some sleep, dear. And you need to be with your husband."

"Thank you for talking with me. For listening. For always being there for me. I love you, Clara," Natasha said, rising.

Clara rose as well and stepped in, hugging Natasha, her head coming only to Natasha's shoulder. "I love you too and missed you so. I'm so glad you're here, and I look forward to meeting Bane."

They walked to the front door. Clara lightly touched the Fatima on Natasha's wrist. Her eyes welled up as she spoke. "Fatima's hand channels good, healing energy. Allow yourself to be filled with the blessing of joy and peace. Open your soul, dear. Embrace hope and trust your heart. Sleep well." She hugged Natasha one more time before closing the door.

in the trenches

الحركه بركه.

⊠ ❋

Movement is a blessing.

❖

chapter 12

"**C**OFFEE?"

"Yes, I have coffee. I also have tea," Natasha said curtly, taking a break from her dates, tea, and pastry in the kitchen. "Sorry," she mumbled, looking down immediately and busying herself with her skirt while taking him in surreptitiously. "I also went to the bakery. The pastries are in the sack."

Bane stopped in his tracks and rubbed the back of his neck. "Um. I don't want to put you out. Whatever you have ready is fine."

"Tea."

"Tea is good. Thanks." He helped himself to several pastries and added a small pile of dates to his plate, then sat down at the table.

Natasha presented her back to him as she ate at the counter, so he took the opportunity to observe her. She was exquisite. Delicately boned without seeming frail. A natural linen skirt flowed to just above her shapely ankles, with a loose red tank tucked into it. Her narrow waist, which he could easily span with both hands, was accentuated with a colorful woven belt. The tank set off her burnished-sepia complexion and lean, toned arms. Her sun-kissed brown hair was piled into a loose knot, highlighting the fine bones in her face. He ached to unpin it and run his hands through the silky-looking curls. Oversized sunglasses perched on top of her head and large loops hung from her ears, almost matching the silver color her eyes changed to when her emotions ran high. Her silhouette was elegant, regal. What would it be like to run his tongue over

her jawline and the column of her neck, graze her beautiful skin with his teeth?

As if she heard his silent question, she turned, regarding him with a slate stare that rivaled polished gunmetal. He noted that she wore a shimmery rose-tinted gloss on her full lips. That he would like to kiss that color off her lips also passed through his mind before he uttered, "Simon will be here shortly. Will you be ready?"

Natasha placed her cup on the counter too roughly, spilling the tea. "Of course I'm ready," she scoffed, wiping up her mess. "Are you?"

"Someone is a grumpy girl this morning." Bane chuckled. "Have another pastry."

"Look," she said, putting her hands on her hips and glaring at him. "I'm tired and I don't like this... this cover... one bit."

He chased his pastry down with a swig of tea and wiped his mouth, volleying back, "Well, sweetheart, neither do I. But it's part of our assignment. We have big dangerous fish to catch and fry. Don't fuck it up. There's too much at risk, as in me and you."

"I don't fuck up anything," she huffed, bending over, getting in his face, her narrowed eyes flashing silver.

Bane smiled, enjoying himself. He baited her some more. "You get me stirred up when you get all feisty on me. It's sexy as hell to this Indiana boy."

"Dammit to hell. Just stop."

Bane opened his mouth to respond, then thought better of it and wolfed down the rest of his breakfast and had another cup of tea. The wall clock ticked in the silence until the knocker resonated back to the kitchen. He put his dishes in the sink and grinned at her. "Time to leave, grumpy."

She didn't respond, but her fiery temper licked at him.

He exited at a jog, still grinning, calling over his back, "I still think you need to get laid."

Natasha's sandals slapped the tiled floor behind him. Bane opened the door and ducked sideways as a plate whizzed past his ear. Simon caught it midair like a Frisbee, his expression indicating he had heard some of the exchange. "It seems you're having a rough start to your morning, Bane."

"Morning, Simon. Something like that," Bane said, laughing on his way out the door.

✳ ✳ ✳ ✳

Natasha yanked her tote from the bottom of the stairs and pulled her sunglasses down from her hair and over her eyes.

"Good morning, Doctor."

"Good morning. He's an incorrigible ass, Simon." Natasha's lips compressed in a hard line.

Simon smiled tightly. "Let's go, shall we?"

"I'll sit in back," she said, locking the front door.

"I'm sorry, but that seat has already been taken." Simon inclined his head toward the car.

Bane filled the back seat. Frustration bubbled up in Natasha. She did not relish having him behind her. The man drove her mad. With any luck, he would leave her the hell alone. She was wound tight from a lack of sleep and unwelcome erotic dreams and was not in the mood for his brand of flirting.

Bane tapped on Natasha's shoulder from the back seat. She refused to turn around; the last thing she wanted to do was to get lost in those eyes of his.

She kept her voice even, all too aware that Simon was finding their tension amusing. "Can I help you, Bane?"

"We didn't go over the information again as requested by Emmet."

Natasha responded once she was sure she could sound civil. "I did. All by myself. I didn't see how it was necessary to do it with you." She tapped on her temple. "I've got it all in here."

"I'm not confident you can pull it off. My ass on the line."

"You've already said that."

"Just making sure you heard me."

She let that comment pass.

"Earth to Nat," Bane called loudly from the back, interrupting her thoughts.

It's Natasha. She remained silent, thinking, watching more sand-colored buildings appear among the scruffy vegetation and trees anchored in the sloping hills bordering the road on the outskirts of Rabat.

"Fine. Ignore me. Thanks for having my back, partner," he scoffed.

Decision made, she inhaled deeply. She was going to dive in. "'Scuse me, Simon."

She unbuckled her seat belt and balled up her skirt, tucked it between her legs, then carefully crawled over and none too gracefully face-planted herself in Bane's crotch, her butt and legs akimbo. Simon whipped the car safely to the shoulder. Traffic sped by as Natasha scrambled to get off Bane's lap.

Glee and a blinding smile replaced Bane's initial surprised expression. "You decided to join me."

This was not what she had intended. Natasha flopped around like a fish out of water, ending faceup, her head resting on his growing arousal. She panicked and looked to the front seat where Simon was busy adjusting the rearview mirror, wholly enjoying the two of them. When she succeeded in sitting next to Bane and adjusting her skirt, her face was flushed with exertion and embarrassment.

"That was unforgettable!" Bane laughed hysterically, rendering her speechless. He tilted his head back, eyes crinkled, mouth wide open, straight white teeth exposed, chortling his ass off. He placed one of his large hands over his flat stomach. "Damn, my gut hurts."

Natasha growled at him, which made Bane laugh even harder. He wiped at his eyes.

"Seriously? You found that funny?" Her anger bloomed like algae in a stagnant summer pond.

"Simply the best." Bane erupted into laughter again, almost doubling over. He was clearly fighting to bring himself under control. "Are you okay? I'm sorry. Should've asked first, but having you launch like that. And land as you did—" He started to laugh again. "Shit, Nat. That was the best. Totally unexpected. You made my morning."

Natasha burst out laughing. "You make me so mad. I lose my head. Let me know when you're done laughing at my expense."

His words mixed with his laughter. "Hey. You okay up there, man? Did she clock you with one of her lovely feet while she was going over?"

Natasha snorted.

"I am in one piece. Somehow she missed me entirely." Simon chuckled.

Bane sobered. Still smiling, he shook his head. "Okay. Think I'm done." He twisted slightly to look at her and then started laughing again.

"Seriously, Nat. I never thought I'd see Miss Starched Ass Stick in the Butt do something like that." He took a deep breath and closed his eyes, then opened them again. His concern appeared genuine. "Are you okay?"

"Obviously I am." Best intentions. *Nothing more than a bruised ego.* The admission hurt. *Miss Starched Ass Stick in the Butt. Jesus.* Was that really how he saw her? Probably, and that wasn't good. When was the last time someone appeared genuinely concerned about her? Natasha was unable to utter a word because her heart stuttered around in her chest. *Nat.* She could live with that. It really wasn't a big deal, and actually coming out of his mouth it made her feel... hope. And that felt... good.

Bane grinned. "This will be something we can tell our grandchildren about."

Natasha's breathing slowed as she found herself lost in Bane's hazel depths.

"Relax. It's okay. We're married," he whispered in her ear. He clasped her hand in his and pulled her closer, leaning over to help. "Let's get you buckled up." His deep voice took on a husky edge and he clicked in her seat belt. "Simon, how much longer?"

"Traffic is moving well. About thirty minutes."

Natasha and Bane reviewed their covers and assignment details while Simon drove.

"The archaeological museum is up ahead," Simon announced.

"Time to look alive. We're on. Ready?"

Natasha smiled. "I am."

chapter 13

THE ACQUISITIONS AREA OF THE museum was an enormous windowless catacomb. Natasha and Bane walked briskly behind Ms. Guilford, the curator who had met them at the front desk upstairs. On either side of them, varying sizes of crates were scattered about in different stages of being unpacked, and staff busied themselves cataloging the items and logging them into the museum's network.

Ms. Guilford's heels clacked over the tile, and Natasha noticed how the curator's hips sashayed under her skirt, working to get Bane's attention. *The woman is going to throw her hips out.* Ms. Guilford made a sudden right into a hall and headed through a door. Natasha elbowed Bane sharply and gave him a hard look just before they followed her into the cube of glass.

"*What?*" he mouthed.

"I apologize for the state of my office," Ms. Guilford said, closing the door behind them, her eyes following her extended arm as it swept over the cramped, disheveled space. "Have a seat please, Mr. Rua. Dr. Rua." She smiled warmly and indicated the empty, utilitarian metal chairs while clearing hers of paperwork. "I apologize, Mr. Rua. The chair is a little small for a man of your size." Her tone dripped with female appreciation.

Natasha tamped down her annoyance. "He'll manage. Trust me."

Bane faced Natasha and winked, further elevating her annoyance. He held the chair and bent over as she sat, his hand briefly stroking her shoulder before he moved the other chair next to hers. Closer, he slipped

an arm around Natasha, encouraging her to lean in. His hand slid over her arm and brushed her knuckles. Bane continued until Natasha started to soften, then released her. He leaned back and stretched his long legs out in front of him, wearing a satisfied expression, his hands clasped loosely in his lap.

His simple act lit her blood on fire. Natasha's eyes had a mind of their own as they stared at his big hands parked over his zipper, then traveled up his body—past the webbed belt threaded through the loops of his khakis to his snug-fitting button-down, which highlighted the flat, hard planes of his abs and chest—to his face. Bane's eyes connected with hers, and he flashed a straight white smile.

Ms. Guilford took several folders from the top of the credenza behind her desk and lowered herself to her seat, slipping on her glasses, which did little to detract from the lovely, delicate face framed by silky, long brown hair and bangs. After quickly flipping through the pile and extracting several pocket folders, she pushed one of them toward Natasha and Bane, back in full professional mode. "Per Executive Director Cantrell, I am aware you are working with AFRIPOL. The museum is grateful to you for helping us recover some of the most important artifacts found in recent years. The significance of three-hundred-thousand-year-old *Homo sapiens* remains and the codex could be monumental."

"We are happy to assist and understand the urgency in recovering and repatriating these discoveries." Natasha scooted her chair closer to the desk and pulled the contents from the folder. She noted how Ms. Guilford's pale skin flushed a rosy pink every time her eyes flitted over Bane. Indeed. He had that effect on women.

Bane edged his chair next to Natasha's, brushing against her as he leaned in to better see the documents and photos.

His touch made her burn, and she took a deep, controlled breath to quell her accelerating heart rate before focusing on the photos and field notes. "What exactly are we looking at, Ms. Guilford?"

"Pardon me. I was remiss in explaining. I was unable to be at yesterday's meeting and believed Director Cantrell might have briefed you on this. They are connected to the case you are working on. I assume that's why you are here. Can you tell me your roles in the repatriation?"

Natasha glanced at Bane, immediately wishing she had not. Looking at him flustered her. "Due to the nature of our work, we cannot divulge

the details, but what I can tell you is that we, my husband and I, make an exceptional team. We are very, very good at what we do. I've contracted with INTERPOL's Heritage Crime Division for a number of years, with great success in recovery, most recently in Guatemala. With the cooperation of the Kaibiles—the country's special ops—and the Bureau of Educational and Cultural Affairs, we were able to secure a substantial archaeological site from the American. In fact, we apprehended one of their top people. He remains in custody."

"The American is who is suspected of this, this…" Ms. Guilford sputtered, turning red. "…this theft!" She leaned forward, her forearms on the scarred wood desk, hands clasped. "One of their top people? I was under the impression the American was an individual."

Natasha shook her head. "No. The American is a vast global network. We suspect they are in cahoots with others."

"This is disturbing."

"It most certainly is. It's probable the American has infiltrated archaeologists and the upper echelons of law enforcement as well as local residents, affluent businesspeople, and museums."

Ms. Guilford glowered, and her eyes flickered when Natasha mentioned museums. She fixed her eyes on Bane. "And what is your role in all this, Mr. Rua? North African and Moroccan cultural heritage are being stolen." The curator looked like a lovesick puppy as she addressed Bane.

Natasha wanted to roll her eyes. Instead, she reached for his hand and squeezed it.

Bane's hazel orbs were full of heat as they raked over Natasha in front of the curator. "My wife was remiss in failing to mention 'dangerous' when describing the American." His tone became deadly serious with his next words even though he smiled at Ms. Guilford. "I'll be assisting my wife as a professional freelance photographer, but I do whatever needs to be done. Like my wife, I've worked on numerous assignments with INTERPOL, and now with AFRIPOL here in Morocco. I'm retired special operations. My purview is intelligence, rescue, and recovery."

Ms. Guilford swallowed audibly. "Returning to your earlier question, these are photos of three distinct rock engravings from sites peppered along *Wadi* Draa."

"The photos leave something to be desired." Bane's voice rumbled softly. "But I can see that the sites are rougher than I expected, as if they were blasted."

"Yes. As you can see, the looters do not care how they acquire artifacts or what condition they leave the excavations in."

"And we're looking at these why? We are after three-hundred-thousand-year-old remains that disappeared from Jebel Irhoud and an ancient codex." Natasha tapped her finger on the photo closest to her.

"Yes. We, those of us working at the museum, have heard rumors that the codex you seek was found in a cave within a cave"—Ms. Guilford pointed to the last of the photos—"closest to this engraving." She pulled another from under a sheaf of paper. "This is a photo of the one we think the codex was taken from. As you can see, the cave is dry. We have samples of soil and rock for comparison after you successfully recover the codex."

"I appreciate your vote of confidence, Ms. Guilford," Bane said approvingly.

Natasha asked, "The engravings?"

"Three prehistoric Tazina-style art engravings from the Sahara side of the Atlas Mountains in the region of the River Draa. They were recovered in Morocco several weeks ago."

"From the fishing vessel seized by the Moroccan Navy?"

"Yes, Dr. Rua. Would you like to see them? They are in the early stage of being readied for exhibition."

Natasha stood. "We would, very much."

"Come with me."

Natasha and Bane fell behind Ms. Guilford as she walked the labyrinth to a large, open, and well-lit room. A hush fell over them.

"Here they are. Astonishing really," the curator said, her tone reverent.

"I didn't realize they were so large. The photos did not represent how impressive these actually are, or how many. They're in pieces," Natasha lamented, horrified.

Bane stepped closer and grimaced. "Has Emmet seen these?"

"No. We've only discussed them."

"Can I take a few?" he asked, indicating his camera.

"Of course. Please keep them among us."

"This destruction is obscene." Natasha's blood pressure soared. She hugged herself, unconsciously bolstering her body against the sterile cold of the room and the disquiet seeking to invade her soul. There was

nothing she could do about the devastation in front of her, but she and Bane could do something about future looting and destruction.

"We were told the looters took sledgehammers to the engravings, to help fit them into the crates," the curator said, scowling.

Bane slipped his arms around Natasha's shoulders and drew her close, kissing the top of her head. "We'll get them."

Natasha leaned into Bane, needing his warmth and assurance, glimpsing the curator's fleeting scowl in her peripheral vision.

chapter 14

B RILLIANT SUNSHINE WARMED NATASHA AS she exited through the door Bane held open. "Do you think Ms. Guilford could be part of it? There's talk of museum involvement."

Bane ran a hand over his head and rubbed his neck, considering Natasha's question. "I've heard that too. We've got to consider everyone a suspect, discern what they say, what they don't say. Look for motivations and into backgrounds. That includes our colleagues." He looked down the street to his left and waved. "Simon is pulling up."

"I need items for dinner."

"Any excuse to go shop—"

Natasha put her hand up. "I don't need to hear your opinion, or what you have to—"

"I love this. We're arguing like a real married couple."

"Shut up, Bane," she hurled at him under her breath.

"And to think I was sure you wanted me."

She whirled on him, eyes flashing. "Just stop. You're like an oversexed battering ram."

"Impressive, Nat. Personification of a medieval weapon used to break down walls." He threw his head back and roared with laughter. "Do you feel under siege?" He laughed again. "Is it working?"

She responded acidly. "No. We have a job to do."

"That's what has you upset. What you saw in the museum. The destruction."

"Yes," she cried. "Doesn't it even bother you?" Her voice grew louder and more impassioned with each word. "Christ, it's history and culture being destroyed. Erased. Stolen. Goddamn it!" She was close to tears.

In the next instant, Bane propelled them behind the immense arched column and into a secluded area, out of sight of passersby. He pressed Natasha against his chest, one arm holding her firmly against his heart, which she could feel racing in time with hers. His other hand brushed her hair back tenderly. "You drive me crazy."

She tried to pull back, only to be thrust against his pelvis, against his unmistakable erection pressing into her.

"Don't take your anger out on me. I'm not your enemy, so quit treating me like I am. I'm pissed off about the destruction and looting just like you are. It fucking sucks."

His heady male scent enveloped Natasha. He was everywhere. Touching her, surrounding her. "I don't require your comfort." She tried to pull away again, unsuccessfully.

Bane dropped his mouth to her ear, his lips ghosting over its shell, sending a jolt of sparks and desire racing through her body like wildfire, hardening her nipples and building a delicious ache in her dampening core. His voice was low and quiet. "Gee, just when I believed we were making momentous inroads. Your icy responses intrigue me, because deep down I believe you're amenable to my style of foreplay. We're in each other's blood, but you continue to fight it. You know I'm interested. I see it in the flash of your eyes, when you bite that full lower lip, and I feel how you're responding to me right now. You want me in your bed, and when you decide you're done lying to yourself, when you decide to let me take care of that deep ache you have, you'll be far happier." He leaned away, eyes tightening and holding hers. "How unfortunate that PDA is not okay in Morocco. If it were, I'd kiss you senseless. Let's go," he said, extending his hand toward the waiting car.

Natasha walked to the car.

Bane reached behind her and opened the rear door for her. "The back seat is all yours for our ride to the *souk*."

"Greetings, Simon," said Bane lightly, sliding into the front passenger seat and putting the camera bag at his feet. "My wife needs

to—" He looked over his shoulder at Natasha, his eyes going immediately to her chest, which rose and fell quickly.

Natasha snapped her fingers sharply. "Eyes here, Bane."

Bane pivoted more in the seat. His eyes lit and the corner of his mouth turned up in amusement. "Shop for our excursion. Do you need a backpack?"

"A what?"

"Um… rucksack."

Natasha was sure her prolonged exhale was audible over the cacophony outside the car, but she managed to respond civilly. "I do."

The car moved into traffic, and Bane's blinding smile disarmed her. "Hard to stay pissed at me when I'm looking out for you, isn't it?" He winked.

She glared at him. "Simon, will you please take us to *Quartier Habous* once we get to Casa?"

"Of course."

Bane waited until her glare evaporated before asking, "We're not going directly home?"

"No."

"Because?"

"Since I need to shop, I'm going to do it where I want to. I also should inquire something for a client. *Habous* is one of my favorite *souks*, I haven't been there in ages. Are you all right with that?"

Bane shrugged his shoulders. "Okay."

"Wonderful!" Natasha said, looking forward to *Habous*.

✕ ▨ ✹ ✕

A genuine smile transformed her face, taking Bane's breath away. Christ, she was dazzling. He shook his head and groaned. "Hell, woman. We're not even there yet and you're telling me I have to put up with your shopping in addition to purchasing a backpack."

"You're correct," she said lightheartedly. "I was hoping we could get lunch there too. I expect you're hungry."

"I'm always hungry." Bane smirked before he faced forward. "Simon, does that work for you?"

"I am at your disposal."

"Thanks, man. My dad always says, 'Happy wife, happy life.'"

"Smart man."

"Yup."

In short time, they arrived back in Casablanca. Before exiting the car, they agreed to meet Simon in four hours, leaving plenty of time to browse, barter, buy, and have a leisurely lunch. Natasha and Bane strolled deep into the labyrinth of crowded, narrow alleys of the old *medina,* passing more than one overladen donkey. Bane snapped away with the camera. Sweet-looking beasts of burden carried rugs and bedding encased in plastic and other household goods that extended four feet or more on either side of their backs. Each of their cargos were roped together and seemingly supported by and sitting atop an enormously wide wicker basket that rested on a generous amount of padding over the animal's spine, secured by a cinch around its belly and connected to the noseband of a colorfully corded halter.

A palette of vivid sights and intoxicating scents assaulted them as they entered the *souk*—mountains of deep red paprika, rich brown cinnamon, and vibrant yellow turmeric, beds of fresh mint, and piles of long, thin, red saffron. Baskets of dates, olives, and salted almonds enticed them from farther down the aisle.

Natasha said excitedly, "I am going to cook tonight. What do you like, Bane?"

Surprised to be asked and that she'd used his first name, it took him a second to respond. "I eat anything."

"Do you have a preference?"

"Do you have a specialty?"

"Not really. Mémé and I used to make a fabulous chicken *bastilla.* So I think I'll make that and a vegetable *tagine.* And *harira.* We can buy the bread and dessert from a baker."

"Christ, my mouth is watering."

Natasha laughed. "Well, maybe we should eat lunch first. It's never a good idea to shop on an empty stomach. I can finalize what to make after we eat. And you can help me with preparations—that is unless you have a problem being in the kitchen?"

"I'm down for that. All of it. My mom taught me and my brothers to fend for ourselves in the kitchen. Where to, now that I can't think of anything but eating? I need sustenance."

"You eat constantly," she chided.

"I've always had a healthy appetite. When you're in the military, you eat when food is provided. It's fuel, number one in my arsenal."

"Well then. Come on," she said, pivoting and walking at a brisk pace.

They walked past incense, ostrich eggs, and chickens and chameleons in wire baskets. Natasha made another right at the next convergence of aisles. One held carpets, lanterns, and rows of embroidered leather slippers and other tanned goods. Another held teapots and *tagines*. And another, carved wooden furniture. The final aisle was lined with jewelry and clothing, purses and backpacks. Around them the clamor of metal from workshops punctuated the sounds of vendors hawking their wares.

Bane focused on keeping his eyes up, so enticed was he by the skirt rippling over her firm hips. He observed his surroundings, but he was soon lost in the maze of color, chaos, crowds, and locals shouting to get his or Natasha's attention. There was no hesitation in Natasha's stride as she walked confidently ahead of him. Often he was rewarded with the sight of a trim brown ankle peeking out from her skirt or a soft smile when she turned her head and encouraged him with a slate-gray glance. She made one more turn, and they were outside the *souk*.

The alley was much wider and less congested now, so he was able to walk beside her. "Are we close?"

Natasha stopped and faced him; her round gray eyes full of happiness. She clapped her hands together like a small child. "We're here. Follow me," she said and turned right once more. His eyes followed to where her hand indicated. To their left, tucked into a narrower alley, was a restaurant. "Welcome to Café Rouge."

They walked another fifteen yards and entered through the open door, Bane trailing Natasha, assailed by scents of food cooking in the varying mixtures of spices, baked bread, and cigarette smoke. It was late morning. Tables were available both inside the rustic interior and in the outside garden through the back.

"I see patio seating," he said. "I don't enjoy smoke with my meal."

"Neither do I."

"This place is full of Europeans," Bane observed, signaling for a table outside.

"Yes, and locals too," she said as they made their way to the patio behind the host. Her voice grew animated after they were seated and given menus. "Mémé and Pépé brought my family here when we visited.

They said it was a nice blend of their pasts and present, being French but living in Morocco. I could eat freely with my left hand and not offend anyone. I believe that's another reason we came here."

The sun was warm and bright. Bane pulled a chair out for her. Natasha sat and slipped off her shawl; the warmth of the rays caressed her polished brown shoulders. "This feels"—her mouth curved into a dreamy smile as her eyes tracked her finger drawing invisible curlicues on the tablecloth—"wonderful." She glanced at her menu and made her decision immediately. "I appreciate you being open to shopping and eating in *Habous*." She pulled her sunglasses from her tote and slipped them on, then continued tracing curlicues absently with her finger.

Bane settled into his chair, watching quietly through his shades as Natasha seemed to struggle with emotions and memories. Even though she appeared to be looking at him, she was elsewhere, having drifted off into the past. Bane waved a hand in front of her face. She didn't acknowledge it.

He leaned forward and covered her hand tenderly with his, stilling its motion. "Nat? Where are you?"

She started and her smile was overly bright. "Sorry. Daydreaming."

"Care to share?"

She cocked her head and pursed the full glossed lips Bane ached to explore. "Uh, no. Thanks. Do you know what you want?"

Bane leaned in even closer and lowered his voice. A slow smile spread over his face. "I certainly do."

Natasha's hand fluttered to her throat. Her tongue darted out and touched her lips, and she rolled that damn lower lip and bit down on it.

"Are you aware of what you are doing?" He groaned, easing back and adjusting his pants. "You're going to be the death of me. I—"

"Good day," the waitress said, placing a pile of grilled peppers, bread, and two small plates on the table. "Tea?"

"Yes, please," they both responded.

She waved over a young girl who filled their glasses. "Are you ready to order, sir? Ma'am?"

Bane picked up his menu, then lifted his eyebrows at Natasha and signaled with a nod.

"I'd like the *rfissa* please."

"Make that two." Bane added, "Can you also bring us some kebabs, olives, and an artichoke salad? Thank you."

"Only one salad?

"Yes. My wife enjoys sharing with me." Bane steepled his fingers and enjoyed the scene in front of him. Natasha had pushed some of the peppers onto her plate with the bread and taken a large bite. The juices ran down her chin when her mouth opened in surprise. "Need help?"

Embarrassed, Natasha dabbed at her mouth and chin frantically, finally swallowing her bite. "Does everything have to be innuendo with you?" she challenged, but her voice was light.

"Whatever do you mean? I only mentioned that you like to share. Where's the innuendo in that? I'm merely being conversational."

"Such a big word," she said, taking a drink.

"I'm a big man, babe."

Natasha choked on her tea.

Bane rose from his chair and came around to pat her on the back. "Wrong pipe, huh?" He handed Natasha her glass of water. "Drink. It will settle the spasms." He rubbed Natasha's back until he felt her relax. "All this back-and-forth. It's kinda stupid. I feel like I'm in a fuckin' washing machine. Agitated. Spinning. Or waiting for the next cycle. Can we just cut to the chase?"

"What does that mean, cut to the chase?"

"In this application, sleep with me."

Her body grew still as stone.

"Look at me, Nat."

She shifted to face him.

"I can't see those incredible eyes of yours."

She took her sunglasses off and pressed her fingers to her forehead, her eyes closed. Molten pewter stared at him when she opened them. Her chin trembled.

"Sweetheart...," he murmured, squatting on his haunches. "Damn, you're scared." He slid his broad fingers through his hair. "Nat. I'm sorry." He covered her hand. "Do I scare you? Is that it? I never meant to scare you."

She shivered as she took a long, deep breath. Her words were calm, careful. "You don't scare me. You drive me crazy sometimes. But"—she stopped him with her hand as he leaned forward into her space—"not here. I have thought a lot about what you said earlier. We need to talk. Privately, without the director, or Simon, or in this restaurant. After lunch. After we go to the *souk*. I have a lot going through my head. It's all piling up."

He reached out and stroked her chin. "I can help, Nat."

"We'll talk about it later, at home."

Bane nodded and rose, leaning over to plant a kiss on her lips. "I know. No PDA. But you're a damsel in distress. I just want to make it better," he insisted, stepping back.

Natasha grabbed his wrist and jerked him toward her. "You almost upended our lunch. It's right behind you."

"Quick reflexes. Impressive." He sat as their food was placed in front of them and tore his *khobz* in half. Before scooping up some of the mouthwatering *rfissa* with the bread, he asked, "What else do you have?"

She dished out half the salad, olives, and kababs to him, smiling, clearly at peace with using her left hand, her eyes full of humor. "You will just have to wait and see."

chapter 15

AFTER A PLEASURABLE LUNCH AND spiced Moroccan coffee, Natasha was prepared to haggle the prices individually, knowing the more she purchased the better her bargaining position was. Her first selection was a rugged rucksack she bought in a curated shop off the alley. It was more costly, but it was what she needed.

Natasha and Bane wandered into a shop full of higher-end goods, seeking authentic Dogon figurines, but came up empty.

"I'm in Morocco for a while. Here's my business card in case you come across something. My clients are particular and not price sensitive." She gave the shop owner her ART card.

They ventured back to the center of the souk where Natasha pulled a canvas bag from her tote and bargained with vendors over spices, couscous, dates, olives, and other vegetables and fruit she would need for dinner and for breakfast. She purchased bread and had a chicken prepared and wrapped for dinner.

Bane captured it all in photos, clearly enjoying watching Natasha in her element.

"We can get pastries in the morning," she said, turning to Bane. "I'm done. Ready?"

He capped his lens and reached for her tote and the other bags. "Ready. I let Simon know. He'll pick us up where he dropped us off."

"Thanks. Did you get some good pictures?"

"I did. It was fun watching you shop."

※ ▩ ❀ ※

They loaded their purchases into the trunk for the short drive to pick up their car. The agency had taken care of all the paperwork, so they transferred their purchases and parted ways with Simon, parking the car—a Jeep—in the garage and entering the *riad* through the gate of the private backyard. Bane helped Natasha unpack in the kitchen and then grabbed one of the large canvas bags to use for a beer and wine run, promising to help her after he returned.

"Wanna kiss me goodbye?"

Her answer was to lift her eyebrows and stare down those twinkling bedroom eyes. "Here's the key. Let yourself in."

He winked at her, humming in his deep baritone on the way out.

Natasha opened the spices and poured them into glass jars and pulled out a colander and began sorting the vegetables. Next she flipped through her grandmother's recipe book, taking her time to read Mémé's notes in the margins. A few of hers were in there as well. Mémé had encouraged Natasha to write when she was absorbed in a creation. That thought made Natasha wistful, and cooking in the kitchen filled her with joy.

She preheated the oven and began preparing the chicken *bastilla*, a delicious chicken pie, first because it took longer to assemble. Natasha shook her head and chuckled; Bane was one determined man. She had not missed how he had all but inhaled his food during lunch. What she was making should fill him up. If there were leftovers, they could take them tomorrow and eat them during the drive.

She placed the *bastilla* in the oven and put a *tagine* and its diffuser and a pot on the stovetop, adding vegetable broth to the pot and oil to the *tagine*. After rinsing and chopping the vegetables, she added onions and garlic to the simmering liquid. As soon as those were translucent, she began stacking the vegetables—placing the ones that would take the longest to cook on the bottom—then whisked the *ras el hanout* blend she'd created into a hot vegetable broth. The spices thickened the broth quickly, and she poured it over the vegetables, placed the *tagine* lid on, and set the heat to low.

Loud banging carried back to the kitchen where Natasha was washing her hands after cleaning the counters. Irritated that Bane wasn't using the key, she quickly dried her hands and rushed to the front door, jerking it open, her expression changing from annoyance to surprise.

Her longtime friends, Gianna and Viviane, stood there with upturned faces. *Oh Lord.* How soon would Bane be back? The store was only on the next block.

※ ❖ ❖ ❖

"Ma'am," Bane called to the diminutive older woman struggling with two large bags ahead of him. He walked more quickly and caught up with her. "Can I help you?"

"I can manage, thank you. I'm almost home." Bright blue eyes regarded Bane carefully, then smiled at him when she realized he was the strapping, good-looking man who was staying with Natasha.

"Me too. Let me help you," he said, moving his bags to one hand and taking the two large bags and slowing his pace to match hers. "It'd be hard for me to do anything with my hands this full, you know."

"I know," she tittered. "Thank you kindly. You're American."

"I am."

"You're Natasha's husband."

Natasha's husband. Natasha had shared their cover. Good. "I am. Bane Rua."

"I'm Clara Gervais. It's certainly a pleasure, Bane."

"It's nice to meet you, Clara. Natasha has told me a lot about you and your husband."

"Oliver noticed you in the garden, and of course Natasha has stopped in a few times since you've arrived. Shared your news. Congratulations!" She paused and faced him. Her eyes were warm and merry and the wavy, salt and pepper hair and the lines of a life well-lived etched into her face did nothing to detract from her beauty. "You married one of the best."

Bane beamed at her in response. "I agree with you."

She glanced at the classic metal-studded wood door with a small iron Fatima in the upper corner. "We're here. Do you have time for a quick cup of tea?"

"I'll need to take a rain check. Natasha was starting to make dinner and I stepped out to get some beer and wine. I told her I'd help, but I've been gone longer than expected."

"The green space connects our home and the *riad*. You're welcome to pass through our home instead of going around." She noted the smaller

99

white sacks nestled within the larger ones he held. "It looks like you've been to the bakery."

"Yeah," Bane said, touching one of the sacks and making it rustle. "Nat's got a thing for baklava, so I got her some, and some other pastries for breakfast. I figure it's a win-win." He flashed his teeth. "I'm going to go the long way. Come in the way I went out. She doesn't appreciate surprises."

"So, you learned that about your new bride?" she asked, putting her hands on her hips.

"I have. And more"—an enormous smile broke over his face—"I've got to get back to help Nat, but we'll talk soon. Have a great evening." He backed away and pivoted, walking toward the corner.

"I'm looking forward to it, young man. Soon!"

※ ▨ ❀ ※

"Hey, you two!" Natasha pasted a welcoming smile on her face. "Wow! This is a surprise!"

"Natasha!" they burst out in unison, pulling her in for a group hug.

"Girls! I had no idea you were back in Morocco. How did you know I was in town?" Although pleased to see them, this was not the best time. She and Bane had details to go over and packing to do, and he had been gone longer than expected. Natasha continued to block their entrance without being obvious.

They talked over one another.

"We knew, but we missed you every time we stopped by," Gianna said.

"We took another chance you'd be home tonight." Viviane unwrapped herself from her oversized lightweight shawl and dropped it onto the floor next to her shoes in the *setwan*.

Gianna slipped her shoes off next to Viviane's. "We didn't see a car parked in front, but we saw Clara a couple of mornings ago in the *souk*."

Apparently they are staying. How the hell is this going to go? "My schedule had been crazy. I've been out more than in."

Gianna was tall, only a couple of inches shy of Natasha's five foot ten, and lean, almost boyish in shape. Her smoky, dark-blue eyes were still her best feature and her shoulder-length hair was again its natural dark blond shade. "We could have called, but we wanted to surprise you."

"Surprised?" Viviane asked. Shorter and more compact, she had voluptuous breasts that boys had drooled over for as long as Natasha had known her. She'd maintained the rest of her curves too. Snug jeans and a body-hugging top displayed them proudly now that she had divested herself of the shawl. Viviane's hair remained dark brown, and she wore it in a short, layered bob. "I brought something to celebrate!" Her dark brown eyes were full of mischief as she held up a brown bag and pushed past Natasha, farther into the *riad* toward the kitchen, with Gianna following.

"I really am," Natasha said, following them, stressing about what was going to happen when Bane arrived. *Jesus.*

"Something smells divine. What can we do to help, Natasha? This is perfect!" Viviane announced after they entered the kitchen.

"I'm so glad this worked out." *Where is Bane?*

"It's so wonderful to see you, Natasha. You are more beautiful than ever."

Viviane's eyes flitted over Natasha, but she didn't comment on Gianna's compliment. "I'm so happy Gia joined me this time," she said, using Gianna's nickname. "I pop in a few times a year. Paris isn't all that far."

Natasha scrambled to remember the last of the many jobs Viviane had held. "Are you still in tourism?"

"I am, and I love it. I think it might be my career. Every day is different. You know how easily bored I get Natasha, you've got to come visit when you can find the time to extricate yourself from teaching and digging in the past," she admonished, her smile not reaching her eyes. "Where's your wine opener? Wineglasses?"

Natasha took a wine opener from a drawer and gave it to Viviane with a tight smile, stinging from the barb. She pulled wineglasses from a shelf and set them on the counter, turning to Gianna, smiling warmly. "And you. How are things?"

Sadness flitted through Gianna's eyes. "Not good. My aunt insisted on relieving me when I told her Viviane had called and asked if I'd meet her, and I think my mother would have pushed me out if she was physically able," she said, smiling weakly. "You remember my aunt is a nurse?"

"I do."

"I admit I really needed a break. Florence is closer to Casablanca via Paris, so I spent a few days with Viviane there and then we flew here

together. The cancer is… God, Natasha… It's merciless. Mama rarely complains even though she's exhausted and in a lot of pain. There's nothing more we can do for her, so we just wait, and she wishes to be at home." She blinked her eyes rapidly. "Looking after her has been much more difficult than I realized." Gianna's cracked words were laced with guilt.

"Of course you need a break." Natasha pulled her in for a bear hug. "I'm so sorry, Gia."

"Enough of that, girls. We're all together for the first time in, what, seven years? Let's celebrate!"

"I just wish to clarify that I didn't let anyone know I was coming. Well, except for Clara and Oliver. I didn't expect to see anyone," Natasha admitted.

Viviane leaned toward her and grinned. "Sneaking in, huh?"

"No. I'm here for work," she responded evenly while leaning away from Viviane. It had only been mere minutes, but Natasha felt her old bricks snap into place. When would the time come when she could let Viviane and her words not bother her?

"I've always said you should play more, Natasha."

Always the mediator between the two women, Gianna said softly, "Come on, Viviane." She moved between the women. "Let's keep it light."

Viviane raised her glass and took a sip. "Mm, good." She topped off her glass and then poured wine into the two others.

Gia lifted her glass. "To us! What's for dinner?"

Natasha took a quick sip and put the glass back on the counter. "Um. I have chicken *bastilla* in the oven and—"

Behind Gianna and Viviane, a deep rugged voice broke in. "Sweetheart, I didn't realize we were having company. Sorry I ran late. Stopped to get baklava for dessert since you love it so much, and pastries for tomorrow morning just in case we stay up late. And I helped Clara with her bags." Bane leaned in through the group and planted a full, juicy kiss on Natasha's lips. "Mm," he murmured, loud enough for everyone to hear.

His heat lingered, and her brain short-circuited, leaving Natasha mute.

"Hi, ladies," he said, nodding to Gianna and Viviane, who stared up at him openmouthed and speechless. He slipped his free arm around

Natasha and pulled her close. His other arm was weighted with a heavy canvas bag containing beer and wine, topped with sacks of pastries. "I'm Bane, your gorgeous friend's husband. Nice to meet you. Welcome to our home."

chapter 16

THE WOMEN INTRODUCED THEMSELVES TO Bane, and Gianna insisted that he call her Gia.

Viviane pouted loudly. "Natasha. When did you get married? You never told us!"

"Yes, Natasha. What the hell?" Gia asked, shocked and looking hurt. She stared at the silver band circling Natasha's finger. "I didn't even think to look."

"Bane and I got married while we were on vacation last month. It was a whirlwind." A happy, dreamy smile covered Natasha's face. She looked at him adoringly and her pulse skittered. His expression mirrored Natasha's and encouraged her to keep going. "When you know, you just know," she explained breathlessly.

Bane squeezed her shoulder, which she took as a signal that she was doing great.

Gia hugged Natasha. "It's wonderful! But I would have loved to have, you know, returned the favor, been there for you." A shadow crossed her face, and then it was replaced with a genuine smile. "I'm so happy for you, Natasha. And you too, Bane. You do know you snagged one of the best women?"

"So I've been told," he said smoothly in his deep, rumbling voice while sliding his hand over Natasha's hip and pulling her to him, smiling like a man crazy in love.

Viviane looked Bane over appreciatively, observing how he had pulled Natasha up against him. She licked her lips before addressing Bane boldly. "My, you are a big, handsome one. What did Natasha do to land you?"

Pink dusted Gia's cheeks and her deep-blue eyes rounded as they darted to Viviane.

Natasha's body tightened at the slight, but Bane massaged her back gently and she relaxed. His arm loosely circled her waist after she leaned into his solid strength, feeling protected.

Bane cocked his head and squinted at Viviane, pasting a smile on his face and saying lightly, "All my wife did was walk into the room. I fell hard and fast."

Natasha looked down at her feet, feeling warm and surprisingly pleased by Bane's admission.

"I was teasing." Viviane laughed it off.

Bane freed his arm from Natasha and looked at the women, his voice friendly as he said, "Please stay for dinner. We won't accept no. There's plenty, and I'd like to get to know you. And I suspect my wife would enjoy catching up." He angled his face to Natasha and gave her a beaming smile. "I'm famished, sweetheart. From the glorious smells filling our home, I guess I missed helping you with prep. Sorry, babe. Can I do anything else?"

She was lost in those pools of ever-changing color and grateful he had her back in a way that made her feel protected and cherished. Safe. Natasha gave Bane a genuine smile and spoke softly, like a woman in love. "It's a lovely, warm night. We're going to eat alfresco. You can help me with the table." She pulled dishes, utensils, and linens from the shelves. "Dinner is almost ready."

"I love how she tells me what to do." His eyes twinkled at Natasha before he stacked the linens, utensils, and ceramic dishes in his arms. He inclined his head, motioning her ahead of him.

While Natasha and Bane set up the patio, Gia called home and checked on her mother, and Viviane stepped away to make a quick call as well.

Natasha went back into the kitchen to pull the *bastilla* out of the oven and turn off the stove, and Bane lit the lanterns and came back in to carry out the food and call the women to dinner.

The evening turned out to be enjoyable and dinner was delicious. Natasha and Bane worked in tandem effortlessly, as if they had been doing it for years. Bane was the cordial host, serving food, drinks, dessert,

and clearing the table. He was also the attentive husband. His ease at role-playing as her spouse and sharing his experiences as a professional freelance photographer allowed Natasha to slip into her own cover without overthinking it. He drank beer as the women caught up, observing them thoughtfully. Their conversation never paused, although Viviane carried most of it. Eventually Gia began to yawn and the women decided to leave.

Bane closed the door behind them and shot the bolt, his brow furrowed, staring deeply into Natasha's eyes. "You okay?

"Of course. Why do you ask?"

"You girls polished off two bottles of wine, although I think Viviane drank one all by herself."

Natasha yawned and stretched her arms up. She caught him watching with interest as her tee moved, exposing her stomach and stretching over her breasts. She crossed her arms over her chest and raised her eyebrows. "And?"

"Are you drunk?"

"No, but I had more than I should have."

"Wine happy."

Her mouth twitched. "Yes, that sounds about right. Hey, thanks for taking all the pictures. I'll need to get copies to them soon or the girls will hound me."

"There're some great ones of you three. Gia was able to take some nice ones of us too."

After an awkward moment, Natasha said, "I'm going to do the dishes and get some sleep."

"We didn't go over details, Nat."

So it was back to Nat. "No, we didn't. If you are agreeable, we can spend a little time going over them after I clean up the kitchen."

"Fine. I'll help you."

"Thanks." Fortified by the alcohol, she scrutinized him and asked pointedly, "What else?"

Bane chuckled and leaned back against the door, hooking his thumbs into the waistband of his khakis, his fingers relaxed, pointing at the don't-look-there zone. His eyes captured Natasha's as her eyes traveled back up. Heat and amusement simmered there. "You're learning my nuances. Very good. The 'what else' is that I find the dynamics of your threesome

interesting. You hang back, which is strange. The strong, confident woman I know disappears, sucked dry in the presence of over-the-top Viviane."

She opened her mouth to speak.

He held up his finger and said gently. "Allow me to continue please?"

"Okay," she said, leaning against the wall opposite the door, slipping her hands into the pockets of her skirt and mirroring his stance.

"Gia's role is the mediator. She plays the loyal friend, an effective straight shooter who isn't afraid to speak up. How am I doing?"

"Spot on."

"She navigates Viviane well, but there's something about Gia that I can't put my finger on."

Surprised, Natasha asked, "Like what?"

Bane grimaced and shook his head. "I don't know. Something. Maybe it's just that she's unusually observant, almost as if she's trained. When she did talk during Viviane's mostly one-sided conversation, she asked penetrating questions, like an interrogator, not a friend."

"Gia's always asked the deep, probing questions. Maybe that skill has become more polished now because of what she does."

"Possibly. What does she do?"

"She's a conservator and restorer. Books, manuscripts, art. She's on extended leave because her mother is terminal. Gia cares for her, lives with her."

"Interesting. No help from her siblings?"

"She's an only, Bane. Why all the questions? You seem to be the one interrogating."

He smiled. "I'm trying to sort through what I observed. You've all known one another a long time."

"We have."

"I appreciated that you were recounting some of your history, but I gather some of it was left out?"

Natasha pulled her hands from her pockets and crossed her arms again. "Yes."

"You just closed up on me again," Bane said. "Fine. I'll tell you how Viviane struck me. She's all about herself and oblivious to Gia's skills, simply because she believes she's smarter and cleverer than everyone else.

Overconfidence is her Achilles' heel. What she wants, she goes after, damn the cost of doing so. She's strategic, controlling, and stealthy. Not to be trusted. Her inclination is to go for the jugular. Does she have any idea how accomplished you are? She's jealous of your beauty. That she's lost her power over you more than bothers her, and that I sleep in your bed and have your back drives her nuts."

"You do not sleep in my bed."

"She believes I do. Her perception colors her belief. Viviane is confident in her sexual prowess and is convinced she can make any man drop to his knees. Christ, I think she believes every guy is a tit man. She kept trying to direct me there. She'd act like a whore-dog to get me."

"That's crass."

"Maybe, but astute."

"Are you a tit man?"

"Most definitely not." He beamed at her, pinning her with dark heat. "I appreciate them, but I love me some long, sleek legs and a beautiful, firm ass."

Natasha looked away, flattered by his revelation yet battling the way his words, his brazenness, set her body on fire. She cleared her throat and regarded him seriously. "Are you a psychiatrist?"

"Nope. Just trained to read people. The lives of others, as well as my own, depend on my observations." He cocked his head. "Why is Viviane your friend? I don't get it."

Natasha flinched at the question and the memories it brought to the surface. "Because she has always been, for as long as I can remember. We go back to when we were in diapers. Our grandmothers arrived in Morocco during World War II from France and became fast friends, and our mothers, born here, were also close. They all assumed we would be third-generation best friends, and we were. Until secondary school." Natasha paused and looked out into space, remembering.

"Puberty, passion, and jealousy can produce a toxic mix. What happened, sweetheart?"

"Nothing really. It was a long time ago."

Bane pushed off the door and moved to stand in front of her, lightly grazing his finger over her forehead to her temple. "Yeah, but you haven't forgotten. It's written all over your exquisite face."

Her voice cracked. "It was the first cut."

"The deepest."

"Apparently. I believed I'd moved past all this. I really did, but Viviane showing up like this, acting like everything was great between us, and coming on to you, well it brought some, I guess, long-buried emotions to the surface. It's as if she is blind to the strain and the hurt. Thank you for having my back tonight, by the way."

"Having your back, that's easy." His voice dropped, etched with concern. "What did she do?"

"She betrayed me." Natasha ducked the intensity of his eyes.

He gently pulled Natasha into his arms. "Talk. It doesn't do you any good to hold it in and let it fester."

The side of her head rested in the crook of his powerful shoulder. His body felt like a bastion. She inhaled his sexy scent and absorbed his strength as he rubbed her back. Natasha's laugh was more of a bark. "You sound like my grandmother."

"Yeah, well she must have been a lot like my grandmother, full of love and wisdom."

"She was." A wistful smile spread over her face. "So, Viviane was always flippant and sarcastic. When she went abroad the summer before secondary school with her family, we were separated for the first time. And it was long enough that I realized how her sarcasm had escalated. It was mean and she seemed to be intentional about hurting others. I didn't want to be party to that, so I kept my distance. Are you sure you want to hear all this?" she asked tentatively.

Bane stroked her hair. "I am."

Her voice was muffled against him, but the words came out in a rush. "Viviane went after the boy she knew I had a huge crush on. I was devastated because, well, I thought he was it. The mind of a fourteen-year-old..." Natasha shook her head slightly, then moved it deeper into the crook of his shoulder. *He feels so good.* "Viviane apologized, but it was half-hearted and only after she lost interest in him, which was almost immediately. She seemed unfazed, not concerned about how I felt or how what she had done affected our friendship. I accepted her apology, but then she did something the next day. She gave me a smug look over her shoulder in the hall between classes. She denied doing it when I asked her, so I convinced myself that I imagined it, but it's obviously haunted me or I wouldn't be mentioning it now, over twenty years later. I should pay you for counseling." She laughed.

"Hey, I asked you to dredge up your history with her," Bane murmured into her hair.

"Gia joined our school, an international school, a week later. She moved from Italy with her mother. She just joined us for lunch one day. She was funny, easy, and open, and Viviane's antics washed off Gia's shoulders like water off a duck. I think Gia's sunny nature and her easy navigation of Viviane's personality buoyed me and we grew close. She immediately reached out when my parents and brothers were killed and shared that she had never known her father. It bonded us, along with our fanatical interest in the past. Gia actually went on to study history before she turned to nursing.

"Gia was the one who spent hours with me while I struggled to pick up the pieces, orphaned by the bombings, the one who held me while I sobbed and raged to make sense of what happened, because Mémé and Pépé were emotionally unavailable. I didn't blame them. They had also been destroyed by the deaths of their daughter, son-in-law, and grandsons."

Bane massaged her back more deeply. "Where was Viviane during this?"

Natasha took a deep breath and blinked, fighting the stupor Bane's magic hands created and to keep the emotions out of her voice. "Viviane showed up at the memorial weeks later, effervescent like soda. It was too much. She acted the same way when Pépé died, and when Mémé passed." She bowed her head and focused on the tile floor. "It hurt deeply, but the long history of friendship in our families encouraged me to let it go, accept her for who she is."

"And now? Where do you stand with each of your friends?"

"I was Gia's maid of honor when she married Guillaume after their whirlwind courtship, during the time between the deaths of Pépé and Mémé. And I was with her a year later, after he died in a climbing accident in the High Atlas. Viviane never married but continues to go through men like they're toilet paper. We're in contact a few times a year, phone and texts, but Gia and I saw each other after my grandmother died last year, and we talk frequently, more often since her mother was diagnosed with terminal cancer."

"I'm so sorry. Cruelty is a nasty trait. Viviane appears overly capable, based on what I witnessed tonight."

"She improved as the night wore on."

"Yeah, only because she was intimidated by me and was placated with a bottle of wine."

They stood in silence for a while, soaking up the nearness and the comforting warmth of each other's bodies.

Natasha had to know. "Would you? Sleep with her?"

"Are you seriously asking me that? No fucking way," he said vehemently, separating Natasha from his chest. Bane slipped a finger under her chin and guided her face up, looking deeply into her eyes, his expression solemn. "I believe I've been more than clear who I want."

"You're the first man who's said that to me," she murmured.

Bane searched her eyes. "I find that extremely difficult to believe."

Natasha shook her head and broke eye contact, pivoting away. "It's getting late. We have a full day tomorrow and I'm tired. Let's get the kitchen cleaned up and review our assignment."

hospitality

الشخص الذي لا يسافر لن يعرف ان قيمه الرجال.

One who does not travel will not know the value of men.

chapter 17

*I*RRITABLE AND TIRED FROM TOSSING *and turning, Natasha rose within hours of going to bed, having given up on sleep. Every time she'd closed her eyes, Bane's mischievous expression taunted her. When she had finally fallen asleep, it was him she dreamed of, more specifically of the two of them grinding it out. Oh Lord, the pleasure he'd given her as she slept. Her body felt wrung out, like the aftermath of an intense orgasm. Had she? It was possible. She hoped she hadn't done something as awful as scream in her sleep, because in her dream she certainly had.*

Yeah, she didn't even want to think about how long it had been since she'd been in a relationship, and if she were being honest with herself, it was little more than sex and the sex hadn't been all that great. It had never been the life-altering experience she'd heard and read about.

Natasha had liked the last guy she'd been seeing. He was comfortable, like one of her old college sweatshirts. But that was it, and when he indicated he wanted more, she pulled away. Fortunately, she'd been called away on assignment, and then another, and another.

She made her way down the stairs and toward the kitchen in her silky pajamas, her path easy to navigate by the moonlight filtering into the courtyard.

Deep rumbling greeted her as she entered the kitchen. "Good morning."

Natasha jumped, her hand covering her throat as her heart rocketed. Holy Lord.

Bane sat in her kitchen. Shirtless. Drinking from a mug. He glowed in the moonlight ribboning through the window. Perfection—dark messy hair, lean sculpted muscle, flat stomach. An array of tattoos covered his sculpted shoulders, chest, and torso.

Her response was breathless. Dammit. "What are you doing up?"

"I'd ask you the same, but I suspect I know the answer—it matches mine. It's one in the morning." He left his mug on the table and rose, walking toward her. He watched her as he took her hand gently, the heat in his eyes searing into hers, lighting her blood on fire. "My bed is cold. I want you. In fact, I'm burning for you."

Bane pulled her hand up to his lips and turned it over, rubbed his thumb over her tattoo and his lips over her palm before kissing it softly and slowly, his eyes never leaving hers. He nipped at the sensitive flesh between her forefinger and thumb and then sucked.

It was hypnotic, observing him. His eyes darkened more as he watched her respond. She was entranced, fully under his spell, needing more oxygen to fight her pounding pulse, which was robbing her of her breath, making her soaking wet and dizzy with desire.

"Natasha," he murmured, lowering her hand. His fingers drifted to her neck, below her jaw, pausing lightly on her wildly beating pulse. "Hmm," he breathed out.

Continuing leisurely, he traced her collarbone, staring deeply into her eyes before moving between the swell of her breasts, taking in the taut nipples under her delicate spaghetti-strap tank, begging for his touch. He paused there as if considering his next course of action, his fingers splaying slightly apart, pressing more firmly over her racing heart, then moving to her shoulder and skimming the outside of her arm. Bane took her hand and placed her palm on his chest, holding it over his heart, which beat as furiously as hers.

"I sleep lightly. I heard screaming coming from somewhere inside the house," he murmured. "It was you, and by the time I arrived at your door, you were moaning. My name." His chuckle was laced with sexual heat, and if possible, his eyes glowed even more. "What were you doing in your bed? I know we're the only two here."

Natasha sucked in her breath, blinking her eyes. She gasped. Oh my god. The electricity crackled between them, wreaking havoc to her system. She inhaled deeply to try to master it and exhaled shakily as Bane guided both her hands to cup his straining erection.

The last of her defenses crumbled. Desire. All she knew was raging desire. For this man. Now. Her hands moved over his impressive length and girth.

"How could I sleep when you were asking for me?" Bane leaned in, grasping her neck and drawing her closer. His kiss was tender, soft, yet hungry. He whispered, "I want you, Nat. I want to strip you naked. Outside. In the moonlight." Bane's hand slid over the hot exposed skin of her back where her top had ridden up. "Take my time with you. Slake your need." His hand slipped into her short, loose-fitting pajama bottoms and over her firm ass. "You feel so good," he groaned, his hand sliding lower, kneading her skin. "I ache to taste you, my beauty." His eyebrows rose in question.

Natasha's gaze collided with his and she leaned inward, unable to utter a word.

Bane closed the distance between them. Their open lips were a breath apart. The knocker boomed against the front door, breaking the mood. "What the fuck?" *Bane growled, stepping back, freeing his hand.*

Natasha removed her hands, immediately missing the promise of more.

�штжж

Warm breath tickled her neck and ear. An urgent whisper infiltrated her delicious dream state. "Natasha!"

Why did he continue teasing her? She tossed and turned, wanting to feel him again. Feel his large hands kneading her ass again. *Just touch me.* "I want, I wa—"

"Natasha! Wake up!"

She opened her eyes slowly to concerned, thickly fringed, mossy green eyes. *Oh shit. I'm in bed. Not in the kitchen. It was so real, and here I am, totally turned on and he is in my bedroom. And...*

"Nat," he said harshly and snapped his fingers at her. "Are you awake?" You were mumbling in your sleep, wanting something."

Shit. She was speechless. And mortified. Bane was bent over her, inches from her face, shirtless and, from what she viewed in the dim light of her room, breathtakingly sexy. *Jesus. Even better than I dreamt.*

🗙 ⬚ ✹ 🗙

Natasha's puckered nipples and flushed cheeks registered with Bane, as did her eyes which were still hooded with desire. "It must have been one hell of a dream." He held his breath as her eyes slid over him. tracing the intricate tattoo inking his sculpted shoulder and upper arm, snaking over his chest and continuing lower over his corded oblique, where it disappeared into the navy sweats hanging low on his lean hips. God, how Bane wished it was her fingers or lips trailing over him. She bit down on her lower lip, her gaze passing the waistband of his sweats and coming to a standstill where he tented the soft fabric.

"You can look more later, Nat. We have company." He stood and placed his hands on his hips. "Get up, sweetheart."

chapter 18

THE LOUD POUNDING ON THE front door was as unrelenting as his desire for her. "Mr. Rua! Dr. Rua!" a man's voice pleaded.

"Fuck." His expression became guarded. "Come on," he commanded gruffly, taking in her short pajama bottoms and silky top that left little to his imagination.

"Mr. Rua! Dr. Rua!"

"Coming!" Bane answered.

Natasha followed Bane quietly and hastily into his bedroom, where he became partially hidden by the wardrobe. The bedroom was neater than hers. His bed looked as if it had not been slept in. In fact, the entire room looked unoccupied. Someone passing by would think it was empty but ready for guests. Reappearing wearing a formfitting tee, Bane closed the wardrobe door and tossed something red toward her. "Put it on."

Natasha caught it midair—a much-worn sweatshirt with HOOSIERS in white lettering across the front. "What the hell is Hoosiers?" she asked, hugging it to her chest.

He waggled his fingers at her. "With me. Quietly." Bane flipped off the light and strode back out, moving past her silently, slowing his pace when he came to the stairs. Then he motioned her in front of him and up to the second floor. "Stay there, or in your bedroom," he whispered.

Her head popped through the neck of the sweatshirt. "I don't understand," she said, slipping her arms into the sleeves. Although very

119

tall, she was slender. The sweatshirt hung on her, covering the pajamas he ached to strip from her body.

Bane kept his voice slow as he explained quickly. "We might have a problem. Whoever it is knows you and I live here. There are very few that would address us by our married surnames. I'm being cautious. That's what I do."

"That's what I do too."

"I know. Stay here." He kissed her forehead quickly, then stepped onto the stairs and spoke over his shoulder, his voice low. "If I call you down, come. As you are. You look convincing, like we were in the middle of something." He smirked. "Mm. You look good in my clothes. Go on."

She glared at him.

The pummeling started up anew, although not with the same gusto.

"I'm coming!" Bane yelled. "Bastard," he said under his breath.

From upstairs, Natasha watched him check his back before slipping into the *setwan*. Thankfully she was staying put so he could focus on the person at the door.

"Who's there?"

"It is Rafiq Nasir. I am sorry about the lateness." The man's voice sounded weak. "I need help."

Caution was called for. The appearance of the man on the other side of the door could be a ploy. "ID," demanded Bane through the door. "In the mail slot."

An ID came through and dropped to the floor. Blood splattered on the tile around it.

Bane squatted and scrutinized the ID. It was Rafiq's. He stood and reached back, pulling his Glock from his waistband. Natasha crept behind him.

"I told you to stay upstairs," he said gruffly without looking at her. "Since you didn't listen to me, stay back. Try staying out of the way. I can't see through this fucking door." Bane released the safety, stepped to the side, and slid the long dead bolt back, cracking the door open, bracing and ready to fire. His quick purview showed that Rafiq was alone and that blood leaked down his right arm and hand.

"Inside, man." Bane ushered him through the door, then locked it. He looked up to see Natasha watching him from the lowest steps, her eyes large and intense. "Nat, I need your help." To Rafiq, he said, "Lean on me."

꙱ ꙲ ꙳ ꙴ

Bane flooded the kitchen with light. He helped Rafiq, who was sweating profusely and breathing fast and shallow, into a chair. "What happened?"

Natasha had followed silently behind them in the dim light, dodging the blood splattering to the floor. Once they were in the kitchen, she put a pot with water on the stove to boil, filled a large ceramic bowl with cool water, and pulled out clean towels and kitchen cloths, a few of which she dropped into the bowl.

Rafiq was deathly pale. He held his right arm against his chest, face contorted in pain as the white dress shirt he wore turned deep red.

She approached cautiously with the bowl. "Rafiq, I'm going to clean you off."

"Yes, thank you, Natasha," he slurred before collapsing to the side.

Bane caught him before he hit the floor, cradling Rafiq's head as he lowered him to the tile. "Fuck. He's bleeding like a stuck pig. I need to get a better look." He glanced up at Natasha. "Scissors? Gotta get this shirt off."

So much blood. Natasha was wide-eyed. She opened drawers hastily. "No scissors."

Bane frowned, shaking his head. "No. Get my first aid case. It's in our guest bath, bottom of the cabinet. And my knife, under my pillow. Hurry."

Sandalwood and spice hit Natasha as she bolted into Bane's room. She reached under the pillow closest to her and searched, her body responding with heat as she envisioned him in bed in all his splendor.

Natasha shook her head. "Not now," she whispered.

Her hands closed around metal. She moved into the attached bath— "our guest bathroom," he had said as if it were fact—to retrieve his first aid case out of the cabinet and the *riad's* first aid kit under the vanity. She ran back to Bane with her arms full.

If possible, Rafiq had become even paler during the minutes she was absent. She placed everything on the table and opened both the case and kit, finding sterile packets of gloves—large enough to cover Bane's very large hands, as well as some that would fit her. She unsealed the extra-large packet and handed it to him, then grabbed a packet of mediums and slipped them over her hands. She did the same with several envelopes of sterile gauze bandages.

"Rafiq?" Bane called loudly as he slipped on the gloves.

Rafiq didn't respond.

"Iodine. Get a field dressing ready." He nodded to the smaller first aid kit and extended his hand. "Where did you pull that from?"

Natasha passed him the knife and bandages. "Vanity in your—in the guest bathroom," she said, correcting herself and answering his surprised expression. Her eyes flickered to Rafiq. "My grandparents were rather meticulous about things like this after experiencing World War II. And I had a habit of getting into situations where I needed minor medical attention."

"Really?" He smiled at her, heat flashing in his expression despite the fact that a man lay bleeding profusely between them. "I see there's still much more to discover about you and your family."

Rafiq shuddered, dragging Bane's attention away abruptly. "Oh, no you don't. Stay with us, man. I'm cutting your shirt off, Rafiq. Remain still."

No response.

Natasha's voice rose in alarm. "Bane, is he? Is h—"

"Be ready to move if he moves." Bane studied Rafiq, then released the blade. Its deadly edge sliced through the shirt like butter.

Rafiq's chest was covered in blood.

"Oh my god." Natasha pulled sterile gauze from a packet and dabbed gently. "I don't see anything on his torso."

"Me either." Bane slipped his knife through the right sleeve, which was soaked with blood. He pulled the drenched fabric to the side. "Give me some of that." He nodded toward the gauze. "Rafiq?"

Still no response.

"He's out cold. Shot twice. Muscle in his upper arm," he said, propping Rafiq up enough to survey his arm. He continued his cursory examination. "Missed the bone. Through and through, back to front. Appears pretty clean. We can address that." Blood coated Bane's glove. "Uh-oh. Not good." Bubbling blood from Rafiq's inside upper arm began to spit. "He's losing a lot of blood. I need to get a better look."

He glanced around the kitchen, clearly searching for something, and lowered Rafiq to the floor again, elevating the man's arm above his head. "Come here. Take my place. We've gotta keep him elevated and get him stabilized."

She did as he commanded without thinking, kneeling next to him, her EMT training kicking in. Bane draped several of the towels over her thighs and rotated Rafiq's damaged arm. He guided Natasha's hand underneath the upper arm and pressed her fingers firmly over Rafiq's pulse point. The bleeding did not slow. Crimson oozed between her gloved fingers.

"More pressure. Give me your other hand too." He placed it over her other one. "Press more firmly. You're doing great. I know this is an awkward position." The bleeding slowed immediately. Bane nodded and covered Rafiq's wrist with two fingers. "Good. He's got a pulse. Can you keep the pressure on?" he asked, his expression intense.

Her heart hammered in her chest, her body warring between keeping Rafiq from dying and Bane's touch. "Yes."

"Good. Stay on it, just like that. Do not let up. I'll be right back." He took off his gloves, tossed them onto Rafiq's bloody shirt remnants, and left.

Natasha jockeyed to get more comfortable, continuing to apply the correct amount of pressure to slow the bleeding. The blood no longer spit but seeped out with each of Rafiq's heartbeats. That red color that she had always been so passionate about leached between her latex-covered fingers, coating her gloves. Slick. Sticky. A metallic smell like hundreds of pennies overwhelmed her. She applied more pressure, praying that their care would give Rafiq the chance he needed to come out whole. Bullet wounds were tricky. This was the first time she had needed to rely on her EMT training, and it was her first encounter with gunshot wounds.

Bane returned, slid another pair of gloves on, and poured some of the boiling water over the flashlight he held before kneeling beside her. His head almost touched hers, his scent enveloping her. She inhaled deeply, his nearness throwing her off-balance.

"You okay?" He squinted and assessed her. His eyes—normally a kaleidoscope of brown, green, gold, and red—had evolved to a soft cognac brown infused with brilliant green.

Her answer was breathy as she found herself lost in his beautiful eyes. "Yes."

His eyes glinted. "Hmm." Bane broke eye contact and focused on what he held—a small tactical flashlight and his webbed belt. "The flashlight is waterproof. Boiling water is our best option for combating germs." He handed her the flashlight and worked the belt under Rafiq's

arm, above where Natasha applied pressure. Bane pulled the belt through its buckle, tightening slowly. "Okay, let up."

She sat back on her haunches and released the pressure. Immediately blood sprayed out. Natasha turned her head and regrouped.

"Yeah. It's unnerving to see someone's life force spraying out of them. First time?" Bane tightened the belt slightly more.

"Yes, but I have basic EMT training. INTERPOL required it before my initial assignment."

"I know, but the real thing is much different. More immediate. You're doing great, by the way. Coming across like you're on autopilot."

Natasha gave him a tight smile.

"We make a good team. He's out cold. I need to talk to you about something else. I'm a fan of Clara's."

Natasha's gray eyes held his. "And?"

"She congratulated me."

She studied Rafiq, who was breathing evenly now. "I forgot to tell you I told her. Oliver had gone to bed."

"I'm glad you did." He watched Rafiq as well. "His bleeding has stopped." Bane checked for a pulse again. It was weak but steady. "Good. We've got to keep an eye on his arm and hand, let up if it becomes cool or there is any sign of swelling. We don't want to chance any tissue dying." His fingers brushed hers as he turned on the flashlight she held. "Hold the flashlight steady while I take a look. I'm glad you're here." His brow furrowed as his fingers tenderly touched and dabbed at the leaking hole in Rafiq's arm. "They brought you on again less than a month after your last assignment. That's a quick turnaround." Bane paused his examination and dropped his chin, regarding Natasha seriously. "I heard Guatemala got really intense and that you did a great job."

She did not want to talk about Guatemala. "I did my best."

"That's all we can do." He sighed, then looked up, his eyes pinning hers, penetrating into her. "I just want to make sure you're going to have my back if the time comes."

"Of course." She swallowed again and sought some way to tear her eyes from his. "Your medical training surpasses mine."

"Smooth segue," said Bane, chuckling. He grimaced as he carefully examined the hole in Rafiq's arm. "I see it. The bullet is lodged in the muscle, .45. Appears to be in one piece." Worry coated his next words.

"Dammit. It's sputtering blood. I'm going to have to extract that and close the brachial or he has no chance of making it. Emmet is at least twenty minutes out."

Natasha brought over the pot and more clean rags. "You contacted Emmet?" The director's first name felt funny on her tongue. Her parents and grandparents had drilled it into her to address adults and superiors by last name and appropriate titles until she was invited to do otherwise. The executive director had not invited her to use his first name.

"Re-glove, Nat," he said. "When I got my belt and flashlight. Emmet lives in Bouznika, more or less halfway between Rabat and Casablanca." He glanced around and found the sterile suture kit. Bane opened it and also ripped one of the empty glove packets open and laid it flat.

"Why the glove envelope?" she asked, re-gloving and adding the discarded gloves to the growing bloody trash.

"For the bullet or fragments. Swab the perimeter area gently with the iodine. Don't get any of it in the wound."

Natasha placed the iodine-soaked gauze with the bloody bandages after swabbing, then held the flashlight over the bullet wound, watching as Bane worked, impressed as all hell. His hand was steady despite the hour and the situation dropped into their laps. "You've done this before."

"More times than I can count. In the field and on the farm."

"Farm?"

"Yeah. Can you get me bullet forceps? Second from the left."

Natasha's finger hovered over the instruments, each in a separate vacuum-sealed pouch. "This one?"

"Yes." He continued to talk while she opened the sterile pouch. "I grew up on a farm. Indiana. Midwest US."

She placed the forceps in his open palm, the heat between them sparking when their gloved fingers grazed each other's. Her pulse went into overdrive. *Jesus.* "I know where Indiana is."

"Ever been there? Dammit. It's stubborn," he groused as he continued extracting the bullet.

Natasha laughed. "I would never attribute stubbornness to an inanimate object. And no, I haven't been there. I've been as close as Chicago."

"Got it!" Satisfaction lit his features as he turned the bullet over in the flashlight's beam. "One piece. Excellent. Give me a glove envelope."

"I will do better than that."

She proudly pulled something from the waistband of her pajama shorts, exposing a generous expanse of skin.

Natasha held up an empty Ziploc bag and shook it. "Eyes here," she said lightly as she opened it. "I found boxes of them in the cabinet when I was in search of clean cloths."

Bane dropped the bullet into the clear open bag and pinned her with his gaze for a few heartbeats. "Sweetheart, you are full of contradictions. I want to explore every single one of them."

Her eyes grew big and her lips parted. His ability to slice through her carefully constructed armor was unnerving. "That's not going to happen."

"You actually believe that? You appeared turned on when I woke you earlier. And again when you were checking me out. Want to discuss all the other times?"

"I was not checking you out. You have an overactive, sexed-out imagination." She huffed, looking away.

"Bullshit. You were. I would take your brush-offs seriously if you meant what you said. But you continue to send 'I'm really interested' messages."

"I do not."

"You do indeed. It must be exhausting to constantly be in an internal argument with yourself about what you desire yet fear," he said quietly, leaning over Rafiq, whose color was improving.

Natasha shifted away.

Bane shook his head. "Hand me the field dressing. Please. I need to take care of the through and through." He gave Rafiq an angry look. "This fucker has spoiled my plans for the evening."

chapter 19

ANOTHER HAMMERING ON THE DOOR announced the arrival of the director. Natasha disposed of her gloves quickly and rushed to let him in, forgetting she was still in her pj's and Bane's sweatshirt until after she opened the door.

"Sir."

Emmet's eyes skimmed over the sweatshirt she wore. "It appears you and your husband have had quite an evening." A small group of men filed in behind him and waited.

"Good evening, gentlemen," Natasha said to the men and crossed her arms over her chest, feeling exposed, wanting to flee upstairs and change her clothes. "Um, yes sir. We did what we could."

"Where is Rafiq?"

"The kitchen. Straight ahead, all the way to the back," she answered, indicating with her hand. Two medics entered, passing quickly, guiding a stretcher stacked with medical supplies and equipment.

"Emmet," Bane said, coming toward them, reaching to shake the director's hand. "A lot of excitement around here. This won't take long?"

"No, the cleaners are quite efficient." He addressed the men still waiting behind him. "Please sterilize the Ruas' kitchen"—he scowled and waved his hand at the evident blood trail—"and the splatter. Double-check the walls and furniture for any spray or droplets." He turned back to Natasha. "They do an excellent job. Please inform Matilda of what needs to be replaced or if anything needs to be resanitized."

127

"I will. Thank you."

Emmet closed the front door. "Did Rafiq talk at all?"

"No." Bane scrubbed his hand over his beard, then inhaled. "Let's talk in our office, out of the commotion." He pointed to one of the double-doored *bâyts* on the other side of the atrium. "I'll be back."

Natasha flooded the elongated room with soft lantern light before entering and waited silently with Emmet, closing the wooden doors after Bane returned with a tray of glasses and a pitcher of water and set them on the desk. She dropped into a chair full of colorful mismatched pillows of various sizes—belying how dark the evening had become—and massaged her temples.

Bane poured a glass for each of them, passing them around. "Drink," he ordered Natasha.

She drained it in one swallow.

"Did you hear any of the shots?" Emmet asked.

"Neither of us did." Bane refilled Natasha's glass and handed it to her. He stood next to her and sipped from his, leaning down to squeeze her shoulder. "Emmet, Nasir kept to our cover, pounded on the door and yelled for Mr. Rua and Dr. Rua. Beyond my concern for him is why he was shot and why so close to our residence."

"This is extremely disconcerting. We need to find out what the hell is going on, if this incident is related to your assignment or only coincidental."

"I don't believe in coincidence. Everything in me is screaming that this is related to our mission. We need to discover how and why. We don't want to be blindsided. Or worse." Bane handed Emmet the two Ziploc bags. "Here's his ID and the bullet. As you can see, the bullet I extracted is in one piece. It's a .45. Just nicked his brachial."

Emmet lifted the bag to eye level and peered at the bullet. "That is a nasty bit of business. We'll see if forensics can get a match with this slug."

Bane nodded. "The second shot was a through and through. Nasir lost his strength fast. He was out cold shortly after we got him to the kitchen. I've no idea where he was shot, how much blood he lost, or how in the hell he knew to come here. We applied a pressure bandage. I stitched him up and packed him too."

"Nice work, Bane. Doctor. We will talk to Nasir as soon as he is conscious." Emmet's gaze moved between them. "Nothing compromised?"

"No, sir," Natasha responded, standing and stretching. She felt better after drinking water, and sitting did her no good when her mind and body were on full alert.

"Not that we know of," Bane said at the same time.

Natasha didn't miss the naked interest in his gaze.

Emmet nodded, his eyes bouncing between Bane and Natasha. "Excellent."

Bane grinned. "My wife looks good in one of my favorites, doesn't she?" He wrapped an arm around Natasha and pulled her close to him. "It's getting late. We need to turn in."

Natasha tried to smile through her grimace. "I doubt I will be able to sleep."

The director watched them with fascination, then looked past Bane and Natasha to the stretcher. Tubes snaked from pouches into Rafiq's body.

"How is he doing?" Emmet asked the medics.

The medic at Rafiq's head answered. "He is stable but requires surgery." He nodded to Natasha and Bane. "You did a great job. Saved his life. We have called ahead to the hospital."

They continued outside to the ambulance. The cleaners came forward with black bags and followed the medics outside.

"Looks like we're done here," Emmet said. "We didn't have plans to meet tomorrow, but what happened tonight complicates things. What a bloody mess. I'll see you in the morning. My office—oh nine hundred. Please be prompt." With that, Emmet followed the men out the door.

Natasha ran the bolt across the door, wishing she felt tired instead of revved up. She turned, almost smashing her face into Bane, who had moved up behind her, his gaze crawling over her face, igniting every single nerve ending in her.

"You mentioned you wouldn't be able to sleep." A slow, sensuous smile lit his face. "Where were we before we were interrupted?"

Natasha stepped back and crossed her arms, holding on to her shoulders with opposing hands. She cocked her head and narrowed her eyes. "So that's all you can think about? Getting in my pants? Jesus, Bane. Think with the head on your shoulders." She threw her hands up in exasperation and paced. "This… this night has been too much. I need… to get out of my clothes. I'm sure there's some blood on me. I need to shower. You should too."

After her shower, Natasha went back downstairs. The adrenaline coursing through her kept her awake. So did thoughts about the man staying in her *riad*. Bane lounged with one knee up and his leg extended in the corner of the atrium under a soft lamp with his eyes closed and one arm casually draped behind his wet, spiky hair, supporting his head. He seemed unaware of her.

Natasha tiptoed closer to study him. Soft music came from the earbuds he wore. Classical. His other strong hand lay across the hip of his low-slung sweats. Her mouth watered. His ink and well-defined abs were on full display. Everything about Bane was beautifully masculine and underscored his strength, even his bare feet.

"I can feel it coming off you." He sighed, pulling his earbuds out and opening his eyes. "A whole lotta things are pent up inside. You're wound tighter than a drum." He rubbed the back of his neck and sat up, regarding her. "I can help you release some of it."

Natasha stayed where she was. Her voice grew more agitated with each word. "Seriously? Are you fucking kidding me?"

Bane didn't respond for a while, allowing the silence and tension to build. Just when Natasha was ready to speak again, he stood and approached, speaking quietly, the corner of his sensuous lips drawn up on one side. His eyes sparkled. "Fuck. It's such a great word. One of my favorites. It's remarkably versatile, don't you agree? Think of it. A noun, adjective, verb, or adverb, which you employed just now." He looked down and shook his head, then considered her with malachite eyes. "Hearing it come out of your mouth is promising." His voice dropped low. "I'd prefer to hear it from you as a verb." He raised his brows, his meaning clear.

"Will you stop?" she hissed. "How the hell can you think about sex when—"

"Sex," Bane said with a sad smile. "Is that what you think. Just sex? I want more than sex, Nat."

"We don't even know one another."

"True, but we can. I'm trying. We both know what we want. Can't you try to meet me halfway?"

"Get it through your head. I am not interested," she said pointedly.

Bane stepped closer and she stepped back, brushing up against the wall between two arches, forced to look up into smoldering eyes.

"I call bullshit," he purred. "You know why?" His finger caressed her neck. "Your pulse accelerates when you're around me. The closer I get, or when I touch you, like now." He brushed his thumb across her bottom lip. "You lick those luscious lips of yours or bite down on the lower one. Christ. That about does me in each time." He pinned her with his heated gaze. "Your eyes dilate, turning from gray to gunmetal. I wonder how dark they become when you're on the edge. And your nipples... They tighten, begging for my touch. Damn, how I want to—" Bane's eyes never left Natasha's face. "Want me to keep going?" he whispered.

She stared at him and croaked, "No. Just stop. I need to think. I need space."

"Fine, I'll give you space. Call me when you need me, because you will, my beauty. Nothing and no one will take care of what you need. Just pray I'm around to satisfy you."

"You are so overly confident."

Bane shook his head while giving her a long look, keeping his voice low, his finger a whisper tracing the hot skin of Natasha's neck and collarbones. His eyes had darkened. "Mm... nope. Just honest. This thing between us is intense and hungry. Off-the-charts chemistry. Doesn't it get tiring? Denying yourself?"

Natasha's next words broke the tension. "Nasir was shot. He almost died in my kitchen. He still might die."

"You're right. I'm sorry. I forget how people who aren't used to situations like this might react."

Her voice rose in disbelief. "You don't feel anything? Are you even human?"

"Don't presume to know what I feel," he said, his words clipped. "I've experienced things that I suspect would turn you inside out." Bane inhaled deeply and closed his eyes, then opened them slowly and cocked his head, studying her. His voice softened. "Sorry. That was a bit harsh. I heard about Guatemala, what happened. Spooky as shit. You have every right to be rattled. Most people would be."

She answered cautiously, slightly unmoored by the shifting focus of their conversation, mesmerized by the thickly lashed eyes observing her with keen interest. "You wouldn't be rattled," she said, her voice soft, her eyes glistening. One tear escaped and ran down her cheek. *Dammit.* She whispered, "I was terrified. It haunts me still. I have trouble sleeping

because I see his face. I see that scorched mark covering one side of his face. I hear his cries and screams. I smell but don't see thousands of lit matches in a wet underground cavern. I see a face appearing in the wall. I taste the Mayans' fear and I feel it too. Something dark and evil."

"Fuck," he said, shaking his head. "That's Steven King shit. I might have been just as rattled if I'd witnessed what you did in that very moment. There was"—he took a deep breath—"*is* no explanation for what happened." He wiped at her tear with the pad of his thumb and licked it.

She imagined his tongue on her skin and shuddered.

He noticed and smiled, holding out his hand, which she took without thinking. "Sweetheart, I feel like a fuckin' yo-yo around you. You push me away. You get upset. But then you allow me close, let me touch you, hold you, comfort you. Kiss you." His words hung in the air, pregnant with meaning. "It's like you're playing with me, but then I really don't think that's your intention. My gut tells me intimacy scares you. You fear losing control when in actuality you control what happens between us. I'm paying attention, but this is a dance with some intricate steps." He pulled her to his chest, and when she offered no resistance, he slipped his arms around her and bent his head, resting his forehead on hers before moving slightly so that his lips were close to her ear. His warm, moist breath raised goose bumps over her skin. He murmured, "I watch you react to me. God knows, I react to you. What is it, Nat? Who hurt you? I can help you work through it."

He nibbled on her ear. She still didn't resist but softened and let out a tiny breath.

"Feel it. Face it. Don't allow it to have power over you."

Electricity sparked through her. God, how could she feel such desire for this man during this moment when the shame of being seen as weak coursed through her at the same time? She broke the embrace. "Is that what you do?"

Pain shadowed Bane's features. His voice became gravelly. "I've had to. To survive. We're inhuman, not infallible." He inhaled long and deep. Confidence and a smile coated his words. "Babe, I'm a fuckin' machine. I'm callous from experiencing and seeing things I wish I hadn't. I've done things that I had to in the moment. I've had to reconcile all of it. Otherwise it would drown me."

"You seem fine to me."

"Oh, I'm fine all right," he agreed, brushing his thumb over her knuckles. "My point is you don't need to always be so tough. Lean on me. Allow me to be your partner. It's easier to stand if you have someone to share and unite with. I don't want to hurt you. I want to get to know you, discover what makes the intelligent and formidable Dr. Natasha Jordaan tick. You fascinate me. From the very first moment you walked into Emmet's office, I was blown away. I felt something. I know you felt it too," he said earnestly. "We have an opportunity during this assignment, especially given our cover."

Natasha said nothing, but her eyes never left his. Although Bane teased her incessantly and annoyed the hell out of her at times, she felt protected by this mountain of a man. She felt safe. Her hunger for him was undeniable, so why was she denying it? Natasha understood that his bawdy banter was part of his personality and, despite his sexual overtures, she was in control. Most importantly, he wanted her to have the control. Bane had impressed the hell out of her while he worked on Rafiq. And now he had given her the framework of something more than working together. Was it possible? Could she trust it? Could she trust him?

He gently tucked a curl behind her ear. The movement was tender. "You're weighing your decision, aren't you?"

She gazed at him with wide eyes.

Bane watched her with amusement and heat. "You were thorough showing me around the *riad* I remember the rooftop terrace. You said you needed space. Why don't we go up there? Is outside enough space?"

She nodded.

"You lead this dance." His gaze held hers for a few heartbeats. "I need to hear you."

"Yes."

Bane flashed her a sexy smile and grabbed a few throws from the couch, then followed her up the stairs.

chapter 20

CASABLANCA SLEPT. POLAR-WHITE STARS flickered above, scattered like glittering dust in the blue-black sky. Bane moved under the pergola with Natasha and dropped the throws on the divan, facing her. Tendrils of moonlight filtered through the intricately carved lattice, spilling over them, creating a texture of illumination and shadow.

His voice turned husky, deeper and richer as he gently took Natasha's chin and tilted her head up, searching her eyes, now molten with desire, pleading for him to take control. He slid his hand under her hair, and his fingers trailed over her neck, leaving a trail of fire.

She shivered beneath the oversized sweatshirt covering her slim frame, surrounded by the intoxicating smell of him.

"You're trembling. Are you okay with this?"

She glanced up at him, biting her bottom lip.

"I need to hear you say it."

"Yes," she whispered thickly, placing her hand on his chest. His heart galloped under it, just like hers was doing.

Bane peeled her hand away and kissed her palm, then nipped and sucked the sensitive flesh between her thumb and forefinger. Her breath caught. It was just like her dream. Her nipples were so hard they hurt, and her thighs were damp.

"Damn, you're so fucking beautiful." Bane's lips hovered, ghosting over hers before capturing them. He pulled back, clearly struggling to keep himself in check.

She had wrestled with her attraction to him since they met, and she fought other demons as well, but she was ready for this.

"You lead, sweetheart," he murmured, his thumb brushing along the arch of her jaw. "I'm all in."

She rolled her lip between her teeth, then released it. He lowered his head again and sucked on its fullness. His groan drove her wild, and he languidly traced her mouth with his tongue, then kissed her slowly.

Natasha returned his kiss and opened her mouth wider, inviting his tongue, cautiously asking for more. The roughness of Bane's whiskers and gentleness of his lips made her blood race. She pulled back, stunned, panting.

"Okay?" His expression was full of concern.

"Yes. Just needed to catch my breath."

"Mm. I make you breathless," he whispered appreciatively, the pad of his thumb brushing over her sensitive lips. He smiled his crooked, sexy smile and kissed the tip of her nose. "I like that. Kiss me again."

Natasha slipped her arms around his neck and pressed her chest against his, sweeping his mouth deeply with her tongue, enjoying how his tongue tangled with hers.

Bane grabbed her hips and tugged her snugly to him, sliding his raging erection against her core.

She stepped back, her eyes round. *He wasn't kidding when he said he was a big man.*

His eyes crinkled as he shrugged. "Not gonna apologize about what you do to me."

His eyes followed his hands sliding over her legs, which were visible below the hem of his sweatshirt. She imagined wrapping them around his hips while he moved inside her.

"Your skin," he murmured as he continued leaving feathery kisses on her neck, her chin, her shoulders. "So silky," he groaned. His hands slid up and he lightly palmed her back, then cupped and kneaded her ass, pulling her up against him again, moving her so that they created friction.

"Oh my god, Bane. I can't even—"

His mouth crashed against hers, then immediately grew tender, cutting off the rest of her words. He leaned back and looked deeply into her eyes, his own now malachite in the bright moonlight. "Damn. What

you do to me. Unbelievable." He guided her hand, encouraging her to explore him. Natasha's other hand joined it and soon she was skimming his corded stomach and the flat planes of his chest.

Bane's overpowering maleness made her feel feminine and dainty. Desired. Things she was unaccustomed to. "Please."

"Tell me what you want." He dipped into her mouth again.

"I want," she said between kisses. "I'm on fire."

"You sure are." He breathed hard, pulling away from her. "I want... more... baby."

"I do... too," she whispered, shaking, intoxicated and sizzling with desire. She needed both feet on the terrace to stand upright. Her body was thrumming, burning with need. "Oh my god... I can't... think," she rasped. "Please... I... please..."

"Please?"

She writhed against him. "Please. I want to feel."

His hooded gaze held hers as his fingers skimmed along her clothed arms, then traced along her neck and collarbone. "Hmm." Bane murmured, teasing lightly, slowly, starting under the front hem of the HOOSIERS sweatshirt and silky tee she wore. His fingers patiently whispered in featherlight circles over her skin, whipping her into a fever. Her body undulated, seeking his touch. He skimmed her stomach and stopped just shy of her breasts. "We need to hit pause."

She cried out petulantly. "No."

"Sorry, babe. I'm clean, but my protection is downstairs."

"I'm clean too. On birth control." She wrapped a bare leg around his thigh and rode it, feeling the scorching heat of him even through his sweats. "You don't need to leave."

His eyes flared and he swallowed, then he bracketed her hips with his hands, slowing her motion and giving her a tender kiss. "Too many clothes. Take off the sweatshirt," he panted.

She pulled it over her head and tossed it onto the terrace.

Bane's eyes turned to malachite as he stared at her hard nipples, which she was sure were fully evident under the skimpy top. Nodding, he growled softly, "Take it off too."

She pulled it over her head and added it to the pile, standing proudly in front of him—feral and hungry. His body tensed in response.

His large hands covered her full, ripe breasts. Natasha's dark brown nipples puckered even tighter and Bane milked her breasts reverently. "Perfect."

He lowered his mouth. Blood zinged straight to her core as Bane pulled and lapped, nibbling gently.

"Beautiful," he whispered before his mouth moved to her other breast and latched on.

Her head bowed and her hands gripped his massive shoulders as he sucked. Holding on to him was all that kept her from toppling over, so drugged was she from the heady fog of desire. His tongue trailed with his fingers, over her ribs and stomach, leaving a trail of sparks and her trembling with need.

Bane knelt down. "What's going on between these gorgeous long legs of yours, hmm?" His fingers traced over the back of her knees, then trailed the inside of her thighs and up inside her pajama bottoms. "You're soaked," he groaned. "Look at me."

Natasha's heavy gaze locked on his, unable to look away. She was sure she had never been this wet. She craved him. Her pounding heart and hot, insistent need made her dizzy.

"More, sweetheart?" Bane grinned wickedly, groaning loudly as his finger, then two, slipped into her slick, silky heat, working her slowly, his eyes glittering with lust as he watched Natasha.

She was so close. "Yes."

"Bottoms off, sweetheart. I want to see all of you." Bane pulled his fingers out, putting them in his mouth and sucking slowly, watching transfixed as she untied the drawstring and let her moist pajama shorts drop to the deck before kicking them toward the pile. "Christ. You're so fucking wet for me. I want to bathe in you."

Natasha felt her knees start to buckle as he inserted his fingers into her again. She moaned loudly and rocked against him, gasping as he stroked her with his fingers and then his tongue. She cupped the crown of his head with both hands and held on, breathing heavily. Waves of his dark hair spiked between her fingers, soft, glossy, and thick.

Bane kissed her thighs before rising. "I could come just tasting you, watching you watch me as I taste you. But—" He hooked his thumbs into his sweats and shoved them down over his lean hips. Commando. He was as naked as she was.

Natasha stopped moving and just stared, her mouth partially open, her breath stuttering, her body quaking for him.

"Nat."

Holy hell. She just stared, rendered speechless by his beauty. Bane was a masterpiece. Gifted. Gorgeous. His long, thick erection strained toward her. He exuded patience and power.

He guided her hands to him, the tension snapping and crackling between them. "I want to fill you. I want to feel you shatter while I move inside you."

Natasha's heart galloped in her throat, making it difficult for her to speak. "Yes," she cried, hoarsely. *Oh my god, yes.*

Bane grabbed one of the throws off the divan before pulling her to the deck with him and tucking it under her. They kissed each other passionately, sipping at each other's mouths, their tongues mirroring his movement as he pushed into her fully, stretching her to the point of pleasurable pain.

Natasha wrapped her arms and legs around Bane, urging him deeper, out of her mind with the heat that built deep inside her. "Bane!" she cried out as her body clenched and bucked. She arched and exploded against him, and Bane thrust home, grunting as his powerful release rippled through both of them.

revelations

صطاد في الماء العكر.

�֎ ֎

To fish in troubled water.

✦

chapter 21

"BANE!" NATASHA CALLED FROM THE atrium. She was just about to call again when he appeared at the top of the stairs in front of her bedroom, now their bedroom.

"Yes?" His deep voice rumbled as he came to look down at her from the balcony. He was fresh from a shower—one she had passed on because she'd showered earlier while he slept and had been intent on making him breakfast.

The image of him naked in the shower turned her limbs rubbery, so she leaned against the wall, trying to look casual. What would it have felt like to run her hands over the hard wetness of him? She blinked, willing away the image, sucking in oxygen and speaking more forcefully than she'd meant to. The matter at hand was far more important. "Can you come down here?"

Natasha lost her train of thought as Bane trotted down the stairs and sauntered toward her, smiling as if he had discovered a secret, a white bath towel snugly secured around his lean hips, setting off his olive-toned skin and tats. His scruff was trimmed back, shadowing the dimples she had seen hints of so often when he talked, smiled, or laughed. Natasha flushed; she had some tender areas from where his whiskers had grazed her last night and early this morning.

Bane pulled her against his dewy, sculpted chest and buried his nose in her hair, which was still damp. "Good morning, beauty. You wore me out after that very-early-morning cup of coffee, but I can be had." He untucked the patterned, sleeveless top from the linen skirt she wore and

slid his hands inside her panties, massaging her ass. "Both of us are going to need some shut-eye later. Fuck, you feel good," he murmured against her head, nesting his hips against her.

Her senses filled with sandalwood and spice, and his attentiveness to her ass sent her heart skittering, her entire body thrumming on overdrive. In all honesty, she would prefer to go back to bed with him. She kissed him and stepped back, cocking her head. "Come with me?"

He lifted his head and his eyes narrowed at her serious tone, but he followed her into the *riad*'s office.

"Whoa. Am I in trouble?" He grinned at her.

"Um, no," she responded, standing in front of a massive inlaid wood desk.

The beautiful room, awash with rich color and a well-appointed rug and Moroccan furniture, was a mess. Papers, note cards, and folders littered the carpet. He did a double take. "What are you doing? We have to be in Emmet's office by nine o'clock." He glanced at his watch. "Simon will be here in roughly an hour to pick us up. Are you packed and ready?"

"I am. Have you been in here?"

"Huh?"

"Have you been in here?" She repeated herself with a little edge.

"Hey, easy."

She inhaled deeply and exhaled slowly. "I'm sorry. You didn't deserve that."

"No, I haven't been in here except when you showed it to me. Why? What's with the mess?"

"So, I was going to make you a substantial breakfast, but when I passed the office, I noticed the door was ajar, which was odd, and when I peeked inside, I saw the cabinet door was slightly open. I walked in, and it seemed like things had been moved on top of the desk too."

"Are you sure?" Bane asked while looking at the antique Moroccan cabinet of silver filigree and espresso-brown leather. One drawer was above each of the two larger doors, which opened from the center.

Natasha tapped her knuckles softly against her lips as her eyes panned the room. "No. It's just a feeling."

"Look, you didn't get much sleep. Maybe you're imagining or forgetting things." He backtracked when she shook her head. "Okay, maybe not."

"I began to close it but decided otherwise. All of this"—she indicated the mess on the floor—"was inside, in disarray. Nothing was in its designated folder. Someone rifled through the cabinet. The drawers are disturbed too. But the other side appears untouched."

Bane frowned at her, then nodded at the other door of the cabinet, which was closed. "Is that a mess?"

"No. I'd started to place things back in an organized way when my fingers brushed across a rough, recessed area on the bottom of the compartment, similar to a knot in wood, but this type of wood doesn't have knots. It struck me as odd, so I stopped. I couldn't really see anything, so I took your flashlight from your rucksack." She splayed her hand on his wrist. "I'm sorry. I normally wouldn't go through your personal belongings."

"It's fine." He squeezed her hand, then laced his fingers with hers.

"Anyway, with the flashlight, I discovered there were a number of rough areas in the compartment. As I said, odd." She slid her fingers from Bane's and her hands became animated as she spoke more quickly. "For whatever reason, I started pressing on them. There was a click and the center panel fell out. I thought I broke it at first. But"—Natasha pivoted and took something from the top of the cabinet, blocking what she held until turning back—"it held this." She handed him a leather bag, mostly flat and roughly nine by twelve inches. The entire thing was hand-sewn and tooled, beautifully detailed. "I've never seen this either. It's Berber. It had to be a snug fit."

He examined the leather, which had aged to a black-brown where it was soiled. The finely stitched, once-white leather lacing had mellowed to a peanut brown. Patterns of red and black leather lacing created ornate patterns on an exterior purselike compartment, and the flap folded and rested above it. A decorative forged silver medallion was inserted into the center of the bag, matching the two medallions on its flap. The straps were woven of finer brown leather with silver, resembling ornate bridle reins but much shorter. "Nice. Old, huh?"

"Quite. Look inside," she said, sitting in a side chair and wringing her hands.

Bane reached into the funnel opening created when he pulled up the flaps. His hand closed over the contents and pulled out a sheaf of papers and a smaller, soft-sided leather journal. He studied both. "They're in French. No surprise there."

"Correct." Her face paled. "Keep reading."

"You looked at these already?"

"I did."

"It says—Whoa." He dropped onto the desk and stretched his long legs in front of him. "*L'accord Américain*. The American Agreement. *Cadre.* Framework." Bane searched her eyes. "Is this what I think it is?"

Natasha hated the answer. "Yes."

Bane whistled and shook his head, skimming each of the pages. "This agreement is fully laid out. It details the founding, how the network began. Christ. I wonder how long it took the bastards to expand outside Morocco once they got a taste of the money." He slapped the papers against his thighs.

She yelped, "Please don't damage the papers! And your towel. Is it damp? Be careful about having them on your towel."

"Cut me a break, okay? My towel is dry or I wouldn't be sitting on this desk," he said, running his fingers over the pages. He massaged the back of his neck as he read quickly. "Nat, this is all kinds of fucked up. They agreed to sanction looting. They provided the seed money," he uttered, flipping to the last page and wagging his head again. "*Conclu et convenu ce 23e jour d'avril 1944, à l'Américain, Casablanca, Maroc.* Hmm, okay. 'Agreed and entered into on this day, April 23, 1944, at the American, Casablanca, Morocco.' A handful of signatures. I assume these people were powerful and influential. We may need some help on these names. Do you have any idea what the American referred to was?"

"It's a famous café in the heart of Casa, opened during World War II. It was a favorite of Pépé's. My grandparents took me there often enough. It's still in business."

"I see. It seems this agreement was signed at the American Café and the network adopted the name of the café. Misleading, but also smart. The American is singular, denoting a person, which is who you were after, and you believed to have apprehended, correct?"

"Yes."

"Yeah, I remember your reaction when Emmet told you that the American is a fucking hydra of sorts, all over the place. Local, regional, global. They've been able to hide under that illusion for decades as they expanded, until you apprehended Schaus in Guatemala. You lopped a head off, and now the others are in danger of being discovered. At least one is here. We'll get the fuckers."

"I appreciate your confidence."

Bane ran his hand over his face and opened the small leather-bound journal. "Damn. *Manifeste*."

Natasha watched morosely as Bane thumbed through the leather book that held what she'd already seen—a manifest with pages of archaeological artifacts and recipients, dated shipments, cash payments and receipts.

"What do you think all this was doing in your grandfather's cabinet?"

"I believe Pépé hid it. Or Mémé found it after he died and hid it."

"Why would you think that?" he asked, his eyes studiously searching hers.

She inhaled deeply, then exhaled just as forcefully, not breaking eye contact. Natasha's hands dropped to her lap and her voice was pure steel. "It appears that my grandfather was one of the signatories, one of the bastards you referred to, and the manifest is written in his handwriting. I'd know that small, tight script anywhere."

chapter 22

"PÉPÉ'S SIGNATURE... IT'S THE SECOND one." Natasha's composure cracked as her index finger brushed over tight black cursive. "Here. Henri Louis Allamel. This is..." Her lips fought to form the next words. "I don't know what to—" She stuttered, shaking her head, wiping furiously at her eyes.

Bane jumped from the desk and took her hand, pulling her from the chair and gathering her close. "Maybe you're mistaken."

"I know his handwriting, his signature." Her words were muffled against his chest.

"Emmet needs to be informed."

She pushed off his chest angrily and stepped back. "No."

"What the hell? Nat, he needs to know."

"I will handle this myself." Her eyes glittered, daring him to argue with her.

"Come on. Think this through," he said. "No one expects you to handle this yourself. At the very least, Emmet needs to see what we have discovered. Nat, there's the strongest possibility that this is tied to current events."

Snatching the agreement and journal from Bane's hand, she fired back, "I am not sharing this with the director."

"If you don't, I will," he said tersely.

"Well, you can't." She held them up, and waved them at Bane, her

knuckles blanched from gripping the document and leather book so tight. "This was my grandfather's property and now it's mine," she said, her voice strident.

"Dammit, Nat. Do you understand the predicament that keeping these a secret could put you in? How it could jeopardize any future assignments? Sharing this information"—he motioned at the document and journal she held—"could impact the turnover of billions of dollars of looting annually. We might be able to break their back, or at least cut off a supply chain. I have no idea how Morocco views something like this, but I suspect it won't fly with AFRIPOL or INTERPOL. No way, not with the UNESCO and Hague Conventions in place. Think. You're reacting emotionally to the fact that your grandfather was one of the founders of the American."

"We don't know that he was a founder, Bane."

"Come on. He sure as hell was. The proof is in the pudding."

Natasha snapped at him and stepped closer. "What the hell does that mean?"

"It means you have the proof. You're holding it. You believe one of the signatures is his. We skimmed over the agreement and the attached signatures and only perused the manifest. There might be more in what we found. Clues, family names. Hell, there might be more in the desk." Bane paused and sighed deeply. "Did you look through it thoroughly?"

"I did not. I found these and then I just stopped. I was too stunned," she admitted.

"Totally understandable." Bane gestured to the documents. "You have the resources and backing of INTERPOL and AFRIPOL. Reconsider. I'm talking ethics. Besides, I'll be seen as guilty by association if I back your decision. I will not do it."

"I do not see how this agreement signed in 1944 pertains to the American and its operations today," she insisted, shaking the papers in her hand. "Explain that."

Bane held his hands up. "You're thinking with this." He tapped his heart and lowered his voice, intent on defusing their disagreement. "You have a fucking amazing track record at repatriating lost artifacts. I heard about you long before I met you, a near-hallowed reputation. Are you really going to destroy it?"

Her beautiful gray eyes glittered. She slammed her hand on the desk and dropped her head, whispering, "This is my family."

"I know," he said softly, reaching out. "And it sucks." He pulled her in for an embrace. Her body was stiff and unyielding. "Are you going to listen to me?"

Natasha glared at him, her jaw hard and her eyes icy silver. She inhaled a long, shuddering breath and voiced her decision. "I will."

"Good."

"Goddammit to hell." She sank into the desk chair. "What if there are other names, people I knew or people I know, and they are innocent of involvement, like myself?"

"The fact that someone or several someones have rifled through this cabinet indicates that it's more than likely you're going to know other players. My gut tells me they were looking for this, maybe more. We'll go through the *riad* thoroughly after we get back from our meeting."

"I'm going to clear Pépé's name. I cannot emotionally or logically believe he did this willingly."

"And I will do what I can to help you, but trying to clear him can't get in the way of our assignment. Okay?"

"Fine." Natasha exhaled loudly before handing Bane the agreement and manifest. "You're right, of course. I just wish, how I wish I could keep these to myself, but I can't."

"You've made the right decision." Bane smiled encouragingly at her, kissed her, and then glanced at his watch. "We've gotta get a move on. I need to get dressed. I don't know about you, but I need to eat." His stomach growled on cue. "You wore out my reserves and then some." He winked and gave her his crooked sexy grin.

"Really, Bane?" she chided, lifting her chin and arching her eyebrows at him.

He shrugged and attempted to look sheepish. "Yeah," he said, leaning forward and placing his hands on the armrests on either side of Natasha, effectively pinning her in, his mossy eyes full of heat. "Really," he breathed into her ear. Bane kissed her leisurely, then straightened and searched her eyes. "We're good?"

Natasha tilted her head, shaking her head and grinning ruefully. "You're something else. Thanks for helping me see reason, for having my back. I'll bring breakfast in here while you're changing. We can tackle the other side of the cabinet and the desk while we eat."

"Works for me." He laced his fingers through hers and pulled her up and close. Natasha's scent of honey and lemongrass unleashed vivid images of what they'd done last night and into the early hours of the morning, and her passionate and uninhibited responsiveness replayed in his mind, bringing him to full attention. His hands slid down over her hips and he pulled her against his hard length. "As much as I'd enjoy enticing you into another round, it'll have to wait." He pressed his forehead to hers. "Damn. What you do to me."

Natasha freed herself from him, a saucy smile lighting in her eyes. "Go get dressed." She waved him away and headed to the kitchen.

※ ▨ ✺ ▧

Bane was back and had begun emptying out the other cabinet compartment before Natasha returned to the office with a tray holding coffee, warmed milk, dates, croissants, jam, cheese, and fried eggs. Files, papers, and photos lay around him in small piles.

She stirred warmed milk into her coffee, watching him work. "I didn't ask, but since you had coffee earlier this morning, I went with that."

He stopped working and shifted easily to sit cross-legged, facing her. Patting the rug next to him, he said, "Thanks. Sit?"

Natasha placed the tray on the desk next to a small globe, poured him a coffee, and handed him a full plate and a mug. She spread jam over her croissant. "I think I'll stand. All of this"—she swept her hand across the cabinet's emptied contents—"makes me anxious."

Talking between bites and drinking coffee, he said, "I've gone through all of those already and kept them in order," indicating the largest pile of folders. He leaned against the wall and uncrossed his legs, drawing up his knees and resting his forearms on them. "I'll return them to the cabinet and, before you ask, yes, I checked the secret compartment. I didn't find anything else. I closed it back up."

Natasha murmured, "You're efficient."

"Years of doing this kind of thing." He eyed her steadily, contemplating what else he was about to share. "I found correspondence and other manifests in plain sight. In files labeled benignly, such as Pool, Garden, and *Riad*. I used one of the expanding folders to hold them. Information pertaining to, say, the gardens, had notes like the perfect fertilizer, information on plants, and a blueprint

of the gardens. Clever man, your grandfather." Bane jerked his head toward the folder at his right hip. "He used the labels as codes, kinda like metaphors. Take the 'gardens' again. The folder also contains lists of artifacts, antiquities, and shipments dates. All of them are dated."

"You work quickly. So of course I am curious. What was in the *riad* folder?"

"Well, that's where it gets interesting." Bane pulled a ratty, dog-eared notebook from the expandable folder and stood. "I would have passed on this due to its condition alone, but since we're looking for needles in a haystack, I went through it meticulously. Among the pages about the *riad* and its maintenance and upkeep was a different kind of record. Your grandfather appears to have used *riad* to represent the network. This notebook is a gold mine, a ledger of operatives in the American, from the date of the agreement, listing himself and, I assume, the other signees. It covers decades. The last date a person was recorded as an operative nine years ago." He opened the notebook, flipped through to the page he sought, and ran his finger down the page, stopping on the last entry. Bane glanced up at Natasha when he heard her sharp intake of breath.

"What is it?"

"That's two days before Pépé died. He was found far away, south of Tangier, in Asilah, a coastal village. That in itself was quite a shock. Mémé had no idea he was there until she received the phone call that he'd been found. He had told her he would be in Rabat for meetings and staying the night."

"Why Asilah? Was he from that area?"

"No. France originally. Alsace."

"Beautiful area."

"It is," she agreed. "Pépé was a much-sought-after architect. Asilah's architecture is quite something due to the influences of the Roman, Arab, Portuguese, Spanish, and French. Mémé felt he may have been working on the restoration of the ramparts and the palace. Pépé was often called in to consult on architectural jewels like those, but he hadn't mentioned anything to her, which was unusual. She did share with me years later that Pépé had seemed distracted and forgetful in the days leading up to his death." Natasha pinched the bridge of her nose with her right forefinger and thumb, as if warning off a headache. "Oh my god. Bane, what is the last name in the ledger?"

He squinted at the tight cursive. "It looks like '*le fantôme.*' Does that mean anything to you? It has"—he tapped his finger over the writing— "three sixes after it."

Natasha's cup shattered on the corner of the desk, the milk-infused coffee running off the surface and coating the broken ceramic and rug. Her face paled and she began to tremble.

"Nat?" He stood to pull her against him. "Shit. Easy. I have you." He kneaded her back until the trembling subsided and then kissed the top of her head. "What is it? Talk to me, sweetheart."

"*Le fantôme.* The ghost." Her damp cheek rested in the crook of his shoulder and he rubbed her upper arms. "It was the name of the small blue fishing boat that breached on the rocky beach below the Asilah's medina wall."

"How does this relate to your grandfather and his death?"

"Pépé was found in the boat *Le Fantôme,* heavily tangled in fishing net. He drowned." Tears streaked her face.

chapter 23

"I'M GOOD." NATASHA WIPED HER eyes dismissively, then held up her hands.

"The fuck you are," Bane said gruffly, pushing past them and gathering Natasha to him, sitting on the office sofa with her in his lap. He held her for some time before running his hand over his damp hair, smoothing some of the wild waves. Christ, an unbelievable night with her now followed by this. She had quieted considerably and had gradually stretched out; her breathing was slow and steady. "Nat?" No response. She was out. Between last night and this morning's emotional gut punch, it was no wonder. Once they ventured into intimacy, they hadn't been able to keep their hands off each other. Neither one of them had had more than a few hours of sleep.

He made sure she was comfortable, then set about cleaning up the shattered mess and breakfast before lying next to her. Bane reflected on everything that had occurred in the past eight hours—from Rafiq showing up shot to the most mind-blowing sex he could ever remember to the devastating discovery at hand. They needed more time to go through the desk and the entire *riad* before leaving on assignment.

Natasha burrowed in deeper as he lifted his hips to retrieve his phone from his back hip pocket. He pushed speed dial and waited. Emmet picked up mid first ring.

"Morning, Emmet," he drawled quietly. "We need to readjust our timetable."

"Bane. Good morning. Why are you whispering?"

"Natasha's sleeping and I don't want to wake her. We need someone to stay here while we're out. Can Simon possibly do that? We'll explain when we see you. Trust me, it's imperative."

"I realize last evening was unexpected and challenging." The director cleared his throat. "The two of you need to get out of bed. I have other meetings scheduled this afternoon."

"Emmet, we're not in fucking bed. We're up. Well, she was. We've had breakfast and—" Bane rubbed his eyes and yawned. A full breakfast and Natasha's warmth were making him groggy. "The meeting has to be moved back a few hours—I'm sorry. Also, our departure has to be delayed."

"Bloody hell, Bane. Is this truly necessary?"

"Definitely. There's been a major development."

"Can you—"

"I can't, Emmet. Given the events of last night and today, you'll understand fully when we meet."

"I bloody well hope so," Emmet said. There was a pause, then, "Hold please."

Bane pushed back the soft tendrils from Natasha's temple and kissed the top of her head lightly as he waited. His heart raced. She had to be the most exquisite creature to ever grace his life. He couldn't get enough of her.

Emmet's loud sigh came through the phone as Bane was about to trace the shell of her delicate ear with his finger. "Matilda will take care of my afternoon appointments, and she has reached Simon." The director sounded bristly. "He will arrive as originally planned and plan on staying. You picked up your car?"

"We did."

"Drive that in."

"Will do. We can use Simon's help going through the *riad*. Encourage him to show up casual. Caretakers live on the property. We'll take it from there."

"What does that mean?"

"We'll bring you up to speed when we see you at noon."

"Be prompt, Bane. We'll have a lunch meeting so you and the doctor can share with me what in hell is so important that the timetable has changed and how this affects the operation going forward."

"Thanks, Emmet." Bane tossed his phone onto the rug next to the sofa, then set the alarm on his watch. A nap with Natasha was too good to pass up. He kissed her head and closed his eyes, surrendering to the expanding grogginess, and dreamed of her.

�֎

Natasha's glorious dark hair fanned out around her head as she lay naked against the white sheets of the bed, face flushed, gray eyes turned to molten pewter with desire. Bright moonlight played hide-and-seek in the billowy clouds, casting moving shadow and illumination over her glistening and velvety sepia-brown skin. Her exquisitely dark nipples were erect, delectable, and begged for more of Bane's attention. Her deep, rapid breathing matched his.

"More, Bane. Please," she moaned, her long legs wrapped around his lean hips, urging him on.

Bane came up on all fours, thrusting deeper, fighting going over the edge. She was hypnotic in her arousal, close but not yet there. His fingers grazed her sensitive thighs, making them quiver.

"Sweetheart, wrap those gorgeous legs around my shoulders." He licked his lips and lowered his head to suckle, ushering her body and his to an explosive release.

✖

Bane woke up before the alarm went off, hard as hell, aching for release, Natasha still snuggled up against him, breathing heavily, skin flushed, dewy moisture on her skin. Her hand rubbed his thickened length and she moaned, throwing her leg over his hip. He checked his watch and shut off the alarm, facing a quandary—wanting to act on their mutual arousal but needing to go through everything in the office.

Natasha stroked him again even more firmly. If she kept it up, he was going to cream in his pants like he had a number of times during high school dates, only this was far sexier since he had experienced her voracious appetite, which matched his—unveiled last night through round three. Or was it four?

His hand slid over her hip and gathered up her skirt, bunching it to almost her waist, exposing her thong and smooth skin. Christ, she was stunning. Bane trailed his fingers over her silky texture, wanting so much more.

Natasha tried to encircle his girth, but his zipper presented a barrier. Her chest heaved and her brow creased as if she were frustrated.

157

Bane hissed through his teeth as her leg moved higher, her inner thigh rocking against him. Decision made, he removed her hand and pulled the skirt down over her legs, planting a kiss on Natasha's nose before carefully extracting himself from her delicious, warm form. He moved to a chair and watched her sleep. She did not rouse but burrowed into the couch, seeking to replace his warmth and comfort.

He mulled over what had transpired since Natasha had first sauntered into Emmet's office and come into his life, changing everything. Dating and sleeping with women had never been an issue, but then he'd never met any woman remotely like Dr. Natasha Jordaan. She was far from average, and her complexity fascinated him. Breathtakingly beautiful and extremely intelligent. Wise. The attraction between them instantaneous, like nothing he had ever experienced. Fierce. Off the charts, crackling electricity. He felt it in every pore of his being, and after spending time with her in and out of bed, he was sucked into a soup of emotions that astounded him. The fact that he might be falling in love with her had passed through his consciousness more than once.

Natasha sighed and flipped over on the couch, presenting her backside to him. Her skirt had ridden back up, exposing shapely calves.

"Damn, baby. You're driving me crazy," Bane groaned to himself, rubbing both hands over his face, recalling early this morning when those beautiful limbs of hers had clasped around him, urging them both toward a mutual explosion that went on for some time before it abated. Last night Natasha had allowed him in, but afterward, each time, she closed off. He assumed it came from being hurt and from fear of being hurt again. Lord knew she had suffered through plenty, but he was a patient man. As much as he enjoyed exploring and moving inside Natasha, he craved dismantling her protective emotional walls. He'd made some progress. She felt safe around him, welcoming his teasing and touch. She initiated conversation and physical contact, smiled more often and held his gaze, flirted with him. She showed him kindness and consideration. But trust? That was elusive. Bane yearned for when there would be no emotional reservations. He wanted all of her.

Bane had witnessed how she carried the weight of loss and betrayal in her eyes and in her soul when she told him about her friends and when they uncovered the family history in her grandfather's office. Natasha needed to discover what he saw—that what she had been through was in large part what made her strong. Watching her sleep, at peace, gave him immense pleasure. He stood and stretched and sat gently next to her.

"Beauty," he said softly, pushing her thick hair back from her face. "Time to get up."

She rolled over and regarded him with sleepy eyes, her voice husky. "Hi."

"Hi, yourself." Bane's fingers caressed her forehead before kissing it.

"How long did I sleep?"

He looked at his watch. "Long enough. I moved our meeting back with Emmet given our discoveries. Noon. Also asked for a departure delay. We need to brief him. Simon will be here soon. I felt it best that he stays here while we're out today and also on assignment."

"Good calls, partner," she said, holding eye contact and stretching her arms and legs. "I guess I needed that little nap."

"Neither one of us got much sleep last night." His eyes crinkled at their corners. "Sweet dreams?"

"Perhaps," she said, smiling slyly and stretching. "Did you nap?"

"For about twenty." He enclosed Natasha's hand in his. "I cleaned up the coffee and breakfast. I'll help you put everything up," he offered, inclining his head at the scattered paper and files on the carpet. "Come on."

※ ※ ✳ ※

Natasha and Bane organized everything, separating what they planned to share with Emmet. Everything else was returned to its original place.

"I feel as though we're missing something," he said, pausing after closing the cabinet door and locking it. His eyes passed over the folded drafting table and large swing-arm lamp, walls, and surfaces.

Stone coasters and a candid family photo topped the side table next to the couch. The heavy silver framed Natasha on the cusp of adulthood, her two younger teenaged brothers, and parents. She was dazzling even then, and from what Bane could tell, she, like her handsome brothers, was a blend of their parents' ethnicities. The Jordaans had been a beautiful family. Bane could not possibly fathom what Natasha had felt when she learned her family had been killed or how she had dealt with it. He would have been consumed with grief and anger had it been his family. And now the discovery that her grandfather might have been involved in the American. Bane understood her shock,

159

denial, and the need to clear him. He knew too well about being presumed guilty. Things were not always what they appeared to be.

Bane turned his attention to the neatly arranged desk. A large leather blotter; a chest of detailed inlaid metal and carved wood; a lamp; an older computer monitor; small globe paperweight; and a ceramic cup, seemingly made by a child, that held an assortment of pens and a pair of scissors. He lifted the curved lid of the chest. It held a tape dispenser, stapler, and paper clips.

"What are you looking for?" she asked, standing in front of the wall of framed coins.

"I'm not sure, but my sixth sense is telling me there are more pieces to this puzzle." Bane's eyes swept over beautifully painted wooden shutters that hung on the wall behind the desk. "Are these as old as they look?"

"Yes. They predate the 1900s. I can't remember the year right now. They were a gift to my grandfather on one of his first jobs. The owners were modernizing their property and no longer wanted these. Such a shame because they're a fine example of Berber-style art."

"He had great taste." His focus shifted to the impressive collections of coins displayed in large frames on the wall that Natasha stood in front of. "Those are originals? Antiques?"

"Yes. Pépé preferred to display his collections instead of art."

"You collect coins. What do you think your grandfather's collection is worth?"

"I have no idea without going through the catalog he kept. I know they are very valuable, possibly priceless. A few date back to Phoenician times."

Bane whistled, his eyes sweeping over the coins again. "And you think all of them are here?"

"I am sure of it. He numbered the cases. I checked them while you were examining the desktop. All are accounted for and no coins appear to be missing. Why? Do you think there's a connection?"

"Maybe. Where did he keep the catalog?"

"I'm not really sure. It's a green leather-bound book, complete with receipts. He showed it to me occasionally. The last time was the summer before I attended university. It's probably in here or in the master bedroom somewhere."

"I'd like to see that," Bane said. "Wouldn't you? See what you glean from his catalog now that you're an experienced collector?" He paused, his brows contracting as he considered. "I find it intriguing that the file cabinet was opened and searched, yet a priceless collection, fully in view, was untouched."

"Sometimes things hidden in plain sight don't call attention to themselves. You know that. Or maybe whoever was looking around wasn't interested in the coins."

"I'll accept that. What about Clara and Oliver?"

"Clara and Oliver?" Her hands flew to her hips. "They have worked for my grandparents since my mother was a young girl. They're above reproach."

"Come on, Nat. They have full access to this place. Your grandparents were wealthy as hell."

"No. Absolutely not. You met them—"

"I met Clara, and I like her."

Natasha's voice was icy, and her eyes flashed. "Don't say it like that."

"Like what? I'm only being thorough."

"Leave them out of this. I told you before—I trust them with my life. There is no reason they would do this, and they are very comfortable financially. My grandparents treated them well when they were living and left them a sizable inheritance when they died."

"People have different motives. You know that."

Natasha glared at him, her eyes resembling prowling stormy clouds that were ready to rain hell.

Bane threw his hands up. "Fine. For now."

"This—" She motioned to the desk. "This happened sometime after I locked it. Neither one of them have been here since I arrived."

"You're sure?"

"I am."

"Hmm. I wish to hell the *riad* had a security system. What about Gia or Viviane? Either one of them could have gone through things when they were here for dinner."

Natasha's laugh came out as a bark, and she shook her head adamantly. "No. The only time either of them was out of sight was to make phone calls or use the restroom. Viviane is into men. Period. I don't remember

anything else coming even close to interesting her. And Gia, well, no. Besides, both of them are financially sound."

"As I just said, sometimes there are other motivating factors."

"No."

"Then we continue to ask questions and make observations." He focused on the desktop and inclined his head toward it. "How often did your grandfather work from here?"

She had calmed down some; however, her tone was still guarded. "Every weekday if he wasn't out consulting."

Bane opened the largest drawer. A cardboard box filled most of the space. He placed it on top of the desk and opened it. "Tools of his trade. Not many though. Is this where he would have stored his tools after he retired?" he asked, pulling the drawer and the remaining ones from the desk. They were all empty, but he examined each of them, then carefully scanned the interior of the desk, aided by his flashlight. Bane didn't find any other hidden depressions, buttons, or writing. He returned the drawers and put the box back in the deep one.

"Yes. Mémé said Pépé gave a lot of them away. They would have gone to my father," she informed him, her voice straining.

Bane touched her shoulder gently. "I'm so sorry, sweetheart," he said, tenderly kissing Natasha on the forehead, watching her silently deal with the weight of her grief. How he wished he could make it evaporate.

She picked up on the silence and raised her head, presenting him with smoky eyes and a smile that glittered too brightly. "I'm okay."

"Are you?" His eyebrows lifted with the question. "This is a tough situation. I'd have trouble with it."

"I am. Truly." She walked to the empty corner. "Pépé set up my own desk here when I was little. I used it when my family visited. My brothers were sent outside to play because they were into everything. I was quieter, so I got to remain inside. We talked about everything, or so my young self believed, and I shared my drawings with Pépé at the end of his mornings, before lunch. He was so encouraging and patient with me. After we had eaten, Mémé would usually entice me outside with gardening or reading time," she said wistfully. "I made that pen-and-pencil holder for Pépé when I was eight. I remember when I gave it to him. He acted as though it was the most special gift he had ever received."

Bane ran his fingers over it thoughtfully. "My mom has always insisted that the best gifts were the ones my brother, sister, and I made her,

because they came from the heart and were made with the deepest love and intention."

"I love that. That's how I felt when I made it for him." Natasha ambled back to the desk and lifted the small globe from the desktop. Joy infused her face. "A globe was the first thing Pépé and Mémé gave me for my desk. Mine was much larger than this one and it spun on an axis; it took up half my desk. Eventually the globe became part of my education. Pépé made it fun. There wasn't a day that he didn't pepper me with information about world history. Countries. Cultures. Governments. I enjoyed it so much." Her hand swept toward the coins. "He made the coins part of my geo-history lessons." She stopped abruptly, wide-eyed, before continuing, her voice rising with horror. "Jesus! What if he acquired some or all of his coins through looting? Or the American? What if some of the coins in my personal collection came to me through looting? Mémé and Pépé started me collecting."

"Don't get ahead of yourself or why we're here. The agreement and manifest need to be analyzed."

"You're right of course. This only looks bad," Natasha conceded, and in the act of returning the globe to its spot, something dropped from its base and onto the desktop.

chapter 24

B ANE REACHED AROUND NATASHA TO inspect the heavy stock paper. "What's this?"

He grabbed his flashlight from his hip pocket and swept the beam over its white surface, which was trimmed to fit within the globe's base. The edges appeared as though they had been deliberately cut and fashioned so the paper could be attached snugly. Yellowed crust covered each of the dog-eared tabs, evidence of adhesive. Dark brown felt, close in color to the wood base, was affixed to the other side.

Bane examined the camouflaged cover more closely. "There's writing. "It's difficult to read because it's so small. Maybe French. TA11. No, wait. I think it's a seven. TA17. What—"

"No. It can't be." Natasha gulped, reaching to take the paper from Bane. Her brow creased as her eyes studied the tiny blue cursive. "Those are my initials and my lucky number. The writing is Mémé's. I'm sure of it!" Her fingers traced over the writing endearingly. Her voice dropped into a shaky whisper. "I don't understand."

"Nat, flip over the globe." He directed the beam at the base and pulled out a second folded piece of paper with his thumb and forefinger. He opened it before passing it to her. "It's addressed to Darling Heart."

Natasha glanced at the note. "What in holy hell? I can't. Not here." She tore out of the office.

What the fuck? Stay here or go out after her?

The french door banged shut. Natasha was in the garden. Bane stood and rubbed his hands over his face. *Fuck. What a can of worms.* He stalked to the kitchen and paused, hand grasping the handle, observing Natasha seated at the table under shade of the pergola, the unfolded note in front of her. She read it quickly, fingering the note, staring straight ahead at the vine-covered garden wall. He pushed the lever down and stepped out. Natasha gave no indication that she had heard the door open or that he approached. Bane knelt next to her. Still no response.

"Hey," he said. "Care to share?"

She exhaled forcefully through tight lips. Her glassy eyes searched his as she handed him the note.

Mon cœur chéri, je crois qu'Henri s'était impliqué en secret dans une sombre histoire. Je te laisse ceci dans l'espoir de découvrir de quoi il s'agissait. Cela fait longtemps que je crois que ce qui s'est passé à Asilah avait un rapport avec son implication. Je me suis heurtée à un échec en cherchant la réponse. Le temps n'a pas joué en ma faveur. Souviens-toi de nos moments préférés: nos jeux et puzzles, nos chasses au trésor, l'entretien de nos jardins, nos créations en cuisine, nos chasses aux scorpions la nuit… Il faut explorer, ma douce. Un indice en mène à un autre, et ainsi de suite. Garde Fatima avec toi pour toujours. Elle te portera chance et te protègera. À tes côtés pour toujours, Josette TA17JBA7

Bane pulled the chair behind him against Natasha's and sat. He draped his arm loosely around her shoulders and scanned the note. "What does this mean?"

She continued to stare straight ahead. "It is from my grandmother to me. Her name was Josette. The *B* is for Blanchett, Mémé's maiden name, and the *A* for her married name, Allamel. She called me Tasha. My middle name is Anne. That's why my initials are TA instead of NA. Her endearment for me was darling heart. It seems Mémé is the one who hid the note in the globe's base. It's full of clues." Without looking at him, she translated it out loud.

"My darling heart, I believe that Henri had secretly been involved in a dark story. I leave this to you in the hope of finding out what it was all about. I have believed for

a long time that what happened in Asilah has something to do with his involvement. I ran into a failure in looking for the answer. Time did not work in my favor. Remember our favorite moments: our games and puzzles, our treasure hunts, the maintenance of our gardens, our creations in the kitchen, our scorpion hunts at night... We have to explore, darling heart. One clue leads to another and so on. Keep Fatima with you forever. She'll bring you luck and protect you. By your side forever, Josette TA17JBA7"

�خ

"Hey, I'm fluent in French. Remember? I caught all that." He gently ran his finger down her cheek, encouraging her to look at him.

Natasha's lovely arched brows moved as she fought to bring her emotions under control, her beautiful, expressive eyes changing from turbulent clouds to charcoal gray.

"What I need is for you to tell me what it means, or what you think it means."

"Sorry. The references to the favorite moments are clues, as is the mention of Fatima and our initials followed by our lucky numbers."

"Why lucky numbers?"

"Don't you have one?"

"Um, not anymore. Gave it up during my teens. But I know a lot of people who do. What do you believe this signifies?" Bane asked, pointing at the initials and numbers.

There was so much she didn't know about him and so much he didn't know about her. Would they have the gift of time? "They refer to notes in the books we read together."

"Still confused. I'm trying to follow along here." Bane ran a hand over his neck. "Seems like there is an overabundance of information scattered about. We could end up turning the entire *riad* and the gardens inside out looking for whatever it was your grandmother left. I mean, scorpions, gardening, games, puzzles...? Can you clarify for me?"

Leaning forward and resting her elbows on her thighs, her jaw supported in fisted palms, Natasha squinted as she spoke, focusing on something invisible. "I think my grandmother was trying to find out what Pépé might have been involved in, but she died before she got to the bottom of it. She buried the clues of how far she got in her list of our favorite moments. I believe Mémé referenced them to throw off anyone

other than me. The treasure hunts were my absolute favorite because they weren't as frequent, maybe once a summer. I loved deciphering the riddles. Her reference to treasure hunts is itself a riddle." Natasha lifted her head and faced Bane with a resolute expression. "My grandmother is sending me on a treasure hunt with the clues she collected, and you're going to join me. We need to look in the gardening books and cookbooks, on pages three and seventeen, or possibly on a combination of our numbers, 317 and 173, if the book has that many pages. We used those as well if we ran out of room on pages three and seventeen. Mémé and I wrote in the margins, and we always dated them. A lot of them were to each other. There should be clues, dated closer to her death, and hopefully those will lead us to others." She took a deep breath, then added, "I'm sure I'm correct."

"Interesting. And what about the reference to the Fatima?"

"Simple. Fatima was important to us. We often prayed to her together." Her finger brushed over the tattoo on her wrist. "Door knocker." Natasha stood and refolded the note before sliding it into the pocket of her skirt. "Come on."

"Where're we going?" Bane asked as he followed.

"To the kitchen. We probably need a screwdriver." Hammering reverberated into the office as soon as they entered.

"Expecting someone?"

"No." She paused and waved him toward the pantry. "The toolbox is in there. You grab the screwdrivers. Metal box, on the floor."

"On it."

✕ ✕ ✕ ✕

Bane heard Natasha open the door, followed by the voice of her friend Gia. Thank God sound carried so well in the *riad*.

"Good morning! I was about to knock. A little softer than our friend here."

Viviane chimed in. "Yes. We were in the neighborhood and wanted to see you before we fly out this afternoon." There was a soft rustling sound. "Fresh and still warm. We bought the last batch. Do you have tea on?"

Bane slipped the folder of what Natasha and he were going to share with Emmet, as well as the flathead and cross-recess screwdrivers, into her tote and then headed toward the entrance. The women's timing was not welcome.

"Bane and I—" Natasha broke off, then said quickly, "Good morning. We have coffee, but it's no problem to make tea."

Pushing her way past Natasha, Viviane chirped, "Is he here, that gorgeous hunk of a husband of yours?"

"I am," Bane rumbled softly, eyes narrow, noting how the women had entered. "Kinda early, isn't it?"

"Please excuse us. We haven't seen Natasha for so long that we hoped it would be all right to drop in again," Gia explained, then hesitated before asking, "It is all right?"

What the hell was he supposed to say to that? "Of course." Bane smiled warmly. "And what gift did you come bearing?" He nodded at the sack.

"Excuse me? Oh yes. Croissants. Fresh from the bakery."

"I can always eat. Had breakfast. Exercised—" Bane winked at Natasha and gave her a sexy grin while rubbing the tee over his washboard abs.

Her blatant return of his wink surprised him and he beamed. It also wiped the expectant smile from Viviane's face.

Gia jumped in. "I'm happy to help you with the tea, Bane."

"I've got it," he said, gently prying the sack from Viviane's hand. "You girls head outside. I'll bring a tray when it's ready." He closed the front door but left it unlocked.

"Are you sure?" Natasha asked.

Bane hugged her to him and planted a full kiss on her temple, his eyes moving between Viviane and Gia. He dropped his lips to her ear, murmuring, "By the way, you smile at me like that again in front of someone and we'll need to excuse ourselves."

Natasha drew her head up, pinning him with molten eyes, and gave him a daring smirk. "When I say and not until then."

⁂

"You dropped something, Natasha," Viviane said, bending over and retrieving the folded paper that had fallen from Natasha's pocket.

Bane snatched it from her, smirking. "For her eyes only." He slid the note into Natasha's pocket and bracketed her waist with his large hands, chuckling, his eyes dancing with mischief. "My wife enjoys rereading my love notes."

Clearly uncomfortable with Bane's sexual banter, the two women hurried out the french doors and seated themselves at the table that Natasha and Bane had occupied only moments earlier.

The way Bane played with Gia and Viviane was fascinating as hell, like a cat with its prey. Natasha pivoted, her smile softening her question. "Really? Have you no shame?"

He leaned against the counter, his thumbs hooked in the waist of his pants. "Not when it comes to you. Besides that, I threw Viviane off her game. I'll be out soon. Dumped the folder and the screwdrivers in your tote, by the way. You left it at the foot of the stairs. I'll put it in our bedroom since we don't know who is snooping through the house." His expression grew hooded. "I meant what I said."

Natasha stepped up to him, regarding him frankly. His slouching posture had them almost even in height. "Thank you." She kissed him perfunctorily, focused as she was on their guests, and started to move away. "So did I."

"Uh-uh," he mumbled, pulling her to him and kissing her languorously, turning her legs to rubber.

She responded in kind, her tongue sliding over his, her body pressing against him and catching fire as they deepened their kiss, wholly wanting more.

Bane lifted her chin with his finger, grazing his teeth along her jaw. He stopped and gazed deeply into her eyes. "You are most welcome, wife," he whispered and smacked her playfully on her ass. "Go, or you'll miss your visit."

※ ※ ※ ※

Natasha laughed and sashayed out the french doors. Bane pulled his eyes away from her enticing movement and adjusted himself, mulling over his relationship with Natasha as he prepared to brew coffee and heat water for tea. This provocative, playful Nat was a very welcome side of her, but he was in way over his head. She was everything he dreamed a woman could be, and yet it was so new. They barely knew each other, but the connection between them—fuck, it was hot. The timing wasn't the best, but when would it be? What he felt was exhilarating and scary at the same time. Where would they end up when this assignment was over?

Bane dismissed those thoughts. However, questions about Natasha's friends resurfaced as he searched the kitchen for a tray, cups, plates, and

utensils. He added napkins, cream, loose tea, sugar, jam, and the croissants. The coffee signaled it was done, and he added the carafe and teapot to the loaded tray and made his way outside, bracing himself for the onslaught of Viviane and intending to further study Gia.

※ ※ ※ ※

"Hello!" Simon said, his eyes scanning the group eating and having coffee. "Apparently I'm late. I hope you don't mind that I let myself in. No one answered my knock and the door was unlocked. I left my luggage in the *setwan*."

Bane rose and shook Simon's hand, welcoming him and not missing a beat as he joined in with the improv. "Hey, man! Great to see you!"

"Hello, Simon. Welcome to our home." Natasha pushed her chair back to stand and motioned him over. "Come sit down and help yourself," she said, handing him a plate. "I'll put on more coffee."

"If it isn't too much trouble."

"Not at all. Gianna, Viviane, this is Simon, an old friend of Bane's," she explained as Simon, roughly the same height as Natasha, stood next to her and smiled in greeting.

Viviane popped out of her chair, holding out her hand and smiling broadly. Her eyes shone with appreciation. "Viviane. Lovely to meet you, Simon," she purred, practically drooling, her fingers grazing his as he released her hand.

"Call me Gia, Simon." Gianna waved at him, not bothering to rise, a friendly smile on her face.

Bane clapped him on the back. "How was the drive in?"

"Without hiccups. I parked in front. I hope that's all right."

"Of course," Natasha said, patting him on the arm. "Now sit. I'll be back shortly."

Keeping up the ruse was effortless, especially when Simon had transformed himself like a chameleon. He was totally believable eye candy—at ease, dressed casually in jeans, a leather belt, and a blue-and-white-striped button-down open at the throat with the sleeves rolled up, exposing sinewy forearms. The sun glinted off the tactical watch on his left wrist. Broken-in leather sandals covered his feet. His blue eyes, always alert, were hidden by dark sunglasses, and a day's worth of stubble added to his sex appeal. Simon's earth-brown hair, slicked down to the point of looking

lacquered to his head on the occasions Natasha had seen him, was wavy, bordering on unruly, giving him a dangerously alluring appearance. The director must have gotten hold of Simon before his usual morning grooming.

⁂

The french door opened behind Natasha, drawing her attention over her shoulder. Bane slipped in behind her. Holding up his hands in a defensive posture, he said, "Before you ask, I left the front door unlocked after the hens came in. I felt it would be more believable if Simon entered as a friend."

"Good idea. Are you always so quick on your feet?"

"You have no idea. We're just getting started."

Natasha kept her back to him and remained silent, focused on her task of making coffee, but Bane saw it when she turned her head to pour more water—the way her lips tweaked, not quite a smile, and how her breath stuttered and then rippled through her willowy frame. He sidled closer.

Natasha stilled and rested her hands on the countertop. Her pulse went into overdrive as he traced the nape of her neck with his fingertip. He inhaled deeply, then scented her, his lips ghosting over the delicate skin, raising a wake of delicious tingling that trailed down her neck and bared arms. Bane nipped Natasha's neck where her pulse hammered, and she shuddered.

"I'll get back to our guests," he murmured in her ear.

"Tease."

"You know it." Bane chuckled before he shut the french door behind him.

⁂

Simon and Bane kept the conversation going with Viviane and Gia, who listened with rapt attention. The men concocted a simple and plausible story. Simon was a professional freelance writer. The men met at the beginning of their careers, when Bane was hired on as the photographer for a feature article Simon was writing. Since then, they had worked together on multiple projects all over the world.

He knew that Bane and Natasha were in Morocco for her job, so he reached out. They invited him to stay at their *riad* while he was

172

working, and he offered to house-sit while they were traveling the country.

Viviane's interest in Simon was evident as she addressed him. "Do you know?"

"Know?"

"Natasha and Bane are married."

"Bane told me when we talked a few days ago, when I mentioned I was going to be working in Morocco. Said he'd be here too. With his wife," he said, emphasizing the last words. He set his cup down and pushed back into his chair, shaking his head slowly from side to side, a smile spreading across his face. "Bane Rua commits. Wow. I can see why." Simon sat forward and clapped Bane on the shoulder and laughed. "Congratulations, man!"

Bane nodded, smiling from ear to ear. "Thanks."

"Are you married, Simon?" Viviane asked.

"No," he answered. "Hey, while I'm here, can I use your office?" Simon asked Bane, helping himself to a pastry.

"It's yours for the duration. Our home is your home."

"You and Natasha are leaving when?"

"Looks like tomorrow. She has some last-minute things to finalize here. She has a lunch meeting. I'm going to tag along."

Simon smiled, playing along, shaking his head. "Have a difficult time letting your bride out of your sight, Rua?"

"Fuck yes."

Simon threw his head back and laughed.

Viviane scowled and crossed her arms below her ample chest. "Do you often talk like that, Bane?"

Crow's-feet crinkled from the corners of Bane's eyes, and he gave her a big smile. "Yep. Guilty."

"The other night you didn't talk like that. It's vulgar. I'm surprised Natasha is okay with your language."

"Okay with what?" Natasha called, walking toward the group with an insulated pot and plates.

Bane rose and relieved Natasha of the pot and dishes. "My dirty mouth."

"Oh. That." Natasha cocked her head at Bane and smirked. "Bane

only uses it when he deems it most effective."

"Sweetheart." Bane chortled and pulled Natasha onto his lap. "That's fucking perfect!"

Natasha snuggled back against him and turned her slate-gray eyes on Viviane. Her brows rose and she delivered her next words deadpan. "What can I say? I married a crass American."

Bane laughed even harder. Simon joined in, and then Natasha. Gia giggled, and Viviane sat quietly, taking it all in, clearly confused why the hell *fuck* was so funny.

modifications

نيس القوم خادمهم.

※ ✺

The one who serves people is their master.

✖

chapter 25

"CHRIST, I THOUGHT THEY WOULD never leave," Bane said, pulling out into Casablanca's snarled traffic. It was going to be tight getting to the meeting with Emmet on time. "Sorry, Nat. But a little of Viviane and Gia go a long way."

"I am inclined to agree, but it was good to see them before they return to their homes. Especially Gia."

"They live where again?" Bane asked, his focus on waiting for traffic to clear to make a left turn.

"Gia lives in Italy with her mom. Viviane lives in France. Is Simon actually staying?"

"That's the plan. We'll firm things up after we talk with Emmet"—he nodded to her tote on the floor in front of her feet—"and share what we found. We haven't had time to go through the *riad* or take a look at the Fatima. Simon can help us."

"It could take a long time."

"Yes, but we're packed."

"True, but we will need to stop at the market after we meet with the director." She still couldn't bring herself to call him Emmet. "I need some items for dinner."

"Can do. I'll help."

"That's what you said last night."

Bane glanced at Natasha, smiled wickedly, and winked. "Yup, and look where that got us."

✶ ✶ ✶ ✶

Despite greeting Bane and Natasha warmly when they entered, Matilda's worry was evident. "He's waiting for you. I'll get lunch ordered," she said, ushering them to the doors outside the director's office.

"Thanks, Tilly. Any word on Nasir?" Bane inquired.

She paused, her hand on the door handle, and blew out the breath she had been holding. "We just received an update. Surgery went well, but there were complications. He's been in a drug-induced coma."

Natasha sucked in her breath. "Oh no!"

Bane growled quietly.

"We just hope and pray that he recovers." Matilda knocked once and opened the door into the director's office. "They're here, Emmet," she said solemnly.

"Thank you." Emmet looked up from sheaves of papers covering his desk and glanced at his watch, then removed his glasses and held them where the temples crossed. He looked exhausted. "Good morning. Nothing like the past twelve hours to drive home the seriousness of our mission. Please sit." He gestured to the chairs in front of his desk, then rose and walked to move between them, leaning against it, his hands clasped over his lower abdomen. His blue eyes swept back and forth between Natasha and Bane. "I appreciate your prompt arrival. Matilda told you that Rafiq came through surgery but there were complications after they got him back to his room?"

"Yes, sir."

"Goddammit."

Emmet regarded Bane then Natasha. "His surgeon shared that Rafiq would not have made it to surgery without your attention, so dismiss any thoughts you might have that you contributed to his current status. We have no idea why he was shot. Whether it was random or targeted. We know nothing. Rafiq never regained consciousness. I have our people watching the hospital around the clock and a team stationed outside his room to guarantee no one enters unless they have been cleared ahead of time by us."

178

"Doctor, due to the attack and because Rafiq came to your residence, I am having security installed. He may have been watched. We feel it's necessary to take this step even though you and Bane are leaving shortly. Simon will have it all in before you return today."

Natasha studied her bright red toenails peeking out from her sandals as the images of last night and this morning replayed in her mind. The last thing she wanted was to be an exhibitionist. *Christ.*

Bane slumped back into his chair and crossed his leg over his knee. His elbows rested on the chair arms, fingers steepled under his nose. "Uh, Emmet. Where exactly are the plans for the installation? I believe I speak for both of us that we request a modicum of privacy."

The director's eyes moved shrewdly between them. He cleared his throat and Natasha looked up. "I believe we can stay to the perimeters, the entrance points, and passages for now. Will that be satisfactory?"

"It may not be, sir," Natasha responded, lifting her tote to her lap and reaching in. "Allow me to explain."

✖ ▨ ❂ ✖

Natasha and Bane waited patiently as Emmet read and flipped through the paperwork she had shared with him. His hair resembled multiple roosters' combs, spiking everywhere from the many times he had run his hands through the short, dense white hair while reading over the agreement and ledgers within the journal. After coming to the final entry, he closed the journal and pinched his nose, scowling and lost in thought. Natasha and Bane remained silent.

"I fully understand the urgency of moving our meeting back and your request of Simon's appearance, Bane," Emmet said, glancing at him. "Totally justified."

He inhaled deeply, stood, and began pacing. "INTERPOL has been after the American for decades, but as soon as we felt we were closing in on him, and we referred to the American as such, he disappeared. We have dedicated countless hours of active intelligence and money since the Cultural Heritage Crime division was created in 1946 in response to the massive amount of missing and stolen art and cultural artifacts during World War II."

"Sir...," Natasha said, raising her hand, forefinger in the air.

The director ignored her and kept going. "For decades the trafficking of cultural heritage was relatively low risk, albeit lucrative, but recently

there has been a significant uptick in associated violence as world conflicts have increased. The American is elusive and has long been suspected of the violence and murder. People have vanished in Africa, Europe, the Middle East, and"—he pursed his lips and gave Natasha a long look—"Central America." Emmet picked up the journal and waved it in the air, pinning her with a cold look. His voice shook. "Bloody hell, Dr. Jordaan. Your family is right in the middle of—"

"Sir... sir..." Natasha jumped to her feet and raised her voice, trying to speak. Her face was contorted with a mixture of chagrin and anger.

Emmet rolled over Natasha. "Your grandfather's signature is on the bloody covenant." He picked up the agreement and snapped the papers at her. "Can you be trusted to carry out the mission? And remain objective?" His eyes flashed at Natasha, Bane, and then back at her. "To have your partner's back?"

"That's enough, Emmet," Bane snapped, rocketing from his chair. "Cut the sanctimonious bullshit. Since when did you begin assuming? The analysts need to take a look at everything. This is an attack on Natasha's character. You're assuming she's a guilty party in all this. She most definitely is not."

The silence thickened until Natasha spoke. "Sir, if I may. That you even question my integrity, my loyalty to the mission, is disheartening. I have"—she spat out the next words—"*never* given INTERPOL any reason to doubt me. I am a professional. I do my job beyond what is required." Her eyes were the color of dark, stormy clouds, and she looked as if she were ready to unleash a torrential, deadly storm. Everything that had been building since the shocking discovery in her grandfather's office, everything she had not had time to digest and process, was clearly coming to a head. Natasha's voice was low and menacing. "Goddammit. I'm invested in this. It was *me* who apprehended Eric Schaus, and it will be *me* who helps to lop another head off the American. I want the network expunged. And while I'm at it, it will be *me* who does everything possible to clear my grandfather's name, or to understand fully why he was involved in the inception of the American. The man I knew, the man who helped raise me after my family was murdered, was kind, loving, and good. Pépé's possible involvement is not compatible with his character, with his ethics." She simmered. "We all know things aren't always what they appear to be. I would give my grandfather the benefit of the doubt even if he weren't my relative. I ask the same of you." Natasha marched toward the door. "I need some air. I'm going to walk this off."

Bane dropped into his seat, totally blown away by what had transpired and full of admiration for how Natasha had stood her ground. She'd been strong, direct, and fierce. "Natasha is a fucking force to be reckoned with, Emmet."

"I upset her," he responded, appearing concerned.

"No. You did much worse. You questioned her principles and integrity. This is your fucking mess."

"Bloody hell. I don't know what came over me."

"You realize you may never get her back? You may have to bring in another contractor."

"There is no other person who can fill her shoes. You know that. She's the best of the best, and the clock is ticking."

Rapid knocks on the door interrupted them. Matilda came in, eyes blazing. "What just happened in here?"

"I made a misstep," Emmet admitted.

Matilda parked her hands on her hips and stared hard at Emmet. "Is she coming back?"

Bane glanced at Emmet, then slouched in the chair and laced his fingers over the hard muscles of his stomach. "She might. If Emmet grovels." He smirked.

Silence permeated the room until Emmet conceded. "I'll grovel. Matilda, please cancel the rest of my day. I need to address this situation."

✄ ⬚ ✿ ✄

Natasha's exodus led her to the *Kasbah* of Udayas. She turned off her phone and strolled the uneven, narrow streets of the ancient blue and white-walled neighborhood until she came to the charming Café Maure with its restful garden. There she ordered hot mint tea and took the steps up to the terrace to sit in the brilliant sun and view Salé's *medina* on the other side of the Bou Regreg estuary and the Atlantic in the distance.

She slowly began to ruminate over what had happened in the director's office. Her outrage crept in again. Sneaky. Sour. Alone, Natasha let the tears flow, rubbing her cheeks and chin where they itched from the salty anger.

Had she just made a complete fool of herself? No. The director had crossed the line. Natasha's fury about his accusation pounded fiercely within her, along with the urgency to clear her grandfather of any wrongdoing. She wanted to renege on her commitment. Tell the director

to bring in another person to fulfill the assignment, but Natasha had to get answers about Pépé's ties to the American and explore the blossoming relationship with Bane.

The water churned frothy-white where the Bou Regreg River discharged into the open sea, mirroring what she felt—roiling shame and anger. Natasha's eyes drifted from the agitated water to the action inland, where the river lapped calmly against the ancient city walls below her. That was what she strived for. Calm.

A small, bright blue fishing boat moved into her peripheral vision. After finishing her tea, Natasha watched it for a few minutes longer, contemplating the fact that her grandfather had washed up on the medina's beach in Asilah in a boat of similar color and size. Natasha's gut told her that Pépé's drowning and his entanglement aboard a boat with the same name of the last entry in the discovered ledger were not a coincidence but a warning to others, an example of what would happen if they created issues for the American. The only way she would get to the truth of Pépé's involvement was to see the assignment through. Decision made, Natasha glanced at her watch and stood, ready to begin her trek back to INTERPOL. She was calmer. Refocused and prepared to apologize and talk.

❊ ❊ ❊ ❊

Matilda regarded Natasha thoughtfully. "Did some time away help?"

"It did. I went to the *Kasbah*."

"It's a peaceful view."

"It is."

"They're still in there." She inclined her head toward the director's door. "I've no idea what they're chattering on about. Go on in. Your lunch is still warm. I'll bring it in to you."

"Thanks."

Matilda squeezed Natasha's arm and smiled warmly.

Natasha walked over and rapped on the door loudly enough that it could be heard over the men's voices. Indeed, they were having a rousing discussion about something. She poked her head in first, unsure how the director would welcome her after she had stormed out.

"Come in," the director said, rising from the chair next to Bane, the one she had occupied earlier, a rueful smile on his face and regret in his eyes.

Natasha entered cautiously, her posture erect and tight, hands clasped firmly, eyes flitting to Bane and then back to the director. "Sir—"

"Please, allow me," he said, his eyes holding hers. "I must apologize for how I expressed my utter surprise earlier. I was stunned, and my concerns—" Emmet cleared his throat and glanced briefly at Bane, who was still seated behind him, then continued. "I expressed them quite poorly. I am profoundly sorry. My concerns came across as an attack on your family and your character and integrity, which I know to be unquestionable. I meant nothing of the sort. I hope you will forgive me and that we can return to the mission at hand."

Natasha weighed the director's apology, realizing it had taken a lot for him to admit his blunder. She sensed a presence behind her and smiled inwardly. Matilda. "I do, sir," she said, extending her hand. "I apologize for my language and for leaving abruptly."

The director looked relieved and then chuckled. "I've worked with Bane on a number of missions. Trust me, your language and your response didn't raise an eyebrow. I do have a request." Natasha's guard began to build again, and he clearly saw it because he rushed to offer the last of his appeal. "Please call me Emmet, and if it's all right with you, I'll call you Natasha."

"I'd like that, sir—" Natasha amended her response as soon as his eyebrows rose. "Emmet."

She heard the door click closed behind her.

※ ▨ ✺ ※

"Bloody hell. What you discovered is hugely significant. I'm pulling three of our analysts from their projects to examine these in greater detail. This is now their priority. Matilda will make copies of everything for each of them as well as for each of us."

A knock on the door announced Matilda with Natasha's lunch and more tea and water. Emmet asked her to make the copies and return the originals to Natasha. He directed his question to both of them. "Do you think there might be anything else in the *riad?*"

"Possibly. My grandmother left clues, and we have yet to follow them." Natasha washed down her bite of food before explaining how she and Bane had discovered the documents and journal, her grandmother's note, and what they planned for the rest of the afternoon.

"This is astounding, Natasha. I realize you two are further delayed, but it can't be helped. Keep me informed."

Bane straightened and leaned toward Emmet, his deep voice sending shivers through Natasha. "Emmet, there is still the unanswered question. How did Rafiq Nasir find us?"

"As part of the team, Rafiq had the *riad*'s address."

"Okay, but why would he be close to our residence?"

"That's the answer we don't have. Be extra vigilant."

"Oblige me. I'm playing the devil's advocate here. You trust everyone on the team?"

"I have no concerns. They've all been cleared and I've worked with them in different capacities."

Finished eating, Natasha wiped her mouth daintily and said quietly, "I knew my grandfather all my life."

"Meaning what?" Emmet asked.

She tapped her fingers on the desk and returned the director's hard stare. "Meaning, at this time, my grandfather appears not to be who I thought he was. It looks as though my grandfather was involved in an organization that would grow to be a vast global network that not only loots and sells antiquities and culture but grows increasingly violent. I don't understand. It makes no sense. I can't reconcile it with the man I knew." Her voice dropped and cracked as she shook her head. "Pépé instilled a reverence for cultures and their histories in me. As far back as I can remember. Today Bane and I discovered documents that imply he was a party to raping it. Jesus." She grimaced, her laugh derisive. "Unbelievable, particularly when you consider what my education and training is. I will do all I can to uncover anything that shows otherwise, to clear his name."

"I am very sorry. Disappointment cuts deep, especially when its cause is someone we regard deeply or love. If his involvement is confirmed, your grandfather's choices do not reflect on you. While I admire your passion to prove his innocence, your primary objective is recovering the Ouarzazate Codex and the *Homo sapiens* remains."

"I realize that," Natasha said, glancing at Bane when he squeezed her shoulder in support.

"Sadly, what you have presented me this afternoon is stunning, and a warning to all of us, to be hypervigilant of people we interact with"—

Emmet inclined his head at Natasha, his expression contrite—" including those we have known for a long time, perhaps our entire lives."

Natasha stood and held out her hand to Emmet. "Bane and I will keep you informed. We'll search for the answers and be on our way. Likely tomorrow morning."

Matilda knocked discreetly. "Here you are." She handed all of them copies and the originals to Natasha. She gave Bane a separate large white paper bag. "Be careful," she added, looking deeply into Natasha's eyes, then Bane's, concern etching her features.

After she left, Emmet inhaled deeply, then nodded at the agreement, ledger, and the journal Natasha slid back into the Berber bag. "Keep those in a secure place."

"Yes."

"Watch your backs, and each other's. Since the attack on Rafiq, I've been having a nagging sense of unease. You are not to deviate from the plans unless something else comes up, and then I need to know immediately. You are traveling armed?"

"Of course," Bane responded as Natasha said yes. He added, "We'll check everything over tonight."

"First aid?"

Bane held up the bag. "Tilly restocked everything for me and then some. I think we're good," he confirmed, answering Natasha's big-eyed expression with a wink and cocky smile. "Special ops, sweetheart."

chapter 26

NATASHA, BANE, AND SIMON PULLED the gardening books and cookbooks from their shelves and piled them on top of the kitchen table.

"Let's divide and conquer." Natasha handed each of the men a small pad of paper and a pen. "Write down the book title and what you find on the corresponding pages 3, 17, 173, and 317. I'm going to put on some water for tea, then join you."

Bane placed a small stack of books on the table. "Four gardening books. Does that seem about right, Nat?"

"Yes," she said, setting out glasses on the counter and adding the green tea to the teapot, waiting for the water to come to a boil on the stove.

"There are a lot of cookbooks," Simon said, counting them silently. "Fourteen. Who has fourteen cookbooks?"

"Fifteen. You missed one, a book on sauces," Bane responded as he extracted a smaller, thin book from his stack and gave it to Simon. "Hell, my mom has more than this, probably triple."

"Are you joking?" Simon asked.

"My mom cooks and bakes like she's feeding an army all the time. She's got baking books, seasonal books, Asian, Spanish, Junior League cookbooks from all over the US. She collects them, even though she says otherwise. Oh, and grill—"

Natasha cleared her throat, and Bane whipped his head around. Natasha stood there with arms crossed under her delicious breasts, brows raised and eyes full of laughter, trying not to smile.

"Um. Hey." His eyes drifted to her breasts pushing up against her tee. "You're looking mighty tasty."

Simon stopped what he was doing and observed the interaction between Natasha and Bane. A loud knock from the front door carried back to the kitchen.

Natasha uncrossed her arms and kept her voice neutral. "Simon, get back to it. And you, chatty man. Focus. We are on a treasure hunt." With that, she glided out of the kitchen, screwdrivers in hand.

Simon spoke softly but firmly. "Bane?"

"Yeah?"

"Can I offer some advice?"

"Do I want to hear it?"

"Probably not, but since we're working together—"

"Fine. Offer away."

"Natasha is a fine woman. Sometimes your teasing is a little blue."

"What the fuck does that mean?"

"Off-color." When Bane continued to look confused, Simon searched for other words. "Insensitive."

"I'm only going to say this once, Simon. What's between Nat and me is private. She's okay with me until she isn't. Our communication style works, and trust me, she communicates clearly."

"Right. If you say so."

"I do. Drop it."

A few minutes later, Natasha stumbled back to the kitchen, sounding slightly winded. "Oh my god, Bane. Come with me."

He followed her into the office and closed the door. "What's going on?"

"Sit. You're not going to believe this!"

Bane regarded her intently and dropped into a chair, elbows on knees, leaning toward her, a furrow evident between his heavy brows. Interest filled his hazel eyes. "Enlighten me."

"That was Clara and Oliver at the door, on their way to the market, asking if we'd come for dinner. I said yes by the way. After they left, I

unscrewed the door knocker, and I found this!" she said excitedly, pulling a tightly folded paper from the pocket of her skirt. "Look! It was inside the Fatima." Natasha bent over in front of him and spread the note out in front of him. She drummed her finger on its surface. "Read it!"

"I like it when you're all animated." He grinned, pulling her down into his lap and nuzzling her neck. "You smell so good."

She arched away and pointed to the paper again. "Focus."

"Damn it, woman," he growled good-naturedly and then surrendered, picking up the paper, its musky scent an indication of age. "This is from?"

"My grandfather."

✠

Ma chérie, je me repentis profondément de mes péchés car ils sont grands. J'espère qu'Elle pourra me guider. Je t'implore de me pardonner, lorsque tout sera dévoilé. Ton Pépé qui t'aime.

✠

"*Dear One,*" he translated as he read.

"That's me."

"*I deeply repent my sins, for they are great. I hope She can guide me. Please forgive me when all is revealed. Your loving Pépé.* Short and sweet," Bane mused, cocking his head, his eyes holding hers. "Any ideas?"

"Maybe." Natasha held her forefinger up in the air. "Hold on a minute. I need to check something." She left the office at a jog.

Bane watched her disappear and shook his head; she certainly was excited about something. He went to the kitchen where Simon was writing on one of the notepads and returned with a beer. Bane was taking a second drink and reflecting on the fact that beer might be hard to come by once they were out on assignment when Natasha came back in, out of breath, her eyes shining. She all but skidded to a stop in front of him and bounced up and down on her toes like an eager kid.

"Okay. Tell me. You look like you're gonna bust."

"Open your hand!"

Bane extended his left hand. Something cool, large, and heavy dropped into his palm. A large iron Fatima with a small key attached sat there. His brows rose with his question. "This is from?"

189

"From the courier packet I received in Cape Town."

"I'm not following you. Why are you giving it to me?"

"Look at it, the key."

"It's stamped. L-91. And?" He placed it on the table in front of him.

"I think it goes to a safe-deposit box. I also found this," she said cheerfully. "Put your hand out again."

Bane played along, amused by Natasha's bossiness, enjoying how she cupped her hand into his waiting one. Heat surged through him at her touch. She deposited something cool and metallic.

"Another key."

"Yes," she said, relieving him of his beer and slipping onto his lap, facing him. "Look at it."

"I'd rather look at you. In all honesty, I'd rather do some other things too." He slid his arm around her waist and pulled her in, rubbing her back softly while running his tongue over her collarbone.

"I'm serious," she scolded, drawing away. "Look at it."

"Fine," he groused. Bane examined the key and his expression changed from pouty to surprised. He sat up straighter and grabbed the key attached to the Fatima, positioning the two side by side. "Where did you get this second one?"

"It was tucked inside Pépé's note."

"Fuck. They appear to be twins. Do you have any idea where this box could be?"

"Not at this time."

"Okay. Next question. Do you have any idea what the box might contain since your grandfather apparently had access?"

"No idea, but after we turn this place inside out tonight, maybe."

Bane rubbed at his face in frustration. "You and I are going to have to wait. Let's get a jump on it."

"Are you going to call Simon in?"

"Simon?"

"Yes." She chuckled. "Remember him? Your good friend staying with us while he's here on business and house-sitting while we're traveling for my work? Presently searching through cookbooks in the kitchen? We need to go help Simon with the books."

"I completely forgot about him. Between this and my fascination with you, I'm a lost man."

※ ※ ※ ※

When Natasha and Bane returned to the kitchen, Simon was lounging against a cabinet, well into paging through a cookbook. "I've made some notes. Per your instructions, there was nothing in three of the gardening books. However, uh"—he glanced over the shorter stack next to his hip and tapped on the top book, *The Mediterranean Gardener*—"in this book there was something in the margin on page seventeen that stood out, so I bookmarked it with a scrap of paper and wrote it in my notepad." He lifted up a tome of a cookbook from his lap. *Mastering the Art of French Cooking.* "I found a similar reference a few pages ago, on page 317. Bookmarked and noted it as well. Julia Child. She was something else, eh? My mum attempted to make one or two of her recipes when I was a wee lad, but, well… Mum wasn't much of a cook."

"My grandmother referred to this cookbook as the bible of French cooking. We used it constantly. What was the reference?" Natasha asked excitedly.

Bane still stood behind Natasha and placed his hands lightly on her shoulders. "Simon?"

"Letters and numbers. They stood out because the rest of the notes are just that, in French, such as "added a sprinkle more sugar" or "Tasha's favorite." Some are dated, others aren't. I enjoyed the story you, I assume, and your grandmother created in the master gardening book. It spans about fifteen years. Remarkable," he commented kindly.

Natasha had forgotten about that. Her throat burned and she looked away, blinking rapidly.

"I'm sorry, Natasha. Did your grandmother pass recently?"

Natasha nodded. "This year."

Simon waited a minute before continuing. "What has jumped out at me so far are these notations. L-91, JBA3 in the gardening book, and L-91, TA17 in Julia Child's book. Very similar, and in the same script. Undated and—" Simon stopped talking at Natasha's sharp intake of breath.

Bane directed Natasha to a chair at the table.

"Can I see them, Simon?"

"Sure." Simon rose and stepped next to Natasha with the two books. He laid each open in front of her.

Natasha traced the writing lovingly, her voice soft. "This is Mémé's writing." She felt her resolve returning, and her eyes moved between Bane and Simon. "Let's get on with it."

chapter 27

S IMON PLACED THE OTHER COOKBOOKS on the table. Thankfully, all were considerably smaller than Julia Child's classic, allowing the three of them to quickly examine the margins.

Natasha pushed the surging memories and accompanying emotions away as she read through the marginalia, until she landed on a very personal note in the baking book. The recipe heading was blacked out. In the margin next to it was a red heart edged with scrolling and smaller hearts. Within the heart, her grandmother had written NATASHA'S CAKE. Below it, she had added, "You are the greatest blessing, my darling heart" and a long column of annual recordings of Natasha's birthdays. The last date was before her grandmother died. *Had Mémé made the special, dense chocolate Bundt cake with ganache icing although she had been abroad or just noted her birthday?* Even if her grandmother had not baked her favorite cake, the fact that Natasha had been foremost on Mémé's mind every year she was absent—well, it was too much. Natasha jumped from her chair and flew through the french doors to the expansive outdoor space.

❈ ❈ ❈ ❈

Bane stood behind her and rumbled softly, "Too much, huh?"

Natasha nodded mutely.

"Your grandmother loved you deeply." He ran his large palms over her upper arms and paused, applying gentle pressure to turn her toward him. "You know, you don't always have to be so strong, Nat. So

impenetrable. I know you've experienced a lot of loss and pain. Look at me, sweetheart," he whispered, swallowing as he took in her wet cheeks and tear-filled eyes.

She wiped at her cheeks with annoyance. "I'm fine," she said dismissively.

"You're right. You are fine, but why settle for that when you could be much more? Feeling and reacting is not a weakness. It's healthy. It helps to strengthen a person. Allows that person to better know themselves. Their limits. Their desires and dreams. To trust."

"You are borderline lecturing me."

"Given what you and I are starting here, yeah, I am. Tough shit. I've experienced layers of you when you allow me in, and I'm talking beyond our physical chemistry. Fuck, it's mind-blowing. But then you shut down and I'm reeling. I want you to be vulnerable with me. I ache for you to trust yourself, to trust me."

Natasha looked away, inhaling deeply. When she looked up at him, the steel was back in her eyes, and so was fear. "What are we starting here, Bane?"

He stroked the silky tresses back from her temples and pulled her forehead against his. Bane framed her head gently with his hands as his lips trailed down her delicate nose and captured her full lips. Natasha kissed him back, and they leisurely explored each other's mouths. She cupped the back of his head and pulled him closer as his hands slid down over her ass, molding her to his pelvis and rigid length. Natasha moaned and Bane broke off the kiss before they succumbed to the fire building between them, panting and pressing his forehead more firmly against hers.

"Our future," he breathed.

❇ ❈ ❋ ❇

"Glad to see you have returned," Simon said, looking up from a cookbook. His gaze lingered on Natasha's and Bane's joined hands. He shook his head. "This is mad."

"Sorry. We lost track."

Simon fixed them with a steady look. "That is not what I am referring to. Whilst you were otherwise indisposed, I made some headway. Just about all these books were blank," he said, nodding to the pile to his right.

"Except the one on top. It contained an interesting comment, next to a suggestion of a wine pairing for a delectable ortolan bunting." He glanced at his notes. "Safe choice Casa's Populaire '91."

"What? That makes no sense." Natasha sat at the table across from Simon. "To my knowledge, my grandmother never served that dish. That particular bird, the ortolan bunting, was banned from consumption because it was almost eaten to extinction. I know this because my grandparents and I saw one during its migration when we were on holiday in the Atlas. They told me the bird's sad story. Mémé would have abided by the law."

Simon pulled the book from the stack and held it up. "It's in here," he said, glancing at his notepad. "Page seventeen."

"I don't remember ever seeing that book."

"It's very old, and the front of it is inscribed in English, which is surprising. All the other inscriptions and marginalia in the books are in French. 'To my loving Josette. May you discover how things should come together. Tasha L. '91.'"

"What?"

"To my loving—"

"No! Tasha?"

"Tasha *L* period ninety-one."

"Let me see that please," she said, hand extended. Her brow furrowed as she stared at the words. "The comment is on page seventeen?"

"Yes." Simon handed the book to Natasha.

Bane watched with interest as Natasha flipped to the page and studied her grandmother's writing, then returned to the cover page to read the inscription. She paged slowly through the thin, small book. "There are no other notes in the book."

"No."

Natasha suddenly sat ramrod straight, her gunmetal-gray eyes shining as they bounced from Bane to Simon. "I think I've solved the riddle," she said excitedly, rising and beginning to pace. "See if this makes sense to you. Mémé switched herself and me in the inscription. L-91 is the number on the key I received from the courier and also on the key enclosed in Pépé's note from the Fatima door knocker. Mémé used this book because of the ortolan bunting recipe, knowing it would draw my attention if I found it. Her notation reiterates the number on the two keys, as does the

inscription." Natasha stopped, smiling from ear to ear. "And she gave us the final piece, what we've been looking for. Where the safe-deposit box is. I'm sure of it. *Safe choice Casa's Populaire '91* is not a wine. Populaire is a bank where my grandmother had a private account, here in Casablanca. *Casa.* Casablanca's nickname. Whatever we're looking for is in a safe-deposit box, L-91, in that bank. All these keys open the same lock!"

Bane spoke up. "Makes perfect sense to me. How do we access it?"

Natasha paused. "With one of these keys, I hope." She resumed pacing. "I have access. Mémé had me sign a form for her safe-deposit box when I turned twenty-one. She gave me a key to it, which is in my townhouse in Cape Town. Jesus!" She stopped again. "I didn't even think to look at it because I have never felt the need to use it. Let's assume my key is another duplicate fourth. So who had the key that was found at a cheese farm outside Imouzzer du Kandar? And where is Mémé's?" She exited the kitchen, saying over her shoulder, "I need to check something."

Bane followed her upstairs into the master, where she disappeared into the closet.

"What're you doing?" he asked, following her in.

Natasha slid her finger under a mounted board with hooks and pressed. The board released from the wall. She lowered it to the floor and slid her hand into the small, horizontal recessed area. "Got it!"

"Got what?"

"Mémé's safe-deposit box key." She opened her hand and flipped the key over. L-91 was stamped into it. "This appears to be a match to the two keys we have in our possession. So, with my key, four keys. I certainly hope that's all of them."

Bane's brow furrowed. "Usually there are only two. Why so many, and why the effort to hide this key so carefully? Kinda overkill, isn't it? After all, ID has to be presented at the bank by the person seeking to access a safe-deposit box."

She felt around the recessed cavity some more and withdrew a legal-sized ivory envelope. "I have no idea. Mémé showed me this hideaway and how it worked when I was a young child. She told me the most important things were kept here. I just remembered now that it existed."

Natasha withdrew a paper from the envelope and scanned it. "This letter is a copy of the one I received from Mémé's attorneys upon her death. They handled everything tied to the estate and still do." She felt around with her fingers. "Nothing else," Natasha said, slipping the letter

back into the envelope and returning it to the hideaway before pressing the mounted board until it clicked into place. Facing Bane, she lamented, "What if I'm wrong?"

"What if you aren't? Too many things are falling into place for this to be mere conjecture."

Natasha walked past him and out of the closet.

Bane followed her out and downstairs, talking as they made their way back to the kitchen where Simon continued to work.

"I believe we're onto something. The bank is closing soon, and you'll need proper identification," he said, glancing at his watch. "I'll call Emmet and ask that your passport is delivered tonight. We can go tomorrow. First thing. We still need to go through the *riad*."

"I forgot about the passport. Yes. Thank you." Natasha moved toward the french doors and rested her hand on the lever. "I'm going to let Clara know Simon is also coming to dinner. I'll be right back."

"Wait a minute, Natasha," Simon said. "I think it's best I remain here. I can continue going through the *riad* while you're having dinner and wait on your passport. Let Clara and Oliver know I'm staying here while you're gone so that I don't alarm them."

"I agree with Simon. That makes the best use of our time."

"Clara's a wonderful cook. We'll bring you back dinner," she promised.

"We're finished here." Simon glanced at her. "Shall I reshelve?"

"Please."

"Where should we begin next?" Bane asked, angling his head.

"We went through the office thoroughly and we know the guest room is empty. Let's start with the *bâyts*. Simon, you can continue while we're at dinner. We'll join you where you are after we've eaten. Bane and I can go through the master later tonight."

"You are sure, Natasha?" Simon asked.

Natasha smiled, her gray eyes moving from Simon's and connecting with Bane's hazel ones before she answered, "I trust you."

chapter 28

S EVERAL HOURS LATER, BANE STRETCHED his arms toward the ceiling in the master bedroom, revealing chiseled abs. His jeans hung from lean hips. "I'm happy our search of the *riad* turned up nothing else. But we're pushing back our departure again."

"We have to go to the bank." Natasha sat cross-legged on the bed and unabashedly stared. The ache for him simmered under the surface like an ember just waiting to be fanned into a fire of passion.

He yawned loudly. "We do. Tomorrow morning on our way out."

"What if it's a dead end?"

"Somehow I doubt it since the office was rifled through, we discovered important information tied to the American, and your grandparents went to the trouble to leave a trail of clues for you about something yet to be revealed."

"We may have to delay even further depending on what is in the safe-deposit box."

"Emmet cleared his morning for us, and he'll clear the rest of the day if necessary. Just in case we need him." He ran his hand over his face and yawned again. "Fuck, I'm tired. You comfortable sleeping with me while Simon snoozes in the guest room?"

"I am, and with everything going on, I actually feel better that he's here. And the surveillance is operational, which is comforting too."

"Clara's dinner was great. Nice of her to feed us. They're a wonderful couple."

Natasha lounged on the pillows, alternately contemplating what the need for privacy disclosed to Emmet, her grandfather's possible involvement in the American, visiting the bank the minute it opened in the morning, and how magnificent Bane was.

"They are," she said. "Clara and Oliver loved you. Thanks again for taking pictures after dinner. Can I have copies? I don't have a lot of pictures. How do you stay so lean when you eat so much? And how do you keep all that definition?"

Bane slid his tee up over his head and tossed it over the back of the chair before approaching her with a glint in his eye. "You can have anything you want. You want to know more about my body?" he said suggestively, narrowing his eyes at her, his deep voice dropping lower.

"Well, about you." She fought to repress the delicious shivers coursing through her system as her gaze roamed leisurely over his face and torso, eventually lingering on the series of tattoos covering his left side from shoulder to flank. "And your body is part of you."

"Very astute." He smirked.

"Ha ha ha. So, how do you do it? You eat constantly. You obviously enjoy beer."

"I only had four. We have an early morning."

"Would you have drunk more if we didn't?"

"Probably not." He cocked his head at her. "Why this interest in my beer consumption? Look how big I am. Worried I won't be able to perform?"

Natasha's laugh sounded like a bark. "Well?"

"Genetics, I guess? And I'm very active."

"Active how?"

"I run. Other things."

Fascinated, Natasha sat forward and hiked up her skirt, massaging her calves and ankles. "Such as?"

Bane's eyes followed Natasha's fingers as they moved over her skin. "I'll tell you after I shower. And I'm more than happy to massage your legs, sweetheart. And so much more."

The throbbing in her body intensified. "You're not tired?"

"I am, but I also like to turn in clean."

"Huh?"

"Go to bed clean. My mom always had us shower at night. We were stinking, dirty kids at the end of the day. It became ingrained in me." He unzipped his fly and dropped his jeans and boxers to the floor. Now fully naked and hard, Bane said, "Come on, sweetheart. Shower with me. I'll get a second wind and share it with you. Take care of what I started at dinner."

"What did you start at dinner?" she asked innocently.

"Good try." He smirked. "You were totally turned on during dinner."

"That was underhanded, Bane."

"Perhaps, but you love the foreplay, as do I. Come on. A shower will revive me, and one with you doubly so."

"You seem to be revived already." She grinned, her eyes dropping to his massive erection.

"Hmm," Bane growled. "I promise you'll sleep like a baby afterward."

"You promise?" she asked, breathlessly.

"I do indeed."

Natasha stood and held Bane's gaze. She sauntered past him with an impish smile, casually stripping her skirt and top, moving toward the bathroom in a matching pale yellow bra and boy-cut panties. "Let's get you clean, husband," she purred over her shoulder.

reconnaissance

ذا سقطت المئذنه لا تلوم الا الحلاق.

If *the minaret falls, blame the barber.*

chapter 29

NATASHA AND BANE WERE AT the bank as soon as it opened and were ushered into a banker's office. She presented her credentials to access the safe-deposit box, and the gentleman confirmed that the account had passed to Natasha when Josette Allamel died, per her will.

"Please," he said to the two of them, indicating the chairs across from him on the other side of his desk.

Bane waited for Natasha to sit before lowering himself into the chair next to her.

"Can you tell me when the safe-deposit box was last accessed?" Natasha asked.

The banker pulled up the account on his computer and swiveled the monitor to face Natasha.

She leaned forward and placed her elbows on his desk, then started skimming the entries. Mémé had added Natasha as a co-lessor when Natasha was twenty-one. Pépé had accessed the safe-deposit box the day before his death. Mémé had taken Henri Allamel off as co-lessor mere weeks after he died and also accessed the safe-deposit box. Images of Natasha's signature card and Pépé death certificate were attached to the file.

"Nothing after that?" she asked the banker.

"No. It would be in the record," he said. "Do you wish to access it now?"

"Please."

205

The gentleman rose and led Natasha and Bane through the security door and a room with walls of safe-deposit boxes, then inserted the bank's key and Natasha's and turned them at the same time. There was a muted click, and the exterior door of the compartment holding the box released. Natasha's nerves were on edge as the banker pulled forth a steel-colored metal box, roughly ten by twelve inches and five inches in depth.

Bane squeezed her shoulder and his breath caressed her as he whispered, "Breathe, babe. It helps tremendously."

She inhaled deeply, then exhaled slowly.

"I'll leave you now. Please take as long as you need. Ring the buzzer next to the door when you are done and I will return," the banker said before giving Natasha her key.

"Thank you," Natasha and Bane responded in unison before the man exited, closing the door softly behind him.

"Ready?"

Natasha's key slipped from her fingers and clinked on the bar-height, stainless-steel counter next to the safe-deposit box. "Why am I so nervous?"

Bane stepped behind her and massaged her shoulders. "Maybe because you've had one shock after another? Or maybe because the clues left for you by your grandmother gave you no idea what you are about to see?"

Natasha closed her eyes and bowed her neck as the tension eased out of her shoulders, her mind returning to last night. And this morning. Bane gently worked her neck, his touch lighting her blood on fire. Her pulse went into overdrive, skipping and skittering.

He softly kissed the back of her neck. "Damn, baby." He sighed.

She faced him. "Not here."

"I know. I just have a hard time keeping my hands to myself when I'm around you." His eyes held hers.

"Always direct, aren't you?" She smiled.

"You like direct."

"I do." She grinned, then inhaled deeply, pivoting away from him and dropping her shawl and tote onto the chair next to where she stood. Natasha reached to lift the lid on the box, then pulled her hands back as if it had burned her. "What if it's a Pandora's box?"

※ ❖ ❀ ※

"Come here." He guided Natasha to one of the utilitarian chairs in the stark room, sitting first so that he could gather her in his lap.

Bane pulled Natasha closer, inhaling the heady combination of honey and lemongrass he had come to love because it was hers, tenderly running his fingers through the tendrils of hair that had escaped her messy bun, wishing things were different. He ached to make it all okay for her, but he had no idea in hell what the safe-deposit box held. Bane lifted her hand and rotated it, kissing her tattoo and palm gently before intertwining his fingers with hers and setting her hand back in her lap. "Your grandfather's office was rifled through. You discovered a secret compartment in his office with incriminating documents. We don't know the whys."

"It's surreal. How could my grandfather, of all people, be involved in the network we're trying to destroy?"

"Emmet has analysts going through everything we gave them. We need to get as much information as possible before we assume anything. We also need to bear in mind that things aren't always what they seem."

"True," she acknowledged quietly.

They sat in silence for a few minutes, each enjoying their closeness and contemplating the next possible twist.

Natasha untangled herself from Bane and rose. "You're right though. We don't have all the information. I've allowed my emotions to shape my perspective instead of using my brain." She faced him, her expression resolute. "Let's do this."

Bane stood, cupped his hand around her neck, and inclined his head. He kissed her slowly. Natasha slid her arms around his waist, pulling him closer and deepening the kiss, leaving them both breathless.

"Later," he murmured, the corner of his mouth drawing up into a sexy grin as he ran the pad of his thumb over her full bottom lip. "I want you too. Fuck, I always want you." He nodded to the metal box. "Let's do this."

※ ❖ ❀ ※

At first opening the safe-deposit box was anticlimactic. Only two items lay inside. The flat, smaller one was an envelope addressed to Tasha in Mémé's handwriting. The second item was an unmarked, corrugated white box that took up most of the safe-deposit box's interior.

207

Natasha glanced up at Bane. "This looks like an archival box. Envelope first." She walked away from the counter and paced while reading the note. Natasha's intake of breath was sharp. Her hand flew to her heart and she dropped into the chair they had occupied moments earlier.

"Tell me."

Natasha bobbed her head and held a finger up as she read, wide-eyed, indicating she would fill him in when she was done. "Jesus." Whispering did not mask her disbelief. Upon finishing, she handed the letter to Bane and turned her face away, but not before he noted the unshed tears and the anguish and disbelief warring in her expression.

Bane read through the letter and whistled before laying it on the counter. He squatted in front of Natasha. "Nat?" Silence. "Hey," he said softly, his finger tracing the outline of her trembling jaw. "Talk to me."

She shook her head and continued to look away, wrapping her arms tightly around her ribs and pushing back against the hard chair, clearly fighting for control, fighting to hold together the crumbling walls of her fortress.

"I'll admit. It's fucking unbelievable, like some crazy thriller." He covered her hands with his, observing how their bone structure differed—hers fine, his heavy. "Need a few minutes?"

Bane had to strain to hear her yes. His fingers trailed over hers as he let go and stood. After several minutes of watching her and total silence, he pulled his phone from his hip pocket and texted Emmet.

Something has come up. Will contact soon.

chapter 30

"I THOUGHT I COULD DISTANCE myself emotionally." Natasha's voice shook but she faced him, clasping her hands tightly together. "Instead, I'm cracking. I have to keep perspective." She dropped her hands and inhaled deeply, rising as she spoke. "As you've pointed out, my grandfather's choices do not reflect on me."

Bane gathered her into his arms. Natasha's heart beat rapidly against his chest as he stroked her back gently. She softened into him and rested her head in the crook of his shoulder.

"That's right." He spoke softly into her lustrous hair before kissing it. "You're strong, sweetheart. And remember, you have me for support. Don't hide from how you feel, and certainly don't apologize to me or anyone else for those feelings, okay?"

Natasha's eyes shone up at Bane as she slid her arms around his waist, hanging on for support. "You're good for me, you know that?"

"I most certainly do. I'm glad you finally accept that."

She stepped back and popped him in the upper arm with her fist, grinning. "Cocky."

"Yes." He winked at her, heat simmering in his eyes.

Natasha cleared her throat and gave Bane a penetrating stare. Reaching into her tote, she withdrew a zippered pouch and, with a flourish, removed a pair of white gloves from a clear protective sleeve.

"What all do you have in that thing?" Bane chuckled, indicating her oversized tote. "It's like a bottomless bag."

"You might be surprised," she replied sassily. "These are inspection gloves. I always carry some with me. They're an extra layer of protection when examining artifacts, in this case the box's contents. Fingers have natural oils in them. The gloves also provide friction to avoid an object slipping from my grasp." She slid them over her slim hands as she spoke. "Let's see what my grandfather left at the front desk of the hotel Asilah because his room wasn't ready." She pulled the flaps from the sides where they were inserted and lifted the lid. "Oh! Excellent."

Bane's eyes darted from Natasha to the thinly wrapped item. "What's excellent?"

"It's some kind of book, and this is archival tissue. Mémé thought this through. There's a large tied organizer in the bottom of my tote. Can you get that for me and untie it? Roll it out and place it next to my hand. It has my tools. Yes, you may dig in my bag," she answered in response to his raised brows.

He did as Natasha asked, then leaned his elbows on the counter and watched her work. She was mesmerizing. Beautiful. Confident. All earlier emotions and tension had vanished; she was focused on her task. She parted the tissue gently and gasped. Inside an unsealed bag was an ancient book.

"What is it?" Bane scowled.

"It's a codex," she whispered excitedly. "Remember when Emmet said there was rumor of another codex that disappeared during World War II? Give me my shawl please."

"Uh-huh…," he said guardedly, handing Natasha the colorful shawl pinned under her tote.

"I believe this may be that codex!" She formed her shawl into a supportive cushion on top of the metal counter and carefully placed the ancient book in the center of it, making sure there was ample room on all sides. Natasha gently slid the codex from its unsealed bag.

"Why would your grandfather have had it?"

"I don't know. Between what's in the letter Mémé left in the safe-deposit box and examining the ledger and manifest, I'm hoping we can discover the answer. Her letter recounted what happened. Let's talk it out."

"Okay. Your grandfather told your grandmother his meeting was in Rabat and he'd be overnighting there. She asked him to put her jewelry in the safe-deposit box because it was close to his supposed route of travel."

"Yes," Natasha said, picking up the thread. "It makes sense since they were leaving for holiday that weekend." She paused in her examination and glanced at Bane. "I know for a fact Mémé preferred to leave her jewelry in the lockbox when they were gone for any extended time. So Pépé did. We saw his signature and the date, so he had his key."

"Right, but when your grandfather was found in Asilah, not in Rabat, he only had one key on him. His car key."

"Yes. The hotel Pépé checked into early kept his bag, but he never returned. They delivered his bag to her and, after Mémé was able to cope with some of her grief, she went through his bag and discovered the codex with a note he'd left for her. A just in case note, Mémé called it. He told her to hide the book and never mention it to anyone." Natasha pinched the bridge of her nose, then cupped her chin, her gray eyes turbulent as she looked at him. "Jesus, Bane. Pépé knew. He knew his life was in danger." She wiped furiously at her eyes, then put her hand out when Bane moved to comfort her. "What did Mémé do with the note? I'm okay. It's just... just... Dammit. I have so many questions."

Bane reached for her again. "Nat..."

"I need a moment," she said, ducking her shoulder away from him. "And I have to put on a fresh pair of gloves."

A bit later, Natasha had regained her composure. "No. I'm fine. Really." She regarded the codex with awe. "It's simply exquisite. My grandmother figured out the correct way to best store this. This looks to be a polyethylene bag, which discourages mold spores and spoilage by allowing the book to breathe. The craftsmanship is unbelievable," she declared. "The bindings... Oh my word! See these?" She pointed to the ornamentation. "They are the craftsman's distinctive mark, equivalent to modern-day commercial signatures."

"Interesting. I have a logo for my work."

Natasha paused, leaning on the counter with the heels of her hands. She tilted her head, her expression inquisitive. "You're a craftsman?"

"Uh, yeah," he revealed sheepishly, unsure how Natasha would feel about what he did, what he loved doing when he wasn't under contract for his specialty. "I'm a blacksmith. I forge wrought iron. Started when we needed things replaced or repaired on the farm. It expanded from there with the home-improvement and renovation craze. Gates, fences, stairs, pergolas. You name it."

She covered his broad wrist with her delicate hand. "I'd love to see your work someday."

The idea of a someday with Natasha filled him with hope. Bane didn't answer. It was during these moments—when they were intensely focused on other things, working with and supporting each other, like in the kitchen performing field surgery on Rafiq, and now—that one of them mentioned a possible future between them. Had she noticed?

⚔ ▦ ❈ ⚔

Heat flushed Natasha's insides like rushing water when she realized what she had just said. *Someday.* "We should get back to this." She rolled her shoulders, then flexed and stretched her fingers. Natasha selected a flat and narrow curved microspatula from her tools. "I don't want to chance the codex coming into contact with the counter," she said, answering Bane's questioning expression. "This appears to be in excellent condition. I'm going to try to open it." She took a deep breath and swallowed. "My heart is pounding. Can you video this?"

"Sure." Bane reached for his phone and positioned himself on the other side of the metal table. "Do you need a mask or goggles?"

"No," Natasha responded, reverently trailing her fingers around the edges of the two-inch-thick codex, feeling for the best place to begin.

"Do you have them?"

"I do." She laughed. "Should I put them on to entertain you?"

"Um, no. There are other things you could put on or take off that would entertain me much more."

Natasha rolled her eyes at him and shook her head. She returned to examining the codex. Its binding was one continuous piece of dark brown and surprisingly supple leather. It looked to be hand-embossed and stamped. Gilded gold and insets of turquoise and other stones enhanced the design. "This is incredible," she whispered. "Are you getting this?"

"Yep."

The binding resembled an envelope, its flap secured by a wooden peg inserted into a leather strap that extended from the back cover and over the front cover. The Teflon-coated metal spatula slid in easily. Natasha moved it slowly between the ancient pages at an angle, away from the spine, alert for the slightest hint of friction or worse—a tear—then

repeated the process from a different angle. The pages separated with little complaint.

"Ready?" she asked, glancing at him and letting out the breath she had been holding.

"I'm ready when you are, sweetheart."

The codex opened without issue and the cover rested easily on the table, supported on her shawl.

Natasha's mouth dropped open. "Oh my god," she gasped in disbelief.

"Oh my god," Bane echoed right after her. He stopped recording and raised his phone to his ear. "Emmet, there's been another development."

Natasha closed her eyes and reopened them, only to goggle in disbelief at the incipit of the codex—its first page. The book hand was uncial—a Greek form of capitals, indicating the ancient book was written somewhere between the fourth century BCE and the eighth or ninth century CE. Below the uncial covering, the top half the page was the name of Alexander III of Macedon. Alexander the Great. What they were looking at was the rumored codex that had disappeared prior to World War II. She was sure of it.

The codex in front of her fit the description of the one that had vanished during World War II, mentioned by Emmet during their initial meeting with Rafiq. Natasha shook her head, finding it difficult to believe she was in its presence.

Bane captured it all on his phone. "I uploaded to the cloud and deleted it from my phone."

"What do I do with this?" Natasha pressed her lips firmly together, then spoke. "I'm thinking repatriation. Where should the book's final resting place be? I want to honor that, but..."

Bane lifted his chin. His hands encouraged Natasha to face him. "But what?" He stood directly behind her and rested his chin lightly on the top of her head, his hands on her shoulders. "What do you mean?"

"I don't know how Pépé came to have the codex. Only that he did, and he apparently died because of it."

"The answer may never surface, sweetheart," he said quietly in her ear.

"Look. This is wholly unexpected. Emmet said this codex was of no importance unless it fell into our laps. It seems it might have."

"Might have." He stressed the words. "Say we delay and get a determination. Maybe this is the codex. Maybe not. The *Homo sapiens* are

whisked out of the country, like the Ouarzazate Codex apparently has been. What then?"

Natasha carefully rewrapped the codex in the tissue and returned it to the archival box, then placed the box and envelope back into the safe-deposit box and secured the lid. "We can address this codex later. I'm returning it to the safe-deposit box, along with Mémé's letter. It's not as if they're going anywhere. I'll talk to Gia about the codex, see what she thinks and can do to help. Since this is what she does, I imagine she'd love to take a look at it." She pressed the button for the banker. "Before we get on the road, I want to return to the *riad*. I'd prefer not to have the key with us, given what has transpired."

chapter 31

THE SPRAWLING CAPITAL CITY OF Rabat rapidly disappeared behind them as the Jeep ate up the miles. Natasha stared out the window, lost in thought. She had not spoken since leaving Casablanca more than an hour earlier.

Behind the wheel, Bane asked, "Want to talk?"

She turned her head sideways, everything made darker by her dark sunglasses. "About how I feel?"

"Uh-huh."

"I don't think so. I don't want to sound like an abandoned child instead of a thirty-six-year-old woman," she said curtly, taking a deep inhale.

Bane inclined his head. Natasha felt his interest through the dark lenses.

"Eyes on the road, mister," she admonished with an impish smile. "I prefer to remain in one piece."

"Tough when you're doing that."

"Has anyone ever told you that you are a very lusty man?"

Bane rearranged his hands on the steering wheel. A deep laugh accompanied his words. "Only you."

"Really? Difficult to believe." She grinned, then her tone changed. "My grandfather isn't who I thought he was."

"It's fucking surreal. For anyone. Emmet is concerned about you, and trust me, not much moves him off center."

"He's concerned about the mission."

"Yes, and us. Just accept that he might care, beyond the mission."

"Fine."

"The two of you made major headway after you returned from the *Kasbah*."

"We did." Natasha pivoted in her seat. "You and Emmet have a nice camaraderie, I've noticed."

"Yeah. I've worked with him on other assignments."

"And Matilda?"

A flash of white appeared in his tanned, handsome face. "She's the woman behind the man. It's important to keep her in the loop and happy, and I like her. You know, it's okay to like the people that you work with, that you come in contact with."

"Are you trying to psychoanalyze me?"

"Nope. I'm not qualified to do that, only trained to observe. As I shared that night after we patched up Rafiq, you keep people at a distance because of the tough shit that you've experienced. It's totally understandable."

"And you're going to tell me again that it's all within my control," she said with growing annoyance.

"Yep."

"Well, fuck you." Natasha was sorry as soon as the words were out of her mouth. She had crossed a line, one she'd sworn she'd never even toe. "Do not patronize me. Ever."

Bane glanced behind him and braked the car hard, swerving it to the shoulder and off the pavement. The SUV dipped and rocked until he brought it to an abrupt stop in the desolate landscape, some distance from and below the A2 highway. The motion brought Natasha within inches of his stony, unreadable face. He rubbed the bridge of his nose and took off his sunglasses. "Don't ever tell me to fuck off." Heat poured from Bane's body as he leaned in closer. "You're mercurial as fuck."

"You do not get to tell me—"

"I'm not patronizing you," he said evenly. "I'm trying to reach you, and you're reacting like this because you feel cornered." Bane rolled down the windows and turned off the car. He unlatched his seat belt and faced her. "Let's have this out. Right now."

Natasha reached to unlock her door.

"I wouldn't. Your sandals aren't going to provide much protection."

She paused, her back to him. Rigid. Silent.

"Scared?"

"Look here," she said angrily, whipping around, beating her stiff finger into his chest. Her fury snapped and snarled like a flag in a high summer storm, and along with it, her heat. "You're pissing the shit out of me."

They both felt it the split instant before her mouth crashed over his, out of control. Ravaged. Broken. She claimed and she took. But what Natasha didn't realize was that in the act of taking, she was giving all of herself, exposing all of herself, and giving Bane exactly what he craved. Her hands clawed at his shirt and pulled it over his head, then her nails raked down his back.

Hungry, so hungry. Impatiently and roughly, she undid the buckle of his pants and yanked at his button and zipper. Bane lifted his hips. Natasha wrenched his pants and boxers past his hips and pulled her skirt up and panties to the side, mounting him, sheathing him in one demanding, rough stroke. She glared at him, then kissed him harshly, meeting softness, whimpering as he slid his tongue into her mouth.

He kissed like he teased, with slow and unrelenting skill, caressing her mouth with his tongue and his lips while she battled with her tormentor. Bane moved easily within her juices as she rode him hard and wild, his hands gently bracketing her hips, allowing her full control. Except with the kisses.

Natasha's eyes were glazed with lust. She grabbed his hair, feeling the shape of his skull, and lowered her head again and inhaled his scent. Her lips hovered over his, then she nipped his lower lip and sucked on it. A deep animal moan escaped before she convulsed violently and collapsed against him, spent, gripping tightly. Her heart banged around in her chest, and Natasha panted as if she'd run for her life, which she had.

Bane slid his tongue over the shallow of her neck before sucking softly and holding her snugly, his breathing matching hers, his galloping heart matching hers. Smiling, he parked his chin in her mass of damp curls.

chapter 32

THE AMAZIGH VILLAGE OF BHALIL was nestled in the foothills of the Atlas Mountains and some twenty miles south of Fes. The village featured eclectically colored homes in pastel hues of blue, pink, and yellow and had over five hundred caves dating back to the fourth century. Most of them housed cattle and sheep, but others were shops or homes of Bhalil residents who used the caves as their primary rooms and added bedrooms and private areas above. The cave homes had the same facades as aboveground houses.

Natasha and Bane presented their passports and checked into a cozy boutique guesthouse, the only one in Bhalil and situated on the edge of Old Town.

"We'd like the honeymoon suite," Bane stated.

Imsen, their host, spoke excellent English. "I don't have that, but I will give you my finest room. How long have you been married?"

"One month," Natasha answered groggily. She had promptly fallen into a deep sleep in the passenger seat after climbing off Bane and readjusting her skirt.

"Best wishes," he said, handing Bane the room key. "A farm-to-table breakfast is served poolside daily. You are welcome to take it to your room. Dinner is optional. However, for planning purposes, will you be dining at the guesthouse tonight or traveling out of town for dinner?"

"We'll be joining you and your other guests. Thank you, Imsen," Bane said.

Natasha's eyes traveled their large room—the ceiling, with rough-hewn beams over thin timbers; the built-in, handcrafted cabinets and lampshades; the metalwork; colorful bedding; and rug. "Wow. This is really nice. It's certainly authentic. Thanks for asking for the upgrade."

"You're welcome."

Natasha faced Bane, his simple reply attracting her attention. The air between them crackled. Unable to tear her gaze from the desire smoldering in his, she felt her heart rate spike and an acute ache rooted deep in her belly.

His slow, cocksure smirk widened into a sexy smile. He closed the door behind him and locked it, holding out his hand. "Let's give the shower a go. See how long the warm water lasts."

Natasha took it and followed him to the bathroom.

※ ※ ※ ※

Hungry, Natasha and Bane searched for somewhere to eat in the charming, well-kept village. They were beckoned into a food store where Natasha struggled to feed herself with her right hand.

"You're a slob." He grinned. Having finished eating, he settled back onto his floor cushion.

"You try eating with your nondominant hand."

Bane looked around the tiny space. A half dozen local men sat at the other round table, talking among themselves in a local dialect of Arabic, finishing their tea and blatantly observing Natasha and Bane. "Um. Not here," he admitted with a bemused expression.

Natasha wiped food from her face. "Exactly. I'm doing my best."

"We've already gotten their attention." Bane cleared his throat and raised his brows at her, unseen by the men since his back was to them. "You catching any of this?"

"Yes. You?"

"Not all of it, and what I understand is nothing of interest. They're speaking a local dialect of Arabic, right?"

"They are. I guess that makes me more fluent than you." She laughed. "But you're right, nothing of interest."

"You did notice that Imsen has utensils? Probably to help those of us who can't manage."

"Yes, but I'll still have the left issue."

"Honestly, you should've mastered eating with your right when you were growing up here."

She squinted at him and tried to look mad.

Bane chuckled softly. "Good try." He sobered a bit before offering, "I'll help you tonight if you promise to come to bed with me early."

"You're holding my eating challenges hostage?" she asked in mock anger.

"I just want to make sure we get enough sleep. We have so much more to explore, and we're just getting started."

His innuendo and sexy smile made Natasha weak in the knees. She was going to need help standing if Bane continued.

※ ▨ ❀ ※

After lunch, Natasha and Bane walked for hours. Periodically, they stopped to talk with the friendly residents and artisans or wander into booths in the *souk* to inspect merchandise and ask questions. Bane snapped photos of everything from people to architecture. Later, Natasha browsed in several shops outside the *souk,* seeking priceless artifacts for her faceless, discerning clients who were willing to pay top prices for the privilege of owning unique pieces of culture and history. As always, she left her ART business card, asking the shop owners call if anything of significance came into their shop or on the local market.

"Bhalil claims pre-Islamic Christian origins and is believed to be founded by people from Volubilis," she said.

Bane followed Natasha over another of the rock bridges connecting the narrow, steep streets that meandered along the seasonal river. "If I remember my research, Volubilis was Roman."

"Eventually. The Berber tribal kingdom of Mauritania became a Roman client state after Carthage fell in 146 BC. Volubilis was its capital. King Juba II, married to the daughter of Mark Antony and Cleopatra, was installed by the Romans in 25 BC. Although he was Berber, his tastes were Roman. He built the version of Volubilis that people see in its ruins."

"The history of Morocco is complex."

"It really is. Invaders, empires, and countries have all left their marks."

"I enjoy having you as a personal tour guide." Bane scanned the buildings around him, looking through the camera lens. The camera clicked rapidly. "I want some photos of you."

"Why?"

He viewed the photos he had just taken, then adjusted the lens setting. "Because tourists take them of each other. Because husbands take photos of their beautiful wives. Sweetheart, quit toying with me," he said gruffly in response to the over-the-top sultry look she gave him.

Natasha burst into a fit of laughter. "Poor man."

"Uh-huh. You're playing with fire." He snapped a slew of photos of her, then scrolled back through the images on the screen. His heart constricted. Natasha's guard was down, and the transformation was breathtaking. Welcoming, playful, and relaxed. He looked up and behind her, adjusting his camera to capture the topography in the distance. "What's that peak?"

"Jebel Kandar. From what I remember, it's spectacular."

"You've been here then?"

Natasha adjusted her shawl modestly around her bare arms; it had come loose as she walked. "And here, visiting with my family. My brothers and I were still in primary school. My father found Bhalil charming. Mama and Papa decided a hike would be a special reward for their three active children who didn't enjoy traipsing through the *medina* of Fes." Natasha's smile was sad. "The *medina*. It's really something else. Have you been?"

"No," he said, watching her carefully.

"You should. We explored while Papa worked that morning, then met him back at the hotel. He had the hotel pack us a picnic. It was so much fun. And beautiful. We were exhausted that night." She smiled wistfully, then glanced at her watch. "We should return. It's six o'clock. Dinner is at seven."

❖ ❖ ❖ ❖

"Hold on a minute," Bane said, leaving her alone outside the dining room for several minutes before returning to Natasha and giving her a quick kiss. "Just checking in with Imsen. The other guests are European and American, so no issues with eating as you wish."

Confident they were the only people in the area, Natasha planted a lingering kiss on Bane's lips. "That was sweet. I like you, Bane Rua."

"Mm. That feels full of promise," he said with a sly smile. His phone vibrated. Emmet. "Yes?" Bane nodded as he listened. "Okay. I'll tell Natasha." He disconnected. "Change of plans, sweetheart. Chatter has

picked up. We leave for Tinghir after breakfast tomorrow and meet our contact in the evening."

✕ ✕ ✹ ✕

Natasha and Bane were the last to arrive for dinner. She had opted for pants and a long-sleeved shirt. He wore khakis and a striped button-down, the rolled-up sleeves exposing his strong forearms. Seeing them reminded her how safe and cherished she felt when he held her.

Bane linked his little finger with Natasha's before entering the dining area and inclined his head, brushing her earlobe before murmuring, "And we're on."

Natasha smiled demurely, then made a point to look each of the five people seated around the table in the eye when what she really wanted to do was to go back to the room with him and experience the delicious sparks growing into fiery passion. "Good evening."

"Hello. I'm Bane, and this is Natasha. My wife."

Dinner was subdued at first, gradually becoming more animated as the guests shared the divine meal and navigated each other.

The fit, middle-aged man and woman—Felix, a gamba fisherman, and his wife Aurora—were a married couple from the Catalan region of Spain on holiday exploring, as they put it, the gems of Morocco. They were leaving with a local guide well before dawn and had been promised a spectacular sunrise from the top of Jebel Kandar. They wore cargo pants and long-sleeved travel shirts and looked so similar in height, weight, build, and hair and eye color that they could have been mistaken for siblings.

Loris, a widower, was in Morocco for business and had decided to travel to Fes before leaving. Dressed in khakis and a pale green button-down, he had extended his trip an additional week to hike in the Atlas and visit Ifrane—a small town that reminded him of his home country of Switzerland—and Bhalil. He was driving back to Rabat the next day to fly home.

The two Americans were the youngest, having recently graduated college. They sported unkempt beards, unruly hair, and the overconfidence of the spoiled and entitled. They were eagerly forthcoming about themselves without being asked. The guesthouse provided beer and wine with the meal, which Natasha and Bane declined. The young men took full advantage though, drinking beer after beer until they noticed Bane's frown directed at them.

Zach Cokinos, the dark-haired one, was dressed in a short-sleeved shirt covered in blue and pink whales and seersucker shorts. He had majored in African studies and was enrolled in a postgraduate program in South Africa the coming semester. Connor Ritman, his blond cousin, had studied business and economics and wore long athletic shorts and an orange-and-blue T-shirt emblazoned with the name of a microbrewery. Their parents had gifted them with travel preceding Zach's internship and graduate school and Connor's promise to seek employment as soon as he and his cousin settled in Cape Town. The young men were flying to Egypt and spending a few weeks there, then visiting Zambia and Tanzania before getting situated in their new home base.

With dinner complete, Aurora and Felix and Loris bid Natasha and Bane good night. The young Americans disappeared without saying anything.

"It's a beautiful night. Let's sit outside for a while by the pool," Natasha said.

Bane helped her stand. "I'm up for that. You interested in a glass of wine if it's available? I'll check with Imsen."

"I'll meet you outside." Natasha headed toward the outdoor terrace where she made herself comfortable on the double chaise on the pool deck, pulling her shawl around her. She was transfixed by Bhalil as it glimmered in the distance, growing brighter as the last of the sunset faded and the smoky-soft edges of the Atlas disappeared into the starlit inky-blue sky.

※ ※ ☀ ※

Two beers in one hand and Natasha's wine in the other, Bane checked himself before stepping outside. Natasha was an ethereal vision, illuminated in the soft glow of starlight. Her body was languid—long limbs stretched out in front, arms relaxed over the thin shawl, head resting on the top of the chaise, her glorious hair tumbling over the back as she gazed at the rising full moon and blanket of twinkling silver sequins overhead. He recalled that first night on the rooftop terrace and how he had worshipped her exquisite and responsive body. Their lovemaking was tumultuous and unpredictable. He craved her constantly, if only to be in her presence.

Noise and movement from Bane's right drew his focus away from Natasha. He scowled. The American cousins, dressed in swim trunks with

towels over their shoulders. Each of them carried a partial six-pack of beer, apparently their personal stash. They hailed Natasha before pulling chairs close to her and sitting.

Grimacing, Bane strode to the pool with his and Natasha's drinks, resigned he would have to share her a little longer tonight.

"Here, sweetheart," he said, stepping between Zach and Connor and Natasha, extending the wine to her, then addressing the young men cordially. "Gentlemen."

She patted the chaise and curled up her legs so that he had plenty of room next to her. "Sit, babe." She took a sip. "Nice. Tastes French."

Babe. That was new, and hearing it roll off her tongue did wild things to his heart and head. Bane set the extra bottle on the deck and took a deep pull on his open bottle. "Um. Yeah. Imsen thought you might enjoy it."

Natasha kissed Bane her thanks, then addressed the cousins jointly. "You mentioned Cape Town at dinner. I lived there for a while. Where do you plan on living?"

"Really?" Zach asked, animated. "UCT area. Do you know it?"

"Yes, I'm familiar with the University of Cape Town."

"Where else have you lived?"

Natasha took another sip of wine before answering. "I've been roaming the world most of my adult years, working here and there."

"Why are you in Morocco?"

"We're combining our honeymoon with my work," she explained, resting against Bane's broad shoulder.

Connor raised his beer and toasted Natasha and Bane. "Congratulations!" he slurred.

The men raised their bottles, and Natasha lifted her glass.

Bane drained his first beer and set it down. He picked up the second full bottle and slid his arm loosely around Natasha's shoulders, running his knuckles over her upper arm, remaining expressionless, the quiet observer. He felt her response through the layers of fabric.

"Who do you work for?"

"ART Enterprise Global. I'm in acquisitions."

Zach straightened, his interest evident. "What does that mean?"

"I get my clients what they want," Natasha said with a grin, as if she

were the cat that ate the canary. "Their interests run from art to unique historical items. Their tastes are high-end and discerning. Price isn't an issue, which makes buying for them a lot of fun."

"You travel with an open checkbook?"

"In a manner of speaking. Wire transfers," she explained.

"Have you bought anything for your clients while you've been here?"

"A few things."

"Like?"

Natasha shook her head, smiling. "Confidential. My clients demand anonymity, for them and their purchases. I deliver."

The conversation moved on, marked with laughter and a discussion of places to explore in Morocco.

"This has been fun"—Connor stood unsteadily and dropped his towel on the seat—"but I came to swim." He walked to the edge of the pool and cannonballed in.

Bane unfolded from the chaise. His expression was stormy as he strode purposefully to the pool with Zach following. "Hey, Connor. Not a good idea. You've had too much to drink." Bane turned to Zach. "You need to look out for him. He's this side of trashed. Never leave someone behind."

"Come on, Con," Zach said, crouching and motioning his cousin out of the pool with his hands. "We've got an early morning. Let's go."

Connor waded through the water to the edge and hoisted himself out, nearly falling over before he stood. He grinned drunkenly at Bane and Natasha. "It's been fun."

Zach draped Connor's towel around him. "We've enjoyed tonight. Best of luck to you on everything."

Bane drank from his bottle while he watched the younger men disappear into the guesthouse. He dropped onto the chaise and looked away from Natasha, closing himself off.

✖ ✖ ✖ ✖

This was a side of him she had never witnessed. Natasha placed her hand over his. "Hey."

He acted as if he hadn't heard her.

She patted gently. "Bane. What's going on with you? We were having fun and now you're shutting me out."

He stood. "I'm going to the room."

"No. You are not," she said, yanking Bane hard with all her weight, pulling him back down next to her. "Please. Talk to me."

Bane turned to her. Anguish filled his face.

Natasha felt her breath whoosh out of her. She searched his eyes, her voice cracking. "What the hell?"

He stared back, his jaw flexing.

"Bane," she whispered, stroking his arm. She slid her arms around his strong, solid torso and hugged him, feeling his heart beat furiously against her. She kissed his stubbled jaw. "What happened?"

He shook his head and pinned her with his ever-changing eyes, opening his soul, allowing her to witness the pain he shouldered. He blinked and took a deep breath and cupped her face with his hands. Bane closed his eyes and kissed her like a drowning man. The thickly lashed lids opened, holding her gaze. "I'm going to tell you a story."

Natasha pivoted so she could rest in the corner of the chaise, wanting to give Bane her full attention.

He pushed the soft fabric of her pants up to above her knees, massaging her calves, encouraging her to drape her legs across his thighs. "You feel so good. Silky. Soft." He stopped and searched her eyes.

"It happened in high school. My senior year," he said quietly, slouching down and resting his head on the top of the chaise, looking at the stars and blinking a few times before taking a deep breath.

Natasha laced her fingers through his and squeezed gently.

He continued. "It was graduation night."

Natasha covered his hand with her other one.

"You know. We were just a group of bored, small-town kids, mostly kids of farmers. There wasn't much that scared us. We'd seen our share of scrapes, close calls, and accidents. For the most part, everyone came out of them okay. Maybe a broken leg or stitches.

"That night, we were rowdier than usual. Hell, we had just graduated. Most of us were going to college, many of us were first generation. I had a full ride to college to play tight end." He rubbed fiercely at his cheeks. "We'd all known each other since we were babies. We always had each other's backs, even if we'd just had a fight. We stuck together.

"Alex was my best friend. His older brother, Booth, got us some whisky and we passed it around before the graduation ceremony. Kept it

among our group, under our robes. Our high school was consolidated, meaning other communities in the county sent their kids there. I remember my parents frowning at me during my speech, so I must have had more than a buzz."

"You were valedictorian?"

"Naw. I was elected by my class to give a speech."

"Popular."

Bane tipped his head to smile at her. "Um, yeah." He looked back up at the sky. "Dad asked me afterward why I spoke so deliberately. I couldn't tell him. It would have added to his disappointment, and I couldn't bear more. You see, I was leaving the farm to go to college and play football. Dad wanted me to stay and take over the farm, the family business. I couldn't commit to that. Hell, I was only eighteen and I had another option.

"All of us walked into town after graduation with our caps and gowns on, acting like wild fools. Alex's brother met us with more whisky. He was such a dick. I never liked him. I was as tall as Booth, but he was skinnier. He always challenged me, ever since I flattened his ass in fifth grade for picking on Alex. Fucker.

"Anyway… We decided, me and my friends, about a dozen of us, that we'd climb the water tower in town. We left our caps and gowns in a pile by one of the supports and went for it. The tower took some time to climb. The bottle was passed around once we got to the top, but most of us had slowed or stopped. I didn't drink any more, but Alex and Ryan kept going. The tower was higher than we realized. We still had to get back down to the ground. We hung out there for a while, sitting on the open walkway, leaning against the metal railing. Talking. Laughing. Looking over our town, bigger than life. Being stupid."

"Being boys," Natasha commented.

"Alex chugged the whisky with Ryan. Responsibility was starting to nag at me, so I told them to stop, at least slow down. All of us were trying to get them to stop. They were fucked up and started to wrestle for the last drops. They stood. Pushed each other around." Bane rubbed the heels of his hands over his eyes. "Fuck. The tower had been built over a hundred years earlier. The bottle slipped and they both went for it. The railing was low. Fuck."

Bane was silent but breathed hard.

Natasha relaxed her grip, realizing she held his hand too tightly. "Bane?"

He whipped around and pulled her to him tightly, burying his face in her shoulder. His body trembled and his heart raced, his words moist and muffled against her neck. "I still see them. Going over. Both of them."

She felt him swallow. Felt his anguish.

"I could have stopped them," he confessed.

Natasha kneaded the corded muscles through his damp shirt, not knowing what to say, only wanting to comfort him, to help him banish his monster. Now that he had opened up to her, she wanted to talk more. She wanted more of everything with Bane.

chapter 33

"MORNING, BEAUTY," BANE PURRED IN Natasha's ear. "The sun's rising and I suspect our host and the cook won't appreciate that we spent the night outside wrapped in each other's arms, in full view of their guests."

Natasha framed the sides of his head with her hands and moved it above hers, smiling softly, fascinated by the play of soft orange, pink, and yellow on his scruffy face. She searched his eyes to see how he was feeling. They looked clear. "How'd you sleep?"

"Like a baby. Granted, I may be a little stiff from being in mostly one position all night." He rested his forehead against hers, then kissed her deeply. "Someone was incredibly comforting last night. Thank you, sweetheart." Bane rose and took her hand, pulling her to standing. "Come on," he said, swooping up the empty wineglass and beer bottle. "We have enough time before breakfast."

"To?"

"To clean up. Work out the kinks. You've got to be a little stiff too. I'm lean, but I weigh 220, give or take. That's a lot of extra weight on your slender bones for the evening, despite the nice cushions on the chaise."

"I'm good." And she was.

Natasha missed Bane's heat and how they had fit together all night. At one point she had woken; he slept deeply on his side against hers, his leg and arm flung over her, his face resting in the crook of her neck. Even in

sleep he made her feel cherished and protected. In a very short time, he had broken down Natasha's emotional fortress and situated himself within her heart. The stars above her were brighter than before they had fallen asleep. Among the glittering diamond dust was a star directly overhead, dazzling like a beacon of hope to her damaged heart. Natasha slowly blinked her filling eyes; the tears slid down her temples. She had fallen in love with him. As if Bane had heard her silent admission, his hand grasped her hip and drew her under him. He burrowed into Natasha farther, kissed her neck and sighed. Content and peaceful, she had fallen back asleep. Natasha felt that peace now.

They walked hand in hand to the guesthouse and left the glass and bottle on a tray outside the kitchen door. After a shower and breakfast, Natasha and Bane checked out of the guesthouse with a picnic lunch, courtesy of the cook. They had a day's drive ahead of them, which included at least two stops—the abandoned cheese farm outside Imouzzer du Kandar where the key had been found and the photos had been taken and Azrou to have lunch.

✄ ▨ ❀ ✄

Natasha's eyes moved from studying the grainy black-and-white photos to looking out at the beautiful scenery while Bane drove toward Imouzzer du Kandar, another small town at a higher elevation. Nothing remotely similar jumped out at her. "I'll resume my photo reconnaissance after we are on the outskirts."

The Jeep passed through Imouzzer du Kandar and continued to climb upward. Soon they were surrounded by thick cedar. Natasha was quiet, lost in the lush scenery.

"Nat?"

"Hmm?"

"Okay if I open the windows?"

"Sure. I'm glad we're trying to find the farm. I need to see it, see if it sparks any memories. The photos don't. There're no dates on the photos."

Bane grimaced and shook his head. "I don't know. All the clues we've come across indicate the farm might be significant."

Cool air and the scent of cedar wafted into the car. Natasha grabbed her jacket from the back seat and slipped it over her head. "Do you think the farm is totally gone or built over? That's common."

"I guess we'll find out." Bane began to roll the windows back up.

Natasha waggled her head. "No, don't." She inhaled audibly. "It smells wonderful. The cook told me there's a pretty waterfall on the outskirts of Azrou, in the Cèdre Gouraud Forest, which begins at the junction of 8 and 13. He gave me directions. Want to stop there? Or we could eat while you drive. He packed us lunch."

"I'm up for it after we check out the abandoned farm."

❖ ❖ ❖ ❖

"Slow down! I think that might have been it," she said, waving the photos at him.

Bane pulled the Jeep onto the narrow shoulder and glanced over at the photos. His brow furrowed. "How in the hell did you spot that?" he asked, shifting into reverse, then entering the overgrown road.

She pointed at the decrepit sign hanging by its corner from a tall post barely visible in the tall brush. "You were focused on driving. I was focused on the photos."

The Jeep bumped along the deeply rutted dirt drive, torqueing Natasha and Bane in their seats. In the distance were a farmhouse and outbuildings made from local stone and mortar that had seen better days.

"Over there." Natasha pointed to the building farthest from them.

There were no vehicles or evidence of occupation. Natasha pulled their guns and extra mags from the glove compartment anyway and checked the safeties before handing Bane his. She concealed her SIG in her waistband and got her small flashlight from the bag behind her seat, then pulled the camera from the bag behind Bane's seat.

Bane snapped the Glock into the holster he had added to his webbed belt and pulled his shirt down to conceal it, then reached into the glove compartment again and retrieved a small black pouch and slipped it into the largest pocket of his field vest.

"Keep an eye out," he ordered before getting out and slinging the camera strap over his shoulder.

She exited the Jeep and walked next to him, her eyes sweeping all around them. They stopped at the structure that had been featured in two of the photos. Bane took off the lens cap, and then the camera whirred as he took a series of pictures. Though empty, the building still reeked of musk and urine.

"It smells like fucking piss on steroids." Bane blocked his nose and mouth with his forearm and kept walking. "They must have kept their bucks in here and never cleaned the floor."

Natasha's mouth and nose stung, and she wiped at her watery eyes. "What's a buck?"

"Cover your nose and mouth with your shirt or with your arm like I'm doing. It'll help," he said, his words muffled. "A buck is a male goat. They piss all over themselves and on everything during rut. The sexy scent you're picking up sends the does into heat. That's why goat cheese stinks."

"Jesus. I may never eat goat cheese again. Why the built-in benches?" Natasha asked, looking around. "Hey." She nodded at the dark, recessed area to their left. "Nine o'clock. I didn't notice anything on the exterior of that side of the barn when we walked up."

"I see it." He moved toward it. "Me either." A thin plank door sagged on its hinges even though it was padlocked. He raised the lock to pick it, but something had been shoved into it to prevent it from being opened. "The benches are for the goats. They're loafing benches, helps to keep them relaxed and productive." He raised the camera and took more photos.

No light showed through the visible space where it had pulled away from the jamb. He took photos of the interior before seizing the pitchfork leaning against the far wall and trying to pry the door open. Unsuccessful, he struck the door repeatedly, splintering the planks until the door was in pieces. Bane pulled the flashlight from his belt and turned it on, its light arcing over a darkened area beneath the structure. Dusty, uneven earthen steps led downward, disappearing into a black void.

"Hmm. What do we have here? I don't see a switch. Or a rail. Hold on to me."

Natasha turned on her flashlight, its beam moving between her and Bane's feet, enabling her to see before she stepped through the broken door. "Do you have goats on the farm? You seem to know an awful lot about them."

"My sister had some for 4-H."

"4-H?"

"An organization we were involved in as kids. Experiential learning. She focused on goats, ponies, and those damned chickens. I was focused on the outdoor programs, shooting, and rockets."

"This was in addition to school?"

"Yep. What'd you do in school besides drive the boys crazy?"

"Ouch!" she yelped in a hushed tone.

"You okay?"

"Uh-huh. Bumped my elbow," she said, rubbing it vigorously to get the sting out. "I studied hard and played volleyball. The boys didn't notice me."

Bane faced Natasha and guided her to him, stroking her bottom lip with the pad of his thumb. "The boys in your school had to be blind fuckers. Even when you were young, you were a beauty. I saw the evidence in your grandfather's office, sweetheart," he said, his lips capturing hers hungrily, his tongue thrusting into her mouth, seeking, wanting.

Natasha moaned, her tongue sliding over his, wanting more. Her hands traveled over Bane's ass and she pulled his pelvis to hers, loving the feeling of his rigid length pressing hard against her core. He drew away, panting. It was all she could do to keep herself in check.

"So damned tempting," he panted, resting his forehead on hers, then pressing a kiss to her temple.

Her breathing matched his. "We're too exposed, and this place stinks."

"Yeah," he said, separating from her and sweeping the large windowless room with his flashlight, then directing the beam slowly in a grid pattern. "Watch your head. The ceiling is low and uneven." He took more photos with a flash. The parts of the walls were lined with stone that looked to be the same used on the exterior, likely for reinforcement. The room was full of wooden crates and pallets and metal shelves. Most of them were empty.

"It smells much better down here." Natasha stilled his hand. "Fresh, as if it has its own air supply. There." Her flashlight paused between two rows of shelves, its beam shining through a haphazard stack of crates. Bane's additional light accentuated the subtle difference. "Another door?"

He took photos of the room.

They moved the crates away from the wall and Bane ran his fingers around the perimeter. Nothing. He passed the flashlight over the surface. There, below his knees, where it had been hidden by the crates, was an ancient warded lock in the center of the camouflaged door.

Bane studied it. The camera whirred as the shutter took a series of pictures. "Do you notice a key anywhere?"

"No. Can you just bust it open?"

"Nope. The lock is built into the door. I'm going to have to pick it. Stay alert," Bane said, glancing around again before dropping to his knees and putting the flashlight in his mouth.

He clamped his teeth around it and directed the beam to the lock. He pulled the small black pouch from his hip pocket and extracted a rake tool and tension wrench, carefully inserting them and feeling around patiently, yet working efficiently. *Click.* The lock creaked with indignation as Bane worked the lock and the door lost its valiant effort to remain closed.

"Interesting." The thick wood had been coated with the same treatment as the exposed walls. "Ready?"

"Yes." Another set of steps appeared in Natasha's beam, and beyond where her flashlight illuminated was utter darkness. She moved her flashlight, its ray bouncing off the low overhead. "The steps are really steep," she said, moving forward cautiously.

⚜ ❈ ✴ ⚜

Bane hugged her to him protectively, stopping her movement. "I'll go first." He weighed the challenge that lay before him. It was impossible for him to stand or to squat. "Damn. These were made for a munchkin. I'm going to crab crawl. Light my path as much as you can." He scuttled down the steps slowly, the camera bouncing lightly against his chest, then sat. "I'm at the bottom," he called up, turning on his flashlight, shining it overhead. "I can't stand because the ceiling is so low, probably four feet or less. The room is larger than the shed we came through, but the ceiling is lower. It's earthen. Looks solid." He scuttled around the perimeter of the room, following the beam as he moved it around the space, trying to avoid hitting or grazing his head on the rough ceiling. Piles of Amazigh blankets were folded neatly in corners and along the edges of the room, and there was something else.

"Nat? You gotta see this," he said, animated, flipping over to all fours. It was more comfortable than walking bent over and trying to look up. "Come on down like I did. Take your time and stay close to the steps."

⚜ ❈ ✴ ⚜

Natasha scooted next to Bane and parked herself, her backside tender from jarring herself on a few of the steps on her way down. She cautiously knelt next to him and brushed her hands together, knocking

off most of the debris. Her head brushed the uneven ceiling, so she sat on her haunches. "Show me what has you so excited."

"Tunnels."

"A central access point," Natasha said, scooching backward, straining to see a switch, her eyes following the exposed wires running from each of the tunnels and along the walls where they met the ceiling. The lines merged near the top of the steps and disappeared. She glanced over the side. The male and female connectors dangled unplugged. Natasha broke out in a sweat when she realized she had almost brushed it when clamoring down the dirt steps.

"Possibly hot, even though they're corroded and dirty," Bane said, suddenly next to her, his brow creased, expression serious. He zoomed in with the camera. "Don't touch them."

"The farm is abandoned. I doubt there's electricity."

Bane shook his head. "You never know. Let's err on the side of caution."

"At least it's clean and it doesn't smell."

"There's that. I could see enough with my flashlight to know the tunnels are reinforced." He held her gaze. "I wonder where they go."

She studied everything her flashlight illuminated, which was little but disappearing black voids. Blacker than black. Bane followed her light with the camera. A panicky feeling came over Natasha—the lack of light was definitely unsettling. The wet, sulfurous-smelling black cave that haunted her dreams came roaring into the present. Natasha's heart raced and her throat began to close. "I have to get out of here," she croaked. "I can't breathe."

"You're okay. Focus on me," he said, helping her scramble up the steps to the room with the crates. "Breathe, Nat. I'm right next to you. Look at me. Breathe with me."

Natasha focused on Bane, matching her breathing to his. The panic subsided.

He pushed her hair away from her face tenderly. "Keep breathing. You're doing great. In and out, nice and slow."

"I feel better."

His brows rose. "Are you sure?"

She inhaled and nodded.

"Let's go then." He took her hand and they walked through the foul-smelling shed and into the sunshine where Bane pulled her next to his hip

and walked her to their Jeep. He helped her in and secured her seat belt, then cupped her chin and gave her a long kiss. When he pulled back, his expression was one of concern. Bane pressed his forehead to Natasha's before giving her one last kiss and getting into his seat. They put their guns in the glove compartment and pulled out of the property, leaving a ribbon of dust in their wake.

Natasha rubbed her upper arms briskly. "I'm sorry. That's never happened to me. Oh my god." She sat back and closed her eyes and took another deep breath. "Dammit! Leaving is driving me crazy. I wanted to explore more, but…"

"You really didn't want to go in them, did you?" His eyes darted to her and then concentrated on the tree-lined, curving freeway.

Natasha shook her head. "No."

"They make you think of the cave in Guatemala?"

Natasha nodded hard once. Her breath was shaky as she inhaled.

Bane reached over and squeezed her knee gently.

"How could the team that went in and found the key and took the photos have missed that hidden door?" She opened her eyes and sat up in the seat.

"Remember they were called out."

"That's right, and it was suspect." Natasha frowned as she considered the possibilities. "I think a team should come back out and check the farm, find out where those tunnels lead, what they were used for." She slid her phone from the front pocket of her khakis. "I'm calling Emmet and giving him an update."

※ ※ ※ ※

After trekking through the magnificent cedar trees, Natasha and Bane arrived at the waterfall and looked for a spot to eat their lunch.

"This is beautiful. A nice break in what's going to be a long day," Natasha said, sitting on the mostly flat surface of a large boulder bordering the bank. To her right, shallow water rushed over low rocks, burbling and glittering where the sunlight shone, enhancing the scent of cedar.

"We have company." Bane sounded amused and sat next to Natasha, his hips grazing hers, sending tantalizing chills racing over her skin that had nothing to do with the occasional spray sprinkling her exposed arms.

Natasha followed his gaze, observing a small troop of Barbary macaque monkeys approaching them, their facial expressions evident in the soft-pink skin of their faces—curiosity and confidence. "Unfortunately, they have no fear of humans and sometimes they're truculent. People have been feeding them forever. They're a big tourist draw here."

"Great. They're cute, but I wasn't planning on entertaining or getting into it with apes."

Natasha pulled a medium-sized white paper sack out of her rucksack.

"What are you doing?" Bane grabbed at her leg and steadied her. "Sit."

"Keeping them at a distance." Her hand dipped into the sack and came out with a handful of unshelled peanuts. She threw the peanuts past the monkeys. "That should keep them busy for a while." She dug into her lunch with gusto—smoked aubergine dip, bread, olives, hard-boiled eggs, dates, and figs. "Thanks," she said with her mouth full, then swallowed. "The next round is yours. I'm betting you can throw farther than me." She handed him the bag, which he stuck under his thigh.

Bane wiped a spot of dip off the corner of her lips and sucked it off his finger, the wicked glint in his eyes sending delicious tingles rioting through her body. He smiled knowingly. "Where'd you get the peanuts?"

She cleared her throat. "You love doing that, don't you?"

"What?" he asked innocently.

"Toying with me."

The timbre of voice deepened. "Am I? Or is it you thinking about what we do when we have private time?"

Natasha licked her lips unconsciously as she studied Bane. He was mouthwatering. His powerful, ripped body radiated sexual prowess and was more heavenly than she ever could have imagined. His ever-changing hazel eyes and handsome face were the icing on the cake. A movie of the two of them naked, mouths and hands wild, thrusting, her quaking, played over in her mind. Her palms itched to touch his skin.

He groaned, a guttural sound that made her ache. "Sweetheart, I'm battling a massive hard-on here."

"Oh." Natasha blinked, then smiled lazily and rounded her eyes at him. "Sorry?"

"Sorry, my ass." He leaned in, his breath whispering over her lips. "I'm looking forward to tonight." Bane reared back suddenly. "What the fuck?"

Two stealthy macaques had come up on him. One tugged at the white bag sandwiched under his thigh and glowered at him.

Natasha smirked at him. "As I said earlier, they can be aggressive, and you certainly don't want to be bitten. Let them have the bag."

He lifted his thigh to allow the monkeys to take the sack. They scampered off to a distance and were joined by the others. Wrestling, shrill barking, and lip smacking ensued as they fought over the contents.

"One of the stores in Bhalil."

Bane turned from watching the macaques squabble. "Huh?"

"Where I got the peanuts. Yesterday, while you were so engrossed in taking pictures. Just in case. I was hoping we'd stop here."

He grinned and gave her a quick peck on the lips. "You continue to surprise me." Bane ate with as much relish as Natasha did. "Damn. This is really good."

"Eat up. I have tea in my thermos," she said, unscrewing the top and handing him the cup before detaching the other cup from the bottom. She filled both to just below the brim. Natasha leaned against a large cedar, watching the monkeys that were observing them with renewed interest.

"We need to go. They look like they're going to approach again."

"I'd like to finish my tea."

Bane placed his cup on the boulder and stood, spreading his arms and displaying his empty palms. The macaques moved away, disappearing in the forest of cedar. He sat back down and sipped at his tea, then held the cup out to Natasha for a refill. "You can enjoy your tea now. Tell me what happened at the farm."

"That last room… I don't know, Bane," she said, hugging her knees and holding her cup between them. "It really bothered me. Jesus. It felt malevolent, like that cave under the temple in Guatemala. My nightmare became a daymare."

Bane scooted closer to her. "We're out of there. We're not going back. Don't allow what happened in Guatemala to have power over you."

Natasha gave him a long look as she finished her tea. "Emmet also said Rafiq's people will arrive in Tinghir early tomorrow and it's unlikely we'll see them unless something changes. I wish Rafiq could have been part of the operation."

Bane stood and stepped off the boulder, assisting Natasha to the flatter ground and pulling her into his arms. He locked his hazel eyes on her gray

ones. "Rafiq is recovering; he's going to be fine." Bane glanced at his watch and grimaced. "Let's go. We've easily another six hours of driving."

"You can go without eating for that long?"

"Um, good point. We'll have to stop and feed me. You're going to get hungry too."

"I have another idea. Let's pop into Azrou, top off the tank, and get some more water and food to go." She patted her rucksack.

✄ ▨ ❀ ✄

Once in the Jeep, Bane said solemnly, "There's one more thing before we get on the road." He withdrew something from his pocket and opened his hand. "The edge of this was peeking out from the crevice where the floor met the wall in the tunnel room, practically hidden by one of the piles of blankets." Carefully he smoothed out the yellowed, torn paper on his leg.

le fantôme, Allamel, Asilah

Natasha's words whooshed out. "What in holy hell? This can't be a coincidence."

"No. I don't think so either. It indicates that the key found at the farmhouse was the same that was in your grandfather's possession, the same that was missing from his effects."

"The key to Mémé's safe-deposit box. The same one I received by courier in Cape Town."

"Exactly, and it also seems to support that the farmhouse has been a locale for the American and they overlooked this bit of paper somehow, or it no longer held any significance for the network. The fact that the room was a cool, dry environment must have preserved it."

"The American murdered Pépé," Natasha choked, her eyes round with disbelief, her hand going to her chest. She looked away, her lip trembling.

"Come here," he said, gathering Natasha close and stroking her head, kissing it. She fought her tears, wiping them as soon as they ran from her eyes. Bane pulled her to his broad shoulder and rubbed her back. "Let it go, sweetheart."

And she did.

chapter 34

NATASHA AND BANE REACHED THE outskirts of Tinghir after the last of the ripped tissue-paper pinks and oranges disappeared from the sky. Around them were the fading shadows of the vast palm orchard bordering the Todra River, which created an oasis the city was known for. Farther ahead was the gorge. Natasha was eager to explore Tinghir in the morning.

They arrived at the hotel, presented passports, and took their luggage to the room. The air charged as soon as Bane shut the door behind him. The tension thickened—vibrating, anticipatory. Impatiently, he yanked his tee over his head and tossed it to the floor while walking toward her. His hands drifted to his belt.

"Clothes off, sweetheart. It's been a long day. We need each other. I want to fill you up, feel you milk me dry as you come undone."

His olive-toned skin glowed and the tattoos inking his skin took on extra definition in the moonlight. His jeans and boxers cascaded to the floor and he kicked them aside. He was naked. Glorious.

Natasha's pulse hammered as Bane's malachite gaze sizzled through her. They had taunted each other all day. She was more than primed and couldn't look away from his long, thick length beckoning her. The punch of arousal made her ache, and a delicious heaviness coiled in her belly. God, how she wanted him, needed him.

His smile was feral, his expression hungry.

A rush of moisture soaked her red lace thong and her hands shook as she relieved herself of her shirt and khakis, tossing them to the chair in the corner of their room. She reached behind to unclasp her matching demi-bra.

"Nice," he hissed though his teeth, his nostrils flaring. "Leave it on. The panties too." His hazel eyes locked with hers with intensity as his fingers whispered over the maddening pulse in her neck and trailed down to the hollow between her collarbones. His fingers dipped inside the top of the lace bra, finding her achingly sensitive nipples.

Bane captured her moan with his mouth, devouring her with his lips and tongue. He guided Natasha's hands to cup him, his heavy breathing matching hers. "Feel how ready I am for you." His fingers trailed across her belly and teased along the fine edge of her thong. "Are you as ready for me, beauty?"

Natasha's thighs quivered and parted, seeking more.

⚜ ▨ ✺ ⚜

Lantern light flickered over their damp skin. Bane had passed out after emptying himself, chasing her shattering release, and slept soundly, tired from driving all day and sated from their lovemaking.

Wide awake, Natasha's mind turned over everything that pointed to the stark truth—her grandfather had been murdered by the American. Her eyes still felt gritty from crying earlier. Her grief over losing him was fresh again, but this time was mixed with anger and questions, one of which was the extent of Pépé's involvement in the American.

She flipped on her side and propped her head up with her hand, sidling closer, seeking the warmth of Bane's skin and his heady, male scent. The delicate skin of Natasha's upper thighs and breasts was chafed where the stubble of his beard had branded her.

Bane's skin quivered where her fingers trailed over his powerful shoulder, the intertwined tattoos that began there and covered his corded upper arm, chest, and obliques. She noticed for the first time the scar tissue skillfully camouflaged within the artwork below his rib cage. What had happened? She lingered on the area, kissing it tenderly before nibbling on his hip bone, her gaze drifting to the vee of his flat lower abs, elusive beneath the rumpled sheet.

Bane ran his finger over the curve of her hip, murmuring in a groggy voice, "Much lower and I'm a goner."

"Hi." Natasha turned her head and rested it on his abs, smiling softly. "You were sleeping soundly. Sorry, mm, I got carried away," she purred, stroking his straining thickness. "So you're awake."

Bane's knuckles tenderly grazed her cheek. "Yeah, that kind of attention quickly brings me to full mast. As much as I'd enjoy another round with you, beauty, I'd like a shower and food. In that order."

Natasha sat up and straddled him. "Are you sure?" She pouted.

He sat up and kissed her as he moved her off him. "Duty calls. We need to be seen and start leaving bread crumbs for anyone who might be watching. Let's walk into the heart of Tinghir and eat."

Natasha drew the sheet around her and settled into the pillows. Her phone buzzed and she checked the screen before answering it. "Good evening, Emmet... Yes. We're headed to a late dinner... I see. ... What?" A shadow passed over her and she sat forward. "That's extremely disappointing. Italy? Are you certain? Okay. I'll share with him. Yes. That too. Bye," she said, glancing at Bane with a ghost of a smile and disconnecting the call.

"Share." Bane drew curlicues over her exposed back, raising goose bumps and her pulse.

"I can't think when you touch me like that."

Bane drew the sheet up to his waist, folded his hands over his crotch, and cocked an eyebrow at her. "Better?"

Natasha gave him a steely look. "The latest reports are credible. There's an active cell operating here that's implicated in the disappearances of the *Homo sapiens* and the codex. Furthermore, chatter says the codex you and I are trying to repatriate is in Italy. Where or with whom is yet to be determined and confirmed. And Emmet said to turn on your bloody phone. He tried to ring you first."

Bane looked over to the nightstand and flipped his phone over. It was dead. Apparently in his haze of passion, he'd forgotten to recharge it. Not good.

"Any word on the farm?" he asked, plugging the phone in. "Or the *Homo sapiens*? Let's multitask." He padded toward the bathroom. "Bring me up to speed on what Emmet said."

Natasha followed, continuing to talk while Bane turned on the shower and waited for warmer water. "The farm was abandoned," she said, trying to focus on relaying Emmet's information instead of recalling that the

scratches marring his skin were where she'd raked his back while she rode him hard in the Jeep.

The lean, sculpted muscles of his back coiled and slid over each other as he moved, mesmerizing her. His torso tapered from broad shoulders into narrow hips and a perfect ass, cut, concave flanks extending into powerful thighs. She secured her hair into a bun with a band lying on the sink edge.

"No recording devices or surveillance equipment. No electricity."

The soft spray of the water hit her face when Bane pulled her in. Natasha blinked her eyes and blew the water out of her mouth.

Bane soaped his body and rinsed quickly, then handed Natasha the soap before stepping out and wrapping a towel around his middle. "He sent more than one team in?"

"Yes, but I didn't ask how many." Natasha showered just as quickly, talking over the water. She turned off the faucet and accepted the towel Bane handed her. "The teams were forced to stop where the tunnels were sealed. We really don't have any additional information than what we already know."

"Except we can assume the American knows someone is nosing around and there is an active cell here in Tinghir."

"Correct." She passed him her lotion. "If you don't mind."

✠ ▨ ❂ ✕

Natasha's mouth watered when the restaurant's specialty of chicken in tomatoes and onions was set on their table. Without thinking, she reached for the bread with her left hand, immediately withdrawing it when she noticed disapproving looks in her peripheral vision. Jesus. How easily she forgot. With her right hand, she scooped half of it onto her plate with the bread, leaving a trail of dribbled sauce all over the table.

"Thanks for leaving me some."

Her silver eyes flashed at Bane. "I did."

"I wasn't sure. You're kinda territorial about it."

The waitstaff was back with skewers of lamb and vegetables, couscous, salad, and other accompaniments. He helped himself to a generous portion and then leaned back in his chair, fully amused. "You want help?"

She concentrated on bringing the food to her mouth, her hand not obeying her brain. "I can manage."

"I can't wait to see this." He chuckled.

Natasha shot him a shitty look and shoveled the food into her mouth. What did not make it in plopped onto the napkin on her lap.

Bane laughed louder. "I've gotta get a bite or two down before you try to take another or I'm afraid I'll choke."

Irritation filled her. She gave him the evil eye and shoveled another helping of the delicious food in as if to prove a point. More of it landed in her lap.

His chair scraped the wooden planks of the second-story terrace as he pushed it back to rise. "You do not disappoint." He smirked, sitting beside her. "Mercurial. Stubborn as fuck."

She swallowed and sipped her tea. "Why are you on my side of the table?"

"I came over to help my wife manage. It's one of the many things a husband does. One of the many ways he takes care of her," he purred, lifting his eyebrows.

"Bane? Really? Here?"

"Sure. No one can hear me but you. No one except us knows how we take care of one another. I've told you, wanting you is a constant. We're having dinner with a number of Europeans, which allows me to push the cultural boundaries. In fact—" He inclined his head and flicked his eyes to the left. "By the stairs. Some people we know have shown up while you were struggling with your meal. Let's invite them to eat with us."

Natasha's eyes swept the busy room as she wiped her mouth with the napkin, then landed on Connor and Zach, who were turned away from them, talking animatedly. *What the hell?* The young men were supposed to be in Egypt.

The cousins turned. Natasha and Bane waved the young men over.

Smiles plastered their faces. "Bane! Natasha!"

Bane stood and gave each of them a man hug. "Join us."

Zach took in the mess in front of Natasha and cracked a grin. "Looks like someone lost the battle."

"That would be me." Natasha chuckled. "I'll win the dessert."

Bane laughed and sat down, motioning to the two empty chairs at their table. "That she will. I thought you two were headed to Egypt."

Zach gave Connor a cool look before answering. "We were supposed to be there, but someone overslept. We missed our flight. So change of

plans. We'll check this area out and grab a flight from Ouarzazate to Cairo."

Connor looked sheepish.

"Have you guys eaten?" Bane asked.

"We did," Connor said. "We were coming in for beers."

Zach stared his cousin down. "But we decided against it."

A waitress materialized next to the table, asking if anyone wanted anything else to eat.

"I'll take some baklava please," Natasha said. "Bane?"

"Nothing for me, thanks. Connor? Zach?"

"We're going to leave you two to your evening," Zach said.

They said their goodbyes and left.

Bane asked the waitress to take a picture of Natasha and him before they left. "I can't have this camera with me and not use it, right?" he said quietly when she shot him a questioning look. "Say cheese." He grinned at Natasha and pulled her next to him, then smiled for the camera. The waitress took a few photos and handed the camera back to Bane. He scanned through the pictures in the display screen with Natasha, then gazed deeply into her eyes. The couple in the photos looked genuinely happy, as if they truly belonged together.

"Winner takes all tonight, sweetheart."

His deep Indiana drawl and not-too-subtle promise made her body hum. "I'm all in." She smiled.

⚎ ⚌ ⚌ ⚎

Natasha and Bane headed toward their hotel, passing by the quiet vendor stalls lining the sidewalk in front of the restaurant.

"We'll visit the *souk* and other shops tomorrow," she said and followed up with the nightly phone call to Emmet.

"We have a fish on the hook. ART has fielded several phone calls. Stay alert."

"That's good news. I'll let Bane know."

"Talk with you tomorrow."

Bane frowned when his phone vibrated. "Emmet."

"Brilliant." Emmet huffed. "Apparently Natasha relayed my message."

"I crashed without charging it."

"I see," Emmet said, his tone conveying otherwise. "There was no charger in your vehicle?"

"Natasha's. We were streaming music through her phone. My portable was in my bag. It won't happen again," he said and meant it. It was a mistake, one that could have cost them. "I don't need to be chastised by you. We'll talk tomorrow. Night."

on the hunt

للي يخاف من العفريت يطلع له.

❊ ❊

Beware of the ghost.

❊

chapter 35

NATASHA EASED OUT OF BANE'S arms and slid on his tee, which hit her midthigh. She opened the doors that led to a lovely balcony and stepped out. It was late. She yawned and stretched, exposing more of her skin to the cool night, then wrapped her arms about her middle and considered their surreal predicament as she gazed at the diamonds sparkling in the deep indigo sky; they had successfully engaged the American. In the distance, the back half of the Jeep was just visible, softly illuminated by an overhead light in the private parking lot.

Natasha pivoted. Bane had spread out on his back, taking up most of their bed, slumbering away, his Glock loaded and on the nightstand. Her SIG was under her pillow. She stared at this bigger-than-life man she had only known for days, this man her soul had known forever.

Natasha traced the Fatima on her wrist. Bane had kissed it earlier, then drawn it into his mouth tenderly, his glowing eyes watching her as he pumped deeply into her. She had cried out, her body quaking and shattering deliciously.

Only after he emptied himself into her did Bane stop nibbling. "Soul to soul," he had whispered, panting, and then kissed her tattoo again. She had nestled into him, sated for now, their pounding hearts returning to normal. Bane had kissed at the juncture of where her neck met her shoulder, his hand splaying her belly, making Natasha feel cherished and protected. Safe.

"You're my heaven, beauty," he had breathed in her ear.

253

Natasha had swallowed her surprise and blinked moist eyes, realizing Bane was her heaven as well and that she had fallen in love with him. She pressed her lips to the Fatima on her wrist and prayed silently. *"Let no sadness come to my heart. Let no trouble come to my arms. Let no conflict come to my eyes. Let my soul be filled with the blessing of joy and peace."*

Natasha closed the balcony doors behind her and secured them against entry. She pulled Bane's tee off and slid under the sheet, naked again, trying not to disturb him.

But Bane clearly sensed Natasha and turned on his side, reaching out and hooking her around her hips, drawing her against him, spooning her. He buried his face in her hair and inhaled, then breathed out. "I love you, Nat."

I love you too. Natasha's heart smiled and her soul filled. She was asleep in minutes.

⚜ ⊠ ❀ ⚜

They rose early, showered, and packed, their plan in place. After breakfast, Natasha and Bane checked out and headed into the town center to find other lodging, sticking to SOP. It was early, so they left their bags with the front desk of a bed-and-breakfast off the long garden square and began reconnaissance in the bustling *souk*, continually sweeping their surroundings for anyone who seemed suspicious. They looked like tourists—Natasha with her oversized tote and Bane with the camera slung over his shoulder. By midmorning they were ready to leave.

Bane veered off at the next right, Natasha at his side, easily keeping up with Bane's long, easy stride. The cacophony of the vendors lessened as they walked farther from the center of the *souk*, and the alley broadened into a narrow street with established shops with more alleys shooting off in other directions. They slowed, then took a left, continuing to take rights and lefts, walking the labyrinth leisurely, cautiously. Occasionally one of them paused at a shop to access the wares while the other watched in their peripheral vision.

"Anything?"

"No, but… Wait a minute. Up ahead." Natasha's eyes moved back and forth. She picked up her pace, her attention on a shop ahead to their left. "I'm going antiquing. Wait a few minutes, then follow me."

Bane slowed and kept an eye on her until she had entered the shop, bringing his camera up and snapping photos of his surroundings. To anyone watching, he was enamored with Moroccan culture.

The first thing Natasha noticed upon entering was that the small shop was filthy and smelled far older than the Amazigh items displayed. String and wind instruments and drums, local pottery and crafts, and bellows, which were much needed by people living in the higher altitudes, packed the place full to bursting.

Her interest piqued when she saw footprints on the dirty floor. They looked to be fresh and of differing sizes; in one set, the right foot dragged slightly and consistently. The footprints passed through the door at the back of the shop, into what appeared to be a storeroom. Her gut told her she was in the midst of a cache created by a serious collector or held by a middleman.

Natasha's eyes grew huge. Ahead of her, propped against the stairs, broken slabs of cave art were revealed through torn white cloth, as well as large carved human figures and a wooden door. She would have to get up close and personal to determine if the artifacts were authentic and ancient, and she stepped forward, intending to examine them.

A shuffling noise to her left stopped her. Similar to the market where the merchants were primarily men, one observed her now, warily from the side of the store, like a cat. He stooped under the weight of age and had a scraggly soul patch on his chin. The eyes in his deeply lined face drifted over every inch of her—from the sunglasses perched atop her loose hair to the long-sleeved cream-colored travel shirt and belted khakis to her sturdy, broken-in leather boots. His eyes then met hers. He scowled and gestured toward the front entrance, indicating she was to leave.

Natasha's eyes flashed at him. In Arabic, she said she wished to speak to the shop owner.

Soul Patch said he was the owner and shuffled unsteadily forward, possibly hoping to intimidate her.

"Do you speak English?" she asked, smiling disarmingly, hoping her hunch was right. How else would the man be able to navigate within the American's network if he was unable to communicate with all parties?

"A little," he said cautiously.

"I'm Natasha Rua. I represent clients who are looking for something special," she said at a slower cadence than normal. "I wish to take a look at your treasures in the back room. Those wooden sculptures, are they authentic Dogon?" She referred to the West African tribal art and offered him one of the ART business cards.

"They are already bought," he said before accepting the card from her.

"I see. May I look at them anyway?"

"I am Amastan." He squinted at her, then read the card. The shopkeeper seemed to weigh his answer before nodding perceptibly and motioning for her to follow.

She adjusted her height to clear the low, scarred header and stepped into the storage room. Dust motes danced freely in the feeble rays of sunlight filtering through the dingy and broken high window. It was enough for Natasha to see that what was in the room was authentic and priceless. She pulled a pair of gloves from her tote to further inspect the two large, carved hermaphrodite silhouettes that had to be close to seven feet tall.

"Exquisite," she whispered, extending her fingers.

A bell tinkled in the front of the shop. Amastan barked, "No touching."

Behind her, she felt Bane's protective presence. His voice rumbled, causing Amastan to jump. "There you are! One minute you were with me and the next you were gone. What'd you find?"

"This is Amastan. He's the shopkeeper of this fine establishment, and we're in luck. He speaks English."

"Great. That will make our talk much easier. Why don't you take a seat, Amastan," Bane quietly suggested to him, pointing to the leather pouf in the corner of the poorly lit room. His size and demeanor were enough to terrify the man, who was markedly shorter than Natasha. "I only want to ask you questions. And my wife… Sweetie, are we buying these?"

"I wish," Natasha said, ad-libbing with Bane. "They're sold, but I want to have a close look. I've never seen Dogon this large outside of a museum."

Bane looked at Amastan and handed him a wad of cash. "Maybe you'll reconsider?"

"No," he muttered, attempting to hand the bills back to Bane.

Bane closed the man's fist firmly around the money and pushed it back at him. "Why don't you just hold on to that for now while we talk?" His inquisition of the shopkeeper proceeded. "How long have you had your shop?"

"Many years," Amastan said, and then his mouth ran like a full-on faucet, muttering between Arabic and Berber while his wild eyes bounced between Natasha and Bane.

"English, Amastan."

"No pictures," Amastan whined.

"Why not?" Bane asked.

Amastan didn't answer him.

"We are going to take pictures," Natasha said, taking several with her phone. "And I promise I'll be very careful with my examination."

"I'd like some too." Bane removed the lens cap and handed the camera to Natasha. "Tell us about your shop. All the way back to its beginning." He leaned against the wall opposite the visibly shaking man and crossed his arms in front of his chest.

"I have customers."

"You do. Us. And we're inquiring about your inventory because we're very interested, aren't we?"

Natasha faced Bane, tilted her head, and grinned. "We certainly are."

"Is there anyone else in Tinghir that has this quality of inventory, Amastan?"

"No. I am the only one."

"Tell us how you came to be the only one."

"People have brought me very old things from Morocco and close countries for decades. A man from Casablanca visited me after the war, after my wife gave birth to our first child. We were very young. I had no money and I had debts. The man paid off my debts and helped me buy the shop—all in Moroccan dirham. I did what he asked. I had a good life."

"World War II?"

"Yes."

Bane whistled appreciatively. "That was a long time ago, Amastan."

"Yes. I am an old man."

Bane massaged the back of his neck. "What was your benefactor's name?"

Amastan shook his head, his skin turning sickly. "No."

"Come on, man."

"He referred to himself as the facilitator. He said he worked for an American. But the facilitator was French and drove a very old car even though he was wealthy."

"No other name?" Bane asked, pushing off the wall and straightening to his full six foot four.

Amastan shook his head back and forth fast.

"Why did you think he was wealthy?"

"He wore an expensive ring." The shopkeeper pointed to his right pinkie finger. "Gold, with a large ruby."

Natasha inhaled sharply and stopped what she was doing.

"Maybe it wasn't," Bane stated, testing him.

"It was. I know value."

He looked around the storeroom and nodded. "Okay, I'll give you that. How often did the facilitator visit you?"

"Only that time. He warned me to never speak of him or to explain my good fortune." Amastan spoke in a hushed voice.

"What happened after the facilitator took care of your debts and shop?"

"My shop became very busy. Things like wood carvings, ebony statues, jewels, and fossils showed up. Occasionally there were taped boxes labeled HANDCRAFTED. I looked in some of them and saw ancient ax heads, pottery shards, and flint stones. Glass beads."

"You are still busy all these years later."

"I am."

"What else has passed through here?" Bane prompted him.

"Bronzes, funerary items, a small Malian terra-cotta ram, human skulls and remains, and many other unique items."

"Human skulls and remains?" Natasha asked, removing her gloves and depositing them in her tote before standing next to Bane.

"Yes. A few times."

"How did those come to your shop?" she asked.

"They were dropped off by Moroccans and foreigners. Always men."

"And what happens up to the time they leave?"

"Each item is logged into a ledger with its arrival date. I store the relics in here and wait for a phone call and instructions. Sometimes once a month, sometimes more often. I am given instructions about when someone will pick up what I hold. I wrap the items for transport. I am paid in dirham before the shipment leaves my shop. I note the departure date, paid amount, and transport code in the ledger next to the item."

Natasha pulled another pouf from the top of a collection of blankets and rugs and sat facing him. "Do you know where any of the items go?"

"No. I was told not to ask, only to keep them safe in the back of the shop until they can be transported and to keep meticulous records."

"You were never curious?" Bane interjected.

"In the beginning rumors circulated within the community that confirmed I was not the only person storing relics to be shipped. A man in Azrou turned up missing after bragging about selling fine things out of his shop. His body was found months later in the cedar forest, his tongue and hands severed. People whispered that the American had killed him." Amastan shuddered. "I was not that curious. I have seven children, many grandchildren and great grandchildren, and a wife."

"So the name 'the American' was known?" Natasha asked, leaning forward.

Amastan looked down and bobbed his head, wringing his hands. He raised his eyes, his expression one of fear. "Are you the American?"

"I'm American, but not *the* American. We're looking for someone we can go into business with. My wife has a number of clients who want unique items, one of a kind. Price is no issue. Does that interest you?"

"I have a partner."

"Maybe you should consider expanding. Let's take a look at your books, Amastan, see if we want to go into business with you."

"I have a computer now."

"Let's see it."

"What happened to the ledgers?" Natasha asked.

"They were picked up by different facilitators. A facilitator never came more than once."

"Interesting," Bane commented.

Natasha narrowed her eyes. "All of them?"

Amastan's eyes flickered to the left. "Yes," he stammered.

"Aw, come on," Bane growled. "Lying isn't something you're good at, Amastan. Where are they?"

"In the cellar."

"You're going to produce the ledgers and show us the files. Now." He pushed off the wall and assisted Natasha to her feet.

Natasha held out her hand. "Give me the shop key, Amastan. The shop will be closed until we leave."

Amastan stared at Natasha with disdain.

"Do it," Bane said, pushing up into his full height. "Everything will be fine if you do as we ask. Up with you."

The shopkeeper's hand quaked as he extracted his key from his loose-fitting shirt and deposited it in Natasha's open hand. "I would like some water," he croaked before unfolding from the cushion and standing unsteadily.

"I'll go get water for all of us," Natasha offered. "There's a food store across the way." The bell above the front door rang as Natasha shut it behind her.

⚏ ▩ ❀ ⚎

Amastan led him downstairs into the tiny cellar and to a closet without a door that served as an office. The ceiling was low, forcing Bane to move while bent over. He glanced around, noting that Amastan had made a thick sleeping pallet out of blankets in another corner of the cellar. A small squat table covered with a beautiful cloth was next to it, and on top of it was a tea set and oil lamp on a metal tray. "You sleep here?"

"Sometimes deliveries and pickups are scheduled very early or very late. It's easier to stay here than go home."

"I see. Where are the ledgers?"

"I will get them."

"You tell me where they are. Have a seat." He motioned the shopkeeper next to the wall where he could keep an eye on him.

"Under the table."

Bane knelt down and lifted the covering of the table. Underneath was a metal box. He opened it, finding two books in bad condition that resembled the ledger Natasha had discovered in her grandfather's office. "Any others?"

"No."

Bane pulled the pallet apart and checked behind the papers littering the walls. He examined the walls, floor, ceiling, and solid steps. The desk Amastan used for his computer was planks of wood assembled without drawers or doors. Nothing.

"Okay. Get up. Open your program."

Amastan sat at on the spindly stool in front of the computer and began typing. The program appeared on-screen.

Bane stood behind Amastan, who was seated and sweating, taking photos of the entries. He tapped a pen on a torn sheet of paper next to the computer. "Now write down your log-in information and shut it down."

"What?"

"I'm confirming you gave me the correct information. Just in case I need to access it later if I have further questions. After all, we are considering a new business venture."

Amastan stared at Bane with dread, bobbing his head furiously as he scribbled the information on the paper and shut the program down.

"Make yourself comfortable," Bane said, setting the ledgers on the desktop and carefully straddling the small stool, unsure if it would hold his two hundred and twenty pounds. He opened them, the camera whirring as he took pictures of the log-in information and the numerous pages in the ledgers. He checked the images on the display screen as he went. "Good."

Amastan returned to where Bane had made him sit earlier.

Not long after, Natasha came down the steps as he was logging into the program.

"Low ceiling," she commented, unable to straighten.

"Yeah." Bane focused on what he was doing.

"Fill me in." She handed him a water and opened one herself before giving the last bottle to the sulking shopkeeper.

Bane whistled. "Look at this."

Natasha leaned over Bane. "Jesus!"

"Where are the others?" she asked Amastan.

Bane sat upright and stretched his back and opened his water.

"The facilitators took them when they came, and I was given a replacement."

Natasha fired another question at the shopkeeper. "So how is it you have these two?"

"There was a fire. I cook here because I am here during the day. The fire destroyed most of the merchandise, but I found these when the shop was being fixed, in that box that was under the table. It was in the

261

storeroom. I brought it downstairs. I think because almost everything was gone, the facilitator didn't ask for them. I have kept them hidden. The next facilitator set me up with my first computer."

"Let's head upstairs. It's time for you to reopen your shop, Amastan."

"Thank you for your hospitality," Natasha said, giving him his key back once they were back in the back room. "Maybe you'll reconsider the Dogon?"

"No. I told you the Dogon are sold."

"When is all this being picked up?" Natasha asked, motioning at the cave art, Dogon figurines, and door.

"The cave art and another large box are being picked up by two men today. They called to say they would be late."

Bane cocked his head and watched Amastan intensely. "Do you know who they are?"

"No. Only that they will be late."

"Did they give you a time?"

Amastan glanced at his phone. "An hour."

"We'll get going then," Natasha said, moving away from the relics. "Let you get on with your day. We may be back soon to try to talk you out of those Dogon even though they're sold. Offer more. My clients would love them for their collection."

"Regardless, we'll be in touch, Amastan. Keep the money. We look forward to doing business with you," Bane said, reaching out to shake the shopkeeper's hand before opening the door. "Enjoy the rest of your day."

⌗ ▨ ✦ ⌗

"I think we stay and wait, Nat," Bane said as soon as they left the shop. "See what the fuck this is. Maybe we've hit the jackpot."

"I agree," she said, crossing the narrow street.

"Where're we going?"

"As it so happens, there's a restaurant right next to the food store, where we can eat and keep an eye on the shop. See who shows up and what they leave with."

"You checked it out already,"

Her eyes rounded. "How'd you know?"

"I was watching you lick your lips in the cellar. Baklava?" He quirked an eyebrow and gave her a wry grin.

Natasha laughed guiltily. "They serve lunch too. We can eat on the balcony. I imagine you're hungry."

"Damn, I want to thank you properly for thinking of me."

"Later, handsome."

Bane groaned as they entered the restaurant.

chapter 36

NATASHA AND BANE WERE LED to the restaurant's small balcony, which they had all to themselves.

After ordering, she said, "So, let's have a look."

He brought up the first image in the display and handed her the camera. "There's a lot to scroll through."

"There's a lot here. The ledgers resemble the one from Pépé's office, although much worse for wear." She continued scrolling through the images, stopping on one that looked different. She enlarged it and moved it around on the screen with the arrow toggles, examining it closely. "Do you think Amastan will sing?"

"I think he'll be very careful. He has a large family and he kept the money I gave him."

Natasha inhaled sharply. "Where was this?" She handed Bane the camera.

He glanced at the image. "It was inside the back cover of the ledger. There was one in each of them."

"It's an ink stamp, *à l'Américain*. Signed and dated. There's a series of numbers and letters on the line above the American, maybe how the network kept track of their transactions," she said, bringing her chair next to his. "Oh my god! Look at the handwriting. It's Pépé's, and his initials. HLA. A different date and another series of numbers and letters."

"I'm betting this same stamp is on your grandfather's ledger. We didn't look through the entire ledger, just the first pages."

265

"It was him, Bane. Pépé was the facilitator. He wore a signet ring. Gold with a large ruby. It was missing when he was found," she stammered. "Why would Pépé risk these, of being incriminated?" she asked, aghast.

"I noticed your reaction in the shop." Bane covered her hand with his and rubbed the back of it with his other. "If your grandfather was the man you say he was, and I believe he was, sweetheart, he may have been coerced. Had something incredibly important held over his head to force him to do what the American wished."

Natasha's rounded eyes locked with his. She whispered, "His family."

"Yes," he answered, stroking her cheek softly.

❈ ❈ ❈ ❈

Thirty minutes later they observed Zach and Connor from the small balcony they had all to themselves. Zach pulled a large rolling cart with old rugs. Connor walked beside him and they proceeded at an unhurried pace as they came closer.

Bane looked through the viewfinder of the camera and adjusted the lens. *Snick, snick. Snick, snick.* "I'll be damned. Their frat boy act worked," he said admiringly and reached into the camera bag at his feet for a different lens.

Natasha slid off her chair and squatted, taking pictures through the balcony's latticework with her phone. She sent them off to Emmet immediately.

Bane took a few more pictures after he changed out the lenses, then laid the camera back on the table in front of him, waiting. "Call Emmet."

Zach parked the cart to the side of the shop's entrance and went inside. Connor kept watch, but he never looked up or he might have seen Natasha and Bane. Satisfied, he entered the shop.

"I discounted them too," she said, pushing her tagine away, hoping for another piece of the baklava she had had earlier. She rubbed Bane's broad back while he continued to watch the shop front and called Emmet to explain the current situation and the photos as well as what Zach and Connor had told them at the guesthouse in Bhalil and during their brief visit the night before in the restaurant. Emmet assured Natasha that the analysts would be on it immediately, then disconnected the call.

❈ ❈ ❈ ❈

Bane's phone rang not ten minutes later. "Emmet."

"The photos Natasha sent were helpful. We have positive identification."

"That was quick."

"Our analysts are among the best. The young men are mules for the American, recruited by their university professors who have ties to the American. Zachary Cokinos was recruited by Joseph Gates, a dean of African studies, and his cousin Connor Ritman was recruited by Miles Seager, the dean of the economics department. The professors came to the attention of INTERPOL two years ago. Also, and this is interesting, there are familial connections. Gates is Cokinos's maternal uncle and Segar is Ritman's. Natasha kept an eye on both of them until she was pulled off late last fall to watch Dr. Eric Schaus at another university. At the time, it was thought that he was the bigger fish."

"She's going to flip."

Natasha looked at Bane with concern, who held up a finger at her.

"Pardon? Sometimes I can't follow you."

"It's American slang for becoming upset."

Natasha mouthed *speaker*. Bane shook his head and hit the Mute button instead. "I'll fill you in ASAP. Keep watching," he said, then unmuted and continued listening to Emmet.

"INTERPOL's decision paid off. Regarding the cousins, what they told you and Natasha about their backgrounds checks out. Except for their itinerary and future plans in Cape Town. For some reason, they recently missed a scheduled flight to Cairo. Their travel destinations and dates coincide with the suspected American activity, most specifically the disappearance of the codex and the *Homo sapiens*." Bane heard a rustle of paper. "Either Cokinos and Ritman are not good at covering their tracks or they are supposed to deceive you, possibly to lure you and Natasha into a trap. They have been in Morocco since mid-May, just after they graduated, squeaking by, I might add, moving about in-country except for a recent trip to Italy aboard a private yacht. It looks as though they delivered the Ouarzazate Codex to a middleman in Italy who then sells the stolen artifacts. We're working on those details. Your focus now is solely on repatriating the *Homo sapiens*. That's all I have. We'll talk soon."

⚎ ⚏ ❊ ⚎

"Dessert?"

Natasha topped off their mint tea and smiled. "Of course."

Bane finished Natasha's meal and told the waitress who appeared that he and his wife would like baklava and the check.

Within minutes Amastan, Zach, and Connor came out of the shop with the unwieldy paper-wrapped cave art and carefully nested it within the blankets, then situated the box on top, securing all of it with rope and talking some more. They pointed toward the direction they had come from. Amastan shook his head and extended his hand, gesturing in the opposite direction.

"Directions?"

"Looks like it," she said, standing, pulling money from her pocket to cover the meal. "Let's go."

They met the waitress on the way down the stairs, exchanged money and baklava, and followed Zach and Connor at a safe distance back the way they had come.

※ ※ ※ ※

The young men took turns pulling the heavy cart over a mile away, along streets lined with numerous tired-looking, baked-clay buildings, and stopped in front of one in slightly better condition than those around it. An immense, dark wood door next to the overhead door was its only adornment. Connor beat the ringed knocker impatiently against the door until a face appeared behind the small grated window. Words were spoken and the overhead door opened. It shut immediately after they pulled the cart through. Natasha and Bane were unable to see anything else from their vantage point.

"As I see it, these are our options," Bane said. "We can go in tonight, without reconnaissance, not knowing if they patrol the building. Or we wait until tomorrow night when we have more insight. Pick your poison."

"Let's come back later tonight."

Bane gave her a long look and considered. "Tonight could go sideways. You ready to face that possibility?"

"I am. Based on what we've seen, there's a pattern of carelessness. One, Amastan was able to hold on to two of the ledgers, and two, Zach and Connor showed up with a cart in broad daylight. My gut tells me the level of carelessness extends to the building we're going into tonight. We

268

can take the day to read though the ledgers and take notes. Plan and prepare. Let's walk along the river on the way back, okay? It's roughly the same distance." She turned back.

Bane fell in beside her. In fifteen minutes, they arrived at their bed-and-breakfast and were given an early check-in.

※ ▨ ❀ ※

Once they were on the outskirts of the city center, the night became as dark as pitch. Cloud cover had moved in, extinguishing ambient light. It was their friend, providing additional cover for their purpose. But the darkness also slowed them down as they traversed the uneven surface of dirt, concrete, and stone.

Natasha kept her flashlight at her side, illuminating the ground just in front of her until she and Bane were close to the building Zach and Connor had entered with the overflowing cart. She and Bane wore small black tactical backpacks that blended in with their dark clothing. Natasha turned off the flashlight, latched it to her belt, and pulled the infrared goggles over her eyes. The IR illuminator Bane had affixed to the goggles enhanced detail and dimension. She could see Bane clearly in front of her, his heat signature giving him form.

He stopped, raised his left arm at a right angle with an open hand, and dropped into a crouch.

She stopped and dropped behind him. What had he seen or sensed? She hadn't picked up anything other than small rodents.

They stayed like that for several minutes until he stood and raised his arm above his shoulder, close-fisted, and pumped it in the air.

Natasha scurried behind him and flattened against the building and whispered, "I didn't see any heat signatures other than mice."

"They're fucking rats."

"Oh." Natasha gulped. Jesus, she hated rats.

"Something was moving. Uh… I can make it out now. It's some type of fabric. Let's go."

The front door was locked from the inside, as expected, so they went around to the back. A wall, roughly twelve feet at its tallest point, made of clay, straw, and branches, extended from the back, bordering a small outdoor space. It was in rough shape—sections had sheared off and standing in the rubble next to it was difficult.

Bane shook his head in disbelief. "This is bullshit. Nothing like an insecure perimeter."

"Maybe that's the point. The appearance negates anything of importance."

"Careless. Easy to breach."

"Yes," Natasha said, using her knife to test the softness. "I think we can scale it if we make footholds and use the branches to pull ourselves up."

Bane jabbed at the wall with his knife. "Shouldn't take long."

It took less than thirty minutes to create the necessary footholds, placing them where straw and branches provided more support.

He pulled paracord from his backpack and tied both lines to a scrappy tree, then tugged to make sure it would hold. "You go first since you're much lighter. If we have to, I'll bring you back immediately. Okay?"

"Okay."

They secured the cord to each of them, and Bane helped Natasha to the first foothold. She scrambled up quickly, clearly impressing him with her agility.

At the top, Natasha's hand slipped on the crumbling wall and she teetered, dropping to the other side and landing on her back in a pile of dirty blankets. "Oof! Jesus Christ!" She flipped up her goggles and did a mental inventory of her body after the hard fall. Nothing broken or sprained, but bruises and stiffness were going to be her constant companions in the coming days. The impact had jarred the goggles over the bridge of her nose. She might end up with black eyes too. Great.

"Nat?" Bane peered down from the top of the wall. He pushed up and over, sinking deeply into his landing next to her. "You okay?"

"I'm fine. Just had the wind knocked out of me," she said weakly, releasing herself from the paracord. "Give me a minute. I meant to land like you did, but the wall is falling apart. Dammit. I'm going to have some bruises."

Bane unhooked himself and glanced around. He knelt, leaning over her and flipping his goggles up. His thumb stroked her cheek, his eyes full of concern, pinning hers before he kissed her slowly.

She deepened the kiss, then pouted when he pulled back.

He sighed and kissed her again—perfunctorily—then helped Natasha to her feet and off the blankets. "Come on. Let's go exploring."

The back door was secured with a heavy chain and two padlocks. "Seriously?" Natasha whispered hoarsely. "Are you going to pick it?"

"Fuck no," Bane said, pulling a compact bolt cutter with folding handles from his backpack. He snapped the handles into place and cut through the chains easily. He folded the bolt cutter back up and slipped it back into his pack, then looked at Natasha. "If an escape is needed, remember there are no side doors, only the overhead and other door in the front, and no cover for us. Ready?"

"Yes," she said, pulling the goggles back over her eyes, then popping the snap on her holster and drawing her gun.

Bane drew his Glock, then opened the door. It creaked on its hinges, sounding ungodly loud in the silence. They waited a few moments. Nothing.

Natasha slipped inside first, her goggles not registering any heat signature or movement. She flipped them up and pulled her flashlight from her belt, balancing the gun on top. She slowly swept the room with the beam of light, ready to fire if necessary. *Holy God.* Natasha whistled appreciatively. "It's a warehouse. We've got a mother lode."

Whoever oversaw this leg of the operation within the American network was sloppy. Artifacts filled the enormous dusty room, which was roughly half the size of a soccer field. Two smaller rooms were off to Natasha's right—one appeared to be an office and the other a bathroom. The floor was covered in dirt and dust, and rough walls were cracking in many places. Many of the artifacts were strewn about without any seeming regard of their cultural and historical importance, yet others were organized on shelves made of wood planks and clay bricks against the long wall. Larger items leaned against the ancient walls—slabs containing cave art and engravings and a stone obelisk in a corner, at least fifteen feet tall. Next to them was what looked to be the cart Zach and Connor had delivered earlier in the day. Overhead lighting and a single large fan had been installed, certainly helpful in the windowless room. There was no evidence of cameras.

Natasha strolled over to the shelves to get a closer look at what they held. Behind her, she heard Bane do the same. He took photos of

everything that their beams illuminated, checking often to make sure the details were sharp.

"There're easily several moving vans of stuff in here."

"I know," she said, taking in the overflowing shelves. The enormity of what was in the vast room was stunning. Items from all over Africa, among them a bronze sculpture and plaques, an elaborate filigree-designed gold crown, soapstone birds and animals, and carved wood sculptures. Boxes of coins. Piles of human bones, bone fragments, and human skulls. One skull stared at Natasha, eye level. It seemed as if it was speaking, crying. She shivered and let out a shaky breath. "Do you think the *Homo sapiens* remains are here?"

"I don't know." Bane started to approach closer. "Safety your gun."

Natasha bobbed her head, too overcome by the level of theft, the looting of culture, to speak. She wanted to cry. Scream. Destroy the bastards.

"Nat..."

"Yes." Natasha holstered her SIG, then gazed at him, her soul filled with sadness.

Bane drew her into his arms and rubbed her back. His solid form helped her to calm down, to breathe more slowly.

"I'm good, thanks," she said, easing out of his arms. She approached the large metal cabinet between the two small rooms, pulling a drawer open and rifling through it. She searched more drawers, finding nothing of interest. The last drawer was locked. "I need your assistance."

Bane popped the lock easily with his tools and opened the drawer. Inside were several ledgers with papers tucked into them.

"These papers resemble those attached to the artifacts." Natasha angled one of the small papers and read it, then another and another. They were attached to the items with heavy thread. "The cataloging system, I believe. It must correlate to something else. I'm hoping the answer might be in the office," she said, walking toward it.

Bane followed, clearly anxious to leave. "We need to hurry—every minute we're here increases our risk."

"You sense something?" she asked, moving her beam over the computer on the scarred wooden surface of the desk. It was cool to the touch. She opened it and entered Amastan's password, sure there was no chance in hell it would work. "You've got to be kidding me. This is

their security?" She shook her head, clicked through a series of files until she found the one that stopped her. "Are they just lazy, or what?" She asked rhetorically, pulling a USB from the zipped inner compartment of her backpack and inserting it into the computer. She prayed the download was quick.

"Just a feeling. This has been too easy. It's bothering me. What do you have?"

"The more recent logs. We can compare them to Amastan's."

He inspected the printer and placed his hand on it. Cool to the touch. The tray was empty.

The file had downloaded.

"I certainly didn't expect to be able to access with Amastan's password." She had ejected the drive and was turning off the computer when a loud sound broke the silence.

"Front door. Let's go."

Natasha's heart pounded in her throat as she slid the slim books and drive into her backpack. She turned off her flashlight and adjusted the goggles over her eyes, following Bane out the back door, closing it as more noise sounded behind her. Someone had entered the building.

Bane hooked both of them onto their paracord, then walked the wall, pulling himself along until he reached the top. He flipped his leg over and straddled the wall, staying low.

"Up. Now," he whispered urgently.

Natasha scrambled up the wall, going over with Bane's assistance.

He jumped, again sinking deeply into his landing; it was a longer jump on this side of the wall. He unhooked himself and began gathering the cord. "Jump. I've got you."

Alarmed voices could be heard inside the building. Multiple men.

Natasha jumped, Bane cushioning her landing, unhooking her, and simultaneously gathering her cord. She freed the cord from the tree, and they took off at a dead run, staying against the buildings.

Behind them, the back door banged against the exterior wall and men yelled loudly. More banging. Car engines revving. Bane ran to the palm grove and down to the river, Natasha on his heels. The sound of the vehicles faded, and they slowed, heading toward where they had left their clothes and Natasha's tote earlier.

After making sure they were alone, Natasha fished around inside the backpack, sweating until her fingers found the USB and transferred it into the more secure compartment in her tote. They changed their clothes and secured the guns and knives and ammo in the tote, then placed her backpack in Bane's.

They kept to the river. Bane carried everything until they were a block from their bed-and-breakfast. The streets were quiet.

Natasha reached for her tote.

He pulled it away from her. "It's kinda heavy with guns, knives, and extra ammo in it."

"Only because you've been carrying it for fifteen minutes." She put her hands on her hips and asked, her eyebrows raised, "Am I weak?"

"You're fucking fierce," he said with admiration, handing the bag to her.

chapter 37

"THEY'RE DEFINITELY CONNECTED," NATASHA SAID, looking over Bane's shoulder. "Same cataloging system." She squeezed his powerful shoulders, then leaned over him, inhaling his clean, intoxicating scent, wanting to fall into bed with him and lose herself in all the sensations and emotions that he made her feel. Natasha exhaled and refocused, then traced her finger over the ledger pages displayed on the tablet. "Looks like a late-evening flight out of Ouarzazate tomorrow. And these numbers must be items that will be on the flight. Going where, I wonder?" She stood back up and stretched. Midnight had come and gone. Her earlier quick shower had not done much to address her aches.

"Switch places with me, Nat. I'll scroll through the camera, give you items with their tag info. You see if there's any corresponding info in this flight list and write it down." He sat on the bed.

Natasha got her notebook and a pen and placed them next to the computer. "Let's see if we have anything."

✄ ▨ ❀ ✄

Within thirty minutes it was clear that the majority, if not all, of the items in the warehouse were shipping out on the Ouarzazate flight. Transporting the items to the airport was going to take a number of trucks, trips, or a combination of both. The Ouarzazate airport was the largest in the area and was about two and a half hours away.

Natasha scrolled through the ledger. The final pages of entries were different, noting buyers, sometimes by name, usually by a number, and on occasion both. Locations as well as dates for shipping, payment, and receipts of items filled the corresponding columns to the right of the notations. "I have a number of entries here with the shipping date of two days out. Let's cross-check."

They were able to come up with over two dozen buyers.

"Are these buyers the collectors or more middlemen? All this information could be people like Amastan and warehouses like this. Where the fuck does this end?" Bane growled.

"Jesus! It's worse than a hydra. It's like a goddamned tangle of yarn." Natasha's fatigue and aching body were getting the best of her. She pivoted in the chair, stretching her stiffening body, which was beginning to throb in areas. It was two in the morning. She was tired and frustrated. "I need a break," she said, twisting her still-damp hair into a messy bun and fixing it with a clip while rising, accidentally moving the cursor to another page.

"Uh, sweetheart," Bane said, rising from the bed, his eyes fixed on the screen.

She frowned and turned back to the screen, falling back onto the chair, unable to tear her eyes from the blinking curser. *Le fantôme. The ghost. Six six six.* An item had been delivered days ago. To Italy. "This can't be! He's alive," Natasha said with disbelief. "The person who killed my grandfather is alive." Her breath came in big gulps.

Bane knelt next to her. His brow furrowed as he studied the entry. He stood and pulled Natasha into his arms, rubbing her back until her breathing returned to normal. "Come on, sweetheart. Let's call it a night. Tackle this after some shut-eye and with fresh heads."

She leaned into his strength. Once again, Bane was calming her, supporting her as she dealt with a flash of emotions. Natasha gazed up at him and was drawn into his hazel eyes, the level of intensity making her heart race.

His hands moved from her back to her bare arms, his fingers skimming her skin like soft feathers, sending electricity coursing through her. Her belly tightened when his hands slid over her ass and cupped her cheeks, pressing her core firmly against his thick, hard heat. A moan escaped her, and Bane applied more pressure, grinding her against him again. He felt so damned good.

"I feel how wet you are for me," he murmured before capturing her bottom lip and biting it gently.

"I want you," she whispered against his lips, then dipped her tongue into his mouth, deepening the kiss, running her hands over his back and ass, urgently stroking his raging erection with her core. She was so wet, so hungry. She was ready to explode.

Panting, Bane broke off the kiss and grabbed her hips, pushing her away from him. He pulled off his tee. "Slow down, sweetheart," he said gently, running his thumb over her swollen bottom lip. "You're going to make us both blow. I want you slow and deep." He pulled the clip from her hair. "Arms up."

Natasha lifted her sore arms, her nipples tightening in anticipation as Bane slid the silky camisole off her.

"You're so fucking beautiful," he said, voice cracking, watching his fingers whispering over her full breasts, teasing her senseless. His thumbs brushed over her hard nipples, making her moan. Bane lowered his head and drew her into his mouth, sucking long and hard. He gave equal attention to her other breast, then dropped one hand, his fingers tracing barely there serpentines over the contour of her belly, teasing her to madness.

She was on fire. Her body thrummed with need and her core ached to the point of pain. She tried to grind against him, but Bane caught her hips and held them apart from his. Natasha pressed her thighs together to staunch the leaking wetness.

Of course he had noticed. "I'm sorry I've made you so fucking wet." He smirked, pulling down her silky pajama shorts. "Get them off," he said, sliding his fingers deep within her and pumping slowly.

Natasha shimmied out of her shorts as she rode each thrust, trying to pick up the pace, aching for release that was so close, panting furiously.

"No, sweetheart." He pulled his fingers from her and sucked on them, his eyes locked on hers. With his other hand he pulled off his athletic shorts.

A whimper escaped Natasha. Bane was masculine grace, magnificence, and the sight of him wanting her had her on edge. "Please, babe."

Bane took her hand and led her to the bed, still sucking on his fingers, motioning with his eyes that he wanted her to lie down. He withdrew his fingers from his mouth and climbed onto the bed, hovering over her, panting. He stilled and his eyes glowed, pinning hers. Trust and love

pulsed between them. Natasha stilled and their breaths merged into one just before their mouths crashed together, and Bane thrust deep into her, taking them both over the edge.

※ ※ ✲ ※

Natasha sat up and inhaled the morning air sharply between her teeth. Jesus. She felt as if an elephant had trampled her.

"Hold on," Bane said, hopping out of bed naked and wide awake.

Natasha hurt everywhere despite falling asleep feeling like putty after two rounds of soul-shattering sex with Bane. She heard the shower go on before he came back out of the bathroom, shutting the door behind him. "Swallow," he said, handing her water and white pills and watching her with concern.

"What are these?"

"Acetaminophen. You fell harder than you realized last night. Sorry my massage didn't help much, sweetheart. Give it twenty minutes to kick in. Can you handle a hot shower if I help you in?"

She smiled. "Yes, thanks. I'm just a little stiff."

He raised his eyebrows.

"Fine. Very stiff."

"And?"

"Mighty sore," she admitted as he helped her secure her hair up and step into the shower.

"I'll be right back. Breakfast is on downstairs. Something baked?"

"Yes, please."

"Tea or coffee?"

"Whatever. Thanks."

"Nat…"

Her heart flipped and her breath caught. His face was full of concern. For her.

"Stay in until I can help you out, okay?"

Natasha studied the suds gathering around her feet with moist eyes, overcome with emotion, not trusting herself to look at him, and nodded.

※ ※ ✲ ※

278

She felt better after the shower and the acetaminophen kicked in.

Bane insisted on checking her over again and massaged some ointment into her back that he claimed was magic.

By the time they went downstairs to have a second breakfast, Natasha's pain had dulled considerably and most of her stiffness had disappeared. She moved more freely, and that impacted her outlook.

"We'll keep you moving so you don't stiffen up, and you'll need to take more acetaminophen through the day," he said, trailing her up the steps to their room. They were staying another night before leaving for Ouarzazate in the morning after picking up a rental.

She unlocked their door and stepped in. "Yes, doctor."

Bane chuckled and kissed her upon entering the room.

"So let's get to work. I was mulling things over in the shower. What if the item is the codex we're to find and repatriate? We already know this artifact is in Italy." She hugged him before sitting on the bed. "Let's see what else we can determine from Amastan's and the warehouse logs."

***

"That's it. I've gone through all of them." Bane closed the tablet and pushed back from the desk, leaning the chair on its hind legs. "How're you doing?" He settled the chair on all four legs and reached for Natasha, pulling her into his lap and pushing her wild hair away from her delicate face, looking into eyes that captivated him. Right now they were a cloudy gray, and she smiled, trying to mask the pain showing in them. "You're hurting again."

"I'm fine."

His finger touched the hollow of her throat and he whispered, "Do you really think you can lie to me?"

She compressed her lips, then sighed. "Apparently not. I hurt, but nothing like I did when I woke up."

"That's what I thought. Let's break"—he looked at his watch—"get some more acetaminophen in you, eat lunch, and make plans."

"I have another idea. We can eat and plan while we stroll the palm grove to the east. I'd like to see it in daylight. One, it will keep me moving and loosened up. Two, fresh air and scenery will clear our heads and help us focus. Three, even though we're working, we should take in part of this oasis. It's supposed to be remarkable. Four—"

Bane silenced her with a slow, wet kiss, leaving their breathing labored and wanting much more when he stopped. He pressed his forehead against hers. "You had me at idea."

✖ ▨ ✿ ✖

During their stroll, Natasha and Bane decided they would pay Amastan another visit and explain that they knew about the shipment and wanted to look things over, possibly offer significantly more money than had already changed hands. Natasha had a buyer who was willing to pay significantly higher for something impossible to come by.

After returning to their room, Bane phoned the director. "Hey, Emmet," he said cordially, putting him on speaker mode.

"Good enough then. We had two more calls to ART, asking about the two of you, specifically what qualifications and knowledge you have that your clients trust you to shop for them in such a unique market."

"Good. We're making inroads." Bane caressed Natasha's palm with his thumb, sparking her blood. "We're renting another vehicle tomorrow. SOP," he said. "The keys are at the front desk."

"Roger. Name?"

"Mr. Repo."

"Your idea of humor, I take it?"

Bane let it slide. "We'll be in Ouarzazate tomorrow. There's a big evening shindig at the airport. We're going as ART Enterprise Global employees interested in a piece of the pie. We'd like to invite other guests. Late. Twenty-three hundred."

"Ours will be there, along with Rafiq's. Be safe."

Bane disconnected the call and kissed Natasha's palm. The wicked glint in his eyes was accompanied by a lopsided smile. "We've a few hours before dinner. How about some exercise and a nap, you know, to address your aches and lack of sleep?"

Natasha slid her arms around his neck, her eyes turning molten, and playfully nipped at his mouth, her lips ghosting over his, breathing, "I'm all yours."

chapter 38

"IMPRESSIVE. KINDA LIKE A DESOLATE mirage in the middle of nowhere."

Natasha laughed and massaged his sculpted thigh. "Oh, come, come. Ouarzazate is known as the gateway to the Sahara. We came here when my brothers and I were little. Rode camels out into the desert. Got spit on by camels. Ugh. Camped in a big, fancy tent. It was really boring. And hot."

Bane chuckled. "I imagine so for little kids. Sweetheart, keep rubbing my leg like that and we're going to need to find a private roadside stop."

She placed her hand in her lap. "Sorry, babe. You make me forget myself sometimes." She glanced out the window at the passing terrain, indeed dry-looking and desolate. They were on the outskirts. Bane exited off N10 and into Ouarzazate, in the direction of the small airport.

"Let's check out our surroundings and then find a place to stay." Bane drove by the entrance to the airport and circled back to an area close to the airport.

"There." Natasha motioned to a nice *riad*. "It's close enough to be convenient but not on top of the runway.

"I doubt there's a lot of air traffic." Bane parked the small SUV.

"You might be surprised. A lot of people enjoy the desert tours, especially when it's cooler, like now."

A room was available, although not the honeymoon suite, so they presented their passports and, for a little extra, they were allowed an early check-in. They grabbed their gear and bags and left them in the room,

heading to *souk* and shops, asking questions about acquiring artifacts for their buyers and leaving Natasha's card, anticipating that INTERPOL would be fielding calls. Natasha and Bane found a great café for a late lunch. Their table allowed them to watch the foot traffic while having their backs to the wall.

Natasha's phone vibrated. "Hello?"

"Emmet here. The Jeep has been picked up. You two have garnered a lot of interest. ART's phone is ringing off the hook. Be careful. You have the wire info?"

"We do. We're ready."

"Let me speak to your husband please."

Natasha mouthed, "Emmet" as she handed Bane the phone.

"Hey."

"I won't repeat myself. Your wife will fill you in. Rafiq's people are in place and ours will arrive within the hour. I want to remind you of how deadly the American can be and wish you great success. I'll see the two of you soon."

"Thanks, Emmet."

※ ▨ ❀ ✖

Natasha and Bane spent the rest of the afternoon going over details. Their room phone rang late.

Bane answered. "Rua."

The man spoke in rapid Arabic.

"English," Bane demanded, then put him on speaker.

"I am Gwafa. I hear that you and your wife represent buyers who might be interested in items I have for sale. That they are willing to pay for unique relics."

"Where did you hear this?"

"A mutual contact in Tinghir," Gwafa said. "I and other sellers will be available at the airport after evening prayer."

"Our clients are extremely discerning. We're looking for one-of-a-kind artifacts, not crap or reproductions. If that's what you're offering, forget it. My wife will know immediately."

Natasha sat on the edge of the bed, listening intently, admiring how Bane dangled the hook.

"The items are one of a kind. They have been acquired carefully and are untraceable."

"I've heard that before. Whet my appetite, Gwafa, or I'm hanging up."

"I have a beautiful Benin bronze."

"Aw, fuck that," Bane snapped at the man. "Do you think I'm an idiot? Benin bronzes are a dime a dozen. You're wasting my time."

Natasha's mouth rounded.

"It is very special. There is nothing like it in any museum," Gwafa said.

"No shit. Call me if you have something exceptional."

Gwafa grew more urgent, and he began listing off other items, waiting a beat before naming the next in line, eager to hook Bane.

Bane didn't respond until Gwafa said it. *Homo sapiens.* "That might be of interest," he said slowly.

Gwafa grew more animated, explaining the remains were exceptional and very old.

"How old?"

"Very."

"I'm gonna pass. 'Very old' isn't going to satisfy my wife's client."

"Wait, Rua." Gwafa came back quickly. "Over three hundred thousand years old."

Bane waited a beat before answering. "Hmm. That sounds intriguing. My wife will be able to confirm the age."

"We have an understanding of her skills."

The American had checked them out. "Do you?"

"We researched you and your wife. We are very careful whom we sell to, as careful as you and the clients you represent."

"How much of this *Homo sapiens* do you have?"

"We have all that was excavated."

"Where's the rest of it?" Bane asked.

Natasha rolled her eyes at him. He winked in response and gave her a cocky smile.

"We have all that was excavated. There was nothing else."

"Fine. We'll meet you tonight."

"We can send someone to the guesthouse to escort you and your wife."

The American knew where they were staying. "Not necessary unless you insist."

"Second hangar, southeast of the terminal, parallel to the runway. We will have a portable machine your wife can use in her examination."

"Good. She'll bring her tools of the trade."

"*Salam alaikum,* Rua."

"*Wa-alaikum salam,*" Bane parroted back. He disconnected the call, then looked steadily at Natasha. "Ready?"

She didn't flinch. "I am."

⁙ ⁙ ⁙ ⁙

Natasha and Bane arrived outside the airport grounds thirty minutes after evening prayer. No one stopped or questioned them, but they felt the presence of someone during their walk in from the guesthouse.

Ouarzazate's small airport was quiet, ghostlike in its lack of activity. A cargo plane sat on the runway across from the building where they were to meet Gwafa and his colleagues, the cargo hold open and ready for loading.

The first person they encountered was at the entrance of the building. Natasha was asked to hand over her tote. The man flashed his eyes at her when he saw the phone. It was one they had purchased in the Tinghir *souk* and served as a dummy, its SIM card empty. He pocketed it and pulled her organizer out and started to untie it.

"Don't touch it," she said in Arabic. "You will contaminate my tools."

He stared at her, clearly intending to intimidate her. Natasha stared back. He finally looked away and motioned for her to put it back in her bag, then waved her in.

"I'll wait for my husband, thank you," she said firmly, again in Arabic.

Natasha's SIG and Bane's Glock were concealed in her compression shorts under the flowing, brightly patterned skirt she wore, their knives in her boots. Bane carried nothing. They had to risk it, expecting only he would be patted down, that rural Moroccan culture should play into their favor. Natasha hoped she could get his gun or knife to him if the situation turned ugly.

Bane was patted down. The man attempted to take his camera, but Bane argued that one condition of the transaction was that his client must see the *Homo sapiens* beforehand. "No photos, no sale." Bane grabbed the

284

camera from the man and stepped away. "Let's go," he said to Nat, turning walking back the way they had come.

They were hailed immediately by another man. "Come back. Please."

Natasha and Bane stopped and waited, watching as the small, wiry man trotted toward them, his djellaba flapping about his pants. "I am Gwafa."

"Rua, and this is my wife, Dr. Rua."

Gwafa considered Natasha for a moment, then bobbed his head at her. He extended his hand toward the building. "Please. Keep your camera."

Bright lights illuminated the interior of the metal building. They followed Gwafa past the crates of items stacked on movable carts on the tile floor, wrapped in heavy paper and secured with layers of plastic wrap.

Natasha's breath whooshed out of her. "Oh my god."

The *Homo sapiens* remains lay on paper within layers of soft cloth on a large rolling metal cart. Next to it was a metal table covered in colorful cloth, and on the other side of it a lab technician with the micro-CT, waiting to scan the remains.

Gwafa handed her a sheaf of papers. "These results verify authenticity. We understand you wish to examine."

"Thank you." Natasha pulled her organizer from her tote and unrolled it, then extracted her inspection gloves and stood over the remains. *Hello. I'm going to take a look at you. I'll be gentle.*

Her body trembled with reverence as her gloved fingers came into contact with the first bone—a femur. She inspected it first, turning it over in her hands, looking for any indication of tampering, then placed it on the covered table. Next, Natasha chose the partial cranium and mandible fragments, each with several attached teeth. Female. The cranium's parietal sutures were closed, confirming the female had been an adult when she died. She placed them on the table, above the femur.

"How much is there?" Bane asked, taking photos while she examined the remains.

Natasha didn't look up but continued her inspection. "Not much, but what is here is invaluable. The human body has two hundred and six bones. Only a fraction of those were found." There was enough of the pelvic girdle—the ilium, ischium, and pubis were fused—to reconfirm the *Homo sapiens* was female and that she had reached adulthood when she died. Natasha scrutinized the ilium carefully. Perforations and post-

birth ossification marring the largest segment of the girdle were evidence the woman had given birth. She placed the bones of the pelvic girdle between the cranium and the right femur and continued to add other bones—several ribs, the right patella, fragments of both humeri and the right tibia, vertebrae, and more—forming an incomplete skeleton. "I wish there was more time to examine her."

"With this few? Like what?" Bane asked.

"Her health. Possibly how she died. But we're not here for that. It would have been incredible to have been present when she was found. There were other clues there." Natasha continued positioning the remains of the ancient woman, making sure none of the bones or fragments were duplicates or were from another individual. "That's all of them."

Bane took another series of photos.

Natasha worked in tandem with the lab technician to process the remains through the large machine, rewrapping them meticulously afterward, and placing them into a wood crate with thick insulation. Gwafa's men stood around impatiently by the open hangar overhead door, waiting to load the cargo plane.

"Well?" Bane craned his neck over her shoulder to look at the information appearing on the screen.

"Truly remarkable," she whispered. "It matches the readout Gwafa gave me."

"This is it?" he asked, helping to nest the remains in the heavily padded crate.

"Yes. This is it."

✂ ▨ ✷ ✂

Commotion and shouting pulled Natasha and Bane's attention away from what they were doing. Men in full combat gear stormed through the open overhead, rifles and guns drawn, the lettering on their tactical vests either identifying them as the Moroccan police or INTERPOL.

"Aw, fuck." Bane glanced around quickly and yanked Natasha behind a stack of crates off to the side of the action where they'd hopefully be out of the path of the fighting and stray bullets. He pushed her to the ground. "Stay low."

Natasha rolled and faced up, reaching under her skirt and pulling their guns from her compression shorts, handing Bane his.

"Thanks," he said gruffly, releasing the safety. "Now stay down. We're safer staying hidden." He partially covered her with his body, and they watched from under the pallet of crates.

Guns flashed and boomed. Bullets flew everywhere, slugging into the walls and the splintering crates. Gwafa's men were undisciplined and inaccurate, shooting often, missing completely. The police and INTERPOL combatants measured their return of fire, striking their targets. Gwafa pulled a gun from his hip, only to take a bullet above his knee. He went down; his scream could be heard above the loud gunfight.

There was no mistaking the sound of another bullet tearing into the flesh of another man. He dropped next to Gwafa, blood flowing from below his ribs. The metallic stench of blood mixed with the acrid gun smoke.

The pile of guns, knives, and makeshift weapons grew as Gwafa and his colleagues were apprehended, cuffed, and searched. The man who'd tried to take Bane's camera earlier made an attempt to run. The largest of the INTERPOL team, who matched Bane in size, brought the gun butt down on his head, and he collapsed to the floor, eyes closed.

"Fucker," the man growled in English.

Natasha's heart pounded. An American. That surprised her even though the contractors making up an INTERPOL team could be from anywhere. She kept her gun trained on the action.

"Drop your guns. Hands behind you," he ordered Natasha and Bane in rough Arabic, kicking their pieces out of their reach once they'd complied, then safetying and securing them in his vest. His helmet, goggles, multicam, and beard obscured his face and made him frighteningly ominous.

Natasha did as she was told. The knives tucked into her boots bit into her ankles and feet. She turned her head to Bane, who spoke quietly to her in French. "American special ops. Breathe, sweetheart. We'll figure this out."

"No talking," he warned Bane in Arabic, tapping his gun against one of the hard protectors covering his knees to drive his point home. "You, belly to the floor, hands behind your back," he barked at the lab technician. "Now."

The man nodded to two of the others with him who were dressed similarly and switched to English. "Cuff the lab boy and put him with the other network lackeys, then go help load everything up on the plane

except that box," he said, pointing to the *Homo sapiens*. "I need your cuffs, Fury."

"Reaper," Fury said, tossing the large man the cuffs, then escorting the stumbling lab technician between himself and the other man.

> ⚏ ⚏ ⚏ ⚏

Only Natasha, Bane, and Reaper remained in the large room with the *Homo sapiens*. He squatted between them and lowered his voice so that it didn't carry outside to where Gwafa and his man were being loaded into a large truck by the DSGN. "I know you understand everything I'm saying to you. Emmet Cantrell sends his regards. I'm going to slip the cuffs on you but not close them. I'm sorry that your positions aren't comfortable, but you need to remain as you are for your safety until the Moroccan police get these men out of here. Got it?"

Both of them gave Reaper brief nods, and he left them where they were.

Natasha's neck was cramping, and the muscles of her back were throbbing.

"Hang in there. I know this is a bitch. We'll be out of here in no time flat."

Natasha gave Bane more of a grimace than a smile. "Do you know him?"

"I don't think so, but he seems familiar. Hard to tell under all the tactical gear."

"You wore all that?"

"Yeah. Sometimes more; sometimes less depending on the nature of the mission."

"I think his appearance is intimidating as hell."

"Needs to be. We go up against the ugliest."

"You said that in present tense. Aren't you retired ops?"

"I am, but I'll always be special ops. Past and current operators share deep connections that come from working collaboratively on the most dangerous missions."

"I get that. You're a tribe."

"Kinda."

"Do you still have all that gear?"

Bane chuckled, then groaned. "This is fucking uncomfortable. No. It was Uncle Sam's. Why?"

"Who's Uncle Sam?"

"US government. Why?"

Heavy footsteps approached. "You can get up. They've left."

Bane scrambled up and helped Natasha stand. He lifted her chin and smirked, his eyes filled with admiration.

"Rua."

Bane's eyes snapped to the man, his expression guarded. He knew that voice and he didn't.

The operative pulled his headgear off and parked his hip on the metal table, careful not to disturb the open box. He crossed his powerful arms, assessing Bane. "I'll be goddamned. We weren't given your names. You know how secretive Emmet Cantrell is." He inclined his head toward Natasha, appraising her with interest. "Introduce us."

Booth Merrick stared at him—eighteen years older, no longer the skinny, older, and bullying brother of his dead best friend. An experienced warrior. His hair had mellowed to auburn with strands of gray, but the blue eyes still burned bright. Graduation night came racing back. Bane braced himself. "Merrick."

"Yes. Reaper to my team."

Bane acknowledged that with a nod.

Natasha wove her fingers with Bane's. She felt the tension in his body and answered Merrick herself. "I'm Natasha. Rua. Bane's wife."

"Where're you from, Natasha?"

"Here, there, and everywhere."

Merrick shook his head and laughed. "Smart and beautiful. Nice to meet you, Natasha Rua. Rua, I think you're in over your fucking head."

"That has crossed my mind more than once."

Merrick rose and extended his hand to Bane. "That night was a long time ago. You weren't to blame. However, I had some skin in it. I'm sorry, but Alex's death is no longer yours to carry. Or mine. He wouldn't want this, and you know it." He kept his hand out, waiting.

Bane finally extended his and shook, and Merrick pulled him into a shoulder hug and slapped him on the back. "A couple of the guys and I are responsible for bringing the two of you back in. Tonight. We picked

your shit up from the guesthouse. It's in our vehicle. Returned your SUV."

"The *Homo sapiens,*" Natasha uttered, heading to the remains.

"The director asked that those be loaded last. Can you double-check the packing on them for the flight please? It's taking off as soon as Fury does the precheck. Everything goes to Rabat. My men will escort all of it to the museum and deliver it to a Ms. Guilford. No need for worry. My team are former SEALs. We served together for years. I trust them with my life."

Natasha wrinkled her nose.

"You know her?"

"We've met," Natasha said.

Bane slid his arms around Natasha and kissed her neck. "Aw, sweetheart. Your jealousy warms my heart."

"I am not jealous." Natasha withdrew and pivoted, bathing him with a scathing look before checking the remains, ensuring they were protected. She labeled the box clearly, and Bane helped her wrap the box in plastic layers.

Merrick observed them, fascinated. "How long have you been married?

"A month," Bane responded. "This has been a working honeymoon."

Natasha elbowed him sharply in the ribs.

Another man on Merrick's team came in. His dark bald head was prominent now that he'd taken off his headgear. "Reaper, the plane's ready. Fury said there was one last thing to load."

"Good. Cutter, this is Natasha and her husband, Rua. Natasha will show you how she wants the box secured in the plane. Follow her directions to the letter."

"Got it," Cutter said.

"Husband, will you carry it, please?"

Bane balanced the box in his arms and walked with her, following Cutter onto the cargo plane.

Merrick cocked his head and chuckled to himself, clearly amused that a woman had heartthrob Bane Rua totally by the balls.

chapter 39

T HEY PULLED IN FRONT OF the *riad*. Natasha had given Merrick the address before falling asleep on Bane, who drifted off an hour out of Ouarzazate, succumbing to Natasha's warmth and the motion of the roomy vehicle.

"Hey, Rua," Merrick called back. "We've arrived. Nice digs."

It was still dark out. Bane stretched out as much as he could in the SUV's second row of seats, inhaling deeply and trying to wake quickly. Out cold, Natasha had made herself totally comfortable alongside his body. His morning wood pressed against the curve of her ass.

He rubbed his eyes. "What time is it?"

"Oh five thirty. We made good time."

"Do you mind going around to the back, Cobra?" Bane asked the driver. "We left our keys with Oliver and Clara, the caretakers. They're early risers. Thanks." *Fuck.* He just remembered Simon was playing houseguest. Bane would have preferred privacy with Natasha. "Sweetheart. Wake up." Bane kissed her temple. She stretched but didn't rouse. "We're home."

Natasha smiled and burrowed into him, her hand running down his zipper, seeking his hard length. He pulled her hand away and clasped it.

She frowned, her mouth pouting.

"Sweetheart, we're in the SUV with Merrick and Cobra," he whispered in her ear.

Natasha's eyes popped open. "Oops." Her slate-gray eyes sparkled with humor.

His lips brushed hers. "I think you knew what you were doing," he breathed in her ear and nibbled the lobe, his eyes darting to the front where the men talked quietly as Cobra maneuvered to Oliver and Clara's home.

✖ ▩ ❀ ✖

Wicked heat flared in Natasha's belly as he trailed his fingers under her skirt, up her thigh, and into her panties. Bane teased her wet entrance.

"I know what I'm doing too," he murmured.

The SUV stopped. "We're here," Reaper announced, getting out. Cobra exited and headed to the back to unload their bags.

Bane's fingers retreated and he sat up, giving them both time to collect themselves before getting out.

After thanking Cobra, Bane exchanged contact information with Merrick and promised to stay in touch while Natasha waited for either Clara or Oliver to answer her knock.

It was Clara, who was wide awake, her face wreathed in a huge smile. She held out her hands and waved Natasha into her arms. "You're home!" she exclaimed, joyfully, wrapping her arms around Natasha. Her tone changed to worry when she saw Reaper and Cobra with Bane. "Who brought you home?"

"Some nice men. They're friends, Clara. We had a little hiccup at the site. We've been on the road most of the night, but everything is fine," she said, noticing the concern in Clara's expression. Natasha hugged her again. "Really. They're on their way to Rabat."

"Bane, bring your friends in for breakfast. I won't accept no." Clara called to the group talking by the SUV, "I have coffee on and just pulled my special almond croissants from the oven. I think eggs and fruit would be simply divine with them. Don't you?" She waved the men toward her. "Come, come!" She reached up to hug each of the big men warmly as they stepped inside.

Bane gave Clara a big smile and a bigger hug. "Great to see you, Clara. This is Reaper and Cobra," he said, indicating the men.

Clara settled the group around her table, refusing help from Natasha. Oliver appeared and kissed his wife good morning and greeted everyone before joining her in the kitchen to transfer the food to the table.

The men went through two pots of coffee and inhaled their food, thanking Clara profusely for breakfast.

A look passed between Reaper and Cobra. "Clara, Oliver, we hate to leave so soon, but we need to head to Rabat."

"You're welcome to freshen up before you leave," Oliver offered. "It might help with the drive. Clara told me you've been driving all night."

Reaper checked his watch, then nodded. "That would be much appreciated."

"I'll get our bags," Cobra said and left.

Both men were showered and dressed in clean civilian clothes within fifteen minutes and ready to leave.

Natasha and Bane said goodbye to the men, then offered to help clean up.

"Nonsense. You two are tired. Get some sleep and we'll visit and catch up later." Clara handed them the key to the *riad*, her knowing gaze lingering on their wedding rings.

Natasha stood slowly, obviously stiff.

"Are you okay, dear?" Clara asked.

Natasha tried to brush it off. "Yes, I'm fine. I had a little mishap. Bane checked me over thoroughly."

"Maybe you should see a doctor," Oliver suggested.

"She's good, Oliver. She just needs some rest and time," Bane responded.

Oliver's words had a bite to them. "And you know this how?"

"I just do, and if I felt she needed more than my care, I'd be the first one to take her to the doctor. I promise."

"Can you tell us more?"

"Not at this time. I'm sorry." Bane slipped his arm around Natasha.

They thanked Clara and Oliver once again and promised they would check in later, then headed over to the *riad*.

▨ ▨ ❀ ▨

A note to them rested on the center of the kitchen table. It was from Simon. Emmet had asked him to leave after Bane confirmed they were in route back to Casablanca. He welcomed them home and hoped he had been a good guest. He was looking forward to seeing them soon.

Bane pulled Natasha close. Her heartbeat synchronized with his.

"I need a shower," she said.

"So do I."

"God, how nice it's going to be to actually move about in the shower."

"Is that an invitation?"

Natasha gave him a saucy smile and proceeded toward the master. Her gait wasn't as fluid as usual because of her stiff, aching muscles.

"You're sorer today."

"Yes."

"The long car ride didn't help. I'll turn the water on to almost hot. I promise to give you my best effort with my magic fingers. Loosen you up," he said, following her into the spacious bathroom.

Natasha and Bane brushed their teeth while the water warmed up. Bane held out two acetaminophen and a glass of water. "They were in my kit."

"Thank you, babe."

Bane kissed her slowly, so tenderly it made her tremble.

Their eyes locked as they took their time undressing one another, savoring each touch, every gaze, the nectar of each other's skin.

They entered the shower together and began to wash and rinse. Tongues tasted and mouths suckled. Teeth nipped.

Bane guided her to face the wall and her hands to the safety bars on either side of the shower. "Does this make you more uncomfortable?"

"No."

"Drop your chin." Bane's fingers moved through the tangles of her thick, wet hair and over her scalp, kneading, releasing the tension she had no idea was there. She dropped her chin lower and moaned in pleasure as his fingers dropped to her neck, working the tension out, the pads of his fingers whispering over her throat where her pulse hammered.

"You have a good grip?"

"That feels incredible. I do," she said breathlessly, almost faint with desire.

"Good. I like you spread out like this, beauty. If you get more sore or uncomfortable, let me know. I don't want to hurt you. I'm trying to ease the pain."

"I ache," she murmured.

One of his hands skimmed her belly and dipped inside her soaking sex. "Here?"

"Yes," she whispered, bucking against his fingers.

"I want you to ache, beauty." His other hand drew feathery serpentines over her belly, then splayed, pressing her against his thick length as he thrust his fingers deeper.

She gasped.

"Burn for me." Bane's fingers worked her slick, hungry channel slowly, then withdrew, leaving her panting. His hands returned to her, massaging the skin of her shoulders and back, gently working over the tender areas, the warm water adding to his sensual attention. Often, his lips trailed his fingers. "How're you doing?"

"Much better. The acetaminophen is kicking in."

"Hmm. Good." His talented fingers pressed on either side of her spine and traveled leisurely down her back to knead the contours of her ass. Bane's mouth joined his fingers and thumbs and he renewed his nibbling and kissing.

Natasha moaned and shivered.

Bane stood and turned her around, moving his thigh between hers, working her legs apart. "Nat?"

"Please, babe." She had to have him fill her.

Bane covered her mouth with his and thrust deep. Home.

⚐ ⚐ ❈ ⚐

Reality hit Natasha with full force when she woke. Their mission would end with their debriefing with Emmet that afternoon. Who knew where either one of them would end up. Bane was American, a Midwest man, an elite, retired military soldier who contracted himself out, intent on bringing down the bad and ugly in this world. She was a South African orphan, raised in France and Morocco, an academic and INTERPOL contractor, a woman without a country.

She loved him more every day, and it had been easier to embrace it after she had acknowledged her feelings that night in Imouzzer du Kandar, when Bane had opened up to her about his past and they had slept under the stars. Their relationship had only intensified, and she wanted more time to learn about him, to enjoy being with him. Bane embodied everything that attracted her—strength of character,

intelligence, humor, honesty, a handsome face, the body of a god. He challenged her to be a better version of herself, to face her past and her truths, to understand herself. In turn, she gave him a solid foundation who listened and didn't judge, and she met him as his partner.

Bane slept on his stomach, his powerful limbs splayed out over most of the bed. A body that could kill in an instant or be incredibly tender and make her entire body come apart. His dark and light layers fascinated her.

Natasha pushed her hair back from her face and glanced at her watch on the nightstand. It was noon. They had to get moving. She padded into the bathroom for something to secure her hair, then pulled Bane's HOOSIERS sweatshirt from the top of the chair and slipped it on over her nakedness.

"I like that much better on you than me, beauty." His deep voice rumbled as he watched her out of one eye. "Come here." Bane flipped over and pushed up to lounge against the many pillows, the sheet beneath his washboard abs loose. He studied her intently. "What's bothering you?"

Natasha approached, stopping at the edge of the bed.

Bane's fingers slid along the hem of the sweatshirt. "Sweetheart?"

Natasha shook her head, unable to speak, and her chin trembled.

"Sweetheart," he whispered sadly, gathering her into his arms and rubbing her back. His phone vibrated, and he grimaced when he saw the number. "Yes? Okay. We'll be ready." He disconnected, then slid a finger under her chin, lifting her face so that her eyes met his concerned ones. "Simon is picking us up since we don't have a vehicle. He'll be here in about seven minutes."

⚜ ⚜ ⚜ ⚜

Natasha and Bane sat in the back seat, holding hands, silent all the way to Rabat. Simon periodically glanced at them in the rearview mirror. Both of them looked out their respective windows, seemingly distracted by the passing landscape, lost in their individual thoughts.

"We've arrived," Simon announced.

Natasha smiled a sad smile. "Thank you, Simon."

"Thanks, man." Bane clapped him on the shoulder.

They were processed by security and entered the elevator, silent to the floor housing Emmet's office.

Matilda's joyful smile was replaced with a frown when she saw Natasha and Bane. "Welcome back, you two." She ushered them into Emmet's office.

Emmet spread his hands out. "Please sit. Welcome back, and congratulations on a successful mission."

Natasha nodded and smiled.

"You sent in reinforcements. That was unexpected but welcome."

Emmet made himself comfortable, sitting on the edge of his desk between them, squinting, his eyes bouncing between them. He could obviously sense that something was off.

A light knock on Emmet's door announced Matilda with tea and pastries. She poured each of them a cup and left.

"Yes. I'll address that, but first the debriefing." And Emmet dove in, directing the session until he was satisfied that every point and detail of the mission was discussed and understood. "The items, including the *Homo sapiens,* are with Ms. Guilford at the museum. Well done! She and her people are working diligently to get the artifacts sorted. Unfortunately, the Ouarzazate Codex is in Italy. We still don't have more information. The ops team that came in to assist us has been reassigned to Italy by INTERPOL because the Ouarzazate Codex is as priceless as the *Homo sapiens* you brought back and"—he took off his glasses and looked through them, wiped at them with a tissue from his desk, then put them back on—"because I received a notification after you left Casablanca. Eric Schaus escaped."

Natasha gasped. Bane turned and reached down, weaving his fingers through hers.

Emmet studiously avoided looking at their linked hands.

"How can that be?" Natasha asked. "Eric Schaus was a broken man when I last saw him. The man I saw couldn't have possibly recovered from the extent of his injuries and escaped on his own. He had to have had help."

"He did have help. A number of people were found dead in the wake of his escape, likely to keep them from talking. We have no idea where Schaus is."

"His disappearance makes me feel as though the Guatemalan mission is again incomplete."

"I can understand why you might feel that way, but you're wrong. You found and apprehended him. Your work was exceptional. The American

has people everywhere. He has had interest in other countries beside Guatemala. INTERPOL has issued a Red Notice. It has an updated photo of Schaus with that hellish black whatever-it-is on his face. He can't be moving about too easily between that and the injuries he sustained."

"So now what?" Natasha asked.

"We wait and we listen," Emmet said. "A new team has been assigned to him. Your notes and insights will be extremely useful." He stood. "Our meeting is concluded on my end. Any questions?"

Bane frowned. "Many, but not now."

Natasha shook her head. "Not at this time."

"Brilliant. Matilda has your paperwork. Please complete it and get it back to her pronto." He addressed the elephant in the room. "Do either of you know what you have planned next?"

"Nope, just a vacation."

"Some real time off," Natasha responded.

"Simon will take you both back to your *riad,* Natasha. I expect Bane still has some of his belongings there?"

"I do."

"Also, the apartment is rented for only one more week, so plan accordingly." He shook hands with both of them. "It has been my utmost pleasure to work with you, Natasha. And you again, Bane. This was my last bit with INTERPOL. I retire in two weeks."

They both congratulated Emmet, who asked that they please stay in contact. He escorted them out to where Matilda waited to exchange Natasha's passports.

Her eyes were full of sympathy. "Simon is outside with the car. I'll see you soon."

Bane smiled, but it didn't reach his eyes. "Thanks, Tilly." He pulled her into a bear hug.

"Thank you." Natasha dodged looking directly at Matilda, barely holding herself together, afraid she would start crying.

Bane and Natasha stepped into the elevator.

✄ ▨ ✳ ✄

"They didn't return the bands," Emmet said, watching the elevator doors after they had closed.

Matilda smiled. "I noticed."

"They have a bloody problem."

"They certainly do. I just hope both of them aren't too stubborn to admit it."

※ ❖ ❖ ※

Bane found Natasha on the rooftop terrace, watching a spectacular watercolor of yellow, pink, and orange. He switched on the lanterns hanging from the pergola.

"Beautiful sunset," he said, handing her tea and sitting beside her.

"It is." Her lashes dusted her cheeks as she sipped.

"You've been avoiding me all afternoon, Nat. What's going on?"

"I'm just thinking about things."

"Am I part of those things?"

Her eyes snapped to his. She had been crying.

Bane faced her on the large lounge and pulled her forward to nest between his legs. He put his tea on the table next to him, then hers. "Tell me, love." Bane's thumb brushed her cheek and then he leaned forward, kissing her gently and cupping her head in his hands.

"It's over."

"What's over?"

"Us."

He swallowed, then grimaced, searching her eyes. "Is that what you want?"

Natasha wagged her head, trying to drop her chin, but Bane held firm. "Look at me, sweetheart."

She lost herself in Bane's eyes, now malachite, the color they became when he experienced deep emotion. Natasha blinked and tears ran down her cheeks.

He stopped them from going any farther with his thumbs. He felt as though he had been kicked in the gut. He had brought this on by skirting his feelings. Because he was scared shitless. "I love you, sweetheart."

A range of emotions passed over Natasha's beautiful face as she processed Bane's words. Confusion. Surprise. Joy.

"I love you too, babe. So much it hurts."

"When I said you were my heaven the other night, that I loved you, I wasn't in a post-sex haze."

She shifted closer to him and placed her palms on Bane's stubbled cheeks, her forehead on his, and nodded. Holy Lord, she loved this man. She unfolded her crossed legs over Bane's extended ones and slid her hands around his back, bringing her core to his, her chest against his solid form. Bane's heart jackhammered. Like hers.

"We'll need to figure this out, sweetheart. We've been two wandering souls for a long time."

She sat back and regarded him. "We have. What do you suggest?"

"What do you want?"

"I want you, Bane. Period."

He chuckled. "And I want you. I want your face to be the first thing I see every morning and the last I see every night. I want to go into forever with you."

The last of the dusk and lantern light illuminated Natasha's enormous smile and her shining silver eyes. "I can't imagine not waking up with you, going to bed with you, spending my days with you." She kissed him deeply and Bane's stomach growled. She laughed, untangling herself from him and standing. "But first I need to feed you."

Bane stood. "Okay. After dinner, let's talk vacation, as in leaving as soon as possible so that we can begin exploring our future in depth."

Natasha picked up the cups and emptied the cooled tea over the wall, leading her love back inside and forward to a new future.

glossary

adhan—the Islamic call to prayer

baklava—a sweet pastry of honey and chopped nuts made from layers of phyllo

bastilla—Morocco's version of a savory pie

bâyt—the elongated rooms lining the perimeter of a riad's inner courtyard. These are typically public and dining rooms. Each has an open arched passage that faces the courtyard.

BC—Before Christ. Long used by archaeologists as a reference point for dating artifacts

BCE—Before Current Era. Sometimes used in place of BC (Before Christ). A way to express date without referencing Christianity.

BP—Before Present. Refers to 1950, when radiocarbon dating and calibration curves were established. Used in archaeology to determine the date of an artifact. January 1, 1950, is used as the commencement date. A date such as 5000 BP means 5000 years before 1950 AD, or 3050 BC.

CE—Current Era. Sometimes used in place of AD (Anno Domini, year of the Lord). A way to express date without referencing Christianity.

djellaba—a long, loose-fitting robe worn by both men and women, typically over other clothing

hamman—bathhouse, an ancient and important aspect of Moroccan culture. Can be any combination of simple, modern, old, and ornate.

harira—a tomato soup with a beef stock or lamb stock base, full of lentils and chickpeas. Rice or broken fine noodles are often added.

hijab—veil or head covering

kasbah—castle

khobz—round, flattish bread used to scoop up stews, soups, salads, dips, and more

left hand—considered unclean. Delegated for bathroom and other dirty chores. Considered rude to use it for any other reason.

Maghrebi tea—Morocco's famous mint tea, a green tea steeped and served with leaves or sprigs of spearmint

medina—the old section of a town or city

numismatics—the study or collection of coins, paper currency, and other money

ras el hanout—a complex blend of aromatic spices. It's also known as mrouzia.

rfissa—a Moroccan comfort food of stewed chicken and lentils seasoned with fenugreek, saffron, and ras el hanout

riad—the traditional stately Moroccan homes of the wealthy. Typically two or more stories, living is inward focused for privacy with the rooms facing an interior courtyard/garden with a fountain.

sahrîdj—fountain in the center of the inner courtyard/atrium/garden of a riad. Water is considered a sacred and vital life-force of a riad.

setwan—the modest sitting area where guests can be received without disturbing the inner riad

SOP—Standard Operating Procedure

souk—a marketplace within a medina, often open-air

tadelakt—a traditional Moroccan water-repellent surfacing technique composed of lime plaster and black soap from olives. Commonly used to make sinks, water vessels, and baths. Also used for interior and exterior walls, ceilings, roofs, and floors. It has no seams or grout limes, making it naturally mold and mildew resistant

tagine—slow-cooked stew with countless options. Named for the clay or conical ceramic dish it is traditionally cooked in. Traditionally eaten directly from the cooking vessel with pieces of bread.

wadi—seasonally dry river

zellige—individually chiseled tiles, typically in geometrical patterns

zouaq—colorful, hand-painted wood used in architecture

introspections & acknowledgments

"He lives doubly who also enjoys the past."
Marcus Martial, 1 AD

I was born with an insatiable curiosity about the tapestry of culture, beliefs, and traditions and how they have impacted the past and frame the present and future. Anthropology, forensics, and history were destined to be my fields of study and my lens for our great world. I've been fortunate to travel extensively and to immerse myself in culture, appreciating and connecting to the people I've met and the places I've experienced.

The seed of *Afraid to Hope* germinated during an archaeological trip in Morocco some years back, where I observed someone helping themselves to an ancient shard in Volubilis. (Yes, I said something.)

I'm grateful to Ishmael, my delightful Moroccan guide, who was unfailingly open during our discussions as we roved and explored the northwest area of Africa. Thank you to my friends Najwa, Loubaba, and Elke for translating the Arabic and French within *Afraid to Hope*.

To the Goddesses—Enid, Kassie, and Marjie—what would I do without you? Chewing over writing and edits with love, laughter, and sarcasm with you is simply the best. Karen, your eagle eyes and even sharper mind astound me. I appreciate your being fabulously honest.

To Ally and Anne, thanks doesn't seem enough. You helped me bring what was in my head to lovers of story and romance. I'm beyond appreciative for your creativity, skills, and patience with me.

Lastly, to my husband and our four kids, there isn't a day I don't thank the universe for you. I love you beyond words.

what to do now

Afraid to Hope is Book 2 of the Ancient Passages series. I hope you enjoyed Natasha and Bane's story. Won't you consider leaving a review on Goodreads, Amazon, or Barnes & Noble?

Do you have friends who'd enjoy *Afraid to Hope?* Tell them about it—call, text, post online. Your recommendation is the nicest gift you can give an author.

more by sutton bishop

Afraid to Fall, Ancient Passages Book 1 (Ari and Luca's story)

To find out about new releases and to receive free and exclusive bonus content featuring characters from this series, sign up for Sutton's newsletter at www.authorsuttonbishop.com.

find sutton online

Website: www.authorsuttonbishop.com
Facebook: www.facebook.com/sutton.bishop.37
Instagram: www.instagram.com/authorsuttonbishop/
Twitter: www.twitter.com/SuttonBishop2 (@suttonbishop2)

about the author

Sutton Bishop enjoys having a foot in both worlds—real and make-believe. She has degrees in forensics and anthropology and a minor in world history. Her writing is inspired by her travels and life experiences. She lives in the Midwest with her husband, their four kids, and a passel of pets.